LEGACY
OF
TRUTH

BOOK TWO IN
THE DRUID'S BROOCH SERIES

CHRISTY NICHOLAS

GREEN DRAGON PUBLISHING

Table of Contents

Pronunciation Guide and Glossary

Irish, a language in the Gaelic family, has several rules of pronunciation that are different from English. For instance, if some letters are followed by H, they are softened. An example from English is S, which softens to SH, or P which softens to PH.

In Irish, this is true of BH and MH, which become V, while DH becomes a very soft YH, barely discernible. TH becomes H, while GH and CH become a rather guttural H. FH is silent.

Another difference is in the slender vowels, I and E. When some letters are around these vowels, they become lenited as well. For instance, SÍ is pronounced SHEE, and SÉ is pronounced SHAY.

An accent draws out the length of the vowel and makes it slightly broader (like from cat to caught).

Below is a list of some of the words and names in the story that are pronounced in a way that might not be obvious to someone unfamiliar with Irish.

Aisling—ASH-ling
An Ceann Dubh—an kee-ann doov ((the black one)
An lucht siúil—an LOOKHT shooil ((Travelers))
Aodh—Ay
Aoibh—Eve
Aoife—EE-fuh
Ban Sídhe—ban SHEE (wailing woman who portends doom)
Bóanna—BOW-anna
Bó—bow (as in bow and arrow) ((cow))
Bodhrán—bow (as in take a bow)-rawn ((hand-held drum))
Booley—BOO-lee ((summer village/pasture))
Cailleach—KY-loch ((witch or hag))
Caoin—kay-OHN ((to keen, wail in grief))
Clachan—kla-KHAN ((winter village))
Cú Chulainn—COO Hu-luhn, also COO Cuh-luhn ((Culann's Hound))
Dubh—dove ((black))

Eithne—EN-yuh
Fiachra—FEE-khruh
Fionn mac Cumhaill—FYON Ma Cool
Fionnuala—finn-NOO-luh
Geis—GESH ((a curse or compulsion))
Gráinne Ní Mháille—GRAWnya nee WHALL-eh
Liath Luachra—lee-uh LOO-uh-khruh
Manannán mac Lír—MAN-nuh-nahn mac LEER
Mo chailín rua—muh KHA-leen ROO-uh ((my redhead lass))
Mo chara—muh KAR-uh ((my friend))
Mo chroi dorcha—muh KREE ((my heart))
Mo chuisle—muh KOOSH-la ((my pulse))
Mo ghrá—muh GHRAW ((my love))
Mo ghrá dubh—muh GHRAW duv ((my black-haired love))
Mo ghile mear—muh GILL-uh MAR ((my gallant darling))
M'iníon—min-EEun ((daughter))
Níamh—NEE-ev (also spelled Niabh or Níamh)
Oisín—UH-sheen
Poitín—po-CHEEN ((moonshine))
Sídhe—SHEE (the Faery Folk)
Síbín—SHEE-been (makeshift pub)
Tír na nÓg—tear nuh NOHG (an otherworld, or Land of the Young)
Tuatha Dé Danann—TOO-ah day DAN-in (the Faery Folk)
Úna—OO-nuh

Dedication

I lovingly dedicate this book to my husband, who has indulged me with many trips to my soul's home, Ireland. He has supported me through my growing pangs as a writer. And sincere thanks go to my beta readers and fantastic author group—without your help, this would never have happened!

I also dedicate it to those who cannot find solace in solitude; those who face the terrifying black pit of depression on a daily basis and yet still manage to pull out of the horror and carry on for one more day.

Foreword

The world has always been a dangerous place. Sometimes the danger is from the outside. War, violence, hunger or greed prey upon the innocent in any place and in any time. And these are logical things to fear; injury, illness, loss are universal. People do die, and people do fear the manner and agency of that death.

Sometimes, however, the fear and danger are on the inside.

Part One

Prologue

Ardara, County Donegal, Ireland
March, 1787

Éamonn

Éamonn Doherty moved the cat and eased onto the old rocking chair beside the crackling fire. The March wind howled outside, as fine a tempest as he'd ever seen. As soon as he settled, his grandchildren bombarded him, clamoring eagerly for a story from their grandfather.

Well, he had only himself to blame. Whenever he returned from his wanderings around the country, he told them a tale of Ireland's past or his own. They expected and loved the tales. So did he.

The bairns settled around his feet. Esme and Eithne, the twins, looked stark and thin with shocks of wild red hair and too many freckles to count, the soft glow of the fire silhouetting their young faces.

"Eithne, that's my spot! I always sit there, and you know it!"

Eithne scowled at her sister. She turned to Éamonn and blinked with innocence.

Esme shoved her sister, but Eithne braced for it. She glanced over her shoulder with disdain.

Fuming, Esme crossed her arms and pouted.

In the far corner sat their youngest sister, wee Brighid, with her arms wrapped around her knees. Everyone called her Bridey. Her solemn green eyes peered out, owl-like. And their cousin, little Níamh, whose parents died of a fever. A brown wren, still a toddler.

Éamonn would have preferred grandsons to pass his stories to, but his son and daughter-in-law, Brian and Shona, gave him only granddaughters. Still, he loved them all dearly. His two other children had dedicated themselves to the church. Éamonn glanced at the girls and decided a story of a manly hero would be best.

He fixed his eyes on wee Níamh until she giggled nervously. Éamonn tousled up his thick white hair until it looked like a lion, and she laughed out loud.

They all watched him, eager for his tale. With a roguish smile, he began. "Tonight our tale will be of a hero of great fame, for who has never heard of *Fionn Mac Cumhaill*, leader of the Fianna, Warriors of Ireland?"

Timidly, Bridey raised her hand.

Éamonn cocked his head. "Yes, child? What is it, my dear?"

In a small voice, she said, "I haven't heard of him, Grandfa."

Éamonn closed his eyes, reaching for patience. "That's all right, *mo chuisle*. I'll be telling you now, so?"

The girl nodded and wrapped her hands more tightly around her knees until she looked like just a pair of feet, arms, and a curly mass of red hair sparkling in the firelight.

In a flash, Éamonn went back in time to the memory of his dear, long-dead wife, Katie. Her hair had been so wild and bright.

The windows rattled as the wind howled.

"The Fianna were a band of warriors, pledged to protect the shores of Ireland from foreign invaders. Fionn's father, the leader of the Fianna, sent his son to be raised by a warrior woman. Have you ever seen a warrior woman, Eithne?"

"I have! There's a woman who hunts in Bunbeg. Alan said she came into his da's bake shop one day!"

Esme glowered at her twin. "I heard that first! He told me first."

"Girls, that's enough. Would you like to know about this warrior woman?"

That did the trick. All four children looked up at him, expectant. Éamonn grinned and got back into the rhythm of his tale. "This great woman, named *Liath Luachra*, stood as tall as me, with long muscles and longer hair. She kept it in thin braids, which went all the way down to her knees. The fierce warrior always wore fox fur and wolf skins, and she taught Fionn her martial arts. When he'd learned all he could from her, he left to join the Fianna.

"But the Fianna knew Fionn for his father's son, and worried about his youth and lack of wisdom. They told him he must leave, as they could not protect him from harm. This angered Fionn, so he left in a fiery temper.

"When his anger cooled, he sought a Druid to teach him wisdom. He found one named Finnegas, who'd spent seven years trying to catch the Salmon of Knowledge. He'd finally succeeded just before Fionn found him. The mythical salmon roasted on the fire, and Finnegas told Fionn to watch it while he got more firewood.

"Fionn watched the fish as it bubbled and popped, sizzled and squeaked."

Níamh let out a squeak of her own to help with the sound effects.

Éamonn chuckled with a smile for the girl. "A great blister formed on the skin of the salmon, growing larger and larger, about to pop. Fionn pressed his thumb to push it back down so the skin wouldn't be blemished. As he did so, his skin burned, so he stuck his thumb in his mouth." He demonstrated with his finger and looked around until each child did the same.

"But this was a horrible betrayal."

"Why so horrible, Grandfa?" Bridey asked, her eyes wide. "He only touched the fish!" She replaced the thumb back in her mouth absent-mindedly.

"Ah, that's true enough. But, you see, by placing his thumb in his mouth, Fionn tasted the flesh of the Salmon of Knowledge, and he now received the Salmon's great wisdom. Finnegas, seeing the truth when he returned with firewood, grew furious and chased him out with a club. However, the damage had been done. Fionn now had the knowledge and wisdom he needed to lead the Fianna fairly."

"In the end, he controlled his own fate, and therefore found his joy. That's all that anyone can do, aye?"

Bridey piped up. "But did he lose the magic?"

He gave her a wide grin. "We all keep the magic he found. One must search for magic in the hidden places. The thin places. The whisper of a butterfly wing. Under the shade of a hawthorn bush. In the rush of ocean waves. Each of these holds magic for us."

When Níamh realized the tale was over, she belatedly removed her thumb from her mouth. As she did, Éamonn lifted her into his lap and rocked in front of the fire. He wished his son found joy in his own life. *Brian might not be a good farmer, but at least he kept his children fed and clothed.*

As if summoned by the notion, his son stumbled into the front room, his eyes bloodshot from the drink. He blinked like an owl in the dim light, as if not recognizing his own children. When Brian shuffled out again, Éamonn let out a sigh.

He sang a sad, low song of lost love and broken promises until each child fell asleep on the soft, white wings of fantasy.

The next morning, Éamonn tightened the straps on his horses' leather packs. Footsteps behind him made him turn to see three redheaded cherubs looking at him with expectant expressions.

"Now, I've got gifts for all of you, but you must promise to be good and listen to your parents, all right, so? Here, Eithne, this is for you..." He dug deep into his pack and pulled out two bangle bracelets made of bone, too big for her thin arm. At age thirteen, she'd grown since he last visited, but still stood shorter than either of her parents. The bangle had angular marks on it known as ogham from ancient Ireland. "This one says 'wealth and health.' I've another for you, Esme. It says 'blessings and beauty.'"

He handed the second to Esme. A smile crept across her face as she examined it. "Is it magic, Grandfa?"

"Not magic, *mo ghrá*. But something pretty to keep."

Eithne glared at her sister. "Why does she get the one with beauty? We're twins!"

He patted her messy red curls. "That you are, *mo chuisle*, but you get the one with wealth, no? You've already got the beauty, then." Despite her narrow gaze at Esme, Eithne pressed her lips together and nodded. Éamonn looked at Esme, but she seemed content with her gift, spinning it on her wrist so the burnished ivory surface glinted in the spring sunshine.

Esme definitely inherited his Katie's compassion, but not her confidence. Eithne had the confidence without the compassion. They both, however, inherited his dear wife's fiery temper.

A tug at his trousers made him look down to find Bridey.

"I couldn't forget you, my wee girl. Here, this is yours." He handed her a rag doll with red hair, which he'd gotten from his Traveler band. She clutched it to her chest, hugged him quickly, and ran away. Éamonn glanced around. "Where's Níamh?"

Eithne snorted. "She's not your granddaughter. *She* shouldn't get a gift."

He gave her a stern look, into the eyes so like his own. "Níamh does indeed get one, Eithne. Be nicer to her, or I won't bring you a gift next time." Eithne stood her ground for a moment but gave in and shuffled her toe in the dirt. "Yes, Grandfa."

Brian and Shona came out of the farmhouse, just as Éamonn said, "Esme, go fetch Níamh while I say farewell to your parents."

The child scampered off, and Éamonn turned to his son and daughter-in-law. "Will you two be fine, aye? You've the farm now. You can make it work?"

Brian gave him a wan smile and hugged him. "Yes, Da, we will. Thank you again for getting us this farm. I still can't believe we actually own land!"

Éamonn hoped it would work. His son had always been a dreamer and the farm, small as it was, might not support them all if he didn't work it well. He hugged Brian, trying to infuse his talent for making things happen.

The English had only repealed the law forbidding Catholics to buy land nine years earlier, but the land agent still didn't want to make the transaction. Éamonn persevered and spent his savings to purchase this farm, with ten acres of land, for his son and family. The soil needed lots of work. Parts were rocky and difficult. But with effort, it should give the girls some stability.

Shona had tears in her silver eyes. "Thank you, Éamonn, we'll make it work, I swear." He bent down to hug her. At least they had the girls to help, all strong-willed and hard workers.

Esme returned, pulling a reluctant Níamh, smudged with dirt and dust, with a tattered rip in her smock.

Shona tsk-tsked over the rip, but before she could get hold of the child, Éamonn lifted her high up in the air, just to hear her squeal with glee. He placed Níamh on the saddle of his horse, and she giggled. He led the horse around the yard in a circle before lifting her down.

"And that, my wee girl, is my gift to you. Someday I'll come back when you are tall and strong and able to ride. We'll go out on a grand ride along the beach. Is that a bargain?"

Níamh nodded, scooting around Shona to hide behind her skirt.

Éamonn mounted his horse, arranging himself between the packs and bundles strapped on either side. As a Minkier, or *an lucht siúil* in the Irish, he brought most of his wares with him wherever he traveled. Now he must make more trades, to replace his now depleted wealth.

Éamonn had skill at trade, but more at gambling. The dice always worked for him. Not so much that it aroused suspicion, but enough to keep him flush. Like his father before him, he sang and told stories of an evening, often in exchange for a night's meal. However, he traded goods such as cloth, iron, food, jewelry, anything he found for a good bargain.

He clicked at his horse to move. As he glanced back to wave, rising dust made his eyes tear. He'd miss them dearly, this solemn pocket of kin. It might be years before he returned to this part of Ireland. His band of traders usually traveled around the coast of the island, stopping to winter in a different place each year.

Éamonn turned back toward the road so they didn't see his tears.

Chapter One

Esme

"*Brochan tanaí, tanaí, tanaí, brochan lom na súghain.*"

Esme sang along with her father and sisters, as they plowed the field, turning the dirt to plant seeds their grandfather gave them. She loved the nonsense song. Her grandfather learned the song in Scotland. "Thin, thin, thin bare juices of the porridge." The song helped the work go quickly, and Esme always loved singing with her Da. It gave her a sense of belonging, a sense of family. She dreamed, someday, of singing to her own family like this. Esme's very own farm, with children running around underfoot. The song almost seemed like a chant, a magical spell, which tickled Esme's love of the fairy stories her grandfather told.

Her father sang clear and sweet, his light tenor soaring in joy as he worked. Esme held her breath as he hit the high notes. His love of music passed to his daughters with varying levels of success. Though Eithne sang beautifully, she found little joy in it and didn't practice. Esme's soul soared when she sang with her father. Bridey had a lovely voice, but when they sang at night around the hearth, she played the hand drum, or *bodhran*.

Her father stooped, pulling up a clump of tangled weed roots and tossing it on a pile. Then he straightened and mopped his brow, pushing his black hair out of his eyes while he sang the next verse.

"*Thugaibh arán dha na gillean leis á bhrochan súghain.*"

Their father always started projects, like this farm, but he didn't stick to them so well. Even at age thirteen, Esme knew her father failed at a deal with the blacksmith, another with a fisherman, and a third with the baker. Her best friend, Alan, the baker's son, told her of the last one. She didn't know if her Da was just lazy or had no ability to bargain. Their father just didn't have their grandfather's stubbornness to stick to a job until the end. Well, she'd help him stick to this.

"Seo an rud a gheibheamaid o nighean gobh an dúine."

Esme still found it hard to believe her family could buy land. Their grandfather said Catholics weren't permitted to purchase land for a hundred years, because of English laws. The law had changed, but most Catholics didn't have the resources to buy now.

Their old-fashioned farm wasn't a grand place, but they had a home. The land came with a sturdy stone crofter's house with a thatched roof. It had three bedrooms along the back and one room in the front, with the hearth in the middle. With three bedrooms, they had more personal privacy. She didn't have to listen to their parents couple at night, or her little sister cry in her sleep.

The fresh-laid thatch roof should last another thirty years, and large flagstones should keep the mud down inside. Even in the howling winds of winter, it would be warmer than the old place. They had more than many in the village. Even Alan lived in a smaller cottage.

"Brochan lom 's e tana lom, 's e brochan lom sùghain."

Something crawled on her leg. Esme swatted at it and watched the lace bug skitter into the turned loam. She shuddered, but it had disappeared now. The girl bent to dig with her spade, sweat dripping down her forehead into her eyes.

Her sister, Eithne, dug in the next row, far behind her. Eithne worked the least she could get away with. Everyone told her twins should be closer than other sisters, but she didn't get along with Eithne. Her sibling always fought her in a battle with undefined rules Eithne changed at will. Esme found no logic or reason for it, other than Eithne's amusement. She found it easier to keep out of her sister's way.

Esme scratched her leg where the bug had crawled. The grit itched and she brushed the smudge, ignoring other smudges all over her legs and arms.

"Daydreaming, Esme?" Níamh's eyes twinkled, two rows down and grinning at her from under sweat-soaked brown curls. Esme got back to work to keep up with her cousin. Some contests, and some contestants, were easier to win.

Their mother came out with milk. "Break time, girls!" Níamh kept working on her row until her cousins all called in unison. She looked up, startled, and dropped her little stick. Níamh's task was to poke holes in the rows after the older girls plowed. Then their father dropped in seeds.

During that week, the family planned on planting potatoes in the "lazy beds," corn in the next plot, with herbs in the kitchen garden. They planted oats and barley. Three cows and an enormous, pregnant sow stood in their pens, as well as chickens. According to their grandfather, this should feed them all. Even now, before their planting yielded anything, they traded butter, eggs, and milk for bread in the village.

As if summoned by the thought of bread, Alan ran to the gate and waved, his blond hair shining in the bright sun. He held a huge basket over his arm, and the yeasty aroma of fresh-baked bread wafted past her. Esme scrubbed at her face, trying to get the dirt off.

"I've got your loaves, Mistress Doherty! Will you be wantin' them here, or in the cottage?"

Her mother collected the empty cups. "I'll take them in the cottage, Alan, thank you. Girls, finish your milk and back to work."

Would Alan remain after his delivery? She'd almost finished her assigned rows and would love to escape with him. She tried to catch his eye, but he spoke with her mother with his back to her.

Esme sighed and stooped, trying to make quick work of it.

Her father must have noticed her haste. "Straighten your row, Esme. You know better." Esme wrinkled her nose and fixed her clumsy job. When she glanced up again, Alan had disappeared. Eithne made a rude noise, but Esme ignored it.

An hour later, grimy, tired, and hot, despite the cool April breeze, Esme found consolation in knowing Eithne would also be grimy, tired, and hot. While not the most charitable thought, she relished her twin sister's discomfort. They took turns at the water bucket, sponging off the worst of the dirt. Bridey scrubbed her face and she returned the favor. Bridey and Esme attacked Níamh's face. They tickled while she squealed, and sudsy water splashed in all directions.

Eithne remained aloof from their childish games and marched inside, her back straight and her shoulders stiff.

Clean and refreshed, with a loaf of bread and a chunk of fresh, soft cheese wrapped in a piece of flannel, Esme ran up to her favorite spot, an ancient standing stone called Owenea. The loaf still felt warm and smelled divine.

Esme often used the stones to escape Eithne, as her twin didn't enjoy tramping around in the wild countryside. Like her grandfather, Esme loved walking the wild hills. She treasured her solitude as a precious gem. As she approached the tumbled ring stones, covered in reeds and grasses on the modest hill, she spied Alan perched on one, his blond hair shining in the sun. Esme treasured her time with Alan even more than her solitude.

Alan helped at the farm often. Despite being only twelve, he had more strength than the girls. Her father needed his help with the heavy work. In return, the girls helped Alan's father in his bakery for parties or weddings.

After jumping off the rock, Alan held out a loaf of bread, wiggling it in invitation. She laughed and fished out an identical one from her flannel.

She broke her cheese in half, offering it to him. "Thanks for waitin' for me. I'm dead tired."

Alan swallowed his bite. "I waited until the work finished. I didn't want to get wrangled into the work."

Esme pointed at a smear of flour on his eyebrow. "Sure and you'll have been up since dawn yourself, helping your own Da." He rubbed at it and stuck out his tongue.

A gentle breeze ruffled her hair as she enjoyed the peace of the day. Several buzzing insects flew around their heads and a sheep baaed. In the misty distance, the sea shone in the late afternoon sun.

Something rustled in the brush behind them. She jumped off their rock, but as she turned, a fat, fluffy ewe burst through the bushes. She gave them a long, low "baa" before tossing her head and nibbling on the grass. The sheep shook herself, perhaps indignant at their presence.

Alan and Esme exchanged a look and burst out laughing. They had no real reason for it, but they laughed until their eyes teared and Esme's side ached.

Esme settled back on the rock next to Alan, close enough for their legs to touch. To the west, islands dotted the gray-blue water. The setting sun sparkled and twinkled on the waves with yellow and peach. Peat bogs and farms covered the land, rocky bits sticking out in hills and cliffs. County Donegal was a rough, wild corner of the country, and every farm required constant work. The village of Ardara sat halfway to the shore, where two roads met in a Y shape, with close-built buildings along each. Alan's dad's bakery sat at the end of one of these streets.

Alan took a drink from his waterskin. "Why do you think these stones are here, Esme?"

They'd made it a game to find new explanations. Esme wrinkled her nose to come up with something. "I think they're markers, for those who wander to find their way home again, no matter if the land has changed."

"Hmm. Might be, to be sure. Maybe heroes from *Tír na nÓg*?" He shrugged.

"The Land of Eternal Youth! But if they set foot in Ireland, they turn to dust, so say the tales."

Alan raised his eyebrows. "They could stay on their horses?"

She rolled her eyes. "And how would they pass water, then?"

That set them off again and the ewe, evidently disgusted by their mirth, gave another "baa" and pushed back through the bracken.

She let out a deep sigh and rocked sideways, hitting his shoulder with hers. "I should get back, Alan. They'll be looking for me soon."

Alan's blue eyes turned wistful, staring at the village below. "I suppose I should, too. Time for cleaning up at the store."

Esme let out a deep sigh. "Same again tomorrow?"

"If I can. Da's got a big bake this afternoon, for the church gathering."

"If you can."

Chapter Two

June 1787

Esme

Bridey's voice drifted from around the back of the farmhouse. "No, it's not yours! It's mine! Give it back!"

Eithne must be acting the maggot again. Their parents went to town, leaving Esme to keep the peace.

Bridey spied her as she came around the corner and ran into Esme's arms, nearly bowling her over. Tears streaked down the younger girl's face, leaving trails in the dirt.

"What's this then, sweetling? What happened?" Esme stroked her little sister's hair where it escaped its bun.

"I found a magic stone and Eithne stole it!"

Esme glanced up at her twin. A faint tug of the twin bond they shared pulled her attention. Esme didn't always relish their shared link.

Eithne looked back, her face as prim and still as carved rock. "I stole nothing. I found it on the kitchen table. I found it, so it's mine." The mental tug strengthened, drawing a tendril of will away from Esme, but she pulled back. It became a struggle of resolve within their twin bond.

"I put it there! It's mine!" Bridey sobbed, her blotchy red face scrunched with frustration. Esme shoved Eithne's bond away and she slid out.

Eithne gave Bridey a hard, angry glare. Bridey stood firm for longer than Esme thought she would, but turned away and buried her face into Esme's skirt with another sob.

Esme's twin rolled her eyes and let out an exasperated sigh. "It's just a stone with a hole in the middle. Rubbish. If she wants the bit of trash that bad, she can have it." The older sister tossed the object in question into a pile of other stones pried out of the ground as they plowed. It skittered down the pile, causing others to cascade. Bridey screeched and rushed to the stones, digging to find her precious relic.

Eithne wiped her hands on her skirts, lifted her chin, and strode away.

Esme squeezed her eyes shut, asking God for patience with her twin sister.

According to their grandfather, a stone with a hole in the middle had magic, a Faery Stone. One threw it into the ocean to grant a wish or bring luck to whoever held it. Esme doubted her cynical twin kept faith with such tales. Esme's rational mind said the magic couldn't be real, but their grandfather also cautioned them to keep an open mind. Bridey, aged ten, still believed in magic.

"I found it!" Bridey cried, holding her stone above her head, triumph shining on her tear-streaked face.

Esme sat on a log and patted the space beside her. "Come over here, Bridey, and tell me how you found it."

While her sister recounted her tale of their day at Maghera beach, playing among the sand dunes, Esme considered Eithne. Her twin went too far. Eithne bullied anyone younger than her, though she acted like an angel for their parents. They never gave credit to tales of Eithne's cruelty, ascribing it to good-natured sisterly spats.

Esme grimaced and let out a humorless chuckle, interrupting Bridey's disjointed story about the beach visit. Alan's older sister didn't bully anyone. Neither did the girls in their hedge school class. They were all short for their age. Still, Eithne more than made up for her lack of height with a huge attitude.

"Don't worry, Bridey. We'll get Eithne back."

Bridey shook her head, her face screwed up in a grimace. "But how? Eithne's so mean! I don't want to be mean like her."

After putting a hand on her little sister's shoulder, Esme gripped it. "We don't have to be cruel, but we might show others how cruel she is. Does that sound better?"

Bridey nodded and wiped her nose with her hand.

They attended the hedge school once the planting finished in the spring. They didn't have a formal schoolhouse, like the Protestant children went to. Instead, they met in an abandoned barn along the Portnoo Road, and they learned Irish, English, maths, history, and money from the old schoolmaster. He had three books filled with exciting tales like her grandfather told. Esme did well with the Irish and history, but not so well with the others. Eithne did best with maths and money.

As Catholics, they weren't allowed to attend a "real" school. But they spent three hours each summer morning learning. Her parents didn't read or write in English and only a little in Irish, though they spoke both well. When Esme found out their father couldn't write, she offered to teach him.

He chuckled and shook his head. "No, *mo ghrá*. It's too late for an old hound like me to learn a new trick. Just learn it well yerself, and that's well enough."

And tricks abounded, when Eithne came around. She seemed to be the ringleader. Her sister had Meg and Fionna Nesbitt in tow, and together, they made the younger children miserable. Nothing would happen while old Mr. Connell watched, but as soon as he turned his back, no one stayed safe. Eithne might pluck Esme's hair (the ones in the back near the neck hurt the most), steal her food, or dip her braid into their inkwell. Meg might stomp on her instep, or steal her slate. Esme'd get it back, but she must pay something, like a favor, an apple, or some humiliating act of contrition.

When Esme complained to Mr. Connell, he shrugged it off as nonsense. He'd leave soon enough. He traveled around Donegal, spending a couple of months in each town, offering his teaching services at the hedge schools.

Adults offered no help. Esme must figure out a way to deal with her sister's growing power and abuse. If only she had magic powers, like in the fairy tales. Alan might help her, and she'd enlist the other girls' help, as well. Perhaps her grandfather would suggest something the next time he came around. He was much better than any adult.

A few days later, Esme crept away as Bridey and Níamh stood, trembling but holding hands, against Eithne's snide insults. Alan crouched, hidden in the bracken behind the barn, in case things got out of hand. Esme ran to get either her mother or father to witness.

However, as Esme approached the farmhouse, raised voices halted her. *This one sounds pretty bad.* They spoke with intense, angry words.

Her mother's voice wailed with despair. "There's no way this will work."

"Shona, you must trust me…"

She let out a snort. "You, I trust. Your work ethic, on the other hand—"

"Are you calling me lazy?" Esme had never heard her father speak so harshly to her mother.

"Not lazy, no. But you know you never finish projects. This season, sure, we'll be fine. But what if a crop fails? What about next year?"

Her father let out a deep sigh. "We have the girls to help and Alan when he can."

"Alan's not your son, and you have no right to command his labor like that."

"I don't command him! He comes over when he's done at his da's shop. Besides, he and Esme are inseparable."

With a frustrated groan, her mother said, "You shouldn't have spent all our savings on the seed. It was short-sighted."

"No, holding back is short-sighted, Shona. Please, bear with me for one season, and then we'll see, aye?"

Esme crept away. Eithne and her bullying would be the least of her parents' problems.

Her father sounded so weak and pleading. Like he tried to convince himself everything would be fine. Like he didn't have faith in himself any more than her mother did.

Some days, Esme thought her parents didn't know what they were doing. They drifted along on a wave of fate, with no way of steering or paddling, floating to wherever life took them.

The talk about the farm failing made Esme's blood chill. She remembered days, even weeks, they'd gone without food before. Esme still remembered the sharp pain in her stomach when they tried to eat grass. She'd prayed so hard for food that day, but God never answered her prayers.

Esme vowed her own life would be different. First, she'd improve her stitching to always have something to sell. Then she'd find a husband who had a trade, not like her father. Then she'd have lots of children, so they'd help. Her own farm would never fail.

Alan had skill at baking. He'd make something of himself.

Their farm did fine now, but she'd never looked ahead to another year. Esme understood famine. Mr. Connell had taught that Ireland had them often. While she knew crops failed, they'd never owned their own farm before. Her father had always worked on someone else's farm and tended their horses. Before that, he wandered with their grandfather and *an lucht siúil.*

As she moved closer, Esme's emotions boiled in a stew of confusion. Her parents' argument had shaken and scared her, so she didn't watch where she stepped. She almost tripped over Alan, still crouched in the bracken. He shushed her, motioning to get down out of sight. Eithne heard her, though, and she halted her tirade on Bridey. She whirled around and spied them.

"Spying on me, now? Is that how it is? Well, just you wait until I pay you back for that, little Mistress Esme. And Alan, too! Don't think I don't see you there!"

While she berated Esme and Alan, Bridey and Níamh scampered to safety. Eithne turned back to an empty clearing, huffing so hard that Esme fancied she saw puffs of dragon smoke coming out of her sister's nostrils. After throwing her hands up in exasperation, Eithne stomped off in another direction.

As soon as Eithne left, they ran after the two younger girls. They laughed at Eithne's reaction, but when Esme related the fight between Ma and Da, they all sobered.

Níamh's brown eyes grew round in horror. "Will we have no supper, then? Will Eithne take my bread again?"

"We'll have supper tonight, little wren, no fear about that. And I won't let Eithne steal your food ever again." Esme embraced her little cousin tight and didn't let go for a long time. Alan put his hand on Bridey's shoulder with a grin.

That evening, after a meal of porridge and eggs, the family gathered around the hearth as their father added another peat log. Everyone had a project in their laps. Their father whittled pegs for a stool. Níamh and Bridey tried to spin thread with a spindle. Their mother had just taught them, so the thread came out coarse and lumpy, but they might use it for rugs. Esme, Eithne, and their mother did needlework of various types. Eithne found embroidery easy, but boring. Esme had to work harder, but loved the fine stitches and bright colors. They might not be practical for the workday clothing, but she still loved doing them, despite having to spin her own finer thread.

Their fat, orange-marmalade tomcat, Boru, jumped onto their mother's lap without warning, upsetting her embroidery frame and scattering spools of colored thread. The spools rolled in every direction. Esme grabbed those heading straight for the hearth to keep them from the smoldering ashes while Eithne chased the others.

Her parents didn't look at each other and still seemed upset from their earlier argument. Maybe if she could get her father to sing, it would make things better. Esme swallowed down her nervousness. "Da? Will you sing Three Ravens?"

Her mother loved that song. Brian stopped his whittling and cleared his throat, taking a healthy swallow of small ale.

"There were three ravens sat on a tree,
Down a down, hey down, hey down."

They all knew the song, a grim tune about ravens deciding which bodies on a battlefield they should feast upon. They joined him on the chorus.

Their mother put aside her rectangular embroidery frame and stroked the cat as she crooned under her breath. His purr grew loud enough to drown out the crackle of the peat fire.

Even Eithne looked content. She studied her needlework with an air of satisfaction and approval. Esme's dislike of her twin eased.

Eithne looked up and noticed Esme staring at her. Eithne's lip curled into a sneer, and she came over to examine her sister's work. "Hmm. Not bad, Esme, but it's sloppy over here. And you used the wrong blue there, see? Someday perhaps you'll be as good as mother and me."

That destroyed Esme's good mood, but she held her tongue. She wanted to scream at her sister, to knock the ever-so-smug look off her face, but she shouldn't. Esme didn't wish to add more worry to her parents. She huffed with rage and ignored Eithne. She picked out the stitches. They *were* too loose, darn Eithne! Esme redid the stitching in a silent simmer, ignoring the story her father told.

When he mentioned standing stones, though, her head snapped up. Her father spoke of a druid who turned to stone when a saintly monk lit a fire on Beltaine Eve, at the beginning of May.

Their father gave a dramatic pause. "And that very stone stands to this day, up on the hill near Owenea. You've likely seen it yourselves, playing around the area while the silent, ancient druid stands frozen, watching eternity pass him by."

A chill wound down Esme's spine, a snake of ice stealing all warmth. *Was the stone truly a Druid, transformed by God's miracle?* She pondered the shape of the stone, squarish and squat. Perhaps he'd been a very short druid? An absurd giggle escaped, even as she shivered. They shouldn't play around that stone any longer. Druids had friends among the faeries, and places of the faeries should be left alone. Still, the story drew her in.

"Would Grandfa know about the stones?"

Everyone stared at her, and she looked at her feet. Perhaps she asked a silly question. Esme's side grew warm as Bridey snuggled against her. She put her arm around her little sister and remembered her parents' argument. If they didn't grow enough food, would she have to watch her sister fade away into nothing, like a druid turned to stone? Would Bridey's bright smile become brittle bone and translucent skin?

That night, Esme tossed and turned in bed. She kept warm enough, nestled next to Eithne. Bridey and Níamh shared the smallest alcove. Their bed had a thick canvas bag filled with softened heather and rushes. Not as soft as a down mattress, but soft enough after good use. Every move made a rustle, so they learned to sleep still.

Esme's parents murmured in the next room, a low susurration which ebbed and flowed. She couldn't hear words, just tone. Their voices stayed calm, broken by an occasional giggle. This reassured her, and sleep claimed her.

Legacy of Truth

Chapter Three

January 1792

Esme

Though Esme had told Alan the story many times, they still argued about it every time they visited the stones. With her arms crossed, she scowled at him. "Da said a druid, I swear! It may have been a long time ago, but I remember his story word for word."

Alan pointed to a couple of white marks on one side. "That's no druid. See, here's the marks where someone cut it with a chisel or something."

A chill wind whipped through and she gathered her cloak tight. "Perhaps someone cut it recently? Someone who wanted a piece of a magic stone, or someone who wanted to leave his mark?"

"If he was a druid, why doesn't he wake up? Surely the monk who transformed him died. His magic would die with him, wouldn't it?"

Esme shrugged, frowning at the standing stone. "But what if he used a miracle from God? God's not dead. He's eternal."

"So are miracles stronger than druid's magic?"

Throwing her hands up, she stalked a few steps away. "I don't know! I think the druids had stronger magic at first, but God took over."

He cocked his head. "Took over how?"

She glared at her friend. "How am I supposed to know? I'm not a priest."

Alan peered at the stone, one eyebrow raised. "Neither am I, but I'd like to know the answer. If more people in Ireland believe in God, then maybe He grows more powerful?"

The power of faith was strong, but simple faith didn't make things appear out of thin air, any more than it fed hungry people. The power of the druids must have been strong at one point. Her grandfather and their father had told them hundreds of stories about druid magic and how ancient gods fought battles and won wars with their magic. As Mr. Connell taught them, the priests brought Christianity to Ireland over a thousand years ago. But Ireland was much older than that.

Esme asked, "Do you think Saint Patrick had more power than the druids?"

With a reverent hand and a wistful expression, Alan touched the shoulder of the stone. "One perhaps, but sure, not all of them."

"Then how did he win?"

He gave her a half-smile. "He converted the High King, didn't he? At Easter? And the King employed the druids, so they had to listen to him."

"How do you think their magic worked? Can anyone still do magic?" The possibility that magic still existed made her heart soar.

Alan stepped to the nearest tree and patted the trunk. "How would I know? They worshipped in the forest, so did the trees help them?"

Esme shrugged. "They might have. And he got turned to stone because wood might still give him power?"

She loved arguing with Alan. They could get as angry as they wanted, but remain good friends. Someday, she wanted a husband like that. Esme glanced sideways at Alan. Would he make a good husband? He might be worth thinking about.

As they talked, they sat upon a crumbling stone wall built years ago by an optimistic farmer. Alan handed Esme a small loaf of fragrant rosemary bread he'd brought and she gave him the butter she'd swiped from the storeroom, pinched into an earthenware bowl. They munched on their meal, kicking the wall with the back of their heels, and thinking about the legends.

"Hey, what if the stones in this wall had been Druids, too?" Alan patted the flat, square stone he perched on.

Esme let out a giggle. "Now those'd be some short Druids!"

Bridey came running over the hill, out of breath. She stood, heaving, with her hands upon her knees. Esme jumped down and hugged her shoulders. "Bridey? What's happened?"

She sputtered, taking harsh breaths between every few words. "Da's fallen... off the ladder... Eithne ran to the village to get... Healer McHugh."

Alan and Esme exchanged a glance as her heart grew cold with fear. They all bolted back to the farm house.

When Esme entered, she shoved down her feeling of helplessness while staring at her father. He didn't look like Da. He seemed drawn and ashen, his flask by the bedside. He smiled bravely as she sat on the stool beside his bed. Motes of dust swirled around his head, twinkling in the wintry sun which struggled to get past the hide windows.

On their thatched roof, a net tied over the thatch to keep the wind from pulling the straw away. Stones tied on the bottom held down the edges of the net. One stone had fallen out and the rickety ladder tipped as her their father tried to retie the stone.

They'd have to spread his work to the others. When she had her own big family, she'd have to assign work. Esme might as well get used to that now. If she didn't take charge, Eithne would take over. Scrawling some notes on their slate, she showed it to her father. "Eithne and I will take the harder things and let Bridey and Níamh feed the chickens, sweep the house and clean the dishes. Does that sound good, Da?"

He nodded once, the lines around his eyes tightening.

When she showed the list to Eithne, her sister pursed her lips. "Your list is easier!"

Esme said, "It is not!"

"Is!"

"Fine. I'll switch lists. Happier?"

Eithne flushed and paused as if she wanted to argue further, but she snatched the other list and marched off with a sniff.

The next day, her father acted in a foul mood, yelling at them for making noise, complaining, or not doing something right. Their mother yelled back at him. Esme just wanted to escape all the anger. With plenty of work to do, she found a task outside.

One cow got it in her head that she wanted to be with the chickens, so she trampled the wire fencing into a crumpled heap. The work to repair the damage made Esme sweat, despite the biting January chill. She stopped to mop the sweat off her face.

Esme tilted her head, sure she heard a giggle. Níamh? After halting her work to listen, she heard a boy's voice, followed by Níamh's giggle again.

Níamh had a boyfriend? She wondered who it might be. Perhaps the butcher's boy, Colum? He followed Níamh with love-struck eyes, but never seemed to have the courage to talk to her. The boy laughed, a low chuckle. Not Colum. He'd never be bold enough for such a thing.

Esme crept around the hedges to peer through the branches. She glimpsed their hair, brown and black, as they perched on the cow byre fence. Brown-haired Níamh with someone she didn't recognize. *He seems much too old for her.*

Níamh only had thirteen years. The boy looked tall, with his long hair pulled into a thick ponytail. He bent his head as he examined something Níamh held.

The bracken snapped, making Esme catch her breath. They both glanced toward her with guilty expressions.

"Esme! Come meet Seán! He's a Traveler, like Grandfa! See what he brought?" Níamh held up a purple object, delight shining on her face.

Esme gathered her dignity about her like a tattered cloak and strode out with her head high, reaching her full five feet in height.

She nodded to the swarthy young man, dressed in a patterned vest and bright-colored trousers. "I'm pleased to meet you, Seán. And your family name?"

After jumping off the fence, he swept a low bow. No one had ever accorded her such an honor, and her cheeks grew warm. "Fitzgeralds, we are. I'm Seán Fitzgerald and me da, he'll be Oisín Fitzgerald. Pleased to meet you, Mistress Esme."

Esme had to admit, this young man had manners. She'd met many Travelers with none. Her grandfather Éamonn was a Traveler, or *an lucht siúil*, as he preferred. He warned her away from other Travelers, as a rule. But this boy spoke with pretty words, to be sure. The young man's mouth quirked up at one corner in a roguish half-smile.

Níamh's eyes grew wide. "Oisín? As in the stories?"

"Not the same man, mind you. Da's not gone off to *Tir na nÓg*. Not yet, at any rate." His impish smile revealed a dimple on his right cheek. Esme had to return the grin, and her cheeks grew warm again.

"But see, Esme, see what he gave me!" Níamh held up a lovely pale-purple shell with a hole in the center. A round hole, smooth and even.

"I thought it only polite to bring gifts for the fair ladies of the house as we come asking favors."

"What favors?" Esme narrowed her eyes in suspicion. He ran his hand through his ponytail, playing with the ends.

Before he answered, Níamh held up her shell. "Is it magic, like the stones with holes?"

The tall young man bent over with a smile. "Indeed and it is, young Níamh. You must keep it safe until you make a wish. When you have a wish, you hold it tight as you can in your right hand, make yer wish, and toss it as far as you can into the incoming waves of the ocean. It must be the ocean, mind you, a lake willna do. And if you can catch the seventh wave, the wish will have the greatest power. Go, run off now and hide it somewhere safe until you need it."

Níamh ran while holding both her cloak tight against the icy wind and the shell close to her chest. The younger girl bobbed along the trail toward the house like a rabbit.

Esme turned back to Seán. "Are you in the area long? Which band do you travel with?"

"We'll be here a couple of weeks, at least. It's just me, Ma, and Da, no band. We've business in the village for a few weeks, and Ma says there's a storm coming. She's never wrong about such things. We're like to hunker down before it hits. Éamonn says there's land up near the old fort to suit us."

"Éamonn? You know Grandfa?"

He gave a warm smile and his eyes crinkled. "Sure and who doesn't? He's known the width and breadth of the land, he is."

Well, if Grandfa Éamonn told them they might stay near the old stone fort, it would be churlish not to take him home and introduce her family. If they'd be neighbors for several weeks, she must be polite.

Esme stole glances at him as they strode to the farmhouse. Once he noticed, he flashed her a wide grin. She fixed her eyes in front, though her cheeks blazed.

She hoped her father would be in a better mood than earlier. With a tentative hand, she pushed open the door. Her father didn't rise to greet the newcomer. His pain at both his leg and his inability to be a proper host showed plainly on his face. Esme glanced at the flask, lying on its side, empty.

"Ah, tha's nae bother, sir. You lie sound there, and I'll go back and set us up for the night. When we're done, we'll come by and have a proper meet. We'll bring food and I'll introduce my family. There's just the three of us. We'll be no bother to you good folk."

Eithne entered with a large basket in hand, filled with tangles of rushes to refill the beds. The wind whooshed in when the door opened, making the candle flicker. Their father pulled his covers up tight to his neck.

She stopped dead in her tracks at the sight of the stranger and narrowed her eyes. "And who might you be?"

Seán bowed low to her. "Seán Fitzgerald at your service, Miss…?" He looked with confusion between Esme and Eithne.

Esme answered him sulkily. "That's Eithne, my twin, if you couldn't tell."

"Mistress Eithne." He bowed again to her and back at Esme and Níamh. "I'm off to the campsite, ladies. We'll be by around dusk, and we shall bring a feast!" He made the last statement with a flourish of his hand, like a Moorish magician summoning the djinn.

With that, he exited, letting in another whoosh of cold air. This time, the candle blew out completely.

They supped well that night, no mistake. Seán brought his parents, Oisín, and Ciara. His father stood tall and slim, like Seán himself. Esme saw where Seán got his dark beauty, though his father's hair seemed a rich brown rather than black. His mother, stout and fair, giggled a lot. They wore bright colors with lots of bangles and jewelry on their wrists, and brought fantastic treats. Brined olives from Italy, a sharp cheddar cheese from England, rice from the far Orient. The rice tasted bland, but she enjoyed trying new things. Eithne turned her nose up at it, making rude comments about the offerings.

Oisín had her parents laughing at a story while Esme studied Seán. He played with the end of his ponytail and kept glancing at her. When he did so, she pretended she looked at the wall past his head, or studied her plate. Still, she got the sneaking suspicion she hadn't fooled him in the slightest.

Seán must be the most exotic man she'd ever seen, with his dark-tanned skin. A stranger from Scotland once came trading horses, and a French man traveled with Mr. Connell one summer, but few people visited this far-flung northwest corner of Ireland. He made Alan seem like the dullest of plain potatoes.

He raised an eyebrow when he saw her looking at him. "Are you not interested in Da's story, Mistress Esme?"

She stifled a giggle behind her hand at his formal address. Girls in fancy manor houses got called Mistress, not poor farm girls. "I just wondered why your hair's so dark? Your parents both seem much fairer." She tried to seem interested without simpering. He had a lovely smooth voice, like water in a brook.

"That would be thanks to my father's father. He'd been a dark Irish man from Galway. Descended from the Kings of Spain, so they say." He sat up straighter, though Esme felt certain he remained unconscious of his posture change.

"Do they say so, then? How fascinating. Have you never gone back to claim your birthright?"

He colored, his dusky skin turning a deeper tan. "No, no, it's too far down the bloodline for such as that. We've no claims left."

Eithne let out a mocking snort.

Esme instantly regretted her teasing. Those who brag of their ancestors seldom have much to be proud of in their own life. She mumbled an apology and stared at the two tart green olives left on her plate.

The burst of salt and sour on her tongue made her pucker. Even the pickled seaweed from the beach didn't get so strong, but she liked them. Esme mopped up the last of the juices with soda bread. The bread made her think of Alan.

When she glanced up again, Seán stared at her. She flushed and dropped her gaze.

A movement out of the corner of her eye caught her attention, and she spied a tiny black spider crawling up Eithne's skirt. Esme suppressed a smile. "Eithne."

Her sister ignored her.

"Eithne."

Still no reaction.

In a sing-song voice, she persisted. "Eithne! You've got a visitor."

This got her sister's attention. Her head shot up to see who arrived. When no one appeared at the door, she scowled at Esme.

"Not there, silly. There." Esme pointed to the spider on Eithne's skirt.

Eithne jumped up and screeched, batting at her skirts, dancing around like a fly on the water. Esme didn't hide her grin, but then turned to see Seán watching her. Eithne stopped gesticulating and smoothed her skirts to sit again.

Esme gulped and cleared her throat, horrified that he'd seen her smiling at Eithne's distress. He'd asked her a question. "I'm sorry. I was miles away. Could you repeat that?"

"I asked if you were free tomorrow afternoon for a walk, Mistress Esme? I'd be delighted to escort you to town, or…?"

Esme glanced back at her father. He'd need her for chores. Eithne drew herself up straight and gave Esme a dismissive glance. "*I* wouldn't mind a walk."

Seán glanced at Eithne as if just now noticing her. He looked her up and down, admiring, but then gave a lopsided smile. "I so apologize, Mistress Eithne, but I asked Mistress Esme."

"Hmph." Eithne pressed her lips together and brushed at her skirts again.

After dinner finished, as she walked their guests outside, Seán took her hand. "Tomorrow, then? Just past noon?"

Esme swallowed, and glanced back at the farmhouse. "I'll have chores to finish. You should take Eithne after all."

"As I said, I didn't ask Eithne. I asked you."

"Still, dismissing her like that may not have been wise, Seán. My twin doesn't forgive insults."

Seán shrugged. "I've known her sort before. That one's all smoke and no fire. And she's not the company I'd prefer."

"I'd like to, I really would, but, well, Da still can't walk, and he'll need me."

His dark eyes grew sad. "Perhaps another time, then? Promise?"

"I promise. Another time."

His smile brightened the evening as he sauntered down the lane.

February 1792

Eithne

Eithne slipped out of the house before dawn. She'd complete her morning chores so her mother wouldn't miss her. She hoped she'd get there on time. Hugh wouldn't wait around.

A twinge of suppressed excitement shot through her at the idea of her secret meeting. It would be the first time they'd be alone together and the day held so many possibilities. The widower had many years on Eithne, but he also had wealth and property. Certainly better than that filthy tinker boy, Seán. Hugh would be her best chance to escape from this wallowing pit of filth.

She gritted her teeth as she finished mucking out the cow byre. Someday, she'd be a rich lady, sitting in a palatial home, away from the shite and mud of any farm. Some might wish for true love or great fame, but Eithne dreamt of wealth and comfort above all.

Hugh O'Hagerty would get her there. His family earned their money from a fleet of fishing boats. He didn't even look too bad, for an older man. Often, he brought her gifts, a pretty scarf, or a carved bone comb, things she hid away from her family. If Esme ever found out, she'd ruin everything out of sheer jealousy.

There, all done! Eithne cleaned up and snuck back into the house. She changed into a fresh skirt and pulled out the glass bottle of expensive scent Hugh gave her last month. He claimed his cousin got it in Paris. Eithne dabbed sweet scent behind each ear and the nape of her neck. She added some to her chest where her breasts swelled, and smirked. He should like that.

As Eithne left the house, still full of stealth, she stole a glance at her sleeping sister. Esme met her little baker boy down at the standing stones, and those dirty Tinkers still camped out at the old fort. Would they never leave? The boy said they'd wait until the storm passed, but a month had passed now. Esme, Níamh, and now Bridey hung about whenever the young man, Seán, showed up. Her sister must be besotted by the boy. He had dark charm, but owned less than her parents did, without even a proper home. Such a waste. Her lip curled and she let out a snort of derision.

After testing her footing at the edge of the bog, she hiked up her skirts. She stepped over the white skull of a sheep. Esme hated the bog and avoided it. She once got trapped in one when they traveled to Portnoo. Eithne found her, honing in on her fear. No one had figured out how she'd found Esme. That's when the sisters realized that not everyone shared their bond. Eithne wished she didn't have it. If Esme twigged onto what Eithne planned today, there'd be hell to pay.

She'd arranged to meet Hugh at an old barn three miles from her home. Eithne didn't want to meet at his place, as his servants might talk. This barn had been boarded up and abandoned, so offered them a measure of privacy.

Eithne glanced over her shoulder, assessing the time. The sun peeked over the horizon, streaks of light skipping above the clouds. The colors blossomed in peach and lavender and for a moment, she caught her breath at the spectacular sight. That glorious sensation when Hugh kissed her felt like this. She breathed deep and focused, picking her way down the tiny path to her rendezvous.

Hugh waited for her on a wooden bench in the barn, the only thing resembling furniture in the whole place. He stood when she creaked open the door. Eithne shut it behind her and turned to him, her back flat against the door. An unaccountable panic shot through her, unsure if she did the right thing, but she shoved it away. She had no time for fear.

He gathered her into his strong arms. "Ah, my dear girl. I almost gave up on you." He wasn't tall for a man, but she fit into his warm embrace.

Hugh held her at arms-length and looked her up and down, a smile growing on his face. One hand remained on her waist while the other explored up her torso. As his touch brushed her breasts, her skin shivered and pebbled with anticipation.

She licked her lips, moving her hands up his back, and down to his buttocks. Eithne enjoyed his reactions when she touched him. It gave her a sense of power over him.

When he kissed her, the over-sweet pomade he used tickled her nose. She tasted a faint touch of tobacco and bacon on his lips. She melted into him in surrender.

Hugh's hands wandered around her waist and buttocks, and she pressed herself against him. Eithne wanted him to touch her everywhere, to make her shiver. She'd even made her own stays so her breasts pushed higher.

As she helped him unlace her stays, she paused. Perhaps she shouldn't do this? He might just discard her once she gave in. But his wife had died a few months before. He'd need a new one to run the household. Once they laid together, he'd want her.

Perhaps sensing her hesitation, Hugh brought her in for another passionate kiss. He continued down her neck, her breasts, and back to her stay ties. He pushed her down into the hay. Eithne lay back while he fondled her breasts, then her waist. His hands felt smooth, but his grip got rough.

Eithne loved the reaction he brought out in her, the tickling and shivering he evoked. He kissed her breasts, his stubble scratching her tender skin. After moving farther down to her nipples, he pinched one between his fingers, and she gasped at the sharp pain. He glanced up, but she didn't see concern or apology, just a smile of satisfaction at her response. Her nipple grew hard and his smile widened into a feral grin.

He yanked down her knickers and buried his head between her legs. His pomade-slick hair tickled her thighs. She tried not to squirm, but couldn't control herself and let out a low moan. He clutched her hips and licked her, moving his tongue within her. Eithne had never heard of this, but it felt so wonderful, she didn't want him to stop. This kiss didn't make babies. She'd grown up on a farm, so she knew how that happened, but it felt so delightful. While digging her fingers into his hair, she rode the wave of pleasure as her breath came fast.

Eithne lay, spent of energy and hoarse from moaning. She raised her head as he sat back, lighting a pipe. He wore a smug smile, full of satisfaction.

"What... what did you do?"

"That, my dear girl, was a special sort of kiss. It's much less risky than other things, you know. Perhaps you might return the favor?"

Eithne caught a glimmer of what he meant and a slow smile spread over her own lips. She didn't bother lacing her stays back on, but knelt down in front of him. She may not have much experience, but she must make him need her.

He helped her by removing his trousers. At first, she stared at him, unable to bring herself to touch him. She'd seen horses and cows, but they didn't do it that way. He took her hand and placed it on his shaft, and she explored the strange, smooth skin of his manhood. Her hands moved tentatively at first, but grew bolder with familiarity. After switching to her tongue, then her mouth, the salty sweat of his skin filled her mouth. His moans gave her great satisfaction, almost as much as when he gave her pleasure.

Hugh pushed her head down further than she intended. She almost gagged as he pumped his hips toward her mouth. Eithne had trouble breathing and tried to pull away, but he held her tight. A few more pushes and he spewed his seed into her mouth. She tried to back off, but he held her in place until his body finished pumping and he relaxed with a moan. Both panting with breath and effort, she sat next to him, her mouth aching and her lips tingling.

Once they rested and dressed, she glanced down at his now hidden manhood. "Less risky, you said?"

He winked. "I can't get you with child that way."

"Oh." Getting her with child meant he must marry her. "Might we, perhaps, take the risk... another time?"

His feral grin returned. "An anxious little minx, aren't you? Hmm. Perhaps, another time. But you know I can never marry you, do you not?"

Eithne's head spun and she grew dizzy. Her plans all required marriage. "Never?"

He snorted and rolled his eyes. "I'd lose my lands if I married a Catholic girl."

Catholic. Catholics were poor, and Protestant were rich. She'd known that all her life. With sudden inspiration, she blurted out, "What if I converted?"

He laughed. "Don't be silly."

"No, Hugh. I'm serious."

Hugh's eyes grew wide. "You'd change your religion, for me?"

She nodded with vigor, not trusting herself to speak. He gave a few thoughtful puffs on his pipe before answering her. "If you converted, then we might talk. But don't delay. I need to find a woman to manage the house soon. The maid's been filling in since my wife died, but she can't handle it all."

"How much time?"

Hugh rose, staring down his nose at her. "Immediately." With that, he strode out of the barn.

Eithne sat in the hay, thinking. She'd never been fervent in her faith. Eithne went to church because everyone did. She'd be in big trouble if she didn't. Her mother would pray over her soul and her sister would cry. Eithne laughed. This might even be amusing.

She stood, relaced her stays, and brushed the bits of straw from her skirts when the door opened again.

Esme stood in the doorway, outlined with the sun behind her and floating bits of hay dust dancing around in the sunbeams.

"I saw Mr. O'Hagerty leaving, Eithne. What in the name of all that's holy have you been up to?"

"That is exactly none of your business, Esme." Eithne moved to push past her twin, but Esme stood her ground.

"It *is* my business, and there's straw in your hair. Did you lay with him?"

"And what if I did? Are you going to run home and cry to Da?" Contempt dripped in her voice, but she patted her head to find the straw.

"I won't need to, not if he's gotten you with child. Well, you've made your bed, so to speak. You'll have to lie in it. I hope, for your sake, it's a comfortable one." She whirled out and slammed the barn door.

Eithne sat on the bench again, hard. The wooden planks jarred her spine. Would Esme say anything? She'd have to tread with caution until her plan worked out. That meant she'd need to be nice to her sister until then. The sickening notion made her stomach turn sour.

Esme

While hobbling around on his walking stick, their father slowly cleared the room and placed chairs and stools around the central hearth. The big wood-block table on one side would hold all the food. It wouldn't be a grand party, by any stretch of the imagination, but twins didn't turn eighteen every day.

Esme rushed to help her father with a chair he'd knocked over. "Da, you aren't supposed to be on that leg. You'll hurt yourself again. We can help with this. Sit!"

With a sheepish smile, her father sat in his favorite chair, with threadbare upholstery stuffed and re-stuffed over the years. "I am going mad with nothing to do, Esme. Give me something."

"Here, have some rushes. You can braid them into Brigid's Crosses."

He rolled his eyes. "Brigid's Day passed six weeks ago."

With a shrug, she pushed the straw into his hands. "So we'll have some made for next year."

"You remind me of my mother when you do that, Esme." Caitriona O'Malley Doherty had died years before, but Grandfa said she'd been a spitfire of a woman. She had plenty of backbone, but Esme decided it must have skipped a generation.

Esme turned as the door opened to reveal Seán and his parents, Oisín and Ciara. Oisín brought an enormous bowl of turnips, a flitch of bacon, and spring onions to add to the feast. He also brought his fiddle and Bridey clapped at the sight of it. Alan arrived with a basket of bread left over from the bakery. Their mother and Eithne arrived behind him, and the farmhouse seemed crowded with joy.

Soon, they had everyone laughing with witty stories. Only Eithne remained subdued. Her sister seemed distracted, and Esme sensed strange feelings through her twin connection. Their father assured her all young women had moody and sullen swings. But she'd become withdrawn and secretive, more than ever. Esme must discover what Eithne plotted. Had she seen Mr. O'Hagerty again?

Their grandfather hadn't arrived yet, so they set food aside for him and started supper.

Her father told the story of *Gráinne Ní Mháille*, the pirate queen of Ireland, while they ate. "She lived two hundred years ago and commanded a fleet of pirate ships. Her father had been a shipping merchant, so she inherited all his ships and trade. But she turned this business into a mighty empire of marauders and pirates. Gráinne owned over a thousand head of kine and horses.

"When the English governor of Connacht captured her sons and brother, she went straight to Queen Elizabeth herself. Can you imagine such a meeting, between two such powerful women?"

Eithne rolled her eyes, and their father shot her a glare. She ignored him and played with the half-eaten turnip on her plate. Níamh and Bridey stared at him, entranced by the story.

"A thief stole from her, so she chased him until he ran into a church for sanctuary. She waited for him to either starve or surrender. Can you guess what happened next?" He raised one eyebrow at Níamh until she giggled.

"The thief dug a tunnel under the church and escaped! She shouldn't have tried to capture someone in sanctuary, you see. That would be sacred ground."

Another grunt came from Eithne and Esme glared at her to behave.

Esme divided her attention between the dark, handsome Seán and her best friend, Alan. She sensed an undercurrent of tension. She'd spent time with both in the last several weeks, taking long walks along the shore, despite the chilly March weather, or picnics at the standing stones. While Alan warmed her soul, Seán made her heart flutter.

They acted like two strange dogs meeting, almost growling at each other. Esme even considered trying to see which one would do more for her, but she dismissed the thought as too much like something Eithne would do.

Her mother clapped for attention and brought out the pudding. She'd traded buttermilk with Alan's father for a sweet cake, complete with sugar icing. Eithne loved anything strawberry, and their mother found a few early wild strawberries to decorate the top. Despite all this, Eithne wore a sour expression.

After cutting the cake into slivers, her mother passed them around before she took her own. She ensured the pieces for Eithne and Esme looked the same size.

Bridey already ate her slice and smeared her finger along the edge of the plate, eager to capture every sweet crumb. Their mother rolled her eyes at her youngest child's addiction. Neither Alan nor Seán ate much of their slices.

Esme cocked her head to one side. "Seán? Do you not like strawberries?"

"They aren't the type of sweets I prefer, no." Despite his charming words, he ate a forkful without taking his eyes off Esme. Esme blushed and stared at her plate.

Alan snorted and shoved a huge bite into his mouth. Through a shower of bright crumbs, he declared, "I think it's delicious, Mistress Doherty!"

Their mother's eyes darted between Alan and Seán, narrowing.

Eithne slapped her hands on the table and pushed herself to her feet. "I have an announcement to make." The chair clattered to the floor with her abrupt movement. Her cake remained untouched except for the strawberries.

Their father's eyes grew full of concern. "What is it, Eithne? Is something gone amiss?"

"Nothing is amiss, Father. I only want to announce I am becoming Protestant. I will no longer be attending church with you." Everyone gaped as if she said she'd sprout wings and fly across the ocean to *Tír na nÓg*.

She retrieved her chair and sat as if nothing had happened.

Their mother frowned at her. "Eithne, what do you mean, you're becoming a Protestant?"

She took a delicate bite of the sweet pastry, closing her eyes. "I would think my meaning is clear, Mother, even for you."

Their mother blinked several times as if she had dust in her eyes. "The meaning, to be sure, but not the reason."

Eithne put her fork down and leveled a gaze at her mother. "Must I have a reason?"

Esme stared at her twin in complete confusion. "Yes, I think you must."

She lifted her chin. "Then my reason is I wish to own land someday."

Seán burst out laughing and Alan joined him. Her gaze blazed at Seán's ridicule. "There's nothing funny about that!"

Crossing his arms, their father frowned. "There is, pet, there is. You're a woman and a Catholic. You'll never own land." Her father sounded more amused than concerned, but Eithne's anger and frustration came off her like waves on an incoming tide.

"That's why I'm converting. I can change my religion, if not my sex. Who knows what the future holds? I *will* own land someday, and it won't be this run down, shabby, rock-riddled farm, either. It'll be rich land, with grazing cows, rolling green hills, and plenty of sheep. And I can, too, buy land! They repealed the law years ago."

Alan had stopped laughing, but shook his head. "Just because the law says you can doesn't mean you'll ever have the money, Eithne."

"Just wait. You'll see. You'll all see." She stood with dignity and stalked to the door to escape into the cool March evening.

Or, she tried. As soon as Eithne opened the door for her dramatic exit, she barreled into the imposing figure of their grandfather. She stumbled back, thunder on her face.

His broad grin flashed white teeth, matching his wild, white hair. "I brought gifts for everyone!"

Esme sat with her grandfather next to the old fort. The sun darted in and out of thin clouds in the spring afternoon. She loved spending time with him, talking things out. They spoke of Seán and his family, her own parents and even about Bridey and Níamh. Besides Alan, her grandfather was her best friend in the world. Esme could talk to him about anything. Still, she hesitated bringing Eithne up. He might not want to hear ill of his other granddaughter. It had gotten to where Esme couldn't think of anything *good* about her twin sister, and that troubled her.

When she broached the subject, Éamonn frowned. "There isn't a whole lot you can do about her, Esme. She'll make her own path in this world, that one. You're not your sister's keeper, after all. Ye've heard the priest say so, have you not?"

Esme bowed her head, understanding the truth of his words. She didn't have control of Eithne, any more than Eithne had control of Esme. But the way her twin acted galled her, as if only Esme had any sense in the family. "I want to protect Bridey and Níamh. Eithne acts nasty to them. I can hold my own against her, but the girls aren't as strong, and Eithne has brought them to tears, more often than not." She let out a short bark of laughter. "I should go to the Druid Stone over there and ask the Fair Folk for special magic to help."

Éamonn blinked a few times, regarding Esme with solemn eyes.

"What? What are you thinking, Grandfa?"

He pushed aside a stray curl which fell over her eyes. "What if you had magic? Would you use it?"

Esme stared at her grandfather as if he'd grown a second head. "Now that's a silly thing to ask, Grandfa. We have no magic unless you count your card tricks and dice. That's magic to those who lose to you, no mistake."

Éamonn's eyes widened with an enigmatic grin. "But if you *did* have something, a special power?"

Esme shifted in her seat. "What sort of power?"

Her grandfather shrugged. "Whatever you like. This is make-believe, is it not?"

She bit at her lower lip. "I think… I think I'd want to make food appear. So none of us would ever be hungry. I don't want Bridey or Níamh to ever have to worry about not having enough food."

Éamonn stared at her for another long moment and then bent to his saddle pack, slung over a nearby rock. After rifling through it, he pulled out several objects, placing them to the side with grunts of dissatisfaction. Finally, he held something up, standing with an expression of triumph. He handed her the velvet pouch.

Curious, she opened it and pulled out a heavy piece of jewelry. Esme traced the exquisite design with her finger, noting the detailed filigree work of stylized birds in gold and silver. Cabochons of purple stone gleamed. The penannular brooch had a circle with an opening along one edge. A long pin fit around the circular portion and through the space, to affix cloth through it. The beautiful piece looked far more valuable than anything she'd ever held. "It's lovely, Grandfa." She tried to hand it back.

He closed her fingers over the brooch. "No, you keep it, my dear Esme. It's meant for you."

Aghast, she stared at him. "I don't understand. Why in God's sweet name would you give this to me? What do you mean, 'meant for me?'"

While settling back down on the rock, he crossed his arms. "It must go to someone of my blood, and you're the best one for it. You said you wanted magic. This is magic."

"It's *what*? Grandfa, did you find a cache of whiskey somewhere?"

He gave a rueful chuckle. "No, I'm not drunk, but I *am* lucky. That's the magic it gave me. I can read people's emotions, which means I win at gambling. It'll be something else for you. The power's different for each person, so you don't get to choose getting food for everyone. But in order to be accepted by the brooch, each person must seek the power, and they must want to use the power for a good purpose."

"All this just because I asked for special magic? Grandfa, I only joked. Your tricks are amazing, and your luck at dice is legend, but magic?"

He lifted her chin to gaze straight into her eyes. "Not just because you asked, but because you don't want power for power's sake. You want it to help people, not to hurt them."

Éamonn took the brooch from her and stroked the edges with his thumb, outlining one bird. "It's an ancient relic we've had in the family for generations. It belongs to one person at a time, someone who has sought the magic. Your questions mean you sought it, no matter how tenuously. Some seek it with powerful will, overcoming incredible barriers. Others seek it without knowing what they're looking for. You're young for it, but I have faith in you. Esme, you're the strongest of your sisters, and the best of the lot."

"I still don't understand. What's so special about it?" Esme wanted to ask "what's so special about me," but didn't dare.

His face showed mock indignation. "You mean, besides the fact it's a gorgeous piece of jewelry?"

She rolled her eyes. "Stop teasing me, Grandfa. Yes, besides that."

"Family legend claims a druid gifted us the brooch, back at the dawn of time. One of our ancestors helped him, but we've lost the true story over the years. As repayment, the druid gifted this brooch and its powers to our family. It imbues you with something, I don't know what. For me, I can sense emotions or intentions. Just a bit, mind you, nothing dramatic."

Their grandfather told so many tales about druids and their role in ancient Ireland. Magical men, priests, lawyers, bards, historians, all rolled into one. Chiefs kept druids as his most honored advisors. They faded away over the last thousand years, after Christianity came.

She stared at the brooch as if a live snake would uncoil and strike her. "What if I don't want it?"

"You *do* want it. You wouldn't have asked if you didn't, deep inside." He patted his chest over his heart.

Her eyes grew wide. "What power would I have? Would it help against Eithne?"

"I can show you how to find out. Tonight, after supper."

They tramped up to the old stone circle as evening fell, despite the chilly drizzle. The mists embraced them in a thick woolen blanket, drowning out all sounds. It isolated them from the world. Esme shivered under her cloak from a trickle of water crawling down the back of her neck. Tramping around the peat bogs in April held dangers. The day stayed soggy, and bogs shifted without warning. Their feet slipped and sunk into the wet ground. Besides the physical chill, ice gripped her heart. She shouldn't be taking part in this pagan magic, even if her grandfather showed her. It seemed wicked and dangerous, something she shouldn't meddle with. The thought made her shiver worse than the cold.

She trailed behind her grandfather, watching each spot, alert for sucking mud. The loamy earth and sere grasses tickled her nose as her feet crushed them. The odd, sweet smell of fog caressed her.

Éamonn halted and she bumped into him. The stones loomed, stark and dim in the low light. The mist made them seem almost alive, menacing and broody.

Éamonn threw off his outer cloak, revealing a colorful robe of deep aqua like late autumn skies. His thick, white hair stuck up at odd angles after he removed his hood. He raised both hands and held an old-fashioned, ornate pewter goblet. It glinted through the gloom as he walked around the circle, outside the stones, in a clockwise direction. Esme followed, certain she would burn in Hell for this. Under her cloak, she crossed herself for protection.

He chanted, but she didn't understand the words. It sounded Irish, but not quite, like someone from County Kerry. She understood the words "light" and "shadow," perhaps something about the sun? No sun penetrated the gloomy twilight.

Éamonn stopped at the point he'd begun and brought the cup to his lips. He turned and offered it to her. She glanced inside at the dark liquid, and up at Éamonn, who nodded with an encouraging grin. She sniffed it, her hands on the goblet growing warm. Where had he kept this? She hadn't even seen him pour it.

The earthy and alcoholic liquid seemed full of ancient power. Her head buzzed with just one sip. Éamonn gestured for her to drink the rest. The strong drink punched her in the gut. She coughed and sputtered.

Éamonn pulled out the brooch. The jewelry shone with a bright, blue glow through the haze. No, green, or perhaps both? It pulsed with light, sending out beams of jewel-bright color in all directions. The fog reflected the light back until the entire clearing flashed, as if the Northern Lights had invaded this pocket of mist, within this ancient stone circle. A loud hum tingled through her feet and hands. A smoking, burnt odor came, like a tree struck by lightning.

Éamonn held out his hand, the shining brooch flat on his palm.

All the prayers and vows of renouncing Satan crowded into her mind at once. She backed away, shaking her head. "No! No, I can't do it, Grandfa!"

Her grandfather raised his eyebrows. "Can't, or won't? Did you not say you wanted magic? You've already supped from the goblet. The ceremony has begun."

Her eyes grew wide. "What happens if I don't?"

He grabbed her shoulder, his gaze intense. "I don't know, *mo ghrá*. I truly don't know. But to do so might very well anger the Fae. And that, as you know from all the tales, is a dangerous thing."

Esme didn't like it one bit. But her grandfather wouldn't lie to her. Besides, it'll all be nonsense anyhow. With a final fervent prayer to all things holy, she touched the brooch.

A buzz, a tingle, and a flood of pain flashed up her arm and into her body. The blue glow crawled through her, settling in her heart and belly. The heat and light pulsed, then froze and sparkled. She cried out, but it morphed into music, a sweet, clear, tuneless note, like a blue songbird to the heavens. Eithne flashed through her mind with a skeptical sneer, but then her twin disappeared.

A figure appeared in the mists. She squinted to make out details, but it erupted so brightly, she had to turn away.

Esme's hair stood on end and the blue light shook her. She trembled as if she would break in two. A frenzy of delight and terror warred within her, flashes of battle and conflict, divine retribution and heavenly joy.

The world turned black.

Esme's eyes wouldn't open. She tried to move her leg, but it refused to obey. Panic rose in her heart, but voice didn't work, either. Her finger? Yes, her fingers moved. Several of them. She clenched and unclenched her hands, shaking out her fingers.

She turned her wrist, bent her arm, and brought her hand up to her face.

Dried mud cracked on her eyes. How did mud dry so fast? "Grandfa? What's on my eyes? What happened?"

She pried it off, crumbs falling down her stays and shivered. The bog had soaked her back and her hands sank into the earth as she pushed herself up.

A hand emerged from the swirling fog, a familiar, wrinkled hand. She grasped the fingers and he pulled her up. He hugged her close until she grew steady on her feet. She peered at the now dormant brooch. The stones, originally purple, now shone deep aqua in the dim light.

"Are you well, Esme? It hits you hard the first time. You'll recover soon, I wager."

Even though she had no reason to doubt him, the truth of his words showed as plain as if he held a sign over his head.

"I.... I can tell." Her eyes widened as she realized what she said.

He raised his eyebrows. "You can, can you?"

She nodded. "Yes, I know. You told the truth."

"Ah, so that's it, then. I hadn't heard of that one, but it might prove useful. A mixed blessing, though, to be sure." Éamonn regarded her, his expression sad and sympathetic. She didn't understand his sorrow. *This power can be a wonderful tool!*

Chapter Four

March 1792

Eithne

Eithne clenched her fists against her stomach. "I don't understand, Hugh. You said—"

"I *said* I wouldn't marry a Catholic. I did *not* say I would marry the first Protestant roundheel who came along."

Hugh *did* say it, before she ever asked the reverend about converting. That they'd be together always if she converted to Protestant. He'd said yes, hadn't he? Eithne's eyes burned with anger and shame, but she refused to let him see her cry. "But I've defied my family and gone through all the steps…"

He waved away her protests. "That's as may be, but you're still a poor farm girl, when all's said and done. Your grandfather is a Tinker, for God's sake. You've no family name, no connections, and no wealth. How would I increase my wealth if I marry you?"

Eithne wanted to die from mortification. She'd done what he asked, hadn't she? She'd renounced her Catholic faith, gone to the Protestant priest—no, the reverend—and declared her intention to convert. Eithne even took classes with him to learn the precepts, passed his test, and gotten confirmed. That act alone felt like she'd taken a giant step up the social ladder.

But now Hugh claimed she hadn't done enough. Eithne's face burned with shame and rage. She'd done it for *him*. "I hate you, Hugh. You disgust me!" She pummeled her fists on his chest.

He pulled her into his arms. Eithne struggled to escape, but he held her tight. Eventually, she relaxed and sobbed against his chest. He stroked her curls, picking bits of straw and flicking them away.

Hugh kissed her on the forehead and tipped her chin up. Her eyes burned with tears and she wouldn't meet his eyes. Shaking his head, he disentangled himself and left the barn with a shrug.

Alone, she paced, her stride getting larger as her temper increased. Sparks of despair shot through her like gunshots as she pounded a fist on the wooden wall. What should she do next? The late morning sunlight streamed through the slats, illuminating the bits of straw dust they'd disturbed in amorous activities. The scent of their bodies and the dust made her nose itch. Eithne eyed a spider on the wall with suspicion.

At least Eithne finally convinced him to move past his "special kiss" into the full act. She treasured the power lying with Hugh gave her, the control she had over his body and emotions. The experience gave her power and pleasure. He lost any semblance of sense when he finished.

Her secondary plan hadn't yet worked, despite her efforts. She hadn't gotten with child. Eithne halted mid-stride. He wouldn't know. She'd just "lose" the child later, as so many women did. A sly smile crept across her face.

Would he react as she expected? Hugh had his own sense of honor. He should consider it his duty, despite her poor origins.

Eithne brushed her skirts of the last bits of straw and strode out of the barn, straight into her grandfather. She fell back several steps, her eyes wide.

Éamonn studied her, one eyebrow raised in question. "And just what're you doin' out here, Eithne? This isn't our land."

"Looking for Níamh. I thought she might have hidden out here. We had a fight." Eithne clutched her skirt.

"Níamh is at home carding wool. I just left there. What's your real reason?"

"I... hadn't seen this place in a while and wanted to make sure it still stood." She patted the doorframe as if testing its strength.

"Eithne." His voice brimmed with tension.

She blinked in feigned innocence. "Yes, Grandfa?"

"I just spied Hugh O'Hagerty leaving, not two minutes ago. Would you like to change your story again, or will you tell the truth this time?"

Eithne set her chin in a stubborn lock and refused to answer.

They stood like two ancient stones, staring each other down, a battle of wills. "Have you given yourself to him, then?" His voice turned gentle, disappointment clear in his tone.

Unwilling to reveal the slightest inkling of her plans, she kept her lips clamped shut. Her father might interfere, but she had no faith in his competence to do anything. Still, better to stay silent.

"Is that why you had this mad notion of turning Protestant? Oh, Eithne, did you imagine he would marry you, then?"

More silence. Eithne ground her teeth to keep from shouting *yes*.

Her grandfather shook his head. "You're well aware his sort don't marry our sort, Eithne. You're a fool to hope otherwise."

Her eye twitched at being called a fool, and her jaw ached with clenching, but she kept silent.

After letting out a sigh, he pointed toward their home. "Back to the house, young lady. Your father will deal with you later."

Eithne stood a moment longer in defiance, then stalked off, skirts in hand to clear the brambles surrounding the barn. One foot splashed down into a mud puddle, ruining her dramatic exit. The Irish girl spit a nasty word which earned her another glare from her grandfather.

Esme

Esme turned into the cow byre, muck bucket in hand, intent upon her chores. She didn't notice Seán leaning against the back of the wall until she almost ran into him. Her heart skipped a beat and she placed a hand over it with a gasp. "And just what are you doing out here, young Seán? Haven't you chores of your own?"

He chewed on a piece of straw, his black hair shining and perfect. He gave a half-smile, dimple showing, and pushed off from the wall. "I've been waiting on you, fair flower. Would you like help with your bucket?" He bent to take it from her hands.

Esme shuffled back out of his reach. She wouldn't let this slick young man get her into his favor so easily. "I can manage on my own, thank you kindly." She strode to the slop pile, turned her back, and half-emptied her bucket.

He placed his hand on her hip. Shocked, she whirled around, flinging the rest of the muck across his chest and legs. He jumped back, cursing and wiping at the cowshit. It just smeared across his shirt

Giggles burst from her, despite herself. Esme grabbed a clean cloth from her pocket to clean off the muck. "You should watch where you're standing, Seán!" She wiped the worst of it from his chest, then stopped, unwilling to wipe farther down. With a gulp, she handed him the soiled rag to complete the task.

He gave her a sly glance. "You're not drying the rest? I'd be grateful if you did."

Esme sniffed and draped the stained rag over his arm as he had made no move to take it. Esme picked up her bucket, emptied the rest in the pile and turned to leave, just as Alan came around the corner.

"What's going on here, then?"

Esme opened her mouth to answer when Seán drawled out with an impish grin, "My girl, Esme, here, cleaned my, uh, trousers for me."

Aghast at such a bold answer, she spun around. Alan's face turned red, then purple. He looked about to burst. Before she had a chance to explain, Alan launched himself at Seán, spluttering, "Esme's not your girl!"

Seán still stood close to the slop pile, so they both tumbled into the mess, writhing and wrestling like a pair of pigs in a frenzy of rage. The horse in the barn whinnied, which set off the chickens.

Torn between paroxysms of laughter and horror at two boys fighting over her, she fetched a clean bucket of water from the well. They'd want cleaning when they stopped behaving like jealous fools. When she returned, they still fought.

Seán held Alan's head in the mud, while the local boy lashed out, clutched at the Tinker's leg, and yanked him off balance. Alan then leapt on the other boy, a well-placed punch connecting with his jaw. Seán roared in rage and grabbed Alan's neck, pushing his face back into the mud.

Did they fight over her? The notion both excited Esme and made her nervous. She winced as Alan took a punch to the face, but then he got his own back by kicking Seán in the groin. Esme didn't know which she wanted to win.

Growls and grunts emerged from the writhing bodies, increasing the porcine illusion. The clamor attracted Níamh and Bridey from inside the house. Níamh held a spindle and had bits of wool sticking to her shirt and skirt. Bridey had straw in her hair from cleaning the horse barn.

"A fight?" Níamh's eyes grew wide. "Are they fighting over you?"

Esme bit at her lip and nodded. "I'm pretty sure Seán provoked Alan on purpose." *Sweet Lord, they're a right mess.* Every square inch of their bodies got covered in mud, straw, and muck. The laughter bubbled up through her nose.

Her giggles set off Bridey and Níamh. This brought their mother out, and she joined the merriment.

The chorus of laughter penetrated the fog of the two combatants, and the struggle slowed. They stumbled to their feet, gave each other sullen looks, and faced the line of laughing women.

After wiping the muck from his face, Seán gave Esme a half-smile and sauntered off to his own camp, his head held high. Alan, however, dipped a cloth into the water bucket and scrubbed at his face, sluicing the worst of the filth off. With a final giggle, Esme helped, sharing a smile with her muddy friend. Níamh and Bridey fetched two more buckets of water and upended these on Alan's head, much to his surprise.

"Hey!" He blinked as the water dripped from his hair.

Her mother shook her head and chuckled. "Well, at least you're cleaner now, Alan."

More squeals and laughter abounded as Alan and the girls played with the water. Thoroughly soaked and in great spirits, they cleaned their mess and returned to the farmhouse. Esme threw a glance at Alan, as his shirt clung to his chest even more than Seán's had. Bridey made a great deal of fuss about drying him off.

Later that afternoon, Seán cornered her in the pasture. His eyes glittered with anticipation. "I'm not joking, Esme."

No, Seán didn't joke. But she couldn't answer him, either. Not yet. She shook her head, and escaped into the house.

She could tell if someone was joking, now. After testing her theory with a game, using Níamh and Bridey, Esme now spotted the truth when people spoke it. She had them tell tales and one in three must be true. Esme guessed right each and every time, so much that Bridey accused her of cheating.

Esme noted how often Eithne lied. Esme had always sensed when her twin spun a tale, from their twin bond, but now she observed the lie, as bright as day. A sullen light glowed on her sister's face. Esme didn't even need to have the brooch with her. It may be the Devil's work, but it helped her keep Eithne's lies in check, and that must be a good thing.

She noticed when the baker fibbed about how long ago he baked the bread, and when her father assured them the farm would succeed. It made her sad how often people lied.

But Seán spoke the truth.

From what he said, he wanted her to run away with him, marry him, and be his wife. If she didn't have the brooch, she might dismiss him as a debaucher, only interested in bedding her. But Seán didn't lie to her.

Traveling didn't sound like a terrible life. Esme might enjoy journeying around the country, meeting all the interesting people. Seán, with his handsome, dark flashing eyes and wavy hair which always fell into his face. He always told delightful tales. Once, he claimed to be descended from Spanish Armada survivors, and no lie shone through. Esme wasn't certain if that meant it was true or that he believed it was true.

Esme trusted her grandfather's judgment and wanted to ask about Seán and his family. His parents seemed kind enough, but their wagons looked threadbare and worn.

She sighed and returned to her task, her wooden loom shuttle clacking back and forth, back and forth. The mindless activity of weaving allowed her to think at the same time.

Esme considered Alan. She'd always imagined she'd marry him, but he never asked and Seán did. Alan only thought of her as a friend, not as a wife. But then, why had he fought so hard for her? She might be happy as his wife, but he—

Her mother's sharp tone cut into her musings. "What are you doing over there, Esme? You're huffing and puffing like a hound in a rabbit hole."

"Just thinking, Ma."

"Well, don't think so hard you forget your place."

Their mother brushed the cat, pulling out teasels and burrs from its long, orange fur. She must have pulled too hard, because it hissed and struggled out of her grasp, bolting for the door. Her hand bled from a long scratch. "Bloody cat."

Rain sheeted outside, so everyone worked indoors. Bridey repaired a rag rug, rebraiding the ends. Níamh dangled her spindle, while Eithne scrubbed the dishes with sullen industry.

Bridey piped up, "When will Da be back?" He'd promised her a gift when he returned from the market.

Their mother shrugged. "Not until the rain eases up. He wouldn't want to get stuck in the mud."

Bridey pouted at her delayed gift but shrugged. "Can we sing a song?"

With a smile, their mother sang in her clear, high soprano.

"Ar m'éirighe dhom ar maidin,
Grian a' tsamhraidh 'g taitneamh."

The song did little to occupy Esme's mind, however, as she knew the words to *Seán O'Duibhir a' Ghleanna* well.

Esme kept thinking about Seán… and Alan. The exciting man who would take her to travel all over Ireland, or the comfortable friend who she'd laugh with every day.

Eithne

As they lay naked in the hay, Hugh crossed his arms, his eyes cold. "You're lying to me."

While forcing herself to keep her chin high, Eithne held his gaze. "I am *not* lying. I should have started my courses three weeks ago."

"You might be mistaken. I've heard women miss them sometimes."

Eithne laughed. "Old women, perhaps, when they're almost dried up and done with their mother years. But young women are regular." This might not be true, but Hugh wouldn't know any better.

He stood silent for several moments. Eithne held her breath as her back and shoulders ached from the tension.

They'd made love in their barn and lay next to each other, with their limbs still entangled with sweat and scent. The May afternoon left them sticky with their love-making, and she clung tight to his body. A raucous bird squawked outside the barn.

Hugh made a noise, and she tensed again, but he remained silent, pondering his options. After several minutes, he stood, pulling her to her feet. He studied her naked self, as if appraising a prize thoroughbred horse, or a mule for sale. He ran a finger around her nipple, his hand moving along her waist and hip, examined her hands, and then each part of her body.

Hugh tapped his lips several times before he grunted with decision. "You will bear me at least two sons. If you have a girl, you must try again. If you don't complete this task in five years, I shall divorce you to get heirs with another woman."

Affronted, Eithne retreated from him, grabbing her clothing and clutching it to her bosom. "Divorce? And what would I do then?" Protestants allowed divorce, but this sounded like a business transaction, not a marriage proposal.

"That's not my concern. I need sons for my estate. If you can't give them to me, you are of no use."

Eithne bit her tongue on a sharp response. She must grasp this chance. She wanted to be married to a man of wealth. No sense now in queering the deal with misplaced notions of romance. She stared at him, as he stood perfectly at ease with his own nakedness. Still clutching her clothing against her naked breasts, she gathered what shreds of self-possession she had. "I shall be your brood mare, Hugh O'Hagerty. I shall give you your sons. But you *must* treat me with respect and dignity."

"I shall observe all proprieties, never fear, Eithne." He examined her again, up and down. With one finger under her chin, he moved her head to the left then to the right. "Do let us hope you're presentable when you clean up, hmm?"

Esme

Seán's back flexed as he rode the horse ahead of her. Esme wondered what those muscles would feel like under her hands. His dark hair and flashing eyes reminded her of tales of Spanish pirates. He acted as if he expected each girl to swoon over him. At least he didn't expect her to perform such foolishness. He seemed to accept her friendship with no demands.

They rode horses out to the Maghera Beach sand dunes, a few hours' ride each way, for a relaxing afternoon together. A road wound down through town and out to the dunes, but they had to walk through the dunes for quite a while to reach the shore. The wind blew chilly, but the sun shone brightly. They knew better than to squander such a fine chance for an outing.

Esme rode a placid mare, a cob from Seán's father's string. He rode a mare named Nuala, more spirited but still biddable. She wasn't an expert rider by any stretch of the imagination, so appreciated her own mount's docile attitude.

Seán reined in at a rising dune. "Here?" Long seagrass, whipping in the wind, crowned the dunes.

Sand blew up and scoured her face, making her splutter. "Someplace more sheltered?"

The Tinker clucked at Nuala until they found an alcove of high dunes. He found a sheltered pocket of peace from the winds.

Once the wind eased, Esme exclaimed, "This is perfect!"

Seán hopped off his horse and pulled down the basket of food and ale. "Your wish is my command, my lady!" He set things out while Esme climbed the next dune to gaze at the sea.

Maghera Beach sat on the edge of a long, low tidal inlet which reached toward Ardara Town. A magnificent maze of dunes higher than even her father's head guarded the land, so high she might get lost in them as the tide came in. While the tide stayed low, they had little danger of getting caught, but she reminded herself to pay attention to the sun.

Esme removed her shoes and stockings to walk on the sand, squishing it between her toes, so sensual and unusual. Despite the cool, soft sand under her feet, the whipping wind sent her back down into the safety of the private alcove. She stood, staring out at the ocean.

Seán came up behind her. "Are you enjoying the view?"

"I am. How far away is America? Can we see it from here?"

Seán let out a full belly laugh, long and loud.

Hurt, Esme frowned. "I didn't make a joke!"

"Esme, dear, America is thousands of miles across the ocean. There's no way we'd see it from here. We can't even see Iceland, and that's not even halfway across the sea."

Though sheepish at her ignorance, she didn't wish to show it. "Legends of Hy-Brasil might have been glimpses of America in the mists."

He sat on the blanket, stretching out his long legs. "Ah, well, it might've been the islands off the coast, or perhaps men high from spirits. We'll never know, but it wouldn't have been America."

Esme made a face at him. After reaching for the biggest chunk of bread, she tucked a bit of ripe goat's cheese with honey into the center. The creamy sweetness made her close her eyes in pleasure. She grabbed a bottle of ale to wash down the gummy mess.

He glanced at her from under lowered lashes. "Here, have the berries. They're tart yet, as it's early, but great with the cheese." The couple enjoyed a companionable silence as they ate their meal.

Seán had a puzzled expression. "Why did you want to see America?"

With a shy smile, she brushed sand off her knee. "It's a place of mystery, a land of strange creatures and people. Like tales of the Fomorians. A place filled with wild savages and mountains of gold. Who wouldn't be captivated by such tales?"

Seán laughed again. "And if you believe half of what you hear about the place, you're even more naïve than I imagined, Esme Doherty. Mountains of gold!"

Esme clenched her jaw. She wanted to believe in mountains of gold, or at least, the promise of an unknown land. There must be something better than scraping a living from the earth like they did. And who was Seán to laugh at her innocence? He may have traveled, but he was no man of the world.

The sun reached for the water and the wind died as they packed up the horses. The late afternoon sun turned the air balmy. Seán stopped and turned to her, gripping both her arms. "Esme, what do you want from your future?"

Startled, she resisted the urge to give a glib answer. He wanted something more than, "wealth and happiness." He wanted something from the heart. "I want a husband, children, a house of my own. Someplace I can call home. Seán, you're hurting me."

"Oh, sorry." He let go of her arms but took her hands. "What about the place you live now?"

Esme frowned, glancing back toward Ardara. "That's Da's home. I mean a place of my own, away from my sister. A place where I run things."

"Greedy for power, are you, then?" Seán grinned, taking the sting out of the comment. She flung a chunk of grass from the dune at him, but he ducked.

"And what about you? What do you want from your life?"

Seán stared into her eyes, taking a deep breath. He smelled of sand, musk, and sweat. He said nothing for a long time and let his breath out again. "I want much the same as you. A good business in trading, a family, a place to call home."

Her eyes grew wide. "Home? But you love being a Traveler. Tinkers don't have homes."

"That's not true. Our wagons are our homes. We just take them with us." He brushed sand off the blanket near the strawberries and chose one from the pile.

"I wouldn't want to live like that. We'd always be moving to a new place." Seán laughed at her and she grimaced. "What's so funny now?"

"Constantly moving to a new place. That's what it is and what makes it so wonderful."

"*Hmph.* I don't see it that way. What I see is constant chaos. I want a place where I can have my things about me, in their proper place. A hearth I can sew near, in the long summer nights. Horses in the barn. Children playing around me. Food on the table."

He tossed a strawberry green over his shoulder. "Ah, well, I suppose I'd have to find you such a place."

Esme straightened her back. "You? And why should that be your duty?"

Seán grinned at her. "Who else? You've no older brother to help and your da is, forgive me, on the feckless side."

Furious at his condescension, she clenched her fists. "You've no right to sit judgment on Da!"

He pulled back. "I meant no disrespect, Esme."

She pursed her lips until he gave her a strawberry as a peace offering. Relenting, she bit into the soft flesh. "And you don't have any brothers or sisters?" Most Irish families had plenty of children. He must have some older siblings out on their own.

"No, though Mam wanted more. She can't have any now. Mam almost died with me, and Da would rather have her than more children. At least, so he always says when she bemoans her barrenness."

"Good for him." Esme wanted lots of children, more than anything, but so many women died in childbirth.

"Well, it makes things easier for me, at any rate. I don't have to fight with any brothers for my parents' regard. I don't have to vie to be the favorite." He gave her a rueful grin.

And he'd inherit all they had, not that they had much. Her blood grew cold. Had she turned as mercenary as Eithne? Thinking of her twin gave her a brief shimmer of their connection, but she pushed it away.

Still, it didn't sound like so bad of a life. Would Seán make her happy? He made her skin tingle when he touched her.

The next day, as they walked along the path toward town, Alan scowled at her. "I don't like him, Esme. He's up to no good."

Esme rolled her eyes. "You're just mad I spent yesterday with him."

He stopped walking and gripped her arm, his expression fierce. "I'm serious, I don't trust him."

Esme had learned to discern between faith and factual truth. Truth had several shades. Just because someone believed something, like the sky being green, didn't mean it was true. It only meant they truly believed it.

So while the truth shone plainly on Alan's face, that didn't mean his mistrust was valid. She pushed at Alan's belief, to see which type of truth he spoke. "What makes you say that?"

In a low voice, as if talking to himself, Alan said, "I don't like the way he looks at you." He looked up as if surprised he spoke.

Dealing with such complex problems took time, and her head ached working it out. Alan didn't help matters by whining. "Look, I'm not with him this afternoon, Alan. I'm with you. Can we just enjoy our day without fighting?"

His knuckles turned white on the basket he carried. She hoped he wouldn't break the handle on her good basket. Esme packed a couple of strawberries, cheese, and the loaf of onion bread he brought.

Their friendship had grown rockier as summer approached. Seán wasn't even courting her. But Alan never asked to court her, either, so he had no reason on God's green earth to act jealous.

They walked past the village toward the long, low sandy inlet at low tide. Alan arranged a rag rug to one side and sat on the end. Esme stood with her hands on her hips, waiting for him to notice her annoyance.

He pulled a strawberry out and his mouth opened to bite into it when he noticed Esme hadn't joined him. He looked comical with his mouth wide, upper teeth touching the pink flesh of the fruit.

Alan removed the fruit from his mouth and cocked his head at her. "What's the problem, Esme?"

She sat, crossing her legs, and fiddled with the edge of the rug, pulling on a frayed bit. "That would be my question for you. You've been a right pest, and I want to know why."

"How have I been a pest?"

Esme stopped playing with the fringe. "You keep needling me about Seán when there's nothing going on between us."

His eyes narrowed. "Nothing?"

"Nothing. He's a neighbor and a friend, and that's it, Alan Gallagher. Can't you get it through your thick skull?"

His eyes got narrower, and he held her gaze as he bit into the strawberry. "Aye, I suppose I can. Promise?"

"Promise? What would you like me to promise, Alan? That we're just friends? Yes. That I won't allow him to take me away and get married on some windswept moor, like an outlandish tale out of the *Book of Invasions*? Yes, I can promise those. What more do you want from me?"

Alan laughed at the image and she joined him. They laughed harder, goading each other on until Alan tossed her the other strawberry. Esme bit into the sweet flesh, and a dribble of juice running down her chin.

"Here, let me." Alan yanked a piece of cloth from the basket and dabbed her face with a gentle hand. Like a lover's caress.

Alan's blue eyes seemed brighter. Esme stared at them for an eternity. "Alan…" at the same time he said, "Esme…"

They both halted and she giggled. He touched her cheek again, this time without the cloth. Her skin tingled with intense anticipation and she closed her eyes. He kissed her, a soft kiss, barely on the lips.

Alan's kiss was sweet and lovely, but not what she'd hoped for. Esme wasn't sure what she wanted, but the kiss was like one a brother might give, not a lover.

What's worse, when she kissed Alan, she pictured Seán. She mustn't marry Alan and think of someone else. It wouldn't be fair to him. "Alan…"

Panic showed in his eyes. "Esme, please, give me a chance."

She stared at the rug. "We shouldn't." A maddening thing she'd discovered about her talent, her own truth came plain, too, if she bothered listening.

Alan turned away, his face flushed. "Ah, no, well." He shuffled around with the basket. "Here, have a cheese. It tastes good with the strawberries." The bright glint of a tear might shine in his eyes, but she must have imagined it.

Her grandfather had been right. Knowing the truth sometimes hurt.

Esme squirmed in the church pew as the priest intoned the Latin Mass. The words barely registered. Her mind churned with uncharitable thoughts and disappointments.

Ever since her grandfather gave her that wicked, pagan brooch, she saw the truth in every face. It showed as a bright glow to their skin, pulsing with colored light, depending on the person and the lie. Maybe a good Catholic should trust everyone, regardless of their lies.

Before, Esme wouldn't have understood how horrid this would be. Eithne's every word seemed to be a lie, but that didn't surprise Esme at all. Or her mother and father lying about the farm's success. She had eyes and understood that truth without the druid magic. But when she went to market day, a series of rude surprises awaited her.

Everyone lied. Constantly. The lies infected everyone. A man selling fruit lied about how long ago he'd picked his apples. The butcher lied about how long he'd aged the beef. A woman buying bread lied about how many coins she had, to get a lower price. Even the priest lied. Esme realized he was only a man, but a priest should be a mouthpiece for God, and rise above petty things. He lied to the congregation in his sermons. He lied to individuals about having a lovely time at tea.

Esme experimented with her talent, trying to push the limits of what it might reveal. With considerable effort of will, she might force someone to tell the truth. However, this exhausted her to the point of passing out, so she didn't do it often. Besides, sometimes she didn't want to hear the truth she compelled.

Coming to terms with all the lies grew difficult. Life itself was one big deception. What's the point of a life full of lies? Esme found nothing but greed and fraud on a universal scale. Even when tiny, insignificant in the grand scheme of life, Esme saw these lies as a filthy scum upon every soul she met.

As the priest droned on, her head ached from the incense. Crowded and close, breathing became hard. The man in the pew in front of her smelled of onions. He must have eaten them while walking to the church service to stink so much.

Throughout the service, she sat like a sullen lump as the priest spoke lie after lie. Her parents didn't notice. They tried to keep the squirming younger girls still. Bridey and Níamh wanted to be out in the sun while it shone. They had no mind to spend the bright, warm May day in church.

After several sharp words and slaps on the hand, the younger girls settled down. Esme avoided greeting the priest on the way out, not wanting to shake the priest's hand and be sullied with the sham.

On the walk back to the farmhouse, the younger girls ran ahead, their mother running to catch up with them. Their father walked beside Esme, still limping from his injury, furrowing his brow. "What's the matter, Esme? Isn't this a glorious day?"

Cynicism dripped from her voice. "Yes, the *day* is glorious."

"Then why are you walking as if you're slugging through mud?"

Esme glanced up at him. "Da, why does everyone lie so much?"

Her father halted. "Lies? Who's lying to you, my dear child?"

Her temper snapped at this condescension. "I'm not a dear child. I'm a woman grown! And everyone lies. The priest lies, the butcher lies, even *you* lie!"

He took a step back, and her mother joined them. "Esme, dear, what on earth are you babbling on about?"

Throwing her hands in the air, Esme let loose. "Everyone lies, every day. About tea, about food, about how nice someone's dress looks, even about what a *glorious day* it is." She gestured up at the lowering clouds in the sky. She didn't mention the most serious lies, like her sister's, or when her father assured them the farm would be fine. "Why can't everyone just tell the truth?"

Her father's eyes grew sad and tired and he placed a hand on her shoulder. "It's not as easy as all that, my dear. People don't *mean* to hurt others with little lies. It's the grease that keeps society polite, that's all."

Esme clenched her fists and pulled away from him, unwilling to be comforted. "And the truth isn't polite?"

After shaking his head, he dropped his hand to his side. "Not always, no. If I told Shona her hair looked a mess, it would hurt her feelings. Instead, I tell her she looks lovely and offer to brush her hair. It makes relations more diplomatic." Her mother narrowed her eyes and touched her head self-consciously.

"But it's still a lie, Da! It's still telling an untruth. I can't understand why it's so bad to tell the truth!"

"You'll understand when you're older, *mo chuisle*, to be sure."

"'When I'm older.' Da, I'm eighteen and a woman! How much older do I need to be to understand things?"

He glanced at her mother, but she just shrugged.

Esme stared at her father, unwilling to credit his words. She considered pushing for an answer but then decided not to chance it. She suspected she wouldn't like the answer.

As her anger built, her father gave a sad smile. "You don't understand, my dear daughter—"

She didn't want to hear empty words, so she ran. Esme knew running made her a melodramatic brat, but she didn't care. She spoke the truth, at any rate. And truth seemed in short supply.

Esme ran past the brambles of gorse, blooming yellow and full of thorns. She ran past their home and farm, as the cows mooed. Then she ran up the hill, to the stones of the old fort, one of her refuges. She'd forgotten Seán and his family still camped nearby until she spied him. He sat on a stone, repairing horse tack. The young man glanced up as she approached, flushed and mussed from her flight.

"What's going on, pet? Is a *ban sídhe* chasing you?" He grinned at his joke but lost the smile at her expression. "Hey, lass, it can't be all bad. Come, sit here with me and tell me what's amiss."

She panted, leaning against the fence. He placed the harness down and put his arm around her shoulders. His embrace felt natural and warm, protective and safe. She sighed, trying to keep it from becoming a sob.

"Tell me, pet. I'm here for you. You can trust me."

He spoke the complete truth, and that fact shone on his face. This simple truth gave her a spark of hope through the bog of despair she sank into.

The tears took over. She might be crying for the betrayal from the lies, or from the joy at Seán's truth.

Seán stroked her hair, bits of red locks curling up to crackle under his hand. "Shh, shh, *mo chroí*… I'm here."

Esme's eyes ached and she had a stuffy nose. He held her tight, his shirt getting soaked with her tears and snot. She pulled back, but he held tight. When she glanced up into his eyes, so dark brown they looked black, she might peer through his eyes into forever. "I'm just so tired of everyone lying. Everyone lies. All the time."

He gripped her shoulders so hard it hurt. "I promise I won't ever lie to you, *mo chroí*."

The words struck into her heart like an arrow. The full truth shone on his face. She grasped this as a precious gift, a present she'd never received from anyone in this world. Again, she sobbed against his chest, this time in utter relief.

Seán stroked her hair again, mumbling wordless endearments. He kissed her forehead, and she lifted her face to look at him. She must look a mess, eyes red and swollen from her tears, but he didn't seem to notice. He brushed a stray tear from her cheek and brought it to his lips. As he outlined her face with the same finger, her skin tingled, like when her grandfather gifted her the brooch in the stone circle. She shivered at the memory.

His voice sounded heart-breaking and tender. "Does my touch frighten you, Esme?"

"No, it gives me the shivers. But good shivers. Would you do it again?"

His smile reached his eyes, and she fell in.

Seán kissed her, long and sweet, on the mouth. Esme closed her eyes and spun, as if the earth below her feet moved faster. He pulled back, and she almost sobbed at the parting. She pulled her soul back from the swirling confusion and opened her eyes.

He lifted her chin and gazed into hers. "Would you allow me to court you, Mistress Esme?"

A ball of fire burned in her belly. The fire must show in her cheeks. Didn't she want to take control of her own life, rather than riding the wave and seeing where it took her? This would be her chance. "I would like that. But, Seán… how old are you?"

"I'm twenty-two. Am I too old for you?" His anxious expression betrayed his concern.

She'd imagined him much older, from his confident manner. "No, not too old."

"I've a good business, with the horses, you know. I've three mares now and a stud. The rest are Da's. When I marry, I'll have my own trading business. It'd be enough to keep you well in style. You won't starve?" These last words formed a question, as if he begged for her faith in him.

Esme would have to leave her family, but one less mouth to feed might make the difference between success and failure. "Would I have to travel with you? And learn how to… be a Tinker? To trade?"

"You'd come with me, or…" Her expression must have changed, as he hesitated, "we might set up a home for you, as you like."

Excitement rose in her voice as she clapped her hands. "A home? Of my very own? Truly?"

"Truly." She almost didn't dare examine the statement, but still the truth shone bright.

Seán placed his hands on her cheeks, forcing her to gaze into his eyes. "Who has lied to you, then? Was it Alan?" His face clouded with anger.

She blinked, surprised. "Alan? No, no, Alan didn't lie to me, but it's been everyone else. Da, Father Logue, Eithne. Well, of course Eithne. That's no surprise." The words sounded bitter in her ears.

Seán sighed and rolled his eyes. "No, Eithne lying is part of the way of things, I'm afraid. Your sister's a bit of a sneak, Esme."

Letting out a rueful chuckle, she nodded. "More than a bit. She tries to manipulate everything into her own view of the world."

"I'm just glad she didn't set her sights on me. She seems to be entranced by that O'Hagerty fellow."

"He seems to be her current obsession. He's not been her first, by far, but he seems to have lasted the longest. Is that why she wanted to convert?"

"Likely, yes. Though if she traps him into marriage, it won't be because of her religion and that's a truth you can rely on."

Chapter Five

May 1792

Éamonn

Éamonn smacked the wagon in frustration.

"Brian, the girls need more food than they're getting. You can't go on like this. Even with Eithne off in the big house with her husband, you aren't surviving. You're shrinking. Look at Bridey over there. She's thin as a rail and getting thinner. None of the girls are tall or strong. You've *got* to consider other options."

Éamonn seldom lost his temper, but seeing his grandchildren in poverty made him angrier than he'd been in many years. He loved Brian with all his heart, but he had to face the fact that his own son was fair feckless and not providing for his family. Éamonn ran his hands through his white hair, leaving it mussed.

He thanked his stars Eithne married Hugh O'Hagerty and would be well provided for. The man had a cruel set to his mouth, but at least she'd never starve. Already in the family way, she looked plump and pleased with herself.

Esme found a young man as well. They planned on getting married next month, when Seán and his parents came back from the Donegal horse fair. She wouldn't be as well off as Eithne, but she'd survive. Seán seemed a good, sturdy lad and he doted on her.

Even with the two eldest gone, though, the farm wouldn't support the rest. Éamonn glanced at the bare fields, the skinny cows, and the molting chickens. A bad summer storm flattened their oats, barley, and corn. The potatoes survived, but that wouldn't be enough. Brian and Shona had no vision, no initiative to improve things. When something broke, the mending took a long time, and never done well.

He must get them out of here.

Brian sat with his head cradled in his hands. He had no defense. The man hadn't even shaved, his clothes ripped and worn. The house needed sweeping and one shutter hung from its hinges.

"Brian, my dear lad, look at me."

His son raised his head, the desperation clear in his eyes.

Éamonn let out a deep sigh. "What if I sent you to America?"

Brian blinked several times, owlish and confused. "America?"

"America. I can get you on a ship. You, Shona, Bridey, even Níamh. I know folk out there, in New York and Ohio. People who emigrated years ago, established on farms. I'll give you money for a stake, to make a new life there. Get husbands for the girls. There'll be more choices out there."

"I can't go to America, Da. What would I do there?"

What indeed? If Brian acted feckless in Ireland, would he not be feckless in America?

But America would be the land of opportunity. It held so much land for so little money, even an eejit like Brian could make enough to survive. He'd known ne'er-do-wells who set themselves up in New York. Even his own brother, Ruari, a hard worker but far from clever, thrived in America. The simple man found a partner in New York and ran a bustling shop in Five Points. Ruari's partner would send Brian and his family onward to Ohio.

"I've a friend in Ohio, Brian. His name's Ewan Donahue, and he owns a farm near Canton. He's a good Ulsterman, despite being from a Scottish family. His wife's name's Fiona Ellison, and they've a young son, named Dominick, about Bridey's age. He emigrated twenty years ago from County Fermanagh and has a fine spread. He writes that he's always looking for steady help. Will you go there and be steady help, Brian? Can you do that much for your wee girls?"

Brian sunk his head into his hands again and his shoulders shook. Éamonn had never seen a grown man cry before and felt a wave of unaccountable rage and disgust at his son. *What had he done wrong that his son turned out so useless?*

"Look, lad, I'll buy the farm from you and sell it later. Esme and Seán can keep it going until they're ready to set up their own home. You take the money, take the family, and go. I'll even get the tickets for you. Just pack up. You can't take too much, mind. I'm not wealthy, but you can take enough to make the new place seem like home."

"But you gave us the farm, Da. It's not right you should buy it back."

Éamonn threw his hands in the air. "Fine! I'll take the bloody farm back and give you a gift of the money. Just take it and go, for the girls' sake, Brian!"

Shona entered, surveying the scene. Her husband sobbed into his hands, and Éamonn's eyes blazed with anger.

With a deep breath, she asked, "Right then, what's all this?"

Esme

Esme didn't want to think about her family leaving. She understood the logic, but still felt guilty as her mother packed her cedar chest full of linens and precious keepsakes. Her own kin emigrated while Esme kept the house. It didn't seem fair.

"Mother, can I help with anything?"

"I don't need your help, Esme. Ye've your own household to plan for, after all. Here, this is the bracelet your grandfather gave you." Her mother wouldn't mean to sound cold, or dismissive, but the chill in her words cut deep.

Esme held back the sharp words as she took the carved bone bangle, placing it on her wrist. She didn't want to part with her mother on sour terms. She'd never see her parents again, nor her sister or Níamh. Her heart broke, but she shoved the feeling down, under a thick woolen blanket of procrastination. It kept peeking out, but she kept shoving. She walked outside to clear her mind of such things. Birdsong and the aroma of fresh hay greeted her.

She watched as Níamh said goodbye to their oldest cow, Bóanna, named both after a goddess in ancient lore, and the word cow in Irish, *bó*. Esme gave a sad smile at the whimsy. Níamh had tears in her eyes.

People who left for America sometimes wrote back. Sometimes no one heard of them again. Once in a while, someone made the perilous journey back to Ireland. The dangerous voyage took several months. Storms, disease, and starvation all plagued the trip.

The ocean terrified her, as living near a fishing village taught her the sea might be a furious and tempestuous foe. One turns their back on the sea god, *Manannán mac Lir,* at great risk.

Would Esme even know if her family died on the journey? If she received no letters, it might mean they got sick, didn't write, or the letters went astray. The landlady in Ardara didn't get a letter for a year from her son when he emigrated. She despaired at all the possibilities. Esme wished the brooch had gifted her a talent like speaking across distance, or seeing someone far away.

They discussed giving an American wake, a tradition many Irish held, a mock funeral for the people who left. A send-off in the realization they'd never see each other again. But the passage Éamonn booked loomed, and they had no time or funds.

Where had Bridey disappeared to? Her quiet little sister barely said two words since the announcement three days ago. She snuck off often, but no one knew where.

Eithne didn't come to help. Already well ensconced in her new husband's house, she disdained association with her poor family. Scorn pulsed from Eithne's mind when they met in town. Esme no longer spoke to her when they passed on the street. She hadn't written nor sent any word, not even a goodbye to her own parents. Eithne had gotten entangled in her new life, not even wishing her own sister and cousin a good voyage.

A loud crash from the back of the barn made Esme run. The gate had snapped off the fence and landed on her father's foot. She rushed to help him. The two of them muscled it off. He sat on an overturned bucket. His expression turned gloomier than she'd ever seen, full of failure and resignation.

"Is your foot hurt bad, Da? What did you do?"

He flexed his ankle once or twice, wincing. "It'll be grand, my dear." He blinked in the rising dust.

With a swallow, Esme blinked back tears. "Da? You'll write when you get there, won't you?"

"Of course I will, my sweet Esme. I'll write every week, I promise."

He wouldn't. The lie shone clear on his face. Her father didn't even believe the lie. Although she might push him to admit the truth, she didn't. He wouldn't have the time, the postage, the energy, or even the will to write to the daughter he'd abandoned. He only said it to make the farewell easier. This made her angrier than if he admitted he'd never write again.

She grabbed his hand. "Da, don't go!"

Her father cocked his head. "You know we have to, pet."

Esme clenched her fists, disappointed and angry at her father for accepting his fate. "No! You don't. Stay and work the farm. This is your land, Da, your very own land! We can do it if you just tried harder!"

He just shook his head with a sad frown. "Esme, go find Bridey."

Éamonn should arrive soon with a horse cart to Donegal Town. A boat would take them to Galway and from there, a ship to New York, then overland to Ohio.

Esme didn't want to fetch her sister. She wanted to run away and scream in the wind for all the things she couldn't change. Maybe if she had a better talent from the brooch, she'd be able to stop all this. She stalked away toward the stones to find some peace.

Bugs came out in force at midsummer. Esme swatted at several as they buzzed by her ear. She pushed through bushes and sedge grasses until she came into sight of the stones. Bridey sat next to Alan.

Alan? What did Alan want with Bridey? They hadn't heard her, so she watched, trying to figure out what spoke of.

Alan bent to whisper in Bridey's ear, and her sister giggled in response, a surprisingly sensual tone to it.

The blond boy handed her sister a flower, purple and dark. Instead of taking it, Bridey shook her head. Alan placed the flower in her hair, behind her ear. Her sister blushed, then Esme gasped as her sister, her little sister, kissed Alan. A deep, passionate kiss.

Esme crept away. She didn't want them to notice her spying on them. What an impossible romance. Bridey only had sixteen years, and left for America tonight. Alan had eighteen years.

Alan and Bridey? How long had that been going on? She hoped Bridey didn't already carry his child. Jealousy reared into Esme's heart, but she stomped on it. She had no business being jealous of Alan. He'd asked her and she'd turned him down. Seán had pledged to her. Still, she loved Alan as her best friend, and experienced a twinge of loss for what might have been.

Picking her way down the hill, she must trust Bridey to return on her own. Esme didn't want to go back to the farmhouse, but she did. No one would let her help, and she stood around like a useless stranger. As if she waited for someone with a long, lingering disease to die.

As the sun dipped into the horizon, painting the world with orange and peach, their grandfather arrived. They packed the cart with their worldly goods in silence. Esme's tears leaked down her cheeks.

Seán wouldn't be back from his trade for several days, which meant she'd be in an empty house for days, subject to melancholy and the ghosts of her family. The idea terrified her. She'd never been truly alone in her life. She pleaded with her father. "I can come with you down to Donegal, at least. Grandfa Éamonn can bring me back."

Her grandfather shook his head. "Sorry, lass. I won't be coming back in this direction for a while. I've business to take care of in Fermanagh before I can return."

"I can help!" Her voice sounded so petulant to her ears, and she steeled her spine to be more dignified.

"No, sweetling. It's man's business. Not someplace I would take my granddaughter."

She hugged Bridey with fierce affection. Her little sister still had the now-wilted purple wildflower in her hair. She stared at it and Bridey blushed.

Níamh had cried most of the day, which set Esme's tears flowing. She patted her cousin's head and crooned to her, as she used to.

Her mother's hug came stiff and cold. How would she mend this rift after they moved so far away? They'd fabricated their pain from resentment.

Esme saved father for last. "Da, be safe, don't die. I love you." Her terror made her breath catch. He sobbed and clutched her tight as she willed him not to abandon her.

She breathed in his scent, that she might remember every detail. He smelled of cow manure and sweat, of dust, salty tears, and regret.

"I'll miss you, *mo chara.*"

And the sad truth shone on his face.

Esme tried to mend her prickles with Eithne. She didn't want to shut herself away from her only kin left in Donegal. She and Seán worked on the farm, with occasional help from Alan, but Eithne remained aloof at the big house.

Today, though Esme sent Alan with a note, requesting her to come. Seán helped her scrub the farmhouse, repair and make the place as presentable as possible. Esme must sift through the things left by their parents. She asked Eithne to come to take any keepsakes she might want. Material things motivated her sister. Perhaps this would crack open a door to her friendship, or at least a workable truce.

Most people claimed twins were inseparable. Two bodies with one mind. Others said twins must be unnatural, evil, or unlucky, but Esme never believed such things.

God must have taken all personality bits from her parents and given half to Esme, with the other half to Eithne, rather than copying them.

Esme sat at the wooden block table, fresh-scrubbed with sand. She brushed her hand over the smoothed surface, enjoying the silky texture of the pale wood. Seán worked outside, tending the cows and pigs. The items her parents left sat in a neat pile next to the hearth. No fire burned, making the house seem lonely.

Esme examined the pile, leftovers from a pair of lives, things they no longer wanted or didn't fit in their baggage allowance. It didn't amount to much. They'd left most of the furniture, many of the tools and cooking pots, but a few special pieces might intrigue Eithne. Rugs and blankets, a few ornaments. Several fine needlepoint pillows her mother made. She had—no, *she has*—fantastic skill at fine needlework. A lovely wood carving her father made of a selkie, the seal body melding into a woman's torso. People used to called her father a selkie, for his black hair and pale skin. The tears burned behind Esme's eyes and she blinked them back. She refused to greet Eithne with eyes reddened with grief.

Seán greeted someone outside. Eithne's presence flooded her mind, all smug and superior. Esme stood, squared her shoulders, and prepared herself for battle.

As she reached for the door handle, it flew open to reveal her twin.

Eithne had changed in the past month. She seemed taller, plumper, and more finely dressed. She wore a deep russet gown with green piping and slashing peeking from the skirt folds. She'd arranged her hair with precise pins and a frilly bonnet. She gazed at Esme with expectation and disdain.

Esme opened the door wider and stepped aside. "Come in, Eithne, please. Would you like ale? Seán just brought it in from the river, so it'll still be cool."

Eithne brushed past her and glanced around. Her sister chose a chair to perch on, sitting on the edge so she'd touch as little as possible. She wrinkled her nose. "At least you've attempted to clean the place."

Her sister may have married up in life, but her manners hadn't improved in the slightest. "I've sorted through the things they left. I thought you might like some. Would you care to go through them together?"

Eithne laughed. "What would I want with any of this old trash? Really, Esme, I assumed you knew me better."

"Well, yes, but I imagined you might like something to remind you of our parents. Something they made, perhaps?" She held up the selkie carving, the smooth bog wood gleaming black in the sunlight streaming through the kitchen window.

The dismissive, haughty look Eithne gave her slid down her body. Esme wanted to fling the statuette at her sister's head. After clamping down on this urge, she extracted one of her mother's pillows. The embroidered scene showed colorful flowers entwined on a background of leaves. The colors had faded, but the extraordinary details remained.

She matched her sister's haughty tone. "Something more decorative, for your salon?"

"Do you have anything of value to offer? No, of course you don't. If our parents had anything of value, they'd have flogged it to feed us for another month. I do remember a rather pretty trinket you had, a brooch. Do you still have that, or did Da sell it off?"

Esme stiffened. She'd never give Eithne the druid's brooch. Both Eithne and Bridey had glimpsed it once, but Esme hid it in an alcove below the chicken coop, to keep it safe from greedy hands. She wouldn't lie, but she wouldn't give any information to her snake of a sister, either. "Brooch? What brooch?"

Eithne waved her hand. "Oh, that trinket Grandfather gave you. It should have been mine."

Esme steeled herself to keep from glancing toward the door, to where she'd hidden it, and shrugged stiffly. "I'm not sure. He gave us lots of gifts."

Her twin narrowed her eyes, glancing around the house. "No matter. I'm sure it had no real value. Esme, is this all you wanted me here for? This is a complete waste of my time. I realize you've nothing better to do than wallow in disgusting melancholy, but I must get back."

Esme'd had enough of diplomacy and peace-making. She pushed against her twin, using the brooch's power to extract more truth from her. "Back to your society luncheons, is it? Or are you redecorating the ballroom?"

"My society luncheons, as you call them, are quite useful. We discuss politics, philosophy, and religion. Sometimes we speak of state policy and how to shape the future. We speak of world affairs. A far higher quality of conversation than *you'll* ever understand." Eithne flicked an imaginary speck of dust from the shelf next to her with a grimace of disgust. She hid something. Esme sensed it through their twin connection and the brooch's power.

While she'd invited Eithne here to mend their rift, she'd had it with Eithne's arrogance. She pushed her will more strongly, to force an answer from Eithne. Esme didn't keep the scorn from her voice. "Aren't we all high and mighty, then? You're moving in the important circles. I'm sure you're listened to like the high-born ladies?"

Eithne flushed and Esme knew she'd hit home. "I don't venture many opinions yet. I'm new to society, so I must study the situations before I make my voice heard."

Esme's eyes narrowed. Eithne spoke the truth, yes, but something else hid behind the flush. She didn't quite understand it, so she pushed harder. Eithne grimaced and mumbled, but Esme didn't hear the words. She pushed again.

"What? Do you want me to say they snub me, is that it? Fine. They do. Are you satisfied? For now. They'll come around soon enough."

Esme crossed her arms, glaring at her sister. "And how do you figure that?"

With her chin raised, Eithne's voice turned prim. "It's a matter of time and propriety. They'll come to see the value of my views."

Esme's anger seethed beneath her calm exterior. Hadn't she wanted to mend things between them? But all the old pain and arguments took charge of her thoughts. "Your views, is it? And what of your religion? The one you abandoned when you abandoned your family?" Esme's rage bubbled and steamed, like a pot on the hearth. Though she kept her voice even, the sharp tone cracked on the last word. Using her power to compel truth drained her energy, and she gripped the chair to keep upright.

"I did not abandon the family. I moved out. It's what young ladies do when they come of age. If they're smart, they move up and out. Obviously, you didn't, but then, you never had much intelligence. And as for religion," Eithne waved her white-gloved hand in a gesture of dismissal, "religion is for the weak-minded. Reason is the religion I follow. I claim to be Protestant because it's expected to follow a church. This one happens to be convenient."

The truth glowed on her twin's face. Her sister didn't posture; she believed herself. Pity replaced her anger at her sister. Eithne would find no solace in God. "And what does reason tell you the purpose of life is, Eithne?" Esme suspected the answer would disappoint her.

"The purpose of life is to survive and have children. The best way to survive is to have wealth, so when disaster strikes," and she glanced around the farmhouse pointedly, "you possess the resources to ride out the storm. Not like the poor, who need charity to survive. This is why our parents failed and why I shall succeed."

Eithne stood, dusting her skirts to rid them of imaginary dirt. "It's already too late for you, Esme. You will fail, too, mark my words. You haven't got what it takes to survive this world or the storms you will face. I never want to see you again. This family is dead to me. You are dead to me." With that prophecy, she slammed the door and left Esme in the late afternoon light, dust motes glinting in the sun.

Eithne's dismissal cut deep, as if she'd cut off Esme's arm. Sure, her sister had never shown compassion, had never cherished her like Bridey and Níamh had, but for her to just leave hurt to the quick. The rising exhaustion from pushing for the truth dragged her to the floor.

She cried into her mother's pillow. Hot tears soaked into the fine embroidery. Her heart snapped, and the break ached like fire. She'd lost a precious piece of herself and she didn't understand how to get it back. Or if she wanted it back. A loss which might never heal.

Seán

It seemed like Seán had stood here before, standing next to a horse cart filled with their worldly belongings. Esme must have experienced a huge wrench when her parents left like this, the month before, and now her grandfather sold the farm to new owners. But Seán had vowed to take good care of Esme, and he would. He put his arm around his fiancé and hugged her tight. She got quieter after Eithne came over and stormed out fit to set the grass on fire last week. He remembered being startled by the slamming door, and watching his love's twin stomp away to her own pony trap. Imagine using a pony trap to travel the mere two miles to her own house. But she had grand ideas about her own place and privilege.

Seán had done his best to comfort Esme, let her know he'd always be there for her. Sometimes she seemed such a fragile creature. He must handle her with tender care. Still, she showed strong will and bravery, if she'd only believe in herself. He wanted to protect her, wrap her up in a warm blanket, and shield her from the cruel world.

Especially from her own family.

Seán had a family and loved them well, but they'd scattered to the four winds in Ireland and abroad. His parents had already gone on their annual circuit, leaving him to take care of Esme.

They gifted him his stake in the family business. Three fine breeding mares and a stallion, as his father promised. Enough to start his own trade missions. While he dreamed of living on the road as his parents did, Esme didn't seem to care for the idea. If she didn't take to his beloved Traveling, he would get Esme a cottage in Achill, near his cousin Tomás's house. Tomás would watch out for her while he went up the coast, selling the horses, buying things to trade, and buying more horses with the trade receipts.

His family had lived like this for generations untold.

Sometimes, Seán wondered what life would be like as a farmer in one place forever, but this last month disabused him of any fancy notions he once entertained. This farming seemed like bloody hard work. Not that trading wasn't hard work, mind, but it meant dealing with people and using talking skills rather than muscles. More like getting into a customer's thoughts and finding out what that person wanted. If the customer didn't want what he carried in the cart, talking might change his mind. With skill, one did well. Without skill, well… Seán believed he'd do well. He'd handled transactions with his father the last couple of rounds.

Éamonn came around from the house, the last pot in his hand. "I think that's the lot, young lady. Is there ought else in the house you'll want?"

"No, Grandfa. We've got everything we'll need and a few keepsakes besides. The rest can all go to the buyers." She patted the canvas-covered cart, all that remained of her worldly belongings.

"You'll not wait around to meet them, then? They're kind folks, and I think you'd like them." Seán opened his mouth to respond, but held his tongue, glancing at Esme. He pulled the end of his ponytail with nervous fingers.

Esme paused a moment, then shook her head. "No, we should be getting on. I'd rather not see strangers invading my only home. I hope they take good care of all the animals." Their cat, Boru, disappeared when her parents left. Hopefully, he found another home nearby.

Her only home. He'd never considered that. After living in dozens, perhaps hundreds of places, he never thought someone might live in one place all their lives. Sure, she had eighteen years, but to have never explored this land? He didn't understand that notion.

"Aye, well, I'll pass on the profits from the sale once it's complete. You said Achill Island, right? Derreen's where you're headed?"

"Grandfa, this profit should be yours to—"

"We've talked about this. You'll need the funds. I'm sending some to Brian. I must send some to you as a wedding gift, aye? I kept my stake, not to worry." He gave a wide grin.

Seán nodded. "Derreen, that's right. I've a cousin who lives there and we'll set up a permanent home."

Esme insisted she'd need a place to stay, at least at first. She might go with him on missions until she could handle the road full time. He'd asked if she wanted a place nearby, to be near people she knew, but she shook her head. "I need to be elsewhere, Seán. There's nothing for me here anymore."

Éamonn stuck out his hand, and Seán gave it a firm shake. "I might come down with the funds myself, but if I don't, I'll send someone I trust. Keep good care of my girl, Seán."

Tears sparkled in Esme's eyes. She cried a lot, but he found it endearing. She gave her grandfather a fierce hug and he realized this must be the hardest leave-taking of all. The spry old man must be a rock for her, but they'd meet again. He was a Traveler, *an lucht siúil*, and he'd come check on them along his travels.

Éamonn pulled Esme to the side, and they spoke in urgent whispers. Seán turned his head to give them privacy, patting the nearest mare on her neck. Nuala, a sleek, roan cob mare, had a sweet temper. She'd been the first mare his father gave him when Seán got engaged. Next to her, Teaga stamped her hoof, a high-stepping and spirited gray mare. Next came stolid Orla, dun with black. The stallion, he was the real prize. He'd studded before and always bred true. The Connemara cob had a black coat except for his white fetlocks. They'd named him *An Ceann Dubh*, the Black One, and from his snuffling and snorting, he didn't wish to wait any longer.

Seán strung the horses together in front of the wagon, though only Nuala and Orla wore the harness. He'd never wagon-trained Dubh. His value remained as a racer and a stud. Teaga still spooked too much for such duty.

Esme hugged her grandfather goodbye again and Seán lifted her into the seat. It had a canopy over the driver seat, a necessary feature in rainy Ireland, with the back covered in oiled canvas. The trip to Achill should take three days. He prayed for mild weather on their journey. Someday soon, he'd buy a proper wagon, with a wooden roof, like his parents had.

With a last nod to Éamonn, Seán flashed a half-smile and grabbed the reins. He almost bounced in the saddle, so excited to be off on his first real adventure, no longer tied to his parents. He'd be married as soon as they settled in Derreen. Then he'd be brilliant in trade and would shower his wife and children with the finest gifts and luxuries, proving his worth to all.

With a *click-click* of his tongue and a rattle of the reins, they set off as the first drops of rain splattered on the oilcloth.

Esme

Esme wiped her face for the hundredth time, wet despite the wagon canopy. The downpour continued most of the day and well into the night, and the wind blew it past any barriers. With the wagon full of their worldly goods, Seán set up the lean-to tent with quick work as the late summer dusk fell. The nights grew longer past midsummer.

Esme huddled in her cloak, chilled from the rain. *What have I gotten myself into?*

Only a day's journey from her home, and she already felt utterly lost. Her family had gone, either across the wide ocean or a in rift of anger and jealousy. Esme wanted so much to hide her misery from Seán, dear Seán, her *ghrá dubh*, her black-haired love. He hopped around, trying to make sure she stayed as dry as possible, comfortable under the tent. He wrapped his warm arms around her, rocking her and crooning like he would a babe. Despite this, or perhaps because of this, tears pricked behind her eyes.

Esme had never traveled more than an hour away from Ardara. She knew the same shop owners, the same villagers, all her life. The new town would be full of strangers. Esme's stomach curled into a ball of fear.

She took a deep breath and counted her blessings. Seán, her loving husband-to-be, cherished her. Her grandfather loved her and she'd see him as he made his rounds of the land. She had her brooch and her abilities. *For all the good they'd done.* Packed in the cart were those few things she treasured from childhood, and she had health and youth. That should be plenty, and more than others had.

Esme said a prayer to Saint Christopher as she traveled, with a wish to arrive in Achill safe and sound. She closed her eyes, hearing the *drip drip drip* of a leak in the tent. The drops landed on her left shoulder, and she squirmed to escape it. *Drip drip drip.* How would she ever sleep in this?

"Come, *mo chuisle*. We'll get some sleep, then."

Is he divining my own thoughts somehow? But she lay next to him and they wriggled down to a spot not too waterlogged. Despite the close space, they had enough room. They found a nice niche and Seán put his arms around her again. He felt warm, and she snuggled into his chest to take advantage of the heat.

"Seán?"

"Yes, Esme?"

She couldn't answer. What would she say? Despite his warm arms, she felt miserable, cold and wet? That'd be no way to start off a new life. "Nothing. Good night."

"Good night. It'll be grand, *mo chailín rua.* Just you wait and see. Once we get the home in Derreen set up, you'll learn to love Traveling. It's not all like this." Esme had an intense urge to jump out of the tent, leap on a horse, and gallop back to the farmhouse, new owners or not.

Sleep found her, but it proved to be a fitful embrace. Seán's endearment, calling her his Red One, must have lingered, for she dreamt of red people. Beings with red skin, not just red hair, leaping around her, throwing water in her face. They laughed and leapt, jumping and frolicking, having a grand old time. She didn't get upset by the water, not in her dream. She laughed and splashed it back, making a game of it. They turned purple, then blue, and cycled through the colors of the rainbow. This delighted her, seeing people in so many hues, as if she traveled the world in this circle of her unconscious.

A loud whinny woke her in the early dawn. The first horse set off the others, and soon the racket grew deafening, setting off a flock of crows. Seán leapt up at the first sound and checked on the hobbled herd. She heard him comforting them as he'd comforted her the night before, with low, even endearments, mumbled in a mixture of Irish and English. *No wonder he's so good at calming me. He has lots of practice with fractious mares.*

The idea of mares distracted her. Esme had refused to lie with him until they were wed. She and Seán had gotten into an argument just after they got engaged. She had no wish to follow her sister's example.

Despite her firm stance, she wondered what it would be like. What would his hands feel like on her bare skin? His lips seemed so full—she pushed away that train of thought. Such imaginings would only make him harder to resist.

Seán promised he wouldn't press her until they married and they wouldn't marry until she had a place of her own. He'd enough goods to buy the lease on a cottage. Esme hoped it had a view of the ocean. She loved watching the ocean.

The horses grew quiet and she untangled from her cloak and bedding to see what kept Seán. When she poked her head out, she spied Seán feeding the stallion.

She tried to brush down her wild hair, but the red curls insisted on going everywhere. "What happened?"

He shrugged, giving Dubh one last handful. "Not sure, but whatever he heard, it's passed now. Did ye get to sleep?"

She wrinkled her nose. "I did, despite myself."

Esme struggled out from under the lean-to and gasped at her crumpled skirts. She'd never been vain about her appearance but she wanted to look presentable. She despaired at the impossibility of such a thing while traveling.

When she glanced up, her breath caught in wonder. Seán looked behind him to see what made her gasp.

Before them, a panoramic view of the ocean gleamed, cliffs rising from the waves like giant's fingers. The sky was a deep summer blue, without a cloud. The sun touched the top of the mountains with glittering splendor, burning off the morning dew. Seagulls dipped with plaintive cries. No wind blew, a true wonder for the west coast of Ireland.

The sea always lifted Esme's spirits. Nowhere in Ireland stood too far from the ocean, but she'd grown up an hour's walk from the shore. She could touch the endless water whenever she wished, to give in to the primeval urge to be part of the ocean. Part of her soul and joy belonged to the sea.

This morning, her soaked spirit soared upon the wings of the gulls and she turned to Seán with a wide grin of delight.

"Ah, you can't be doing that, *mo chroi.*"

She blinked, confused. "Doing what?"

"With your smile shining like the morning sun. It makes me want to take you to my bed right now and love you for days, and I can't be doing that just yet, so?"

Esme's cheeks flushed and she dropped her gaze, staring at her shoes, at her hands, anywhere but at Seán's grinning face. "Ah and now you're being shy." He took her hands in his. "I'll be gentle when the time comes. I vow this to you."

She gazed into his eyes, and the truth shone bright. Not that she believed he'd be cruel. She'd seen cruelty on Hugh O'Hagerty's face and Eithne's. Seán didn't have a cruel bone in his body.

Esme stood on her tiptoes and kissed her husband-to-be. It surprised him, but he leaned into the kiss. Something stirred within, an insistent warmth curling through her. They stood locked together until Nuala snorted and whinnied.

When they broke apart, Seán busied himself with harnessing the horses, while Esme packed the lean-to, shaking out the worst of the morning dew. She mustn't allow it to get mildewed. And it would do her no good to linger on what she wanted to do with Seán.

They journeyed south of Donegal town into the village. The day remained bright and, for a wonder, dry. Seán pointed out interesting things along the way, such as the huge farmhouse near Bundoran or the inlet view in Ballyshannon. She tamped down her envy at the sprawling place, not wanting to be grasping like Eithne.

By the time the sun reached noon, the village of Tullaghan loomed, with a beautiful stone high cross in the town center. While the cross sported no fancy carvings or detailed designs, it towered over Esme, making her feel insignificant.

Seán nudged her as they disembarked, pointing to a bakery. "We came on the wrong day for the market, but we could still find supplies." Esme's mouth watered with the idea of fresh bread. Bread made her think of Alan, but she shoved his smiling face from her mind. She'd made her choice.

Esme still gawked at the towering cross as Seán tied the horses to a fence post. He tugged on her arm to get her attention back to the wonderful aroma of baking pastries.

A voice, quavering with age, spoke behind her. "They say the sea carried it in hundreds of years ago."

She spun to find an old, crabbed man, sitting on a stone fence, puffing on a slender clay pipe. From his sunken jaw, he had no teeth. Though his clothes looked worn and faded, they were clean and mended.

Esme touched the sharp stone edges of the cross. "It looks new for that, doesn't it?"

"Aye and isn't anything comes from the sea covered in magic?" The old man gave her a toothless grin, then spat to the side.

While that morning started out bright, clouds rolled in around mid-afternoon and stayed the rest of the day. At first, they brought a light sprinkle, blown away by the winds. By late afternoon, it poured in sheets, slowing the wagon to a crawl. The canopy did little to protect Seán and Esme from the wind, and they huddled together as the horses pushed through muddy roads to their evening destination.

Seán settled on Ballymote for their stop, another market town he'd visited many times. No one set up market stalls in the current deluge, though, and they tried to find a dry spot for the night.

They passed the square tower of Ballymote Castle, dark and grim in the lowering gloom. Esme shivered, and not from the rain. She'd never seen a full castle before.

A pinched look came over Seán's face. "A mob killed Travelers there, long ago."

Esme squeezed his hand. Her grandfather had never mentioned how dangerous Traveling might be. "That wouldn't happen now."

They drew up to an inn, and Seán jumped down into a huge puddle. He let out some heartfelt curses.

Esme stifled a giggle. "Well, you couldn't have got any wetter, but now your clothes are more colorful."

He stuck out his tongue, then offered his hand. She accepted with a gracious nod, avoiding the puddle.

They entered the inn called The Rat and the Parrot, shaking the rain off their cloaks in the doorway. Seán took her hand and pulled her toward the bar. Esme breathed deep, taking in the myriad odors, nervous at walking into the crowd. While loud with laughs and gambling, the place smelled of peat fire, stew, stale sweat, and beer.

He waved at the landlady as she served a couple of mugs of ale to a portly, red-faced patron. "Have ye a room we can let for the night?"

The landlady, lanky with thin, black hair, looked them up and down, from their rain-plastered hair to their sturdy shoes. "Sure and I do have one more left for ye. Have ye beasts for the stable? I've some room left in there."

While Seán haggled for space, food, and stable room, Esme studied the place. She'd been in the pub in Ardara, but she knew everyone in town. An entire room of strangers, most of them large, sweaty men, frightened her. She felt reluctant to leave the side of the landlady, one of the few women in the inn.

Carrying bowls of steaming stew, a large crust of bread, and mugs of ale, Seán found them an empty table near the bar.

"You'll be fine here while I settle the horses. Mistress Higgins will watch out for you." Esme glanced up as the landlady beamed at her. She managed a meek half-smile back. The ale tasted hoppy and bitter. She closed her eyes against the disquieting noise as she savored the frothy liquid.

Her stomach growled as she tasted the chunks of steaming lamb, potatoes, and carrots. Smothering a small burp, Esme savored the delicious meal.

She saved half the crusty bread for Seán, who returned soaked from the rain. He took it with a nod of thanks. "I think the weather wants us to rest, what do you think?"

"I could sleep for a week in a proper bed."

Seán's expression grew doleful. "Esme? You know the cottage we'll have on Achill won't be like your parents' place was, right? At most a small, two-room thatchie?"

She reached for his hand and squeezed. "It'll be fine, Seán. I'm not Eithne. I'd rather have you than a fancy house any day." He smiled with relief and she returned his grin. *Here we are, both grinning like idiots.*

He lifted her hand and kissed her fingertips. They grew warm while the rest of her still shivered from the rain.

He moved to take his cloak off and cover her shoulders. "You're not taking a chill, are you?"

"No, no, it's just all the wet. I'll be grand once I dry off." Despite her protests, she felt glad of the extra warm layer.

They mopped up the last bits of stew with the bread. Warmer and sated, she now noticed individuals in the crowd. Most seemed to be farmers or workers, with plain clothing and floppy hats against the rain. A few women sat in the crowd; one played cards with three men, and the other sat near the crackling hearth, polishing a tinwhistle.

An old man pulled a fiddle from its case, and a third held his *bodhran,* a hand-held drum.

The fiddler tuned his strings, a discordant sound, but one well familiar to Esme's ears. She missed evenings singing with her folks and experienced a stab of loss. She finished her drink to ward off incipient tears while Seán stood to get more ale.

The man with the *bodhran* looked young, pear-shaped with light brown curls. He cleared his throat and hummed, finding his key. The raucous conversation ceased.

Mirk and rainy is the nicht
There's no a star in a' the carry
Lightnings gleam athwart the lift,
And the cauld winds drive wi' winter's fury.

Oh! Are ye sleepin', Maggie?
Oh! Are ye sleepin', Maggie?
Let me in, for loud the linn
Is roarin' o'er the warlock craigie!

The room burst into song for the chorus. Esme almost fell off her stool at the sudden sound.

Esme's father sang this song many times. She joined on the next chorus and smiled as Seán sang along. She put her hand over his again, squeezing. Life seemed bright when warm, dry and filled with tasty food and joyful music.

Later that night, well sated in food, drink, and song, they entered their room. Seán insisted she take the bed, while he made a pallet on the floor near the burning peat in the hearth. She didn't have the heart to argue with him, as she craved a soft, welcoming bed. The cornhusks inside rustled as she lay back. Her head barely touched the pillow before she fell into a dreamless sleep.

Light streamed in the window the next morning, cool and bright. Esme hoped with all her heart it would remain so.

Vendors bustled to set up their tables and wares for market day as they left the town, and Seán made a few stops for supplies. He bought fresh berries, pears, a flitch of salted bacon, travel cakes, and a hair ribbon.

"Whyever would you buy me a hair ribbon, Seán? We don't need to waste money on such luxuries."

"Because the bright blue looks lovely in your red curls, my dear."

She gave him a sidelong glance. While she appreciated the gift, a wife must keep a sharp eye on the purse-strings. She musn't allow him to fritter away their scarce funds on extravagances. "Just this once, then."

He chuckled and stroked her head.

Today, Seán set a goal of Castlebar, a good forty-five miles down the road. If the rain didn't ruin the roads, they might make decent time.

The countryside held a preternatural sharpness after heavy rain, especially when the sun shone bright and everything sparkled. The land seemed reborn in the night, fresh and ready to grow. Esme breathed deep of the grasses, the wildflowers along the road, and the cows in the fields as they passed. One bellowed out to the horses and Nuala let out a whinny in reply.

Seán waved to the cow with a casual flick of his hand. "That old cow reminds of the one I tried to ride when I was eight."

"Oh? Do tell, *mo ghrá*." His tales always made her laugh. While the truth glimmered as he spoke, it dimmed when he exaggerated for dramatic flair.

"My cousin dared me. He claimed he rode cows all the time. It was so easy, even a sprout like me could do it." He grinned. "I was a spindly child, tall but thin like a stick. Of course, the beast had a spavined back, no good for anything but milk, mind you. She was old with no spunk left, but to me, she seemed big and frightening.

"I came up to her side, all nice and easy-like. Her hooves looked hard, and she glared at me as I approached, rolling her eyes with alarm. I brought a stool to help me leap onto her back. Almost made it, too…"

Esme raised her eyebrows, suppressing a giggle. "Oh? What happened instead?"

He chuckled, his hands rolling in demonstration. "I flipped right over the bloody thing and landed in the mud on the other side. Spooked the old girl enough, she almost stepped on me. Oh, how my cousin roared with laughter!"

She burst out laughing at the picture of him, lying covered in mud, trying to avoid the stomping of an angry heifer. Their laughter echoed along the valley, answered by mooing cows.

With fine weather, they arrived in Castlebar with little fuss, as the late summer sun touched the horizon in an explosion of peach and purple.

Esme had never visited a town so large. A bustling place, even without a market today. Several street signs proclaimed their names; Linenhall, Main Street, Staball Hill. Esme'd never seen street signs before. They found Shambles Square and passed a coaching inn with the presumptuous name of The Imperial Hotel. It sounded like someplace Eithne would stay.

Despite the luxury of a bed the night before, Esme decided she must think like a wife, not a pampered child. So, instead of splurging on another inn, they found a camping spot outside town. Decisions like this came easier with fine weather. Esme set up the lean-to while Seán dealt with the horses and prepared supper.

The edges of a long lough wound its way into town. While it wasn't the sea view she craved, the sight was lovely as dusk fell and the birds settled themselves for the night.

Seán built a fire to cook the bacon. The sizzling and popping of the fat formed a chorus to the sounds of the evening. Her husband-to-be crouched over the blaze, his skin dark with a summer tan. That set off his black, straight hair, hanging around his face. She wanted to brush the lock back behind his ear. His looks seemed exotic and exciting, even after knowing him all summer. He assured her his skin tone faded in winter. Esme couldn't believe it would fade to her own pale, freckled complexion. Was his chest the same sun-dark color? Would their children be dark or fair?

He had no siblings, but he didn't say he *never* had any. Children died all the time. Perhaps his mother lost several children. A bubble of melancholy burst inside her. The heartbreak of losing a child must be horrid. Would it be worse to lose a babe, or a child almost grown? She never wanted to find out. Her own mother lost a baby boy, just three days old. The babe had a hare lip and couldn't suckle to feed. They'd tried to feed him with cow's milk, but he wouldn't drink. His weakening cries had been heartbreaking as he faded from life. They baptized the poor wee lad as Padraig and buried him in the church graveyard.

Tears leaked down her cheeks. They might fall for the memory of her lost brother, or her family gone to America, or the realization she'd never see her childhood home again.

Seán knelt by her to hug her. "What's wrong, *mo ghrá*? Are you frightened?"

"I'm… oh, I don't know. I miss home. I miss Mam and Da and Bridey and Níamh." Her eyes grew wide with surprise. "God help me, I even miss Eithne!"

That made them both laugh, but hers tasted bitter.

"It'll be grand, my sweet Esme."

"I should write to them after we get to Achill."

Seán frowned and squeezed her hand. "We need a place to send the letter. We don't know if they've even arrived, much less where."

Esme hadn't even thought about that. She imagined letters just found their way to people, like magic. She sniffled and wiped her nose. "But how am I supposed to find them, then?"

"Look, your grandfather gave me the name of the farmer he sent them to, Donahue. We can write to them, so? Even if your parents don't stay with them, they'll stop there. Never fear, we'll find them."

Seán sounded so sure of himself, and she wanted to believe him. The truth flickered on his face. He only half-believed his words. That glimmer of truth gave her hope, though. She gave a brave smile and wiped the tears from her eyes.

As the fire crackled and hissed, they watched the last light die in the west, over the rolling hills. She wanted to fall into the safety and strength of his arms, to kiss his tanned skin, to feel his hands over her body, but she knew that once they started, they wouldn't stop. She refused to play Eithne's game, and vowed to herself she'd wed before she lay with any man.

That evening, Esme dreamt of a bog she needed to cross. She didn't know why or how, but she must. Her life, her dreams, were on the other side. How could she do it?

Every step slogged her down further, deeper into the mire. She saw the end, just beyond her reach. Try as she might, she couldn't grasp the ledge. She sobbed in her sleep and Seán cuddled her closer, stroking her hair until she rested easy once again.

Eithne

Eithne woke in a cold sweat. Her heart pounded and she gasped for breath.

She had few nightmares, but when they came, they were of her living on that disgusting farm, with no money, wearing rags, and eating rotten slop. This dream had been different, full of fear and marshes and something beautiful.

Her husband snored next to her and she slipped out of bed. She had no wish to disturb him. When he woke in the night, he either had a foul temper or amorous intentions. Eithne had no desire to be beaten or swived just now, though sometimes it amounted to the same thing. She must remember her dream.

Pulling her night robe on over her growing belly, she padded down the plush carpet in the hallway to the drawing room. Even in June, the dark room remained chilly. She sat in the window seat and watched the stars overhead, recalling her vision. Flashes of jewels and gold teased the edges of her memory as she caressed her stomach.

It must be that blasted brooch. Esme had somehow lied to her and kept the bauble, and it kept intruding on Eithne's memories. It tugged at her soul and memory. No matter that Eithne could buy a similar jewel now. That one drew her, despite her wealth. When she first glimpsed it, Eithne had searched the entire house for days. Under Esme's bed, in her clothing drawer, even in the yarn bin, but Esme hid it well. With a grunt of disbelief at her twin doing anything well, Eithne concentrated on her dream. Perhaps it would give her a clue.

Entwined figures twisted in the bog, winding around the silver and gold piece, pulling her mind through the woven pattern. The dull aqua gleam of gems drew her eye, pulsing in mystical invitation. It called to her, pulled at her heart with a strident demand.

The twisting both sickened and fascinated her. Human limbs twined within the writhing figures, but cat eyes also glimmered from the mass. Eyes with inhuman colors, purple and silver, black and gold. Hands groped for her and she reached out to take them.

Eithne felt nothing but the chilly glass of the window. The stars twinkled in the night sky, mocking her failure.

That settled it. She must get that blasted brooch. It possessed something powerful, and she craved that power. It sparked red and orange in her memory, and she couldn't ignore it. The brooch's potential would be wasted in her sister's hands. Besides, Eithne was the eldest, by an hour. Anything that valuable should come to her first, and Esme last. Esme always last.

Chapter Six

June 1792

Esme stared at the strange green terraces covering the mountainside. She couldn't figure any rhyme or reason to the plots. No straight lines or squares. About a dozen croft cottages of various sizes dotted the area. All had low walls and peaked thatch roofs. The cottages formed a distorted oval around a smaller area, like a kitchen garden. Everything seemed deserted.

One old man sat on a stool outside a cottage. He smoked a pipe while whittling and glanced up at their approach. He stared at them, crude knife paused.

Seán pointed to the oval area. "They call it a *clachan*. Everyone lives in these cottages during the cold months. In the warm months, they travel up to the *booley*, higher in the mountain, with the livestock. It gives them both grazing land and growing land. They share within the group."

"So they don't own their land?"

"No, they're all considered one big tenant."

Esme gulped, staring at the tiny cottages. "Would we be living here, then? Or up the mountain?"

"That depends on what we can find, pet. We'll stay in the *clachan* until we can find a place. I can afford a cottage, so the building will be ours, but we must rent the land."

It all sounded so complicated. But her father might have fared better in such an arrangement.

The village, as it looked too scattered to be called a town, sat past the *clachan,* along the shore. A wooden dock, a large building for sorting the fish hauled in each day, and a tiny shop. A *síbín*, like a pub, completed the list. Lone cottages sat scattered along the shore.

They pulled up next to the wooden *síbín*. Esme's muscles felt stiff from the travel. Seán secured the reins and grabbed her waist, lifting her from the wagon seat. She stretched her back after so much time in the cart. They shared a nervous glance.

When they entered, she blinked to adjust to the dim light. A long table ran along one side, with crates and boxes underneath. The other side held an empty hearth and a dozen scattered and unused stools. She hadn't expected the place to be filled at mid-afternoon, but this desolate emptiness disturbed her. Instead of a warm, welcoming pub, this seemed a dead place.

Seán's voice echoed in the empty space. "Hallo, anyone here?" The stink of ashes, stale beer, tobacco smoke, and mildewed thatch tickled her nose. Something scuttled in the thatch, but nothing else stirred.

"This place is scary, Seán. Where *is* everyone?"

He shrugged, his eyes darting to the corners. "They'll be up at the *booley*. I expect they spend most of their time on the mountain in the summer, unless they're out fishing."

"So will we have to buy two places? One up on the mountain and one down here?"

He hugged her shoulder, giving her a reassuring squeeze. "Not right away. We only need a mountain cottage if we've cows to graze, and we haven't any yet. We can raise pigs and chickens, and make do with that this season. Next season, we might expand. Nothing so complicated yet, so?" He gave her another squeeze and turned to the door.

"Seán?" Dread tickled her spine at this place's loneliness.

"Yes, my dear?"

"Nothing." Esme wanted to say she didn't want to live here, but she should give it a chance first. Who knows? Maybe they'd find good friends here.

By peeking into the chapel, they found another human. The priest, Father McNulty, was sweeping. He glanced up when they opened the door. "Aye? Can I help ye?"

Seán cleared his throat. "You can, if you know where we might rent a cottage?"

He did have a vacant cottage for rent in the *clachan*, so he took their coins with a handshake. They couldn't buy it outright, but Seán's cousin, Tomás, lived in that cluster. The priest told them Tomás had left on a trade mission a few months before.

A string of hamlets meandered along the coast. They shared the priest, the church at Kildownet, the fishing dock, and the *síbín*. Extended families often clustered in each *clachan*. Few visitors came here, with poor roads and on the way to nothing.

The cottage—their home, Esme told herself—held two rooms, which made it larger than half the others. The whole place measured twenty feet long by twenty-five feet wide. One door and window faced south, while another door faced north to encourage the breeze through in the summer. The window could do with curtains. The bed was small, but she'd be in her husband's arms, and that would be grand. At least they'd be together.

The walls stood five feet tall, but the thatched roof rose to six feet in the center. Seán had to duck to get in, but he stood straight inside.

On one end, a hearth filled with ashes stood, but no chimney. Smoke rose through the thatch well enough, which smoked out the worst of the pests. Esme frowned at the likelihood of mud on the hard-packed earth floor, but she found a pile of flagstones out back. Seán could place some near the hearth and doors. She'd make this place her home, no matter what it took.

They unloaded the cart in a tense silence. The few pieces of furniture made the cottage seem crowded. The bed, press, and shelves took up much of the space. One wall had shelves built into the stone. Esme spent time arranging her ornaments. As she placed one of her mother's embroidered pillows, she fought back more tears. She didn't remember ever crying so much in her life as in the last couple of months. A new beginning with her husband-to-be in this tiny hovel seemed such a wrench. Everything she'd ever known had disappeared or left her. Esme breathed in deep, squared her shoulders, and finished her task.

That evening, sitting in front of a cheery blaze, her spirits lifted. Seán revealed a few surprises he'd bought at the market. He hung a lovely tapestry on the wall, an ocean scene which reminded Esme of Ardara. After pulling out two sweet-scented candles to burn on cold, dark nights, he lit them for their first evening. She snuggled into his arms as they lay on the floor rug, watching the fire burn.

Esme let out a deep sigh. "When do the others come down off the mountain, do you think?" She must have time to settle in before the place teemed with strangers.

"Not until the first harvest, so another month. I'll be back before then."

She shot up out of his arms. "Back? Where in God's sweet name are you going?"

Seán blinked at her. "To trade. You knew I'd have to. I'll make a quick trip around the island. A scouting mission, to find out what people need, what they've got to sell, and how I might make a good run."

Of course, he needed to trade. She'd be home alone in this tiny, dank place, with Seán out on trips. Unless she wanted to go with him. But she had no desire to sit in that wagon again after five days. Still, she mustn't let her husband realize how uninspired the cottage left her. Had her father been right? Did lying make things better? She said she'd be happy here, and she'd do her best to make it the truth.

Without Seán to help, her plans for the house tasted like ash in her mouth.

"Come, lay back again, *mo chara*. I'll keep you warm."

The next week, Esme wished for her mother. Or Bridey. *A woman shouldn't have to dress herself for her own wedding.* Even Eithne would be of help, with her sense of style and fine fabrics.

She frowned at her tiny reflection. The hand-mirror required her to bend and gyrate to see herself from all angles. She threw the mirror on the bed in frustration.

Seán found her a lovely dress, pale-blue muslin with darker blue ribbon at the high waist. The sleeves puffed and gathered. The gown would have suited a taller woman, but he didn't have many to choose from. The neckline dipped low, making her uncomfortable. But she should be able to show off at her own wedding. *Where had he found the time to buy such things? Perhaps being the wife of a trader had its advantages.*

When Seán pulled the dress from the package, he handed it to her with a grin. "You're ravishing in blue." She held it up, delighted at the novelty of wearing new fabric.

Esme bundled her hair up with more dark-blue ribbon and wore a string of beads Seán bought. While they were only painted blue wood, they complemented the neckline. She considered wearing the brooch, but instinct told her to keep it hidden. She hadn't even shown the brooch to Seán. While keeping secrets from one's husband might be a strange way to start a marriage, her grandfather warned her to keep the magic safe and secret. Not that anyone would believe its powers.

She fussed with her hair, tucking in stray curls which kept escaping. She spit into her hand, smoothing it over her head to tame them, but they refused to behave. Exasperated, she gave up. They'd fly in the wind on the trip down to the church, no matter what she did.

In the week since they arrived, she hadn't met many residents. The old man smoking the pipe was Mr. Conchobar Quinn. His children lived up on the mountain, but he stayed down in the *clachan* all summer. He spoke little, but he had a fine hand for wood carving. Seán already offered to trade his carvings along his route.

The only other summer resident was an older woman, Mistress Maire Lynch. Her daughter lived up on the mountain and her son fished each day. She spent her days weaving endless lengths of green and brown fabric.

They had few wedding guests, with everyone still up the mountain for the summer. Mr. Quinn's cart pulled up outside. Esme took another deep breath and let it out again. *Her wedding day.* This bare ceremony would be a far, far cry from what she'd imagined as a young girl. If they'd married in Ardara, she might have invited the whole town. But then she'd have to face Eithne.

Alan wouldn't be here to share her day, and she missed talking with him. She remembered seeing him with Bridey. Perhaps Alan wished he'd gone to America, too. She took a deep breath against what might have been.

Esme covered her head with a scarf in a vain attempt to keep her hair in order and walked outside. Mr. Quinn offered a hand into the cart as the wind tugged and pulled her scarf, winding its tendrils inside. She pulled it tighter and tied it under her chin. The clip-clop of the horse's hooves on the stone path helped settle her, though the jouncing of the wagon forced her to brace for balance. They descended the hillside to the church.

No one waited outside as they pulled up to the simple stone building. A graveyard stood to the left, with plain stones and a Celtic cross, well-weathered from ocean winds. Quiet crept across the hills, except for the jingling harness and crying seagulls which seemed to fill her ears day and night.

After squaring her shoulders, Esme marched inside. Seán stood at the altar, scrubbed clean and looking anxious. She ached for her father to give her away, but Mr. Quinn ungraciously accepted the job for a pouch of tobacco. Step by step, Esme marched up the aisle. The empty pews glared at her in scorn for leaving her family behind. *But they left me behind! I didn't leave them!*

She swallowed when Old Mistress Lynch in the front pew gave her a glassy-eyed nod. She flashed a brief, nervous smile, and then turned to Seán.

His dark eyes shone bright with anticipation and fear. His hands twitched and he looked flushed.

Seán took her hand and squeezed so hard she gasped. He relaxed his grip, an apologetic look flitting across his face. They locked eyes, let out a deep breath, then turned to the priest.

After years of English persecution of the language, they could get married in the Irish. Esme grew detached as the priest spoke to the empty room, as if he abjured the ghosts of past congregations to love, comfort, and support each other. To care for their children and their hearts. The pressure of the empty room crushed her shoulders, a palpable hand pushing down. She shuddered, which earned her a look of censure from both Seán and the priest.

The priest cleared his throat. "Do you promise to love, honor, and obey your husband?"

Did she? She must. She'd no bridges left to burn. "I will." Esme choked out the words, despite her crippling fear.

The priest asked a similar question to Seán.

"I will." Seán's eyes gleamed in the dark room.

With an avuncular smile, the priest declared, "I now pronounce you husband and wife."

Anxiety and dread crashed against a wave of joy and happiness. Seán banished her fear with a firm kiss planted on her lips. He swung her around for a bone-crushing hug. She laughed and shoved her demons away, at least for today.

As they walked in silence back to their cottage, Esme's apprehension grew. The wedding night both frightened and excited her. Having grown up on a farm, she knew what should happen. She'd heard her parents' tender words and sounds all her life, but they always pulled their bed curtains. She hoped she wouldn't disappoint her new husband.

Seán had been with girls before. He told her this on the journey. He'd been with two girls as he traveled, one in Kerry and one in Fermanagh.

Esme's eyes went wide at this news, her hand covering her mouth.

"I never wanted to marry them, Esme. I swear! You're the one I want to wed. To have my children. The only one."

Glad that she could see the truth shining on his face, her dismay melted before his charm. But had he lied to the other girls?

Esme hoped Seán knew what to do to make the first encounter more… what? Enjoyable? Magical? She just hoped it wouldn't be too painful.

Her mother warned her the wedding night would be painful. But she also promised she'd enjoy it, eventually. Esme hoped her mother was right. Did Eithne enjoy lying with Hugh? Did her Protestant husband treat her with kindness? Esme pushed that thought away. Eithne had no business in Esme's marriage bed, nor she in Eithne's.

Once back in the cottage, Seán brought her a stone bottle of ale. They stood next to the bed, nervous and prickly. She'd slept in the bed all week and him out on the hearth rug. He was a stickler for honor, her Seán was. Her Seán. Her *ghrá dubh*. Esme's face grew warm as she grinned.

He caught her smile with his own, and they both grinned like fools. He placed the bottle on the press and touched her face, his fingertips brushing along her jawline.

She shivered as goose-skin pebbled her arms. Alan's light touch on the beach sprang into her memory. She pushed that away. He had no business here in her marriage bed, either.

Seán stood, fetching a plaid woolen blanket to drape around her shoulders.

Esme grinned at her new husband, so tall and dark. "I wasn't cold, just, well, that felt nice."

"That's fine. This will keep you from the chill, then."

He touched her face again, this time with the back of his hand. She closed her eyes to enjoy the sensation. He touched her lips, then his finger drew a line down to her neck and into the bodice of her chemise. Prickled skin returned, a shiver running down her spine.

The sensation reminded her of the brooch when she touched it for the first time. The power made her back tingle and buzz. The fright and nerves of that experience felt similar to now. Despite her nerves, she didn't want him to stop.

When he halted, she opened her eyes to see why, thinking she'd said something out loud. Her new husband fumbled with the laces at her bodice, so she helped him.

Once free of the bodice, she stood in her chemise in the firelight. She felt like a flitting spirit, insubstantial and ethereal. She perched on the edge of the bed and patted the spot next to her. He pulled his own shirt off and joined her.

His fingers quested around her back and down her spine, across the curve of her buttocks and down the inside of her thigh. She touched the edge of his chin, already rough with stubble, and down the sun-darkened skin of his chest. His body, the smoothness of his skin, and the hairiness of his private parts fascinated her. He touched her in places she'd never touched herself. They explored for what seemed like hours, tasting and finding new places to play with.

When he'd caressed every inch of her skin, he stared at her. His eyes flickered in the light from the burning peat, glittering like the stars in the night sky.

Feeling playful, she lay back, her eyes dancing. "What next?"

His voice came deeper than normal, husky. "What would you like to do next?"

"You're the expert. Surprise me."

Seán kissed her neck with renewed fervor, then down to her breasts. He pushed them together and put his face between them, scratching them with his stubbled chin. Her groom continued lower, circling her navel with his tongue, then farther still. She gasped as he parted her lips with his tongue and squirmed. He held her by the hips so she couldn't get away. He explored and tasted, tickled, and tested until she moaned and writhed, caught between nerves and delight.

Esme had never experienced anything like this. Waves of sweet pleasure rippled through her. She grasped the mattress as the sensation coursed through her body.

Seán glanced up with a satisfied grin on his face and pulled himself up on top of her. He teased her with the tip of his manhood, but she wanted to feel him at long last. Esme pulled his hips into her.

Sharp pain made her cry out. Seán stopped, concerned, but she made him go on. His weight upon her and his manhood inside her excited her, despite the pain.

Sometime later, they lay in bed, enjoying the glow.

"Did I hurt you too bad, Esme?"

"No, no, not too bad. It'll be better the next time, I'm sure." Esme couldn't tell if she lied or not.

Seán looked bleak, but she cuddled into his shoulder to reassure him. She traced the beads of sweat on his hairless chest. Esme had always imagined him to be hairy, but his chest sprouted only a dozen lonely, black hairs around the nipples and none above the navel.

She tickled his belly.

"If you tickle me, be prepared for the consequences!"

She half-fell out of the narrow bed and stumbled to her feet. "Oh, are you going to tickle me back, then? You'll have to catch me first!"

"I'm a Spanish pirate, me lassie! Avast! I always get the girl!"

She squealed and ran to the other room, putting the chair between them. It felt so sinful jumping around the cottage in nothing but hair and sweat.

Seán feinted left, then right, and grabbed her in the middle. She slipped out of his grasp and circled around the table.

He spoke in a sinister voice. "There's no escape!"

She grabbed the plaid woolen blanket and tossed it over his head. While he scrambled to get free, she hid behind the wall of the bedroom, out of sight.

He found her and he hefted her into his arms. They both collapsed on the bed in a shower of sweaty giggles.

"You are a silly woman, Mistress Fitzgerald."

"And you are my silly husband, Mister Fitzgerald."

Éamonn showed up three days later with supplies for their new home, a few comfortable chairs, and a wide embroidery frame for Esme. Esme wished her grandfather had arrived a few days earlier, to give her away, but he said important business detained him in Westport.

"Thank you so much, Grandfa! I can't wait to make something beautiful. What can I make you to repay your kindness?"

Her grandfather gave her a conspiratorial grin. "I only want some time with you, my dear. I need you to come with me somewhere."

Esme glanced out the door, where Seán tended to the horses. "Where are you taking me, Grandfa?"

"To a special place, my dear child, a place with magic. Come, let's get going now before the rain begins."

"I don't understand. Where is this place?"

He shook his head. "You'll see."

"Grandfa, tell me! I don't want to leave the entire day without knowing where I'm going. What if something happens and Seán needs to find us?" For a moment, she considered compelling the truth from him.

"We'll be grand, lass."

Seán wanted to come along, as they'd be passing through Dugort and other towns on the north end of the island, but Éamonn dissuaded him.

It took them most of the morning to ride up to the stone circle. After skirting Knockmore Mountain, they rode along the west coast. Despite living only a mile away, Esme hadn't yet been to Ashleam Bay. The view over the beach astounded her. She tried to count the islands winking in and out of the morning mists, but gave up. Sheep grazed on the cliff next to her and one fat ewe bleated.

She bleated back, and Éamonn laughed. "Come, Esme. We've miles to go yet."

"Is Achill all this beautiful?"

"This is a special spot. We'll head up on the pass north of Knockmore to the main road, then through Bunacurry. Next, we travel up to Dugort and around Slievemore. The stone circle's on the slope of that mountain."

Esme shivered at the memory of the stones. Would it be as bad as last time?

The idea must have shown on her face as Éamonn laughed again. "No, it's never as bad as the first time. Much like the wedding night, so?" He jabbed her in the waist, making her giggle. Her blush rose like the dawn tide, fast and furious.

Her smile deepened at the memory. *That* had *been lovely after the first time.*

Clusters of homes strung along the coast and the main road, like pearls on a string. They passed buildings other than crofter's cottages. Churches, a general store, a blacksmithy.

Could she use the brooch's power for trade? She might become a fortune-teller. For a wild moment, she weighed the notion. But that would be a perversion of the brooch's power, using the magic for her own gains.

Esme screwed up her courage to ask the question burning in her mind. "Grandfa, what am I to do when Seán goes off on trade?" She'd thought about the problem since Ardara and hadn't come up with a useful answer.

She might work her needlepoint for sale. But would anyone be able to afford that sort of work on this poor island?

"Do? Why, you keep the summer garden, the livestock, and enjoy the day. What else can you want?"

"You know better than that, Grandfa. I can't sit around and do nothing. I'd go mad."

Éamonn chuckled. "I know, *mo chuisle*. I brought you that frame, and you're good enough with the needle, even better than Eithne now. You might try your hand as a seamstress?"

A seamstress needed less specialization than someone creating fancy embroidery. She'd need to invest in quality cloth and thread, though. It seemed like a reasonable shift of her skills. She preferred the fancy work, but she'd think about it.

As if echoing her thoughts, her grandfather said, "You could still do the fancy work and have Seán take them on his trade missions."

How odd to think of her husband as a mobile store. She might send out completed work, and he would bring back useful things. Maybe even commissions.

They rode in silence, then Esme blurted out, "Did Grandmother stay home when you Traveled?"

A wistful look came to her grandfather's eyes. He brushed his hands through his hair, scratching at his scalp. "Caitriona was a rare woman, indeed, Esme. She traveled with me, unless with child. She haggled better than many a man. I can still see her eyes sparkle with the thrill of a well-struck bargain." Éamonn grinned wide, showing dimples and his white, straight teeth.

He looked down at his granddaughter. "She wouldn't let me leave her behind. Katie had a genuine love of adventure and a burning need to be on the road. The few times we settled in one place for any length of time, she'd pace like a caged wolf within a few weeks. Her temper burned like fire, and I did what I must to avoid igniting it. However, you'll be a more settled sort. Am I wrong?"

Esme shook her head. "You're not wrong, Grandfa."

He let out a chuckle. "You'll be fine in your wee cottage, my dear. Seán will come back after each run and bring you wonders and stories from all over this land. He's not the first Minkier to take a settled wife and he won't be the last. As long as you're comfortable with your own company, it'll be grand."

Esme didn't think she'd ever enjoy her own company. She wanted her family. Except for her grandfather and sister, though, all her family had gone. Or had they? Her grandfather had other children. "Tell me about Uncle Donal and Auntie Orlagh."

Éamonn leveled a suspicious look at her. "You aren't thinking of moving in with them, are you?"

"No, no, nothing like that. Just curious."

"Ah, then, that's grand. They both live near Kilkenny and are both vowed to God. Donal's a full priest, with a flock of his own, and Orlagh took her vows as a sister in the nearby abbey. They're both sincere in their faith."

Esme frowned at this, having seen the lies in priests before, but her grandfather chided her. "No, they're good people and true to their beliefs. Such folks do exist, you know."

Her cynicism welled up, wanting to deny his words. Her grandfather believed that truth, and pushing for more would do no good. She'd met only two priests, the one in Ardara and the one here, and she hadn't talked to the local priest enough to form an opinion.

Dugort came into view, with a beautiful, wide beach off the road. Seagulls wheeled on the wind, and the surf lapped against the sand in lines of lacy white. A man on a horse rode along the shoreline.

"Could we stop for a break, now or after the stones, Grandfa?"

He chuckled as they passed. "Katie loved the beach, as well. Not so much being in the water, but she loved the beach. You must get it from her. I can't stand sand getting everywhere myself, but we can stop on the way back."

They passed a large quartz stone with markings on it. "Folks called it the Star of Achill. Catholics held secret Masses during the Penal Times last century, when Catholicism was punishable by English law. They'd cover it with a blanket when the priest came to town, so everyone passing by would know when Mass would be."

"Wouldn't the Protestants also know, then?"

He gave a feral grin. "I presume no one told the God-botherers about the signal."

The stones were arranged differently than in Ardara, and looked smaller. Several stones stacked together formed a chamber with a large, flat capstone at the center of the semicircle. The grass grew thick around them, but only bare dirt lay inside the circle. In front of the chamber, two lower, flat stones lay, like an altar one would find in church. One had a series of marks carved into the corner, like a counting pattern. Curious, Esme touched one.

"Those are Ogham marks. Druid writing."

She shook her head. "Druids didn't write, Grandfa. Mr. Connell taught us they memorized everything."

"Yes, that's true. But they commemorated people. To do this, they made a language of the trees. Pictures that represented sounds and concepts. This is the language."

"What's 'commemorate?'" She hated to admit not knowing a word, but her grandfather wouldn't chide her for ignorance. Her country accent sounded so rough, and she wanted to work to improve it. Eithne had done so. Why couldn't she?

He chuckled. "That means to honor someone. To ensure their memory stays alive."

Esme touched each long cut in turn. Some cut straight while others leaned at a sharp angle. She counted thirty marks. "What does it say?"

"No one knows. That secret, along with so many others, died with the druids." Her grandfather's face fell.

As noon neared, the morning mists burned away. White, fluffy clouds scuttled across the sky, and the ever-present cry of gulls pierced the air.

The sea glittered at the base of the hill, and a glimpse of the beach beckoned her. The wind whipped her dress and shawl without mercy. Her hair, though plaited and tied up in a scarf, still escaped to dance in the wind. Esme felt utterly alone on the edge of the earth.

After clearing his throat to get her attention, her grandfather walked clockwise around the stones. He intoned those almost-Irish words. Once he completed the circle, he walked to the center altar stone, touching it with solemn ceremony. A blue glow shone from the stone, traveling up his arm pulse by pulse. Soon, the light enveloped him and he turned to Esme, beckoning her to join him.

Remembering the harsh shock from the last time, she reached out to the altar stone with a hesitant touch. It felt icy cold and sun-warm at the same time. She braced herself for the buzzing, but only felt a low hum, pleasant and almost comforting. The vibrations traveled through the stone and into her arm, shoulder, torso, and the rest of her body. The blue glow flowed and ebbed in soothing music. Esme grew light-headed and dizzy.

The tingling stopped, and she realized she sat on the ground. She didn't recall the transition between the two states. The buzzing stopped when she let go of the stone. Esme touched it again and it returned, though fainter. Concentrating, she could control it, making the buzz stronger, then weaker. With a smile at her grandfather, she reveled in her new ability. He grinned back.

"Learning to work the power, are you? I can sense you manipulating it."

"What makes the stones glow?"

He shrugged. "Not sure. My own Da couldn't tell me, when I asked. It might be the power of who built the stones, or the earth, or the druids themselves. It's to do with the *Sídhe,* the Fair Folk. A few times, I've seen them at the stones." He shivered at the memory. "I've tried to learn more, but without much success. We used to know more, but must have lost the knowledge over the generations. It's not like we can write down the details." His expression grew pinched, but he still glowed blue with the vital energy flowing through him.

Esme didn't want it to stop. The stones made her feel alive and slippery, as if she could prance atop the stones and leap from mountain to mountain, weightless. Similar to when Seán made love to her, a soaring sensation through her body. *Perhaps they have faery magic after all.*

The humming eased then ceased, despite her efforts to bring it back. She screwed her eyes shut in concentration, but it stayed gone. The stone grew icy cold now, a normal chilly rock.

Her grandfather patted her hand resting on the stone. "The energy only lasts a short while. It won't come back until another day. I've experimented with it. Later today the power won't work, either. Maybe the night or the dawn refills it. The moonlight, or the stars, or the 'witching time.'" Éamonn looked at the setting sun with a wistful expression. His snow-white hair stuck out in all directions.

She giggled and pointed at his hair. He grimaced and patted down his wild locks. "Yes, well, it has side effects. Look to your own, my dear."

Esme patted her scarf but it had disappeared. Glancing around, she spied the faded blue flannel flattened against a stone, about to burst free into the wind. She pounced on it and tried to get her own dancing, frizzled hair back under it, getting a faint spark as she touched the stone. Her efforts proved futile.

When she gave up, they headed back down to the beach. "Is it always like that, Grandfa, after the first time, I mean?"

"No, each time's different. But it feels great, so? If you're drained or desperate, the power can settle your nerves, connect you into our land. It gives you a base to build from. No matter what your talent might be, the stones are a place to rest and heal your soul. I know the life of a Traveler can be hard, and harder when you must stay at home when he's gone. This should help."

She didn't know what he meant, but she tucked it away for future information. Esme felt better and more certain about her future than she had in several weeks. She might now have the strength and motivation to make their house a home, even without Seán there.

Legacy of Truth

Chapter Seven

July 1792

Eithne

After sitting down at the breakfast table, Eithne accepted the mail from the butler. She glanced at the invitation from a landowner in Letterkenny, placing it for Hugh to read when he returned from the morning rounds. While Eithne had charge of his social calendar, she learned early on that he and only he should open his mail. She also mustn't eat until he arrived, but she might have tea.

Eithne opened a revolting oilskin envelope to reveal the much-creased paper, black with the uneducated scrawl of her sister, Bridey. She felt a familial duty to read it, so she extracted the letter with some care. They all arrived in America, though Níamh got seasick most of the voyage. Bridey met a farmer on the voyage over and married as soon as they arrived in America. Eithne would lay odds that her child would be born "early." She suspected Bridey already bedded the Gallagher boy, Alan, before they left. Eithne snorted, amused that Bridey had flanked Esme.

They settled on Bridey's new husband's farm, in Ohio, and asked that Eithne pass their location on to Esme. Such homey news bored Eithne. She toyed with the idea of what life might be like on the frontier. She'd no longer encounter the snobbery and staid traditions in what passed for Irish society. But Ohio sounded horrifically backwoods. They must live in hovels and scratch their living from the earth. No different from their life in Ardara. They'd gained nothing by moving halfway across the world.

Eithne dismissed her family from her mind and imagined the Red Indians would kill them all off shortly. Passing on their location to Esme would take too much effort, even if she knew where Esme lived.

That posed a problem. Dreams of her sister's brooch still haunted Eithne. How would she procure it if she didn't know where her sister lived?

Somewhere on Achill Island, that much she knew, but Achill was a large place. Perhaps their grandfather would give her more precise information. He visited every few months.

Eithne breathed in deep, proud of her new life. Hugh treated her roughly, and made his displeasure known with an occasional beating, but he kept her in style as promised. He bought her an entire wardrobe of new dresses in the latest fashions. She delighted in ruffles and silk. In addition, he bought her a collection of fanciful hats, something she'd never imagined owning. She relished the extravagance of the feathers. Eithne loved caressing them just to enjoy their velvet texture.

Hugh made her duties clear. She planned his social engagements, ran the household, and submitted to his needs in the bedroom. Hugh expressed much dismay at her first "miscarriage." However, she conceived a real child soon enough, and it grew in her belly now. She hoped for a son to satisfy her husband.

Hugh returned from his morning meeting with the foreman, sitting with a grunt. He spied the envelope and opened it as the footmen brought in their breakfast. His preferred breakfast consisted of boiled eggs and potatoes, but she liked fruit. She picked at hers while he read the newspaper and ignored her.

Eithne cleared her throat as he perused the words on the thick paper. "Would that be for Lady Allan and her daughter's presentation?"

He grunted with a nod. "Next week."

"Shall we go? I would enjoy a trip to Derry."

"I've got the south field to deal with. But you can go. Make our appearances and my apologies, but don't dally. Take your maid."

She nodded and finished her tea. Without another word, Hugh finished his food and left the table.

Eithne had met Lady Allan at the last engagement. She glowed at the memory, proud of her performance. The lady even listened to her opinions on music, though someone had twittered behind her back. No matter, she made progress. This would be an excellent opportunity to observe how people treated her without Hugh to shield her.

Esme

A betraying tear dripped down Esme's cheek. "Don't both of you leave at once! That's not fair." She sounded plaintive and petulant, even to her own ears, but being all alone frightened her.

No one else would be in the village for another month. Mr. Quinn would be no sort of company. He hadn't said two words to her since her wedding. Old Mistress Lynch must be soft in the head. She talked to herself, mumbling to a daughter who'd moved far away. Besides, she smelled of old cheese.

Father McNulty returned to his bishop the day before. That only left the fishermen who left at first light, came back by noon, gutted their catch, and lugged it up the mountain.

Seán hugged her tight. "You'll be fine, *mo chara*. I'll be back in a few weeks. I'm just going around the island. I have to see what's on offer around here, so? That way, I can set up a proper trade line. Besides, I got you fabric to practice on. Nothing for sale, if you don't want to. Make yourself something pretty. Make me something pretty, if you wish." His dark eyes twinkled with merriment, trying to get her to smile.

Esme turned to her grandfather, desperation in her eyes.

"No, Esme, I've got to be off as well, if I want to make it to the Puck Fair this year. There should be fine horses there. I'll see if I can't find one or two for Seán to sell, aye?" He turned to his grandson-in-law and gave Seán a hearty clap on the back.

Seán patted his stallion's dark flank, eliciting a snuffling and a hoof pawing the ground. "Sure and you won't find anything better than *Dubh*, here, but ye can try."

His look at *Dubh* held more affection than his look for her, but she pushed that idea away as unworthy. Seán loved her well, and she acted childish. She still didn't look forward to the enforced solitude.

"You've books, Esme. You can read when your fingers ache from the sewing. The pig and chickens need care. You'll be surprised at how much the gardening will fill your day."

While placing her hands on her hips, she glared at her new husband. "I grew up on a farm, Seán. I know how much work's involved. This isn't a true farm, it's like a…. play farm. A kitchen garden and a weird, winding plot I don't even know the proper edges of. What if I pull up a neighbor's potato or turnip and get run out of town?"

Éamonn shook his head. "That won't happen, lass. Wait 'til the folks come down off the mountain, you'll see. Your Seán'll be back by then." He raised an eyebrow at Seán until the latter gave a hasty nod. "So you'll have no bother with it."

She still harbored doubts, but she hid her surliness as she hugged her grandfather and husband goodbye. She might use her power to learn the truth, but she suspected it would show they lied, and didn't want that image haunting her as she waited alone.

The prospect of lonely weeks loomed over her as they rode off. She'd argued with her husband several times in the weeks since their wedding.

She even tried to push him, using her talent, but that only exhausted her. If she'd been smart or had any forethought at all, she would have hammered out these details before agreeing to be his wife. But her parents' emigration had drowned out other considerations.

Esme took a deep breath, straightened her spine, and started her new life. Maybe she should start playing cards, like her grandfather. He always won. The brooch's magic would help her there. At least, until someone accused her of cheating or witchcraft. Then where would she be?

The garden seemed in decent shape, for all it had been neglected since the last tenants left. No one had touched it since the rest of the village moved up the mountain months before. Sprigs of rosemary, mint, wild garlic, and basil ran wild. After digging deeper, Esme found chives, sage, chervil, and parsley.

The house itself wouldn't take much work to keep clean. The slope of the hill allowed water to flow through a channel down the center of the front room, to take any waste or rainwater. At least that kept the floors from getting muddy.

Seán left her with good candles, peat for the fire, and enough food to feed her through several months, despite vowing to be back by month-end. They found a storage hole built into the dirt floor to keep potatoes, carrots, turnips, and other root vegetables. She stocked that full and hung the herbs she picked. The chickens laid eggs, and Seán left sacks of flour and oats. Somewhere, he'd traded for a quarter barrel of dried fish. She could feast all day until his return and not run out of food.

Esme busied herself with making the place more like a home before she got into her needlework, beginning with the outside. A little whitewash and the cottage would look fresh and cheery, welcoming for when her husband returned.

Several days later, as Esme knelt in the garden, pulling up weeds which threatened to take over the wild garlic, Mistress Lynch pottered about the *clachan*. She often wandered from place to place, sometimes pausing at a door and muttering to herself.

Esme sat up, stretching her back. "Mistress Lynch? Can I help you with something?"

The woman stared at her through milky eyes and stumbled off to another cottage. Did she need something? Esme rose to her feet, wiping the dirt off her hands with her apron. She walked toward the older woman, placing a hand on her shoulder. "Mistress Lynch?"

The woman whirled around and flailed her arms. "Go away! Ye aren't supposed t' be here!"

Startled, Esme stumbled back, twisting her ankle on a stone. She wheeled her arms to catch balance, hitting Mistress Lynch's shoulder. They both tumbled onto the ground.

A gentle slope can become a steep decline when one has no balance, and while Esme stopped herself, the older woman crumpled down the hill. Esme struggled back to her feet to catch her, but she didn't move fast enough. She stared in horror as the older woman tumbled down the slope.

Esme must get help, and fast. Father McNulty would be at the church. She limped down the path but her ankle stabbed with pain. Should she make sure Mistress Lynch lived first? She turned back toward what looked like a pile of grimy rags. No, she didn't want to know. Best she get help first.

Before she got halfway to the church, she spied someone walking along the shore. "Mr. Quinn! Help, please! Mistress Lynch had a fall!"

He moved too slowly to suit her, so despite her ankle, she hurried to the church and found the priest. Between the three of them, they carried Mistress Lynch into the church.

Once inside, the woman pointed a long, bony accusatory finger at Esme. "She pushed me!"

Esme's eyes widened. "No, no, that's all wrong! Mistress Lynch, I fell, and tried to keep you from falling."

The old woman crawled away from her touch. "Murderess! Get her away from me!"

Truth shone on her face, and Esme staggered back, her hurt ankle twinging. The old woman believed Esme meant her harm. That hurt more than the accusation itself.

Esme gave Father McNulty an appealing look, but he just shooed her out. "Best go outside for now, girl. We'll get it straightened out in the end."

Her twisted ankle throbbing in misery, Esme waited outside for the priest to finish his ministrations. She found a stump and sat to wait, massaging her ankle.

When Mr. Quinn left the building, she rose painfully to her feet, but he just sent her a glare and hobbled away on his cane. Esme sat again, her heart fluttering with worry.

The door to the church opened again, revealing Father McNulty. He wiped his hands and shook his head.

Fearing the worst, Esme rose, not daring to breathe. "Is she... is she hurt bad?"

"Ah, she'll live well enough, but her hip, that's in a bad way. She may not walk again."

Esme's blood chilled. What else should she have done? "I tried to stop her! I swear I did!"

He shook his head, a frown creasing his aged face. "Ah, well, that's as may be, Mistress Fitzgerald. She's not changed her mind about what happened."

She swallowed against the rising dread, guilt, and fear. After deciding it must be a mistrust of strangers at play, Esme gave up and returned to the garden. There, at least, she found solace in the growing things. At least they didn't yell curses at her. And her ankle didn't hurt as much after she wrapped it.

After a few hours, the temperature dropped and the wind rose. With a glance toward the sky, she spied an immense, dark thunderhead loomed above the bay. Sunlight streamed around it with sharp lines. The air held a metallic, heavy scent. The sunbeams blurred and the storm headed for the village. Wind screamed around her now, whipping her hair across her eyes. She scrambled to collect her tools and gathering basket. Esme made it into the cottage as the first heavy drops pelted her head.

She slammed the front door tight and ran for the back door. The wind blew so strong, it might blow the rain in sideways. Esme had no wish to slosh around in the mud for the next several hours. The tiny window in the bedroom needed shuttering, too. A damp spot already formed on her bed.

She lay back on the bed, next to the damp spot, panting with her haste to batten down the house. The wind screeched and squealed outside. She'd never heard such a gale before. Their home in Ardara sat in gentle hills, well-sheltered from the ocean storms. This tempest rattled the shutters and doors. What would she do if the force of it broke the door? Should she brace furniture against it?

With much grunting and shoving, Esme moved the press in front of the bedroom window. In the front room, she cast about for something to use for the front door. The north door wouldn't need anything, as the wind came from the south.

Prying with her fingers, she lifted a flagstone an inch before it fell. Her efforts just got her skinned fingers, torn nails, and frustration. Esme shoved a chair in front of the door, knowing it would do little to stop the force of the wind.

She sat on the chair to add weight. She couldn't work on anything. The daylight had fled with the storm, leaving it too dim to see inside the dark cottage, despite the glowing peat log. She might cook, but the hearth sat too far away. Could she stand without losing the door?

A stronger wind gusted, shoving her chair an inch. With her heart beating faster, she pushed back with her feet. Best stay in the chair. Esme never liked thunderstorms. She shivered and hugged herself, trying to keep both warm and calm as the tempest screamed. The thatch tugged and rustled, despite netting and ties. Seán staked the netting to the stone walls, but a strong enough wind might yank it free.

A song might help her ward off fear. A cheery song seemed ridiculous, but a sad song would do nothing to lift her spirits. At first, she couldn't think of *any* songs. Esme knew hundreds. She closed her eyes to think of her father's favorite tunes.

The first song she could grasp was a silly song her father sang while drinking, about a man who lost his duck. She sang the chorus to get into the rhythm. Her voice didn't work at first. Only a squeak came out. She felt self-conscious singing to an empty room, but cleared her throat and tried again, voice wavering light and off-key.

Oh, my name it is Nell and the truth for to tell
I come from Cootehill, which I'll never deny
I had a fine drank and I'd die for his sake
That me grandmother left me and she goin' to die.

Something *thunked* on the door as she said "die." Esme almost jumped out of her skin. The wind howled and growled around the cottage. Darkness fell, despite the early hour. She wanted to stoke the fire, but if she stood up, the door would crash in.

Esme sang the chorus again. By the second line, a cold, sharp draft shot up her back. Her eyes darted around the room, noting a dim glow through the thatch above her. A large, dirty drop of water splashed into her eye.

Esme didn't often curse, but she'd heard colorful phrases from her father and grandfather. Even Seán exhibited creativity in such arts along the road. She drew upon this hidden treasure trove to color the air. The wet patch grew in the thatch. Another drop splatted on her head, followed by a third. Soon, a thin stream of water hit her head and dripped icy down her spine. She shifted the chair to one side, but she couldn't escape it. A puddle formed at the door and splashed mud on her skirts.

Did the other residents have to deal with this? What if the roof blew off? Well, so what if it did? Would the others take her in before allowing her to drown? Her own tears added to the deluge. How could Seán have left her in this horrible place?

Esme must fix the drip. Frantically, she cast about for a solution. She found a rag she used to pick up the cooking pot. After dashing to the hearth to grab it, she stood on the chair and stuffed it into the hole. The drip stopped, but the water saturated the rag and dripped again. She let out another curse. *At least the hole didn't get larger.*

The chair didn't move during her leap to the hearth, so she added another brick of peat. Everything felt damp and close, but soon a cheery peat fire glowed. That helped dispel a good chunk of her fear.

What a wonder a fire is. Just a little heat, a little warmth, made the world of difference, and lent a spark of hope on a cold, dismal afternoon. The peat glowed in bright shapes, drawing her in and offering escape from her panic for a few precious minutes. She ignored the wind and rain, or what the storm might do to her thatched roof.

How many thousands of generations of her ancestors stared into the fire, searching for comfort? How many eyes followed the dancing flickers of light? The hearth made a house a home. It warmed bodies and spirits in the cold, dark times of the soul.

Water sloshing distracted Esme from her reverie. The channel which cut through her cottage had grown to a river, but at least it didn't wash out the floor. An ingenious thing, for a cottage built on a mountain. It looked about to burst its bank.

After what seemed like hours, the rain eased to a steady beat on the roof. Cooler air caressed her damp skin, despite being midsummer. When the rain died, she moved the chair from the door and, minding the enormous puddle, stepped outside.

The world seemed fresh after a heavy rainstorm. It brightened her soul to breathe in the clean world. Grass glistened in the pink and orange of the setting sun. Mists curled off the mountain. She turned to examine the thatch and spied a patch blown to one side. She might fix that without too much bother. Much heartened, she walked the mile down to the shore to look along the beach, with only a slight twinge on her ankle. Storms might throw useful items on the shore. Good driftwood, flotsam from the shipping lines, even fresh fish would be useful.

Seagulls returned with the sun, but Esme welcomed them as companions after her isolation in the cottage. Great shapes of twisted driftwood dotted the sand. She picked one up, turning it over in her hands. Esme could make one into a clothes-tree, to hang coats and cloaks, and make her house more homey. Torn fishing net, too small to use in the sea, tangled on one branch. She picked it up anyhow, thinking it might be helpful on the thatch or the kitchen.

A group of gulls flew in front of her, squawking over a fish carcass. She stepped around them, leaving them to their supper, and wandered up the edge of the tide line. An unusual stone caught her eye. The reddish stone had a hole in the center, worn smooth and even, like the wish-stone Níamh treasured. She smiled and placed it in her pocket.

Esme glanced at the gulls. They watched her as if waiting to see what she did. Nodding to them in thanks for the gift, Esme kept walking.

Back in the cottage, the bit of netting proved large enough to help with the thatch repair. She found the twine and spent the last bit of good daylight standing on a stool, tying the netting into the remaining roof net. She shook her hands out several times, as they tingled from lack of blood.

The wet netting kept slipping out of her fingers and her stool wobbled. After some more creative cursing, she tied the last knot. She examined her work, testing the repairs. It may not be pretty, but it should stay.

Esme embraced her daily routine with a vengeance, pushing aside her growing disquiet about the patchy thatch roof, Mrs. Lynch, and her new life alone in the strange place. Her ankle now well-wrapped for support, she tended the kitchen garden, pulling weeds and slugs. She didn't just maintain her own portion of the garden, but the entire plot. It might make her intrusion into the community more palatable if she helped while the other residents lived in the summer *booley*, especially with Mistress Lynch's accusations.

After the garden, she fed the chickens and pig and checked around the cottage. Sometimes stones came loose, or a piece of thatch needed resetting. She swept the floor and shored up the drain channel with pebbles.

Next came improvement projects. As the weeks passed, she wrestled several large flagstones into the house and around the hearth. She added one to each side of the doors. This should prevent mud puddles. When Seán returned, she'd have him put flagstones through the house for a stone floor.

In the afternoons, she dried and hanged the wet things if the weather still held. In the evenings, she worked on needlepoint projects or making clothing to sell. Maybe she'd go with Seán on his next trip, selling her own handiwork.

If the weather grew poor, she remained indoors. Esme's pile of clothing for Seán to sell grew high. She tried her hand at whittling, with a driftwood piece from the beach. She made decorative buttons, two tall, thin cups and a few shallow bowls. Her carvings couldn't be called artistic, but functional. She'd ask Seán to find a proper whittling knife, short and sharp.

Her husband, a word which still gave her an odd thrill, should be home soon. At every sound outside, she flinched and rushed to the door, then chided herself for her silliness. She'd hear horses and a cart, making a racket on the quiet mountainside. Still, every time a sheep bleated or a chicken clucked, her hopes soared.

Esme knelt in the garden early in the morning as heavy fog lay across the island. Even seeing two feet ahead proved impossible. The mist smelled sweet and wet, shrouding the land like a wool blanket. Such weather muffled sounds, transformed and transported them to other places. When an unmistakable metallic jangle echoed in front of the house, she grabbed her basket and rushed out.

Her tangled skirts tripped her and she fell flat on her face. Esme's forehead came down inches from the curb stones, and she took a deep breath to regain her composure. Esme sat back with care. This time her ankle had twisted badly. She pressed ginger fingers on her already swollen joint. She didn't think she'd broken it, but it hurt like the very devil.

Much more carefully, she got to her feet. Any weight on her ankle made her whimper. She hobbled and skipped to the back door. After grabbing a driftwood stick she planned on carving later, she used it as a crutch. Esme flung open the front door, searching for her returning husband.

The room remained empty.

She'd sworn she heard the jangle of metal. What else could it have been?

Knowing the oddities of mist, she held onto the doorframe, listening for any sound. Nothing. Gulls in the distance echoed in the fog, and a sheep bleated. Nothing more.

An icy shiver made her shudder and traveled to her fingertips. Her skin bristled with the chill. Did she hear Seán's fetch? His spirit, come back after his death? She must get inside next to the fire. She craved warmth and comfort. With gritted teeth, Esme hobbled to the hearth to light the fire. The flint dropped on the flagstone as she still had hold of the crutch under one arm. "Blast it!"

She'd never talked out loud when alone, but the last few weeks changed that. Esme needed to speak just to hear a voice, any voice. She dragged the stool over, retrieved the flint stones and tried again.

Her hands shook with cold and fear. With numb fingers, she clicked the stones three times, four times, and five. The fire started after a dozen failed attempts, and she let out a long breath, almost blowing the tiny fire out. She crouched a long time, watching the peat glow with blessed heat. Fascinated by the fire, she drifted away in thought.

The swamp from her nightmares returned, but she found a path. Could she cross it? Esme noticed a line of flat flagstones winding into the tall marsh grasses. She placed a tentative foot on the first one and found it reassuringly solid. She shifted her weight and it held.

Esme stood on the stone, appreciating its solid strength. She held that strength inside, something to rely on. Something to cherish.

A snap from the hearth shook her awake. Esme didn't know how long she'd drifted, but her muscles felt stiff when she rose, and her ankle throbbed. She glanced at the door, to see if Seán had shown up, but the yard remained achingly empty.

As the sun eased toward dusk, she picked up her sewing, but put it away again. She'd grown bored with the project. Esme disliked most of the colors, but if she must make items to sell, she should make things catering to other people's taste.

Her stomach growled, and she realized she'd not eaten since waking. Leftover stew from the night before still simmered in the hearth pot. She chopped up a potato to add, with chervil from the garden.

Metal jangled outside again.

Esme took a deep breath and forced herself to stay still, listening hard. Definitely metal. Then creaking wood, jingling chain. Then the *click-click* Seán did with his tongue at the horses.

With her crutch under her arm, she hobbled to the front door and opened it, half-expecting to once again see nothing.

Out of the deepening gloom came a horse's nose. Two horses now, and behind them, a cart. And on the cart, her dear, long-missing husband, Seán. She wanted to jump up and kiss him, but she remained rooted in place, in case she experienced another vision, a shade, or a ghost.

Seán dropped the reins and opened his arms wide. "Esme, *mo chuisle*! Oh, I've missed you these weeks! Come give me a kiss!"

Esme hobbled toward him, and his eyes grew wide. He leapt down and ran to her, lifting her in a bone-crushing hug. Her husband whirled her around, making her dizzy. Instead of letting her down, he carried her into the cottage like on their wedding night. He sat on the largest chair and held her in his lap. She kept her arms locked around his neck, never wanting to let go.

Seán grinned like a loon, his dark eyes sparkled like black diamonds in the firelight. "What happened to your foot?"

"I twisted it this morning. I thought I heard you returning, but I must have imagined it." She wanted to mention the possibility of seeing his shade, but didn't want to worry him.

"Ah, so it's a wound you suffered for love of your husband! I must pamper you, my dear." He nuzzled into her neck. The stubble on his chin scratched her skin, and she giggled.

She squirmed, but couldn't escape without hurting herself. "Mercy!"

"Just this once, then, love. Here, let me go unharness the beasts, and I'll be back in a flash. I've presents for you!"

With tender care, he stood and placed her back in the chair, bringing the stool for her foot. She laughed and shooed him away to the horses, her fears and loneliness forgotten in the rush of relief.

An enormous bag entered the cottage, followed by a somewhat smaller Seán. He laid the bag down along one wall and walked back to the cart for more. This continued until a massive heap of sundries filled a quarter of the room. Seán dusted his hands. "There, that's everything! Safe from bandits, at least."

"Bandits? There isn't a soul around for miles, except the two oldies down on the shore. This place is a ghost town. Who'd be stealing your stock?"

"Perhaps it's safe enough here, but they're all around elsewhere." He frowned at the open door, then shut it. "Do you feel quite safe here alone, Esme?"

She glared at him, angry at his abandonment again. "And if I didn't, what would I do?" She wiggled her injured foot. "This could have been a lot worse and who would have known? It might have happened the day after you left and me unable to make it back to the cottage. My bones might have rotted in the kitchen garden for all you knew!"

He looked drawn and tired. "Ah, Esme, it'll be different when folks return. This place will bustle in a week. It's like a Traveler camp when people are out on missions. It's deserted until they return, then it's bursting at the seams!"

"And next summer?"

"Next summer we'll have kine, and you can go up to the *booley* with the rest of the village. I won't leave you alone again, I promise."

Seán believed his words. Maybe he'd keep that promise. She took in a deep breath and sent a prayer to St. Christopher so he might protect her husband on his travels. After placing her worry with the saint, she gave her husband a rueful grin. "That's all good, then. So, at the risk of sounding like my sister, what have you brought me?"

Eithne

At that moment, Esme's sister enjoyed herself.

Eithne floated amongst the guests at the soirée. Her husband's social circle afforded her several opportunities to attend gatherings, despite the scarcity of society in the backwoods of Donegal.

Her current hosts entertained several nobles, including a baronet and two ladies. Several artists and authors also attended, including one young playwright who paid her gratifying attention.

Of course, playwrights ranked only marginally higher in status than trained monkeys like actors. Still, he had entrancing, pale eyes and a lovely, slim body. Eithne had grown heartily tired of her husband's rotund figure. She ached to bed someone with more muscle, energy, and a wilder imagination.

She watched the young man as he spoke to Lady Ross. He had tied back his pale blond hair with a dark-blue velvet ribbon. She wondered how silky his hair would be if she ran her fingers through it. His long legs looked limber, too.

Hugh must never find out. Eithne shivered at the danger if he discovered her infidelities. Stiffening her spine, she cemented her smile and moved to the next group. It wouldn't do to arouse suspicions. She'd given the young man plenty of clues on how to find her after everyone retired.

While she once disdained the stone circles Esme always haunted, she now found them useful trysting spots. Certainly, Hugh would never tramp up to such a wild place, nor would he imagine finding his wife there.

The playwright beckoned to her from the corner. "Eithne! Do come here and join us. Lady Ross has the most intriguing idea."

While keeping her smile in place, she joined the small group.

Lady Ross placed an over-familiar hand on Eithne's arm and declared, in her high-pitched, ridiculous voice, "Mistress O'Hagerty, I do believe we should hold a concert here."

Eithne cocked her head in puzzlement. "A concert? Of what sort?"

"Music, of course! Young Mr. Lee here has held several, based on his father's work in Dublin."

She turned to the thin young man. "And what did you have in mind, Mr. Lee?"

The stammering man explained about a renewed interest in O'Carolan's music, but Eithne had already stopped paying attention. She imagined her husband's reaction to such a production in their home. He had very little interest in anything resembling culture, and had no appreciation of music whatsoever.

"That sounds most interesting, Mr. Lee. Where would you hold such an event?"

After giving a sly smile, the Lady said, "Why, at Woodhill of course!"

Eithne did her best to look shocked, flattered, and then weigh the suggestion carefully. "Truly? Do you think our house would be up to such an event?"

Lady Ross's piercing giggle rang through the room, cutting across all other conversations. "No, no, of course not! Your house is much too small. I mean up on that hill. There's a stone circle, is there not?"

Eithne's spine grew cold. She didn't think anyone but locals knew of that place. She couldn't meet anyone there, now. "I believe so, yes. But it's a wild place, overgrown with bracken, I'm sure."

"But such a romantic place for a concert! Imagine such a thing! Music under the sky, in the place of the ancients. An enchanted evening! We must go see it the next time we visit. We might host a whole series of concerts there. It should become quite an attraction to visitors."

Eithne nodded and gave platitudes, seething with frustration. With people tramping all around the circle, the hidden aspect would disappear. She'd just have to find some other trysting spot.

Esme

They descended the mountain in groups, pulling wagons and strings of cows. A long line of motley clumps of people and their household goods. Seán and Esme sat on the low wall in front of their house, watching the people arrive, each group finding their own cottage. The strangers nodded to the pair as they passed, but no one said a word or waved. Esme noted threadbare clothing, but clean and mended. These people had pride, despite being dirt poor.

Seán helped her clean up the common walkways in the two days since his return. They both agreed this might help with their acceptance into the community. His cousin, Tomás, still hadn't returned from his trade mission, but the folks here would know him. Tomás had some relation to the rest of the *clachan*. Seán didn't know if he'd married in, or his parents had, but he had no wife or children here.

With this cheery thought, Esme returned to the house to gather the baskets. Seán had brought an abundance of gifts, both for her and for their new neighbors. They'd call upon each and offer the basket in a neighborly welcome. Each basket contained bread, seeds, spices, and a pillow she embroidered. She hoped these proud folk wouldn't see it as charity.

Esme's nerves jangled. After so long alone on the hill, the cluster of homes seemed so crowded. "Should we go now?"

"Give them time to settle in, so. They've been away all summer, right? At least an hour."

She paced, silent and restless.

"Come, sit here. I'll comb out your hair for you. It'll relax us both."

Seán loved combing her hair. The tangles made a right mess today, as the wind whipped strong that morning. The wind blew strong on the island most mornings, to be fair. She nestled down on the floor between his legs and handed him the brush. He worked on the ends, working his way up until her curls grew silky. Esme closed her eyes in pleasure and let out a hum of contentment.

He told her a tale of his childhood, but she didn't pay the words much mind. The soothing hum of his deep voice entranced her as his fingers caressed her scalp. She nodded off with the music of his speech.

Esme wanted to brush his hair out in return. She loved stroking his long, straight hair. Straight hair seemed so odd to her. His fell thick and midnight black, like a horse's mane. She had a quick image of his Spanish ancestor, instead of a swashbuckling pirate, a great, black Andalusian stallion. The giggles bubbled up inside her, and she almost fell backward.

"What? What's so funny?" His eyes grew wide, and he looked so much like a spooked horse, she held her breath, but fell again into laughter.

"I can't… I couldn't possibly… no…." Esme gasped through her laughter. She held her side, stitched in pain.

He narrowed his eyes at her, suspicious. "I know I didn't say anything. Did I tickle you?"

"I… was thinking of your hair…"

He raised his eyebrows. "There's something funny about my hair?" With a tentative hand, he touched his head, searching for a cowlick.

Esme shook her head. "No, no… I can't explain…"

He glared at her then made a noise in the back of his throat. He stood and grabbed the first basket. "Are we ready to brave the first cottage, then? Or are you still paralyzed with hilarity?"

With a few final last chuckles, she tied a scarf over her hair. She tried to keep the corner of her mouth from twitching up whenever she glanced at her husband.

First, they visited the cottage next door. An older couple entered earlier, and the cart they brought down stood empty outside.

Seán knocked three times, pointing at the weathered and warped edges. No one answered at first, but after some shuffling and mumbling, the old woman opened the door a crack.

The woman wore a huge gray checkered wrap and showed just two teeth. "Aye?"

"*Dia dhuit*, mistress. We're your new neighbors, Seán and Esme." He gestured toward her. "We brought a gift to welcome you back to the *clachan*." He offered her the basket. She glared at him, then peered at the gift. Her hand snaked out from under her wrap and grabbed it, staring inside. She glanced up again at Seán, as if expecting him to take it back.

"*Go raibh maith agaibh*." She slammed the door in Seán's startled face.

Esme took a step back at the slam. "Well, at least she thanked us."

Seán stared at the door. "Perhaps I should have mentioned Tomás."

"We'll do so at the next house. With small places, if one person knows, they all know in short order." She told Seán about Mistress Lynch, but he'd dismissed it as unimportant. He might have judged too quickly.

"True enough. Let's go get the next basket."

In the end, their hospitality received a mixed bag of reactions. Even mentioning cousin Tomás, most of the villagers wouldn't chat with them.

One younger couple on the other side of the *clachan* greeted them, but most folks just grunted and closed the door. All took the baskets.

Esme's hopes fell further with each visit. They remained intruders, unwanted guests overstaying their welcome. By the time they returned to their cottage, dusk crept across the island. She wanted to curl up on her bed and sob.

Seán gave her a tight hug. "It'll take time to get used to us, pet. We'll get there. We made the first gesture. Now we act friendly and wait for them return in kind."

Esme wanted to believe him. He'd traveled all around the country and got to know many strangers. But he'd never lived in one place more than a few months, much less in a *clachan* like this. His parents hadn't been part of a larger Traveler tribe. He didn't understand a true community.

They ate supper in silence. Afterward, Esme returned to her latest needlepoint project. Seán had brought back fabric and thread in beautiful colors. Esme dug through them like a child in a sweet shop, eager to create beautiful things with her new stash.

On his trading trip, Seán sold his haul and all but the two mares, Nuala and Teaga. He brought back spices for trade and cooking and supplies to get them through the winter. Seán also had a store of goods for the next trip. He bought two cows but hadn't brought them home.

"When will you get the cows? It'll be nice to have milk to cook with." She didn't want him to leave again, but craved cheese.

"I'll leave in a couple of days. The trip should only take me a day. I'd like to get more horses with my profits, but I'd rather to go to Louisburgh, on the mainland. It depends on how the weather goes this week."

Esme's heart beat faster at his leaving her alone again with this alien village, newly populated with strangers. "So soon? You just got home two days ago!"

"It won't be a month-long trip like the last one, I promise. I'll be back before you know it."

At least his belief in his promise shone bright on his face. "Well, bring cheese back on this one, will you? I've been craving it like the devil this week."

Her husband snorted and glanced toward the door. "I could get you cheese tonight if the rest of the village accepted us as fellow humans."

"Aye, but that's not the case, is it?"

"It will be, pet. It will be."

The cart faded into the morning mists. A wave of mixed panic and anger rushed over Esme. Would this be her life from now on? A few days enjoying her husband before he disappeared again, traveling the country like a vagabond, leaving her to care for their home? Without friends or family, her only anchor abandoned her.

She returned to straighten up the mess left by her husband's morning departure. He took the clothing and pillows she'd made, and most of the coins. He left her a few pence, for paying the rent and other household expenses.

Esme hatched a plan about trading her more basic work for seeds and other staples from the other tenants. Trading would help her get to know them, and be a constant reminder she contributed to the community, or so she hoped.

She surveyed the gifts, spices, seeds, food, and supplies. Now that the flagstones kept most of the mud at bay, she could sew with more confidence at keeping things clean. Touching the smooth linen, dyed a pale sea-foam green, made her smile. It would make a lovely overdress for someone with standing in the community. With a fancy hem and embroidery work around the collar, the dress would command a high price. Esme just started planning a rosebud and leaf design when a shout came from outside.

When she flung open the back door and scanned the communal garden, a cow mooed. One of the neighbor's cows jumped the garden fence and ripped through the thyme. Two neighbors, the younger couple who'd been kind to them, chivvied the beast, trying to get her out of the garden.

Esme ran to help. She plucked a handful of sweet clover, as she used to at her father's farm, and held it out to entice the cow to step over the stone fence. Step by step, encouraged on both sides by the other two, the cow stepped half over the low fence, then all the way over, clipping her back hoof on a stone with a loud *clack*.

Esme led her out to the common pasture area, in front of the *clachan*, patting the beast on the neck as she gave the clover as a reward for her compliance. Smiling at her success, she turned back toward the couple with a triumphant grin.

The young man stood almost as short as Esme, stout with dark-blond hair. He tipped his tweed cap at her. "Ah, well done, mistress. Thankee kindly."

His wife stood about the same height, but less than half his weight. Her wavy, reddish-blond hair flew and tossed in the faint breeze. "Aye, thank you. We didn't have much success. The bait worked grand." Her voice sounded light and sweet, like a bird.

Esme held out her hand. "I'm Esme. We met last night."

The man shook it, but with a tentative handshake, as if not used to such proprieties. "I'm Cormac, Cormac O'Malley. This here's my wife, Aisling. I've a fishing boat down below."

After Cormac's reaction, she didn't dare shake Aisling's hand. "I'm very pleased to meet you, Cormac, Aisling. I'm afraid we're brand new transplants here. We have a cousin, Tomás, but he's out trading, so we're adrift. I've lived here for a month, now."

Aisling glanced at Cormac then back at Esme, her eyes growing wide. "Did you tend the garden, so? Usually, it's quite a job when we return from the mountain. It's my occupation."

"Yes, and I'm glad to have had the work. Seán left trading, so I went near mad with needing a task." She smiled at them both, hoping they could be friends. "Your occupation?"

Aisling gave a sly smile. "I'm a healer, you see. Many of the herbs in the garden are useful as remedies."

"I'm glad I could help, then."

Cormac took his wife's hand. "Would you want to come in for ale? It's a warm morning, so it is."

Esme grinned and followed them. Inside seemed as dark as her own, but even smaller. They had but one room, though they found creative ways to store things. They'd suspended racks from the rafters with ropes, holding bags and clothing. A leak might spell disaster, but the place seemed well-maintained and neat. Burbling in the corner caught her attention. Esme turned to see a trundle bed with a child, perhaps four years old, reaching out with chubby hands.

"Ah, Aoife will be wanting fed. You go sit there," Aisling waved her hand at the sturdy benches near the hearth, "and Cormac will bring the ale. I'll join in a minute. She gets fussy when she's hungry, so she does."

Aisling sat in a rocking chair underneath their window while Cormac handed her a wooden mug. Esme took a cautious sip then a bigger one. The ale tasted good, dark and bitter. Just the thing to raise her spirits.

Cormac's voice was gruff but kind. "So your cousin's Tomás, you say?"

"Yes, well, my husband's cousin, really. I've never met him, myself. We married last month. Do you make the ale yourself?" She didn't spy any barrels, but she noticed a storage pit.

"No, we get it from Sweeney House. They trade for pork and beef in the autumn. This is the last barrel for the summer."

Esme stopped mid-sip, guilty.

He shooed his hands at her to drink. "No, no, drink up. We've still the full barrel."

"Thank you. Could I trade for some myself, do you think?"

"I don't see why not. You've got pigs, aye? And chickens. You should do. Carrick Sweeney always has an eye out for luxuries, too, so good breads go over well."

"What about clothing? I am a seamstress and do fine embroidery."

Cormac rubbed his beard. "He's got no wife, but his old mother lives there. No one sees her much, but she'll come out for a special occasion, like a funeral. A miserable woman, she is, but she does like the finer stuff. She might be keen for fine things. The big house is on the other side of the mountains. Would you like to come when we go next?"

Esme's mind whirled with possibilities and the green linen dress she'd planned shifted to an older woman's tastes. "That would be grand, Cormac, thank you. You said your name's O'Malley? My grandmother was Caitriona O'Malley."

Cormac raised his eyebrows. "Do you know where she hailed from?"

Esme shrugged. "She Traveled with Grandfa."

"Ah, then we might be related, at that. I have Traveler cousins. It wouldn't be close, mind you. O'Malley's a common name." Common it may have been, but Esme felt a connection. Irrational, but she'd take any reassurance offered.

A giggle came from the corner, where Aisling played with their daughter while feeding. Esme gazed wistfully at the domestic scene when Cormac spoke. "I've not seen Tomás for a time, even before we moved up the mountain. Are you sure he still lives here?"

Seán hadn't mentioned the last time he spoke to his cousin. Had he decamped and moved on? "I don't know, Cormac. I'll have to ask Seán when he returns."

"Ah, well, either way, you're here now. We're glad to have another young couple. Most of the folk around here are older, and it's tough on Aisling, especially when I'm away fishing for days." He nodded to his wife and daughter in the corner. She gave them a sweet, sad smile.

"What else can you tell me about the neighbors? We didn't speak to them much when we handed out the baskets. You're the only ones who gave us a nod." Esme ducked her head, embarrassed, but she must grasp the opportunity to learn more about her new community.

Aisling piped up from the corner, "A gossiping mess of magpies is what they are. The men do the work, and the women do the talk. And heaven forfend anyone new come in! We arrived five years ago, and we're still the 'new ones' to the oldsters here."

Esme furrowed her brow. "The women don't work?" On a farm, everyone worked.

"Oh, they work. They'll mind the gardens and the beasts. But the 'real' work, the fishing and slaughtering, that's for the men. And anyone new is here to steal catches from the men, so they say."

Esme shrugged, "Seán's a trader. He won't be competing for the fish."

Aisling let out a cynical snort. "Then he'll be treated as a Tinker and no joy to him for that. Not, mind you, that there's aught wrong with trading, but they'll see it as beneath their high-and-mighty selves. And you're both strangers, as a final sin."

The anger from the older girl came off in palpable waves. The truth shone in her eyes, though Esme sensed exaggeration. Not much, though.

What had they gotten themselves into in this strange place?

Now the *clachan* came down the mountain, Father McNulty reappeared like magic and Sunday services resumed. Esme never considered herself attached to Mass. However, after a month of intense loneliness, she gravitated toward the services like a fly to the flame. Few things brought people together like God. Esme counted on that sense of community.

Everyone attended this first Sunday service. These people survived by scraping their living from the land and sea. Her family did the same, but with help from her grandfather. The villagers survived on the edge of the world with little cushion to fall back upon. Despite that, many dressed better than her own family.

Esme sat in the back pew, watching people as they entered. They came in family groups or pairs. A few shuffled in alone, but someone always greeted them, patting the pew beside them in invitation. Someone laughed near the front of the church, the sound echoing off bare stone walls.

Mr. Quinn came in and gave her a chilly nod. Mistress Lynch limped as she held on to his arm, and they took a pew two rows ahead. Esme tried to catch Mistress Lynch's faded eye, but the older woman ignored Esme with more dignity than the Queen of England. Mistress Lynch's hat had a huge feather. Esme squinted, trying to determine its origin.

The squawk of a child made her turn to see Aisling leading Aoife by the hand. The woman gave Esme a warm look and sat beside her. Cormac came in next, still patting road dust from his good jacket.

He grinned at her, showing a missing eyetooth and a broken front tooth. "Been watching the proms?"

"None of them will so much as acknowledge me. Have I turned invisible?"

Aisling's eyes shifted back and forth, and she spoke in a bare whisper. "Shh, shh, keep your voice down. They can all hear you. The sound bounces around like a ball in here."

Abashed, Esme noticed several of the older women glaring at her. She felt sheepish and chastened. How many of them believed Mistress Lynch's accusation?

A door behind the altar opened, heralding Father McNulty's arrival. He'd gained weight since last month. He had middling height and perhaps around her grandfather's age, but sported a round belly as if he carried a child.

With somber intonation, he began the service. His voice droned and Esme, despite her eager anticipation to attend, drifted away in wool-gathering.

While everyone attended the priest, Esme glanced at the others. A clutch of older women sat near the front, those who looked at her when she mentioned Mr. Quinn. Esme recognized her next door neighbor, who'd snatched the basket and slammed her door. A couple of younger men, fresh from their fishing boats, stood in the back. How many came from her own *clachan* and how many came from neighboring ones? About eighty people filled the place. Countless shuffling and sniffling punctuated the sermon, as they rose to sing.

Esme didn't know the hymn. She tried to keep up but felt foolish for mumbling the words. She hurried to sit after the hymn and sat hard, making the wooden pew echo with the impact. This earned her more censorious looks from the gaggle of ladies up front.

She kept her head down, the very vision of respectful, through the rest of the service. When she glanced up, she caught the eye of an older woman near her. The woman gave her a bare smile. There, she'd done it! She got some approval, no matter how small it might be. With work, she could change how they thought of her.

When service finished and she'd taken communion, she shuffled out with the rest of the crowd, behind Aisling and Cormac, to thank the priest. Every villager needed to catch the priest up on all that happened over the summer. Each person told the same stories a dozen ways. By the time Esme came to Father McNulty, he looked tired, harried, and bored. She imagined he'd love to get off his feet. He seemed the honest sort, and she wanted to help him. Instead of taking more of his time, she simply thanked him.

As Esme turned to leave, the eagle glares of the women still standing in a clutch near the front door of the church bore into her. She nodded in their direction, and they all grew still. While walking away with as much dignity as she could muster, Esme tried hard not to think about their eyes on the back of her head, watching her walk up the narrow path. Aisling and Cormac walked ahead, and she hurried to catch up.

Aisling looked confused. "Are ye done already with the priest? That was right fast, then."

"I didn't want to take up so much of his time. He looked tired."

Aisling clicked her tongue. "You made a mistake, Esme. The hens'll think you didn't like the service, or don't like our priest. Or that speaking with him is beneath you. It's a death knell, that is."

Esme slumped. She'd never figure out this place. She tried to be considerate. The priest would be so tired, wanting rest and relaxation after his homily. Instead, she'd insulted the man.

Once back in the safety of her own place, she gave in to the tears.

Esme had never had to deal with so many strangers before. She'd known the people in Ardara all her life. Who to be nice to, who to watch out for, and who would be compassionate on a rainy day. After being uprooted to this isolated place, so far away from everything she held dear, wrenched her heart. She blamed Seán for leaving her with these people, and herself for not making more friends. She blamed the village for being so rude.

Esme cried the blame out until it ran down her cheeks and onto her arms, leaving puddles on the back of her hand. She rocked on the low stool in front of the hearth, crying until she got the hiccups. Those hurt her throat and made her cry even more in frustration.

She took a deep breath and emerged from her wallowing. At least she found new friends in Aisling and Cormac. She clung to this bright star in her despair like a lifeline. When the tears dried from her eyes and cheeks, and her eyes burned with salt and anger, she walked outside to care for the animals.

Mr. Quinn and a woman she hadn't met sat on a bench next to the garden. They looked up as she passed, but sucked their teeth and returned to their quiet conversation. Esme refused to let her feelings take over again, and entered her chicken coop.

Three of her chickens escaped and wandered down the hill. Esme hastened to gather them, at the expense of several cuts and three enraged hens.

When she examined the coop, she found fresh-cut wires. Esme's blood grew hot, and she wanted to go to every cottage and discover the culprit. She'd see who lied and who didn't, and she'd know.

But then what? She couldn't call them out. That would just make everyone hate her more.

The clucking hens reminded her of the women in the church. With Eithne in mind, she pelted grain at the chickens. After a few unsatisfying throws, she forced herself to be gentle.

Chapter Eight

September 1792

Despite her joy at Seán's return, they got into a horrid fight right away, and he left again. Esme argued he needed to spend time with her between trips. Seán argued he must be on the road so he could afford to stay the winter. He'd left in a huff, as she steamed and simmered around the house until her isolation threatened to undo her all over again.

Still, Cormac and Aisling kept the loneliness at bay. Esme had wonderful conversations with Cormac while Aisling tended Aoife. While his wife would toss in an occasional opinion, she left most of the discussions to them. Fishing in Achill Bay Sound required more craft than she'd dreamed of.

This week, however, Cormac had gone out on his boat. While she enjoyed Aisling's company, her only female friend remained absorbed by her child. Aoife had a sweet temper, but got ill often, so her mother always fussed over her. While visiting with her in the evening, Esme worked on needlepoint while Aisling rocked the girl, fed her, or mumbled into the child's ear. Esme felt like an intruder and didn't come over as often.

When would Seán return? He traveled to a new place this trip, somewhere he'd visited with his parents. She couldn't remember the town's name. Leena? Lenine? Farther south, at any rate.

When she asked him about his last trip, his cheeks had darkened. "Well, I was only seven."

"You must remember. Tell me."

He ducked his head, playing with the ends of his hair. "Well, I remember one thing about it. I got my first kiss there."

She raised her eyebrows, a stab of jealousy shooting through her heart. "A kiss? With who?"

"I don't remember her name. She had a couple of years on me. We worked in the stables, looking after horses. I remember teasing her about hay in her hair. And one thing led to another." He shrugged, the picture of innocence.

Would he find this long-lost sweetheart? The lass must be married now. No need to be jealous of past ghosts.

Esme made practical items, like bonnets, aprons, and shawls. She made luxury items, like decorative pillows stuffed with fragrant herbs and dried flowers, or decorated ribbons to pin on hats. While she thought about making hats, she had no training in shaping the headpiece or affixing the brim.

Nightfall rushed in each evening as the summer died, shortening her working hours. Firelight shone well for the larger stitches in practical garments. Fine embroidery needed good sunlight.

Today, the sun shone with few clouds on the horizon. Esme lifted the baby blanket she worked on. Embroidered flowers clustered in one corner and weighed the wisdom of embroidering the other corners. Baby blankets got lots of wear and tear. Bridey gummed hers many times, leaving long smudges of drool. Perhaps only one corner. The fine flax felt pliable. She closed her eyes, stroking her cheek with the blanket, hoping to have her own baby someday.

Esme's eyes flew open. She counted the days on her fingers, back to the last time she'd gotten her courses. Ten weeks to the day. She stroked her still-flat belly. A baby. A child might make her less lonely here. More work, but more human contact, too. A smile crept across her face at this first step to having the big family she so craved.

Her husband would be so proud. Only three months ago, Seán had brought her to Achill Island.

After tracing the delicate flowers with her finger, she examined the blanket with fresh eyes. This one, she'd keep for her own child. Her own babe. The dark hours of the long winter nights wouldn't be so lonely. Ah, but she wouldn't give birth until March or April. Days would grow longer again. She didn't look forward to spending long winter nights pregnant and alone. But Seán said he'd be with her over the winter, didn't he?

Would Seán be pleased with the news? Esme smiled to herself. He'd best be. He caused this, after all.

The now-familiar drop in pressure told her a storm headed her way. She often worked with both doors open, to catch the cool sea breeze on warm days. Today seemed warm for September, but the wind picked up. Clouds roiled across the bay as she rushed to batten things down. After checking on the chickens and the now pregnant pig, she tested the thatch netting. Once she shut the doors and shuttered the window, she glanced at the pile of dried peat for a long, dark afternoon of heavy storms.

Esme resented late afternoon storms. They stole her precious sunshine and left her with damp, dim evenings. She craved the light as if it nourished her, making her blossom. Without it, she withered into sadness.

Seán brought her a loom on his last trip. Since weaving didn't take as much light as needlework, once she threaded the heddles on her loom, she wove to take her mind off the storm. The intense thunder and lightning here still frightened her. She sang while she worked the loom to keep her mind off the rising wind.

Esme sang a song her father sang, about two ravens arguing over which choice bits of a fallen knight they should eat. Morbid and depressing, it fit her mood. She timed her shuttle to the rhythm of the song. Back and forth, click and clack.

A loud crack and a blinding flash of lightning broke her rhythm. Her hands shook as she gripped the loom. Bright light flashed around the door frame. The earth beneath her feet shuddered. Had lightning struck something? Few trees grew on the windswept mountain. She hoped it hadn't struck a cottage. Even surly neighbors didn't deserve to die in such a way.

Esme kept on shivering and couldn't seem to stop. She rose and wrapped a blanket around her shoulders, but couldn't get warm. While chafing her arms with her hands, she squatted in front of the hearth to absorb more heat. She threw another peat brick on the dying embers, waiting for it to catch. She lost herself watching the shapes glow on the smoldering peat.

When her body stopped shivering, the hearth fire glowed with comforting warmth. A spark flew from the blaze and she hopped back, fearful of it catching her wool blanket. While she drifted, the storm blew out. The air smelled clear again. She took several deep breaths, enjoying the scent. The time after a storm seemed so magical. The world seemed softer after the storm stopped.

Esme needed company, so she walked to Aisling's cottage on the far side of the *clachan*. The twilight grew dim, even with the wind chasing the storm clouds away. She splashed in a hidden puddle. After grimacing at the mud, she skirted the rest, paying better heed to where she stepped. She had a flash of memory of being lost in a bog as a child, but she shook it away.

Aoife wailed inside, and Esme hesitated before knocking. When Aisling opened the door, tears streaked down her face. Esme hugged her tight, taking care not to crush the child. After a moment of shared warmth, she gave Aisling a hard look. "Are you afraid of thunder, as well?"

"No, not the thunder, nor the lightning. It's the storm itself that frightens me. I never know if it's taken Cormac away."

Cormac's boat still sailed the sea, trawling for deep-water fish. He'd left two days past. He often left on three or four day stints.

Esme hugged her friend again, her own fears gone. "It'll be fine, I'm sure. He'll be back when he can."

Eithne

Eithne wandered through the market, fanning herself against the heavy heat. She had no interest in the wares for sale, but she needed to escape that house. When Hugh left on business, or stayed in the fields, she loved being in the house. But he complained of the gout and spent more time in his lounge. That left him much too close for her comfort. She had no freedom to do as she wished and it frustrated her.

At least this market looked larger than the dismal weekly affair. Tinkers invaded the town for some horse fair, so they offered goods from far afield. Thieving Tinkers sold low-quality goods with high prices, but she enjoyed shopping. Eithne caressed the linen of a shawl in sunset shades before walking to the next stall. This one sold jewelry, but not gold or silver. Nothing but glass beads and junk. With a sniff, she moved on.

The tanner booth next door held no interest for her. Rather, the stench made her hurry past as she grew nauseous. She'd been sick often, especially in the mornings. She'd borne Hugh one son already, a stout heir named Harold. Such a sweet lad with an angelic smile. Smiling to herself at the memory of his pink, healthy cheeks, she paid no attention to her path and bumped into an older couple.

The woman cried out in surprise. "Eithne? Eithne, it's been so long!"

Blinking, Eithne stared at them. She remembered their faces, but couldn't figure out from where. Their clothing looked simple and ragged. Certainly, no one she'd met recently. She pushed past them.

The blonde, stout woman put a hand on Eithne's arm. "Do you not remember us?" She looked hurt, but her husband chided her.

"Why should she? She'd been just a young lass then. We're Seán's parents, your good-brother. Oisín and Ciara Fitzgerald. We camped near your farm for a summer."

Of course—those disgusting Tinkers. How could she forget? They'd loitered around her parents' farm for months. She rolled her eyes and nodded, trying again to brush past, but the man stopped her.

"Have you heard from Esme or Seán? We haven't seen them for a while, and Seán's not written to us."

Surprised that they could read, Eithne took in a deep breath to answer, but regretted it. They must not have bathed for some time. A sickly sweet stench clung to them, which made Eithne's stomach roil. "She's somewhere in County Mayo, I believe."

Eithne hadn't been able to find where Esme lived, but she wouldn't tell Tinkers that. She still ached to find that brooch, as it haunted her dreams, but their grandfather Éamonn didn't visit much. Last time, he refused to tell her where Esme lived.

The woman nodded like a loon. "Sure, County Mayo it is."

Eithne affected a nonchalant tone. "Do you remember the town?"

"Oh, we do at that! On the southeast end of Achill Island. But we can't afford..." Ciara swallowed and glanced at her husband. "I mean, Oisín can't travel far anymore, and I haven't been able to get there."

"Well, I've no news of them. Now, I must go." The couple stared at her as she shouldered past. How common of them to discuss finances in the crowded market. Eithne brushed at her sleeve where the woman grabbed her. Their reek clung to her clothing.

The south end of Achill Island. At least she found out where Esme lived. She must figure out a way to get Hugh to let her go to find her sister. And the brooch. She'd have to find some creative excuse to get around his controlling habits.

As she passed a child begging along the road, an idea flashed in her mind. Her sister was poor, and good Christians wanted to help their poor relations. Eithne did charity work, as the lady of a manor should. Granted, she only donated table scraps to the soup kitchen, but that counted as charity. She must keep up appearances, after all. What would be more natural than visiting her sister? Her only family left still in Ireland?

Hugh didn't like her traveling, though. She must find an excuse he would accept.

Seán

When Seán returned a week after the storm, he worried about his reception. He'd left in the middle of a fight. His father always told him never to let the sun set on an argument. But he'd not only let the sun set, he'd gone off for several weeks from his lonesome wife, leaving her among strangers. While Seán agreed with her wishes, that he *should* spend more time at home with her, the days grew shorter. Winter roads could be dangerous, and he wanted to do as much trading as he could now, while the weather shone fine.

Seán missed his bride. He wanted to be with her, spend all his time stroking her soft cheek, playing with her blazing curls, and laughing at her quick wit. But he also needed to pay for her home and bring gifts back to delight her. His last trade had been a disaster, buying a pony who didn't live up to the trader's promise. A stubborn beast, more mule than a pony, but Seán paid a premium price. The mulish pony sold for much less than he'd hoped at Achill Sound. That trade still rankled, but he must make the best of it. Betting on the races next month should help him recover his losses.

He *click-clicked* at Nuala as she turned the last bend. The cluster of cottages came into sight around the mountain. The mists rose, hugging them in cotton comfort.

When pulling up to the thatched house, Seán noticed the chicken coop needed mending again. He'd have to work on it before his next trip. The hens wouldn't fit through the hole, but they'd pick at it if left to their own devices. They weren't smart enough to understand they got better food and care within the cage.

After taking a deep breath, a fine gift of scented beeswax candles in his hand, Seán stepped to the door. Still, he hesitated. Esme didn't throw things, like some wives, but her temper grew snappish. He didn't have enough history to gauge his chances. He took a deep breath and braved the lioness in her den.

The place looked a right mess, with blankets strewn in one corner, dirty cups and bowls near the hearth, and an empty pot sizzling nearby. After grabbing a blanket, he moved the pot out of the embers lest it crack. Aside from the scent of the fire, a sick, sour odor filled the room. What happened to Esme?

As he walked into the bedroom, he spied her curled up on the bed. Had she fallen ill? He perched on the edge, his hand on her shoulder. "Esme? Esme, *mo chuisle*, are you well?"

She didn't move.

Panic rose in his stomach as his heart beat faster. *Oh, God, please let her be alive.* He couldn't live with himself if he'd left her to die.

Seán shook her shoulder, her skin cool but not cold. She lived. Esme moaned and turned over. Tear tracks streaked down her cheek. Her shift looked soiled and crumpled, as if she'd slept in it for a week. Esme shoved him aside and reached for a large bowl from the floor. She retched with dry heaves.

Seán sat back on the bed, relieved she just had an upset stomach. Maybe the sausage hadn't been properly cured? He held the bowl and stroked her hair, mumbling comforting nonsense. "It's all right, Esme, I've got you."

Esme stared up at him with bloodshot eyes, drawn and miserable. She turned to retch again. A dribble of saliva sparkled in the sunlight from the window.

The stink of vomit added to the staleness in the room. The linens needed deep cleaning. How long had she been so ill? "Did the food go bad? Did I bring you rotten cheese, my love?"

"No, no, it isn't the…" she grabbed for the bowl again. "It's not the food." She wiped her mouth with the back of her hand, her lips pressed together. "It's the baby."

The words didn't make immediate sense to him. "Baby? What do you mean, baby?" His eyes darted around as if he'd missed an infant stashed away in the corner.

She gave a wan smile. "Our baby. Or it will be, in seven months or so." She patted her belly, still flat.

Dumfounded, Seán looked from her to her belly and back again. The information must have penetrated his mind. "A baby? You're going to have a baby?"

Her smile grew stronger. "Yes, my love. A sweet, little black-haired boy, I hope. Just like you."

Seán stayed rooted to the spot as if someone planted him as a seedling, and he stood now as a mighty oak. He felt both vulnerable and powerful.

She's going to have our child! His dear wife would give him a son to hold, train, and love. He bent to kiss her, but she halted him with a hand on his lips. Her eyes grew wide and she turned to retch into the bowl again.

Esme coughed and spluttered, wiping her mouth with the back of her hand. She gave him a sweet, weak smile.

"I think the kissing should be later, *mo ghrá dubh.*"

Instead, he hugged her tight. His heart beat fast with excitement, delight, and a touch of fear. He'd have his own family soon, his very own.

When he released his wife, she glared at him with resolute eyes. "Maybe now, you'll stay longer."

Esme

Over the next few weeks, Seán played the dutiful husband, and she loved having him home. He helped Esme with every chore, cosseted her when she got sick, rubbed her feet and cuddled her in the evenings as the weather grew cooler. They sat in front of the hearth, talking with each other more than they'd yet had a chance to. He told her stories of his adventures on the road. She related details of life in the *clachan*.

Knowing he must leave again, Esme treasured every moment Seán spent at home. She had no talent for hiding her opinion. Many times, her grandfather mentioned her face worked like glass, emotions open for any to see.

She just finished milking the cows when Seán popped around the corner of the cottage. "Here, love, let me carry that for you." He reached for the pail, steam coming off the warm milk in the chilly pre-dawn air.

"I can carry a milk pail. I'm not a cripple." Even as she spoke, she grimaced at her waspish tone. She smiled to lessen the sting of her words.

He looked hurt, but grinned back. "Shall we carry it together, then?" He grabbed one side of the pail and she the other. Their differing heights made it awkward. However, she needed a salve for her rebuke, so she managed until they got back into the cottage.

"A chicken escaped this morning. Can you round her up? It's the black one, Betsy. She's talented at escaping. I think she grew fingers instead of talons."

"Right away, Esme. Yes'm!" He flashed her a silly grin and hopped back out the door.

Esme appreciated his help and his company. She didn't want him to leave, but she wished he wouldn't assume her to be a helpless babe-in-arms, unable to do the slightest thing without him bounding in to help.

Despite her frustration, she kept her anger calm. Seán had a tendency of leaving his clothing strewn about everywhere. Where did he drop his shirt from last night? There, flung over the press. And one stocking on the bed frame. The other should be nearby, should it not? No, it lay near the hearth. How in God's sweet name did it get over there? Did he throw it? She gathered the clothing to wash into a basket by the door.

Aisling and Cormac would join them for supper, and she wanted the place to look spotless. Well, as spotless as a thatched roof cottage with a dirt floor could be, even with a few flagstones and woven mats. She walked outside to fetch the broom to remove any spider webs from the inside of the thatch.

Esme paused at the door, listening. She should be able to hear Seán searching for the chicken, but only heard a few sleepy clucks and rustles from the coop. The dawn lightened the sky to a deep but brilliant blue. A faint glow from the east showed calm waters in the bay and dark forms of the mainland silhouetted against the velvet sky. The near-darkness grew quiet, a precious time of her own. The air tasted cool and thin, sweet and salty with grass and sea.

Esme felt as if she stood alone on the mountain, perhaps even alone in the entire world, just the dawn and herself. She breathed in the solitude and let it fill her. Sometimes being alone with oneself might be treasured. Too often, a thing to be feared.

A raucous clash of noise came from the coop, a rattle of the fence, and Seán cursing at the chickens. He must have found Betsy and returned her, against her will, to confinement. The other hens took up the fight and soon all the morning peace vanished.

Broom in hand, Esme returned to the house to finish her morning chores.

Chapter Nine

October 1792

Aisling

Seán opened his arms wide as he told his story. "More people than the eye could see! Every type of horse you could imagine. Tanner stalls, bakers, spice merchants. Anything you wanted, someone had it."

Esme's eyes had grown wide with Seán's description of the horse fair. Had she warmed to the notion of joining her husband on a trip? Aisling hoped so, as the woman seemed so lost when he left on his trades.

Fascinated by Seán's stories and adventures, Aisling spooned more stew into her bowl. "It sounds like an exciting life, to travel everywhere, meeting new people." She loved listening to the dark-haired man's voice.

"Not so much as you might think. More dusty roads and rainy nights under a leaky tent. At least now I've got a proper wagon, with a covered roof, so the leaky tent isn't a problem. Many people figure the Travelers are out to steal, so they feel justified in cheating them."

Cormac cocked his head. "Are Travelers the same as Tinkers?"

"Sort of. Tinker and Gypsy are what others call us. We prefer *an lucht siúil,* or Travelers. The other names have bad reputations, so we avoid them. Sure, there are some who've cheated others, but most are honest. No one remembers the honest ones. If anything goes wrong in the area, folks blame the Travelers, even if they had nothing to do with it." Seán took a long swig of dark ale.

"Even among ourselves, we steer clear of some bands. You can tell by their attitude and the care they keep of their wagons. The dishonest bands' wagons are either flashy or falling apart. If honest Travelers are having a hard time, they keep their wagons in good nick if they can."

Aisling glanced toward the door with a sudden memory. "Did you ever find your cousin, Tomás? He drove a flashy wagon. Bright red with light green leaves in the eaves. Fresh, shiny paint."

Seán wrinkled his nose. "No, he disappeared in the spring. His cottage is empty but for scraps of furniture. No one on the routes has seen him, as if the land swallowed him and his flashy wagon whole."

Aisling imagined a hill opening up like a giant mouth and eating Seán in one huge swallow. Nuala and the wagon would give a scream, and they'd disappear forever.

Just like the ocean might swallow Cormac. An icy finger of fear traced her spine. After taking a deep gulp of ale to shake the feeling, she almost choked. Esme patted her on the back until she breathed again. She smiled at the other woman, grateful for the help. Appreciating Esme's generous soul, she took her hand and squeezed.

Turning to Seán, Aisling asked, "Are you off again soon? Will you search for Tomás?"

"I don't think so, no. If he turns up I'll ask him what happened. But I've a business to run. I'll be off again soon, though. I've more things to fetch before the winter sets in." He grinned at Esme and she blushed, glancing down in embarrassment.

Aisling knew Esme didn't want him to leave again. But they fought like bulls whenever he stayed and that wouldn't be good for a woman with child. It might be better if he didn't stay. Esme got so lonely when he left, though. Aisling craved human contact when Cormac went out fishing. She promised herself to be there for Esme when she needed comfort.

Esme

A couple of evenings later, Esme threaded her loom by the window. She loved the knobbly blue thread Seán brought, but it tangled. She spent a good quarter hour unraveling one knot of it, as Seán came in from feeding Nuala.

When he flung open the door, the strands she'd laid out so painstakingly flew everywhere in the night wind. "In God's sweet name, Seán! Be careful!"

"With what, Esme? I can't control the wind."

She scowled at him. "You could not bang open the door when you burst in!"

Seán threw up his hands in frustration. "I didn't bang anything! The wind ripped the door out of my hand when I opened it."

Esme clenched her fists around the strands she'd rescued. "Then keep a better grip!"

"You're not being reasonable, Esme."

"And why should I be? You're only going to leave again."

He grabbed a shawl from her chair and threw it against the wall. "What in the devil's own hell do you expect me to do when the baby comes, and she has no crib, no blankets, no clothes?"

She jumped up, screaming at him, quivering in righteous indignation. "You can build a bloody crib, Seán. You don't have to *buy* everything. I can make clothes and blankets. Why must you go tramping off into the sunset again, like a grand hero, when you're better off taking care of your family here?"

"I can't take care of a family with no income! You *know* that!"

"The other men here do well enough. You can make money off the land, the kine, and the sheep. You just want to get away from me!" Tears hammered against her eyes. She wanted to hold onto the anger, cradle it and fan the fire until he gave in, but the rage would not stay hidden. It crept into her eyes, stealing into her hot cheeks and quivering chin. Esme turned away so he wouldn't see the streaks down her face. She didn't need to examine it with the brooch's power to know she was just being hurtful. Somewhere in her heart, though, she wanted it to be true. Her own wish for occasional peace meant he must want his own.

"By all that's holy, Esme, I want to care for you. I want to be a proper husband and buy you the things you deserve in life. Why can't you see that?"

She stood with her fists clenched and her back turned in condemnation. What answer could she give, that she hadn't already shouted a dozen times? Esme stood firm, not giving an inch. He told the truth, but she didn't want to give up the fight yet.

Seán stomped into the bedroom and yanked drawers out. He slammed them open and shut, pulling things out while cursing and muttering under his breath. He stuffed things into his traveling bag.

Esme snuck a peek at the doorway but schooled her gaze back to the hearth when he came back into the room. She whirled on him. "You're leaving again, now! In the middle of the bloody night? You're running away, you fecking coward!"

He stood in front of her, fists clenched in rage.

Esme raised her chin. "Go on, then, hit me! If it will make you feel more like a man!"

Her husband raised his fist, but then took a deep breath. His face turned red as he lowered it, huffing like an angry bull. He turned his back on her and stomped to the door.

Esme scanned the area for something to throw at him, but nothing came to hand. The iron pot would be much too heavy and still half-filled with yesterday's stew. Her precious loom would never do. A ball of yarn would have no satisfying impact.

Too late. He already walked through the door. Seán slammed it with a finality that made her jump, and tears burst forth. She didn't know if she cried for anger or loss. Esme sat down hard on the dirt floor and hugged her knees. She rocked back and forth, letting tears flow for what seemed like hours.

When she rose, she risked a peek outside. The wind still blew strong in the black night, the velvet sky studded with stars. No moon shone, but she needed none to see the horse and cart had disappeared. He *had* left her, just like that.

Esme loved Seán, yet he drove her mad. When he stayed home, she both loved the attention and the intimacy, yet hated him second-guessing everything she did and treating her like an incompetent child. When he left, her heart ached and she counted the days until he returned. Half of her was missing.

Did love always work like this? A mix of hate and passion, anger and tenderness? Aisling and Cormac didn't have such stormy encounters. She pulled up half-forgotten memories of her own parents arguing, but they never yelled so much.

Esme wondered if Eithne's marriage worked better. Did Hugh treat her kindly? Did he pamper her like a lady and bring her gifts? And did she regret her choice?

She thought of her parents, Bridey, and Níamh, far away in mysterious America. Had they settled in a new home? Did they prosper? She never wrote to Mr. Donohue. She must remember to write and give it to her grandfather when he visited.

And what about Alan? Would she have fought so much with him as a husband?

Later that night, she sat bolt upright from a sound sleep. Something banged in the main room. Esme grabbed the driftwood club she kept close by and crept out of bed.

If the moon had risen, the clouds hid it. By the smoldering glow of the banked fire, she made out a shape, messing about in the press. She snuck up behind the figure and raised her club when the figure cursed in her husband's voice.

"Seán? Seán, what the devil are you playing at?" Lowering her club, she backed up and blinked, trying to get accustomed to the gloom.

"Well, since you're up, lighting a candle would help." She expected him to sound sullen or angry. Instead, his voice sounded cheerful, almost gleeful.

After fumbling around for the lamp, she grabbed the matches on the hearth and lit the wick. In the flickering glow, his smile reached from ear to ear.

"What will you need for a two-week trip, *mo chroí*?"

"What?"

"If you come with me now and then, you won't feel so abandoned and isolated. Better now, before any weans come, aye?"

After remembering her trip to Achill, she didn't fancy the prospect. It must have shown on her face.

"It'll be better than the trip here. Try it, just this once? I promise you'll enjoy the journey." His eyes entreated her with eager hope. Esme had to give it a chance. That first trip had been miserable, but she'd never been anywhere new before. Now, traveling might be better. And she would be able to pick her own supplies and fabric in the market.

She gave Seán a half-smile. "This one time, then. I'll give it a go."

The grin on Seán's face made her heart melt, and she hugged him tight. After several kisses and mumbled endearments, they made up in earnest.

Esme loved making up after their fights.

Esme stared at the stately Westport House as they strode by. The tree-lined boulevard called The Mall seemed so genteel and posh, walking down the road seemed sinful. But Seán assured her anyone could walk the Mall, and so she strolled, arm in arm with her husband, examining the stalls of the weekly market.

Aisling had agreed to watch over their livestock while they gallivanted across the countryside. This seemed like a holiday from workaday life. The stalls offered so many options, the choices overloaded her. Colors and odors assaulted her with the cries of the stall attendants.

"Fresh meat pies! Dripping with fat and flavor!"

"Good, strong leather work—none better!"

"Buttons and notions, for all your needs!"

When they stopped at the final booth, Esme found bone, wood, and cloth buttons, both flat and shank. Seán warned her not to purchase anything until they looked at all the stalls. While she shopped, he checked which stalls might need his own goods, appraising the sellers and the wares on offer.

She stumbled as a large man barreled into her. "Oh!"

"So sorry, mistress! I didn't watch where I stepped." The educated accent and voice of a wealthy man, from his dress, came as a surprise to Esme. She didn't speak, but nodded in response as he moved on.

She kept her voice to an intense whisper. "Seán, was he a nobleman?"

Seán let out a laugh. "No, no, *mo chailín rua*. Perhaps a footman, by the look of him. A servant in a large house, from the livery."

"But he spoke so posh." She'd never met someone in service to a stately home, except for the boys who worked in the stable at Hugh O'Hagerty's house. The rest of the servants didn't come into town much.

"He'll have learned it from his master. The higher servants imitate their master's speech, as they interact with guests. The lower servants, the cooks or stable boys, don't. They talk more like we do."

Esme stared at the man's retreating back until the crowd jostled her back to her senses. She wanted to fix her own speech. His words sounded so aristocratic.

The afternoon whirled with activity and people. She'd never been in such a mixed crowd. The peasants and servants shopped alongside the wealthy, even if only upper servants or wealthy merchants. These lower social classes didn't behave as she imagined.

Exhausted, she plopped down in Seán's wagon and organized her purchases. Good, pale blue wool and a roll of rougher wool in rusty red plaid. She found linen with a dainty floral pattern, flax, and cotton bits. Silk ribbons, silk and cotton thread, buttons, and findings completed her haul. Esme surveyed her pile with great satisfaction. She could create several attractive pieces with this lot.

A glimpse of red hair caught her eye, and she focused on it. For a moment, she spied herself walking down the street, but the press of people obscured the figure from her vision. That couldn't be Eithne. Why would her twin be in Westport? Plenty of people had red hair. Her imagination must be playing tricks on her. Still, a shiver shot down her spine as if she'd seen her own fetch.

Seán found buyers for most of his goods. Two merchants wanted to see what he had left and make their own selections. He complained about the prices he got, but prices fell on the last day of the market.

They'd meant to arrive a day earlier. However, various delays made them late. In a moment of frustration, Seán yelled that she slowed him down. They stopped for more nature breaks and took longer. Men had it so easy in comparison. A few laces pulled, and instant relief. Women must deal with several petticoats, even if they wore slit bloomers. She didn't like to be in plain sight, so she searched for cover.

Esme had gotten lost in the densely grown forest at one stop. After she relieved herself, every step increased her uneasiness and panic. Seán's voice filtered through the trees. She pushed her way through coarse bracken to emerge, scratched and sweating, from the woods.

"Where in the name of the nine hells did you get off to, Esme? I got worried sick!"

With a sheepish half-smile, she climbed into the wagon. "I lost my way."

"Why do you need to tramp so deep in the woods, anyhow? It's not like you won't hear another wagon coming down the road in plenty of time to arrange yourself into womanly decorum, or whatever you do."

Esme shrugged. Being exposed while vulnerable made her panic, and panic didn't let nature run its course. She needed to find a private place.

Perhaps being out on the road hadn't been such a great idea.

As she packed her purchases in oiled cloth, Seán spoke to a lingering merchant. The big fellow topped Seán's height, and almost twice the weight, with short-cropped blond hair and a reek which made her eyes water. The smell of a pig-keeper. She'd know the stench anywhere. She closed the wagon curtains to block out the pong and tidied up while Seán finished his deal. That man frightened her, but she didn't know why.

The man tried to convince Seán his own market, in Louisburgh, would be a better bet than this one. It ran the same day, but ten miles away. If Esme had a say, she'd refuse him out of sheer sense of smell. But Seán asked him the pros and cons, like a good trader. He didn't say no, promising to consider it. The pig man didn't sound convinced, but grunted as he left.

"Esme? Come on out. He's gone."

She opened the curtains. He grinned fit to crack his face. "Well? Did everything get sold off? Are we done?"

"Sort of."

"What does 'sort of' mean, then?"

"It means, yes, I sold all I brought, but no, we're not done yet." He lifted a box, about five inches long, ebony and carved with delicate birds. The interlacing Celtic knotwork reminded her of the brooch. That stayed inside the lining of her skirt. She didn't want to leave it at the cottage, where anyone might walk in to steal it. To wear it in the open would ask for trouble. So, she'd sewn into a hidden pocket.

"What's that? Where did you get it?"

"This, my dear girl, is my profit."

Esme resisted the urge to open it herself. "What's inside?" Seán liked to tease her, but she wouldn't give him the satisfaction of knowing it worked.

He lifted the lid, revealing a necklace of glowing black pearls. They glittered in the fading sun, tinged with orange from the light. She gasped at their beauty.

Without thinking, she reached out to touch them. They felt cool, like metal. After drawing her hand back, she glanced up at her husband. "So, a good profit, then? Where in God's sweet name are you going to sell those, though?"

"It's why we're not done yet. No one here can turn these into anything useful. We'll have to travel Galway to get a decent price."

"Galway! But that's...!"

"Three days' travel. But we can get a fantastic return there. Perhaps twice as much as in Castlebar or Ballina, if they can even afford the pearls."

Esme hadn't expected they'd be gone so long, or travel so far away. But it was an adventure, right? The first night on the road hadn't been so bad. And sleeping in the proper covered wagon had been a vast improvement over sleeping in a tent on the hard ground or in the pouring rain.

She nodded, wanting to give her husband's way of life a proper chance. "Let's do it, Seán. Galway, imagine that!"

Farms got smaller as they approached the city. How did these tiny gardens feed the people in these houses? Her own cottage didn't have much land, though, instead using fields in the summer *booley*. Maybe these folks had summer grazing space, too.

The city itself was more *everything* than she'd imagined.

The bustling crowd grew thick, despite the drizzly day. Carriages crisscrossed busy streets, people milled about in front of stores, pubs, inns, and official buildings built of brick.

They passed a large building, which Seán called a hospital. "Are there so many sick people here? Do cities get more plague and illness, then?"

Seán laughed. "That might be true, but that's not why it's so big. People come from all over to be treated there, Esme. They have the best doctors, so people seek them out. Some parts are just for travelers to stay the night, like an inn. Also, they take..." Esme looked at Seán, confused at his hesitation.

"They take who, Seán?"

"They take lunatics."

"Mad people?" She studied the solid brick building with concern. Would they crawl out of the window to get her? Would they attack her?

"It's all fine, Esme. They lock the mad up, from the tales. They keep them in cells, like criminals. And many are criminals, from things they've done in madness."

True madness frightened her, making her shudder. She thought Eithne must have a touch of madness to be so blind to love and affection. However, her connection with Eithne convinced Esme her twin was cruel, not insane.

Esme didn't know which was worse. "Let's not linger, Seán. I don't like this place."

Seán peeked into several alleyways until he found one with a stable. He flipped several coins to the stable lad, who unharnessed and stowed the tack.

As they left, Esme glanced back. "Will our wagon be safe?"

"Aye, the city stables have a reputation to keep, after all. If our goods get stolen, everyone will know to avoid the place."

The cobblestoned walkway, wet with morning fog, made her stumble until she got used to them. The William Street jeweler's shop sat just around the corner.

Unlike the market stalls in Westport, the jeweler had a solid building, sticking out on the corner between a milliner and a clockmaker. The sign proclaimed it to be Dillon's, a fine purveyor of gold, silver, and gems.

Inside, Esme entered a different world. The noise and bustle of the street disappeared when the door shut. Impressions of velvet and sparkle surrounded her, with glass cases holding jewels, gold, and pearls. She did a full turn, surveying the glittering display, like something out of her father's tales in the Fae Otherworld.

Esme never saw so much wealth in one place. It made her feel shabby and poor, and she tugged her good shawl about her shoulders to hide her simple dress.

Seán showed no such modesty, as he strode to the counter with purpose. "My good man, I have a bauble to trade you might be interested in."

The man behind the counter's nose rose almost to the ceiling as he looked down at Seán, despite being at least six inches shorter. The jeweler had a snub nose and wore a pained expression. He looked as if he ate most of his profits, judging from his generous waistline.

He sniffed and spoke in a haughty tone. "What could *you* have of interest to *me*, Tinker?" He spit the last word like an insult.

Esme did a quick survey of their appearance. What gave them away as Travelers? Seán ignored the slur and brought out the exquisite box.

Without opening it, he slid it onto the glass counter. The jeweler's eyes widened and gave Seán a suspicious glance. With two fingers, he lifted the ebony lid. When the black pearls shone in the light, his eyes glittered. His attitude shifted to solicitude. "And how may I be of service to you, sir?"

When he offered the first price for the pearls, his lie shone bright on his face. Before she thought about it, Esme raised her eyebrows. "That's much too low of a price, sir."

Both the jeweler and her husband stared at her. "Tell me, how much would you be able to sell these on for?"

When she frowned at his answer, he gave another amount. Each time, his face lied, though the glow grew dimmer each time. Finally, she nodded. "There, that's the true price. We'll work from that."

The men exchanged a glance and the jeweler said, "Very well, to humor the young lady, I'll increase my original offer by a guinea."

After much haggling and hedging, Seán warmed to his task. Esme grew fascinated at her husband's bargaining skills and noted which worked best. She even offered a few comments of her own, and in the end, the jeweler almost doubled his original offer.

Once they left the shop, Seán grinned wide enough to split his face. But now they held a great deal of coin, and every person they passed on the street seemed suspicious. Esme took Seán's hand. "Let's head back home straight away, Seán. I'm not comfortable here."

"One night, my beloved. We'll enjoy a fine meal at a comfortable inn and a night on a featherbed. Then we'll be off in the morning, aye? With good luck, we'll make it all the way home in two or three days. How did you learn to do all of that? And how did you know the right price?"

Esme shrugged. "I watched you and followed your lead." Her grandfather had warned her to never tell others about the brooch's power, though she wanted to tell her own husband. Still, it made her feel warm inside to know she'd helped with the trade.

They ate a delicious meal of salmon and creamed potatoes, and she'd treasure the luxury of the fine inn. After the meal and too many pints, they retired to their room, dividing the remaining coins into several stashes.

"This is to frustrate thieves on the road. They might get my purse and yours, but we'll still have most of the profits in your skirts and hidden places under the wagon." Seán tapped his head. "One thinks of the dangers if one is to survive them, *mo chroi*."

Her father never had such forethought.

The next day, as they passed the road to Cong, Esme sat in the wagon itself, not feeling well and trying to rest as Seán drove the horses. The wagon came to a stop, and she heard voices. Though she sat up, she stayed inside.

Seán spoke pleasantly, but an edge to his voice kept her wary. "Good day to you, gentlemen. A fine day for travel, is it not?"

"Good for some, aye." The unpleasant voice came out like a growl.

Seán clicked at the horses to move, but they didn't budge. The others must block their way.

"Whatcha got in the cart, Tinker?"

"Nothing of interest. I dropped off goods a merchant bought and paid for last week."

Clever lad. That meant he'd be carrying no goods and no money. If they believed him.

"Fancy we'll take a look and see what you've got. Won't we, lads?" Grumbles and grunts expressed consent. Someone fumbled with the latch on the back of the wagon.

"Now, why would you want to disbelieve me? Do I look rich to you?" Seán wore his favorite gray shirt and brown leather vest. Neither looked too clean and his shirt frayed at the wrists. She'd noticed it needed mending the night before.

The man in back cursed in frustration and walked around to the front.

"'Ere, now, let us in, lad, and we'll not hurt you too badly." How many men? Seán stood tall, but his muscles were wiry thin rather than stout.

Esme's eyes darted around for a weapon. The wagon had almost nothing left after the trade mission, but she yanked several blankets over her head, pretending to be a pile of rags. If she couldn't defend herself, she must hide.

The horses stamped their feet as Seán calmed them. The front curtains of the wagon whipped open.

"'Arry, he might be tellin' the truth. Just rubbish in here."

"Make sure before we let the sweet lad go, Tom."

Tom climbed in and stomped around the wagon, pushing at things and making the cart rock with alarming creaks. Esme held her breath as he reached her hiding spot. He jerked the blankets off and let out a shout of triumph. "Hoho! What have we here?"

"What is it, Tom? The lost Spanish Treasure?"

"Oh, it's a treasure all right!" He yanked her arm. Esme screamed and tried to pull out of his grip. He hauled her out of the wagon. Three burly men in dire need of a bath stared at her. They all wore rags and Tom, who dug his fingers into her arm, had breath which stank like rotten potatoes.

Seán stood next to her, holding her other arm. "Leave my wife alone. I've got coins. I'll trade for her."

Esme's anger boiled up, but she knew if she said anything, these sort of men would just hit her.

"Trade for her, he says." Tom laughed, and the wash of odor from his breath almost made Esme pass out.

The biggest one didn't laugh. "How much you got, Tinker?"

"Not much," Seán admitted. "But I'll give you all I have. Just please, leave my wife to me."

Esme hoped his quick-witted tongue would talk them out of this situation, but he seemed as frightened as she. These men might have escaped from the asylum. Her stomach lurched. What would a madman do to her?

Harry held out his hand. Seán gave over his pouch of coins. The bandit dumped them on his large palm and counted them out loud. After several moments, he nodded to Tom.

The third man protested. "Oi! Don't we get a say in this, then? I've not had any in weeks, and she looks like a sweet bit of pie, she does." As he came closer, he sniffed her up and down like a dog. She shivered, her stomach roiling again.

"Leave off, Riley. The coin is enough."

Riley grabbed one of her breasts in a rough squeeze, and she yelped. She clung to Seán's arm, but he stayed stock still.

"Oi, I like it when they make noises, 'Arry. C'mon, let me play, at least!"

The truth shone on his face, and her heart beat so fast, she thought it would burst.

Harry placed a finger on his chin, which made Esme quail further. She cast a desperate look at Seán, but he still froze in shock or fear.

Riley yanked her forward by the hips, jerking her away from Seán. The man ground his hips against hers. His rock-hard manhood jutted out underneath his breeks. She screamed again, pushing against him with all her strength.

Seán finally burst into action. "Stop! Leave her alone!" Tom caught him, pulling his arms behind him. Riley stopped grinding against her and shoved her down into the dirt, fumbling with her skirts.

Esme screeched, batting at him while holding her skirts down. "Stop it! Help! Don't touch me! Go away!"

It dawned on her that nothing would save her. Her nausea grew and she spewed straight into Riley's face.

Disgusted, he stopped rummaging below her skirts and stood, spitting and gagging. "Jesus, Joseph, and Mary. What the hell!"

She curled into a ball, heaving the remnants of her stomach on the ground, sobbing in between being sick.

When she finally came to her senses, the bandits had disappeared.

Seán wiped her face and lifted her into the wagon. By mutual consent, they didn't speak of the incident but hurried home. They didn't even stop for the night.

When Seán left on his next mission, he offered to take Esme along again. He didn't seem surprised when she refused.

Chapter Ten

December 1792

Seán still hadn't returned from his latest departure a month before, and Esme grew worried, rubbing her distended belly. No snow had yet fallen this December, but colder days put more desperate people on the road, making it more dangerous.

Esme rose with care that morning. Her dreams had been disturbing, with visions she didn't remember. An inexplicable dread consumed her as if the earth swallowed her whole. Not her recurring and disturbing swamp dream, but a more nebulous terror, threatening not just her, but Seán as well. She climbed out of the fear and got on with her day, despite her fatigue.

Today dawned pleasant, crisp and clear. A brilliant, deep blue filled the sky. On days like these, Esme might flap her arms and fly, leaving the green earth behind. She resented the chores when sunlight beckoned. The garden needed little work in the winter, but she must tend the animals, along with the house and laundry. By the time she finished her work, dusk crept along the horizon.

Night held little but boredom and fear. During the day, she read, cut cloth, sewed clothing, did fine embroidery, worked in the garden, or took care of the animals. She attended church on Sundays, her only social interaction. She visited Aisling, but the other woman got so preoccupied with her daughter, Esme never stayed long. Aisling talked of little else than the way the child held her head, or gurgled a word, or how her stool smelled. Esme needed a child of her own, before she could participate in such conversations.

Cormac chatted more, but he'd gone out fishing again. The fisherman wanted to net more catches before the January storms. They had barrels of dried fish, but he wanted more for winter.

Aisling told her he'd gone out three days ago, before a rough storm came through. He should return any day now, and Aisling had worry in her eyes. But she always worried. She fretted and fussed with her baby, anxious for Cormac's boat to return.

Esme caught her friend standing on the hillside, staring out to sea, as if her gaze would bring him back. Her skirts whipped around her legs as she stood still as a statue. Esme imagined Aisling's outstretched hand finding Cormac's boat and lifting it out of the water to the safety of the harbor.

The sight broke Esme's heart.

Other folk in the village, such as Mr. Quinn, Mistress Lynch, the Molloy brothers, or Mistress McCann and her daughter Eileen, ignored her. The village still considered Esme an outcast, someone to scorn, despite her acting like an angel in church, weeding the communal garden, and bringing small gifts. None of that seemed enough.

With a wary glance at the clouds moving in the distance, Esme prepared for another storm. She'd gotten better at reading the signs. If the clouds looked light and white, the weather stayed fair. But low, thick clouds with cold, biting winds meant a wild night. Tonight promised to be such a night.

Settling before the hearth, she arranged her embroidery frame. The short days didn't allow her much time for needlework, but now and then, she carved some time for her joy. The fine, detailed crewelwork and needlepoint still gave her the most satisfaction.

As darkness beckoned, it brought on dark thoughts. Esme didn't like her visions of the earth swallowing people whole. They came unbidden as she sat before the hearth. To forestall the darkness, she wove. The *click* and *clack* of the loom relaxed her despite howling wind. It sent her into a trance-like state, detached from her own body. Esme might float into the sky and see the whole cottage from the roof tree. She spied her body below, shuttle passing back and forth, *click clack*, *click clack*. Her fire smoldered in the hearth, and the rain hissed outside.

The fire gave rise to the memory of the form at the stones, that first time with her grandfather. That being of light which came forth, shining and terrifying all at once. What if she'd reached out and touched them?

A loud pop in the hearth brought her back into her body. She checked to make sure a cinder hadn't popped out to burn her or the cloth.

It wouldn't do to fall asleep at the loom. She might fall over from the chair and smash the frame. If she broke the loom, she'd have nothing to do in the long, dark evenings.

The soft hiss of the storm shifted to sleeting rain. The tug of the wind on the cottage thatch pulled, an odd physical sensation. Perhaps she reacted to a breeze in the house or the howl outside, but she became one with the place during such storms. Esme closed her eyes, riding the bob and weave of the currents, almost as if she rode a boat on the ocean.

For a moment, the ocean surrounded her. She stood on Cormac's fishing trawler, and the situation looked desperate. Great waves broached the side of the boat, one after another. Cormac and his two mates lashed themselves to the mast, but it broke and fell with a mighty crack, taking a good chunk of the hull. The icy cold salt water slapped her in the face. Esme gasped, but received only thick brine to breathe. She choked, coughed, swallowed more water. Cold nothing consumed her.

After opening her eyes with a gasp, she sputtered, spitting out sea water. The warm cottage seemed alien. After she caught her breath, she shivered next to the hearth, warming her icy hands. The vision had been so real. Grief wrenched through her. Cormac had drowned in this storm.

What would Aisling do without him? Aisling and little Aoife, alone and bereft of Cormac. How would they survive? Aisling would need the comfort of human arms. The rest of the *clachan* still treated them all as outsiders and would offer no help.

After considering and discarding a half dozen options, Esme came to the slow conclusion she had no way to help Aisling. She could barely help herself, pregnant and alone. If Seán never returned, she'd be just as forsaken. They'd all die of starvation, alone on this blasted mountain. The earth might swallow Seán, and Cormac swallowed by the sea.

A slow thought crept into her mind. She had a way out. She might walk outside and lose herself in the storm. Esme wouldn't have to waste away, starving and alone. She rose and shuffled to the door, her mind spinning with despair. She flung the door open to let the storm in.

The furious wind stung and yanked at her, pulling her through the doorway. Buffeted and battered, she took her first step outside into the maelstrom.

A flutter in her belly halted her. Esme placed her hand on her stomach and it fluttered again. Did her baby just move?

Rushing inside and slamming the door shut, Esme stumbled back to the hearth, every nerve waiting for that tiny movement. She sat on Seán's overstuffed chair, curling her feet up under her. She huddled under a woolen blanket and stared at the fire.

Her resolution to lose herself in the storm had disappeared. Instead, she stumbled to Aisling's cottage. Her friend would need her.

April 1793

Esme had never felt more like a beached whale. While she'd never been skinny, her belly now looked enormous. It stuck out so much she couldn't see her own toes. Despite promising to be home all winter, Seán had to go out on another trade. The money they'd lost to robbery had stolen that dream from them.

Seán wasn't home and she needed something from a shelf in the rafters.

Muttering imprecations about missing husbands, she grabbed the wooden stepstool. Even on her tiptoes, she still couldn't reach the crock of honey. With another curse, she fetched two large books from her precious collection. This allowed her to inch the pot to the shelf edge with her fingertips. Why did they even use these shelves? Every inch of storage counted in the tiny cottage, but Seán knew she couldn't reach so high in the best of times.

Once she gripped the pot of honey in her arms, she stepped off the stool and replaced the books. Now she'd make her tea.

She'd been craving honey in her tea for three days, but she'd put that off. Now her body demanded the sweet treat with a force that brooked no argument. She stirred a healthy dollop in her hot tea and sipped, savoring the sweetness.

A knock on the door interrupted her reverie.

Aoife ran in and hugged her leg. Esme smiled down at the girl. "Child, don't you know it's not polite to rush into someone's house?"

"I knocked. You must have heard me!" Aoife's eyes darted around the room. After spying the knitting project she'd left the evening before, she pounced on it, gave Esme a jaunty wave, and scampered out again.

As she chuckled at the energy of children, Esme creaked out of her chair and stirred up the peat, coaxing it into stronger warmth. The April morning remained chilly.

As she straightened, the ever-present dull ache in her back sharpened. Esme pressed the heel of her hand into the muscle to ease it. That didn't help.

"Aoife?" Esme cried out, hoping the girl remained close.

"Hmm?" A faint answer reassured her. She must still be just outside.

"Aoife, get your mother, please. I need her."

"Yes, Mistress Esme!" The sound of her running feet reassured Esme. She sat again in the overstuffed chair near the fire. She closed her eyes and tried to push the pain away with sheer will. That only worked when she stood in the stone circle, but she tried anyhow. After her vision blurred into dizziness, she stopped trying.

When she opened her eyes, Aisling stood over her, frowning. "Pain in your back, Esme?"

"How did you know?"

With a rueful chuckle, Aisling crossed her arms. "I've been expecting this for several weeks. I think your baby is coming."

Several hours later, as Esme lay in a bed of clammy sweat, she ground her teeth. It sounded so simple. *The baby is coming.* That hadn't prepared her for the pain, the long hours that felt like days, and the waves of nausea ripping through her. Nor the aching loss that Seán wasn't there when she needed him most.

How would he realize she'd deliver today? But he should have stayed home, with her so close to birth.

Esme grunted as another contraction took over her body. The muscles on her belly rippled, pushing the baby out and down. Her grunt became a strangled cry as she tried to keep the pain from consuming her. She panted and whimpered until the pain eased. When she opened her eyes again, Seán's worried face filled her vision.

This must be an illusion brought on by the pain. Esme reached her hand out to touch his face. It felt cool and fresh, not covered with sweat like everything else in the room. She cried out again, but with a cry of joy.

"It's all right, my dearest love. I'm here. I'll be holding your hand."

"Ah, *mo ghrá dubh*. You came back. You really came back!"

After several more painful hours, the babe arrived, red and squalling. She looked like a boiled lobster, with the sweetest face Esme could ever hope for. And the precious look in Seán's eyes when he beheld his daughter tasted sweeter than any honey.

They named her Katy, after her grandmother.

Chapter Eleven

May 1795

Esme loved days like these. The sun shone bright and warm, and the ever-present sea wind disappeared for a wonder. Sea gulls cried in the distance, but the buzz of bees drowned them out. On days like these, flashes of time at the beach in Ardara flickered through her mind. Memories of her childhood home seemed more difficult to recall on the darker days.

Up on the mountain, in the summer *booley*, the sea birds echoed in the distance. She knelt in the garden, pulling weeds. "No, Aoife, pull the other one. Yes, the one with the yellow flower." The little girl tried to pull up a rosemary bush, but the thick stalks grew too large for her little fingers.

"But the yellow flowers are pretty!"

"Yes, but they aren't supposed to grow there. This is where rosemary and chives grow. The dandelions are useful, but they grow anywhere. We don't need to make a special place for them."

Aoife pouted, but played with the yellow flower. She rubbed one against her cheek as Esme watched her with wistful eyes. Would the new child growing in her belly would be a sweet girl like this one? Aoife had blonde hair, bright as a flower herself, wispy and thin like her mother's. She remained thin and given to fevers and chills more than most.

Her own dear Katy had three years now, and had grown into a happy, sweet child. However, Esme hadn't been able to keep any more babies. She'd been pregnant three times in the last three years, none lasting past five months. She stroked her belly, just at the five month mark now. Seán promised to return at least once a month, every month. He mostly kept his promise. A few times he'd been late due to winter storms or a washed out bridge. He should come back any day now.

That night, Aisling and Esme stayed in Esme's cottage. The girls fell fast asleep in the other room as the women watched the fire.

Esme turned to her friend. "Do you think you'll marry again?"

Aisling kept her eyes glued to the hearth. "No. Not that there are any suitors banging on my door. My heart still aches for Cormac."

Esme swallowed. Her heart ached for Seán, but he still lived. She felt guilty for having a living husband while her friend grieved.

Aisling glanced up, her eyes glittering in the low light. "I still crave his hugs, though."

Esme missed being held by her husband, especially when she worried so about losing another baby. His warm arms comforted her like nothing else. Tears leaked down her cheeks, mirrored by those on Aisling's face.

Esme placed a hand on her friend's arm. "You and Aoife should stay here tonight. You shouldn't be alone."

They both slept in the bed, keeping each other warm during the chilly night. Esme didn't fall asleep for a long time. She wanted to remember this sensation of being held, warm and safe. Aisling's breath stayed uneven. She must also be awake.

Esme drifted off, but her dreams grew dark. She tossed and turned. Aisling smoothed her hair and kissed her. Esme didn't know if she kissed back, thinking Aisling was her husband, or knowing who she kissed. It seemed natural to her, an extension of the emotional comfort they shared. When Aisling's hand cupped her breast, Esme's eyes flew open.

Aisling smiled. "If you don't want to, I understand. But if you need..."

All of Esme's Catholic schooling screamed at her to pull back. But she'd already embraced the druid's brooch and its faerie magic. Even the priest took lovers. Why shouldn't she?

Esme slid her hand down her friend's back to her hips and pulled her closer. The night ended in sweet release for both of them. While the affection couldn't replace Seán, it helped Esme get through the rough spots.

Seán returned home the next day, and Aisling took Aoife back to her own cottage.

Her husband treaded carefully while Esme carried a child. Their arguments morphed into something different, more like an affectionate dance, a planned sparring with understood rules. They might throw things, but not at each other. They might grapple or tickle, but no hitting, and neither if Esme carried a child. If tickling led to more interesting things, so be it. If they argued, they must not go to bed upset.

Seán broke these rules when he left in a huff of anger. When he returned after a week, Esme didn't let him into her good graces, or her bed, for several months. He remained home for weeks to make it up to her. They settled into a true partnership. It had bare spots here and there, but the relationship grew strong. Caring for their daughter brought them together when he stayed home, and gave her someone to dote on while her husband left again.

While out in the garden one morning, Esme grabbed leaves from her daughter. "No, Katy, don't eat that!" It wouldn't hurt her, as nothing truly poisonous grew in the summer garden. But it tasted bitter, and the child would be reluctant to eat anything green for weeks. It had happened before.

Aisling grew her medicinal plants in the winter garden, in the *clachan*, which might be harmful. However, she built a stone fence around her section, and no one else dared touch it. The other residents mumbled when she built it, but no one denied her the right. Besides, she did all the healing for the village folk and those along the hillside. She became so renowned, some whispered *"witch"* behind their hands and held up their fingers in the devil's horns as she passed, to ward off evil. But they still came to her for the ague or the croup.

Mr. Quinn's coughing rang across the *booley*, racking and harsh. Esme winced, but Aisling said she had nothing to help the old man. He suffered from consumption. She might ease his pain before he died, but no more.

Aoife glanced up at the cough, then looked to Esme with worry etched on her young face. Esme cast a sympathetic look at the girl, whose mother stayed in the cottage, along with half the elderly population of the village. "Your Mam will be out when she's done, lovey."

"He won't. He'll go tonight." Aisling returned to playing with her flowers.

Esme stared at the girl. Her belief shone on her face, but how did the girl know? Aoife had a slight blue tinge around her, then it disappeared. Did the girl have a touch of the Sight? She had an odd way of acting, always more intense and quieter than most.

"Then we must be sad for him, because he's gone, and pray for his soul." Esme busied herself with weeding. They'd know soon enough if Aoife told the truth.

Aisling didn't emerge until well after the darkness embraced the mountain. She came into Esme's cottage, bedraggled with fatigue etched in her frown. When Seán left, they always shared one cottage now. They didn't have to heat and clean two that way. The arrangement earned more whispers from their neighbors.

Aisling sat in the smaller chair, slumping over in exhaustion. "He's gone, I'm afraid."

"He's out of pain, Aisling. You did all you could." Esme placed a gentle hand on her friend's arm.

"I know, but it still hurts to lose someone. Even someone as crabby and crotchety as old Mr. Quinn." Esme brought her a bowl of steaming broth and fresh-baked bread.

"Aoife, pour your mother ale. She'll need it after this night."

The girl had told the truth, after all. The old man hadn't lasted the night. Did she have faery magic or good instincts?

They sat in silence, each absorbed in their own thoughts, until Aoife gave a mighty yawn.

Aisling shucked off her healing role and burst into being a fussy mother. "Blessed Mary! I just realized you're still awake, sweet thing! Get off to your bed now." Aoife protested she felt fine, not tired at all, but her drooping eyelids belied the protests. Soon, Aoife curled up next to the already slumbering Katy.

"I always forget how long the summer days last. You'd think I'd be used to it by now." Aisling took a long swallow of her ale and grimaced at the bitter hops.

"Were summer days much shorter in Kenmare, then?" The days seemed shorter here than Donegal.

"A bit more. But the winter nights lasted forever. We had a grand time, though. We'd sing and tell stories before the fire all evening. During the days, we'd work, mending or weaving, spinning and carding. But the stories, those I miss those most of all." With a dreamy look, Aisling gazed out the dark window. A stray breeze swept through the cottage, lifting her straight flyaway hair. The reddish-blonde blazed in the firelight, giving her an unearthly glow.

Esme gave her friend a grin. "Shall we tell a story tonight?"

"That would be just the thing. I may not stay awake through the whole thing, mind. But I'd love a sweet story."

Esme dredged through her memory. Most of her father's stories spoke of war and adventures, but he told a few love stories. Many ended in tragedy, in the way of Irish tales. Esme considered several before she found a fun one.

"I shall tell the tale of the Giant of the Causeway. Many, many years ago, a giant named Finn lived on the Antrim coast with his lovely wife, Úna. One day, he discovered he had a rival in Scotland. The rival, Benandonner, towered over six feet tall, so the story goes. This rival would taunt Finn from across the sea, at the place where the two lands are but seven miles apart. They would hurl stones and clods of dirt across the narrow strait, but neither could throw that far. One clod of earth fell in the Irish Sea and became the Isle of Man."

Aisling closed her eyes, but she didn't sleep. Katy let out a sleepy moan and snuggled up to Aoife. Esme's own eyelids drooped, but she kept going. "Finn challenged his foe to a fight. He built a massive causeway of stones across the sea to the Isle of Staffa, where Benandonner lived. As he got near, he realized how truly huge his rival was and flew back home across his bridge. His rival would chase him, so he asked his clever wife for help hiding him.

"Úna dressed Finn as a baby and shoved him into a cradle, then hid herself. When Benandonner arrived, he beheld this massive baby. After assuming the father of such a child would be enormous, he ran back to his home in Scotland in fear for his very life, destroying the causeway behind him. You can still see the remnants of the bridge at the Giant's Causeway in Ireland and the Isle of Staffa in Scotland."

Soft snores came from the chair. Esme placed a woolen blanket over Aisling and caressed her dear friend's cheek, careful not to make noise. She'd hoped Aisling would join her this night, as she craved physical comfort, but her friend had worn herself out with healing and deserved her rest.

Sleep didn't come to Esme. She tossed and turned until she tangled her legs in her blankets. Sweat and wool smothered her. With a curse, she threw them off and walked outside in her shift and dressing gown, careful not to disturb the girls.

The black June night caressed her. No breeze came from the ocean, but the air smelled fresh. She breathed deep, smelling the sea, the garden, and the thatch of the cottage roof. From her doorway, Esme stared at the stars.

Did Seán stare at the same stars tonight? What about her mother in America? Her sister, Bridey? And what about Alan in Ardara? Despite her home full of people, her eyes teared up from loneliness.

Then the world intruded upon her again, stealing her moment of peace. A snuffle in the garden became a pig who nosed her way past the stone wall. A couple of the stones had fallen, so she shooed the sow away and replaced them. She caught sight of Mr. Quinn's cottage and remembered Aoife's prediction.

Was the child faery-touched? It might be a lucky prediction. However, that blue glow reminded Esme of the fairy stone's magic. Did Aoife have power, like Esme? She must ask her grandfather the next time he visited. He hadn't come in over a year.

She returned to the warm cottage. By leaving the door ajar, she hoped it would allow the night air into the place. She prayed her sleep would give her peace.

The next morning, the whole *clachan* came down off the mountain for Mr. Quinn's wake. Folks came from neighboring villages. He'd lived to an impressive age of ninety-one, and outlived all his children. While his grandchildren had long since moved away, he had distant relations all over the island. Though most hadn't liked him, everyone knew him, so they came to pay their respects.

Since his tiny cottage would never hold enough people, the church became the wake house. Mistress Lynch and her cronies prepared the body and the food.

The ladies wrapped him in a snow-white shroud of almost translucent linen. A steady stream of mourners came in to bid him farewell, then retire to the garden. Storytelling, songs, and the serious drinking would come later, at the *síbín*.

The priest spoke to an older lady in a show of sympathy and regret. He didn't mean it, Esme saw it on his face. He said mere window-dressing and platitudes. She didn't know what he did when he didn't perform services, but the priest didn't believe in the chastity and charity he preached. The hypocrisy disgusted her, but the community had little choice in priests.

When her time came to speak to the priest, Esme's frustration at his lies got too much for her to bear. No one stood close enough to hear her ask, "Father, why did you lie to that woman?"

The priest blinked several times. "What do you mean, Esme?"

She gritted her teeth and pulled upon the brooch's power, wanting to hear the bald truth from his lips. "You don't have any regret or sympathy for her. Why did you say you did? A priest shouldn't lie!"

Beads of sweat dripped down the Father's cheek. "Esme, you're overwrought."

He placed a hand on her shoulder, but she flinched away. "You always lie to us. Every day. What do you really feel about Mr. Quinn, Father? What is the truth?"

"I…" he swallowed, and glanced around. In a bare whisper, he croaked out, "I hated him."

As the smile crept across her face, Esme realized she'd used the brooch's power for a horrible thing. The smile disappeared, and she bowed her head, backing away with a muttered, "I'm sorry."

Her stomach hurt, and she pressed the heel of her hand into it. That had been such a terrible thing to do. An act more worthy of Eithne than of her.

Outside, voices rose in an unearthly ululation, mixing with the howl of the ocean wind. The *caoiner* sang. If the deceased had few family, they might hire professional wailers to mourn at a funeral. The wail added a surreal touch to the day.

Esme stared at Mr. Quinn's body, the empty husk of a man she'd spoken to. The man who stood as her father at her wedding, though she hadn't passed a dozen words with him in the five years since. She couldn't see his face, covered by the linen, but he seemed a marble statue rather than a shrouded corpse. Esme's eyes grew wide as her own grandfather's face grew on the shroud, cold and empty.

Her skin rose in gooseflesh. She shuddered and hurried out of the church, into the reassuring sunshine. The wind might blow, but the bright summer day remained warm.

A sense of wrongness gripped her mind and body. She searched for Aisling but the other woman had left the building earlier. Aoife had turned pale, and her mother took her behind the church in case she got ill.

After walking through the green graveyard, Esme rounded the back wall and found Aisling, holding Aoife's hair back as the child vomited on the grass. Katy crouched next to her friend, holding her favorite ragdoll.

Esme held the girl's shoulders as they shook with heaving. Her gorge rose and she added her stomach's contents to Aoife's.

She grabbed onto the grass for support. The world twirled, and she didn't want to fly off. Aisling put a hand on her back, the only point of stability she had. Her head spun, her knees buckled, and she collapsed into the dew-wet grass.

Her mind stopped spinning. Esme swallowed and wished for cool water to clean the sour taste of bile. She wanted to spit, but not on holy ground.

Katy looked at her mother with tired eyes. "Can we go, Ma?"

Esme got hold of herself for her daughter's sake. "Yes, sweetling, we can go. We're done with our duty here."

She picked herself off the grass, her limbs shaky and tired. Together, they marched back to the mountain.

Aisling

The climb to the summer *booley* made their legs ache, though she'd walked it many times before. None of them had much energy after Mr. Quinn's long illness and funeral. They wouldn't be taking part in the wake, not with the girls being ill, so Aisling had little guilt skipping the gathering. As they trudged the last bend and the summer cottages came into sight, Esme doubled over, clutching her middle.

Panic gripped Aisling's heart. "Esme? Esme, what's wrong?"

Her face screwed up into a pained grimace, like someone poked her stomach with a piece of hot iron. Esme grunted in pain and fell to her knees. While curling into a ball, she pressed her hands to her stomach. Katy tried to grab her mother's hand.

Aisling knelt beside her, a hand on Esme's shoulder. "Is it the child, Esme? Answer me, Esme, can you hear me? Aoife, fetch my herb bag, as quick as you can!" The girl darted off to the cottage while Aisling pushed Katy aside to uncurl her friend.

Esme shuddered with chills, her body clamped hard into a ball. Silent tears streaked down her face, contorted with pain and terror. "No, nonononono, not again, please, Blessed Mother Mary, not again!"

Katy wailed with frightened tears.

Aisling tried to get her fingers into place to test Esme's stomach, but Esme curled tighter and let out a strangled cry. She shivered and moaned in waves. A dark blood stain bloomed on her petticoats.

After what seemed an eternity, Aoife returned with Aisling's medical bag. She rummaged through it, searching for a particular herb.

"Esme... Esme, dear, you must listen to me. Here, see if you can chew and swallow this." Aisling tried to push dried Monk's Pepper into her mouth, but Esme cried and paid no heed to Aisling's help. "Aoife, I need to get her into the cottage, but everyone's down at the wake. Go get me the blue blanket. Can you do that?" The girl darted off again, reappearing with the largest blanket they had, a good six feet long.

"That'll be grand, Aoife. Help me lift her, will you? Grab her feet. Then take care of Katy."

The five-year-old didn't help much, but she'd feel useful. Aisling tugged Esme's arm until she wrestled her onto the blanket. Then she dragged her, foot by foot, toward the cottage. At the doorway, she had to jerk a few times to get her over the threshold, but they made it inside. The girls held hands as they followed. Aisling tried to lift Esme onto the bed, but failed. At least they got Esme inside.

After stoking up the cooking fire, Aisling put water to boil for tea. She rifled through her medical bag again, searching for the right herbs. Esme let out a low, dissonant moan.

Aoife's voice sounded faint, wavering. "Ma?"

"Just a moment, Aoife."

"Ma, she's bleeding." Her voice rose with fright. Aisling gritted her teeth at the dark puddle under Esme's still-curled form.

"Jesus, Mary, and Joseph, bless us." She made the sign of the cross and rushed to Esme's side. "Aoife, run down and get the priest. If he says he's busy, you tell him Esme's still alive and Mr. Quinn isn't. She needs him more."

She might staunch the blood, but not much else. The tea might slow the bleeding and strengthen her. Katy sat by her mother's side, stroking her hair. Aisling tapped her fingers on her arm while she watched the water, waiting for it to boil. At every faint sound, her eyes darted to the door.

The water boiled, and she threw in the herbs. One to stop the bleeding, another to dull the pain, and a third herb to help her keep the babe. Another eternity passed until she judged it ready.

While kneeling by her friend, Aisling lifted her head. "Esme, listen to me. You must drink this, Esme. Yes, I know it's hot, but you must try. You need it."

"Die…just let me die, Aisling. I'll never have another baby."

"Nonsense. You're just having troubles. Plenty of women have troubles. You'll be fine, but you must drink the tea."

Esme choked down a few swallows of the bitter, scalding liquid, but she coughed, and her entire body shook. she let out an ethereal moan, as if the earth itself cried out.

Ruthlessly, Aisling tipped the cup to Esme's lips once again, forcing more hot liquid into her friend. "More, Esme. Drink more."

Esme sputtered and licked her lips, trying to rid the bitter drink from her mouth.

"No, drink it, don't spit it. Again, please."

"You're… ruthless when you're healing…"

"Yes, I am, quite. Now, another sip." She held the cup to Esme's lips.

Sip by sip, Aisling got the entire mug down Esme's throat. Her moans grew softer, and Aisling hoped that meant the pain eased. Esme looked down in disgust at her blood-soaked skirts. She sat in a puddle of blood and mud on the floor.

When Esme tried to get to her feet, Aisling pushed her back. "Not so fast, missy. You need to get washed and changed, then to the bed."

"I lost it, didn't I?" Esme's eyes grew wide and glistened with tears.

Aisling didn't want to break Esme's heart again, but she wouldn't lie, not to her friend. She dropped her gaze. "I'm afraid it must be so, Esme. I'm so sorry."

Esme stared at the blood, looking detached as it pooled and eddied with the mud. Guilt colored her expression. "It's all my fault. I must have caused this. What if it's true? What if I can never have more children?" Tears fell in streaks down her cheeks.

Aisling let out a short bark of laughter. "Never? You're twenty-three years of age. There's plenty of time to have more bairns, my dear. You'll be fine. And you have dear Katy already." She shoved all her confidence into her voice.

Esme's spine straightened with Aisling's assurances. With help, she stood and pulled her soiled clothing off. They got her washed, a bandage wrapped around her in case of further bleeding, and in a clean shift before the priest arrived.

Aisling stood with her hands on her hips. She fixed him with a fierce look. "You took your dear, sweet time getting here, so you did. She might have died and gone without being shriven."

The priest took an involuntary step back. "You sent a child. I thought she played a prank at first."

"Since when is a woman bleeding a prank? And who else should I send? Everyone's down at the wake."

Father McNulty scratched behind his ear and ducked his head. He didn't answer her question. "Is the lass all right now?"

"For the moment, yes. However, I want you to tend to her at any rate." She kept her voice low, but it did no good.

Esme's voice rustled like dry paper. "I'm not ready for Last Rites, Father, but I would like to give confession if you have the time."

He cleared his throat and nodded. He glared at Aisling until she left the cottage, grabbing Aoife's hand. She gave a last, long look over her shoulder before she exited, watching Father McNulty sidestepped the muddy puddle on the floor, wrinkling his nose.

As she returned to her own cottage, Esme spoke in her paper-thin voice. "Bless me, Father, for I have sinned. In the name of the Father and of the Son and of the Holy Spirit. My last confession was one month ago…"

Eithne

Her husband's querulous voice intruded on her thoughts. "Eithne, I need you to stay with me tonight."

With a muffled groan, Eithne put down the letter from her parents and climbed into bed. A night of drinking always made him amorous. She didn't fancy his blubbery hands all over her body while he shoved and grunted like a pig. She didn't want him ever to touch her again. "And bring the goose grease."

Eithne wrinkled her nose. Their physician suggested the grease as a gout remedy, and it stunk. Slather rancid goose grease with rye and wax on his foot to relieve the pain. Such a disgusting remedy did no good for the gout, but it drove her off.

She got back out of bed and went to the press, where he kept the stinking nostrum. She'd had to endure too many nights like this one.

Once she'd borne him a second son, she hoped his attentions would wane. Better yet, she wished he'd have no need of her services. Yet still he demanded her attention much too often. In fact, Eithne might even be with child a third time.

At least his attentions finished quickly. After he spent himself, she curled up on the far end of the bed, trying to sleep despite his wheezy snoring. She rubbed at her upper arms where his fingers had dug into her skin. There'd be bruises again. She'd learned how to keep him from bruising her face.

Did Esme experience regret and disgust after her dark Tinker husband swived her? Eithne let out a bitter laugh at the idea. Esme delighted in her poverty. Eithne still hadn't discovered a way to convince Hugh to let her travel to Achill Island. Did Esme even live there anymore? Travelers would always be feckless folk, apt to move at a moment's notice.

With a sigh, Eithne realized she'd never travel freely while Hugh still had command of her movements. Therefore, she must make sure he no longer had control of them.

While hatching her plan took most of the night, she worked out the salient details before the spring dawn intruded on her musings. The final solution made her quail, horrified at the need, but then she decided that this plan would take care of several issues. If she had any chance of achieving her own goals, she must stay the course.

He planned to cultivate the north field that week. While he had a foreman and several other workers, he preferred to do this important step himself. Eithne crept out of the bed before he woke, dressed, and padded into the main barn. The cultivator was ready to hook up to the horse team, so she made some adjustments to the gears. While Eithne had few mechanical skills, she'd grown up on a farm. Her grandfather taught her how to use the equipment. She knew which screw to loosen, and which blade to sharpen. Eithne put that knowledge to good use.

In the end, everyone put it down to poor maintenance of the cultivator. The foreman was beside himself with worry that he'd bear the blame. Eithne smiled at the convenient scapegoat as she sacked him. The other farmhands sighed in relief that it wasn't them. Eithne hired a new man to handle everything to her satisfaction, and wore black for the required period.

Eithne made certain the new foreman was a young, strong man. Tall, blond, and quite biddable.

Chapter Twelve

September 1796

Esme

The year after her collapse, Esme lost interest in life. No one wanted to be with her, not her parents, her husband, not even her babies. Entire days went by and she did nothing but stare at the wall. Seán came home and left again, with her barely speaking two words to him. Katy stayed in Aisling's cottage all the time now. Esme felt so utterly alone and useless.

Aisling did everything by herself, with no help from Esme, so why should she bother exhausting herself with work? Aisling even took care of Katy better than Esme did. Esme's daughter would be much better off in Aisling's cottage. Seán had his trade missions, seeing the world without her. Perhaps if she stayed still long enough, the dark specter of death would come and take away the pain.

Today, Esme didn't even bother getting out of bed. Her entire world contracted to this corner of her cottage. Nothing existed outside of this corner, just a hazy, oppressive gray presence which kept her inside her cocoon. The void pushed on her, gentle but relentless, and stole her silent breath.

Her cocoon vibrated as Aisling came in and lit the fire, but she didn't turn to greet her friend. Why should she bother? Aisling would insist she eat, come outside and take the sun, or do something constructive. She had no interest in any of it. When Aisling shook her shoulder, Esme jerked it out of her friend's grasp and kept staring at her wall. Not even Aisling's embrace at night could rouse her anymore.

The cottage grew quiet again. She dared to look around, and spied a bowl of stew on the stool, congealing as it cooled. She took a couple of spoonfuls and grimaced at the sourness. It must have sat longer than she thought. Nothing tasted good any longer. Ale, pie, stew, bread, it all seemed ashy and dull. The faded light coming through the window proved the sky matched her mood. *Good.*

A familiar jangle came from outside. Had Seán returned already? He'd stolen away in the morning mists over a month ago. Last time, he'd been gone for two months. Each trip grew longer. Esme roused herself from the bed by the time the door to the cottage opened to reveal… her grandfather.

Joy burst into her heart, and she tried to jump up to greet him. Her illness and a year of doing little left her too weak.

She gave her grandfather a tender hug. "I've missed you so, Grandfa! Welcome back!"

"Esme, my dear child, you're a sight for sore eyes. But so thin? What have you done that you're wasting away to nothing?"

She swallowed, unwilling to answer. Nothing she said would sound reasonable. Instead, she took him by the hand. "Come, sit, have tea."

The fire Aisling laid earlier still smoldered in the hearth. She set tea steeping while her grandfather patted the road dust from his long jacket.

Katy burst through the doorway. After skirting the new arrival, the child ran to her mother. She buried her face in Esme's skirts, shy around this stranger.

"Katy? Katy this is your Great-Grandsire, Éamonn. Can you say hello to him?"

The child shook her head, still buried in cloth. She snuck a peek out with one eye and re-buried her face.

Her grandfather laughed a long, low, liquid chuckle. That sound had always been a cure for any dark mood. "So you have a daughter, Esme? That's grand news indeed! And you named her for my own sweet Caitriona! Thank you for that. I've more great-grandchildren to add to the growing list, then."

Esme cocked her head as she patted Katy's hair. It had been so long since Katy had hugged her. "Grandchildren? Who else?" Did Eithne have children, or perhaps Éamonn's other children had bairns?

"Yes, Eithne has two boys already, and another bairn on the way. She's been quite busy."

That her twin should succeed where Esme failed cut her to the bone. An uncontrollable wave of sadness swept over her for her lost children. She'd miscarried so many times, lost so many precious lives. Except for Katy, dear Katy. She pulled in a huge sniffle as the wave of despair swept over her. "Her husband must be quite proud."

"He would be, but he died. I've come from there with the news. A farming accident, they say, but there are whispers of foul play."

A chill ran down Esme's spine. "Foul play? By whom?"

"No one will say, for fear of getting in trouble with Eithne. She quite rules the place now, a queen in her realm. Her eldest lad's but ten, and training as a fine soldier to her whims."

Her grandfather's tone held a strong vein of bitterness. He scratched at his scalp, ruffling his hair, a sure sign of agitation. Eithne had never been the most charitable person, nor the kindest. But for their grandfather to have lost faith in her, she must have become a cruel woman. Esme seldom sensed anything from their twin bond any longer. Perhaps distance weakened their link. Esme took solace from this blessing.

"What else is happening? We're isolated out here in the back of beyond, you know."

He raised his eyebrows. "You get no newspapers or gossip from the Travelers?"

Esme shrugged, inching Katy closer to the chair. Her legs wobbled and she didn't want to fall in front of either her grandfather or her child. "Who comes out here to trade? We get few hardy souls willing to brave the rocky tracks this far out, Grandfa, except you and Seán. And I don't think anyone closer than Galway runs a newspaper." Resentment dripped in her voice.

Her grandfather helped her to her chair, his voice gentle. "Is he not treating you well, Esme?"

Esme's eyes glistened. Her grandfather might not have her own talent for drawing out the truth, but he didn't need it. She sniffled again as Katy curled into her lap. "When he's here, everything's fine. No, that's a lie. When he's here, we fight, and when he's not here, I wish he'd come home so we *could* fight. I don't know how to fix it, though." Her tears escaped down her cheeks, and she made no move to stop them. She trusted her grandfather with such an admission more than anyone else in this world.

"Is he keeping you fed? Clothed?"

She nodded and hugged Katy closer. "He is, yes, but sometimes it's tight. Don't get me wrong, he loves the Traveler life. I went with him once, but I..." She stared at the ground. "I didn't like it. And he's had awful luck in trades."

Her grandfather looked thoughtful and scratched at his chin. "Hmm. Bad luck in trades, is it." He stared into the fire.

"He takes my clothing and embroidery, selling it on at the trade fairs. It helps."

Turning back to her, his face clouded with anger. "So you're working for what he should provide, is that it?"

"Well, if you put it that way..."

He paced back and forth, though he needed to turn after only three strides. "I am, girl, I am. A man ought to provide for his own family. If he can't, he should move on and let someone else do so. You wouldn't stay alone for long, I'm sure."

The world swirled beneath Esme. "Grandfa, what are you saying?"

He halted his paces and took a deep sigh, shaking his head. "Naught but silly thoughts, dear. Pay me no mind. He wouldn't be leaving you anyhow? He's a good lad, just not here often, aye?"

She nodded, distracted. How to get off the subject of Seán? "What's on in the world, then?" After struggling to her feet, she poured the hot tea into two mugs, handing one to her grandfather.

He took a cautious sip. "Excellent tea, Esme, thank you."

They spoke of other things, catching up on the people in Ardara. Esme relaxed into this pocket of the past, a reminiscence of her former life, before her marriage. She almost heard the giggling of Bridey and Níamh playing outside, or Alan's voice calling to the house. She wanted to dislodge her ghosts. At the same time, she held them tight to her bosom, a salve against the swirling darkness.

When Esme had asked Éamonn about Aoife's abilities, he promised to watch the girl. He didn't think it had anything to do with the brooch, but there must be other faery-touched folk in the land.

The next day, Esme had her hand on the door to the cottage to find her grandfather, when she heard him speaking with Aisling.

"Will you not stay longer? She comes back alive with you here. When you're gone, she becomes a ghost. Not even Katy can snap her out of it."

"I would if I had the time, my dear. I've business I must tend to. I will come back soon, though, I promise. I won't abandon her. She's had enough of that in her past."

When her grandfather left the next day, Esme drooped, but the blackness didn't seem as bottomless.

Eithne

Eithne resented the required year-long mourning period, but once it ended, she took advantage of her newfound freedom and searched for her sister. She left her newborn child, yet a third son, with his nurse. The child had Hugh's eyes, and she hated being reminded of his repulsive attentions on her. Her other children looked more like her.

After Hugh died, Eithne dismissed her nursemaid. Mistress Dillon looked much too young and pretty. Hugh had hired her, and Eithne knew the children weren't the only thing she'd taken care of. Not that she harbored any jealousy of his attentions, but she mustn't tolerate such perfidy in her household.

No matter. The new nurse, a much older, simpler woman, worked much better. Mistress Dooley proved to be reliable and steadfast. She wouldn't attract the eye of anyone, especially the young, blond foreman.

Eithne delighted in the adventure of traveling on her own. She stopped wherever she wanted, explored the towns and hotels as she wished, and bought whatever she desired. Her own natural frugality kicked in, now that she had charge of her finances. She'd learned enough from the foreman to manage the accounts. Still, Hugh had used an abundance of caution. "Cheap" came closer to the truth. Eithne could afford a luxury or two.

As the coachman helped her into the carriage, she noted he seemed young as well, but not young enough for Eithne's palate. However, she enjoyed watching him while on a long road trip.

As she passed through Westport, Eithne recalled her last trip there. It seemed so long ago, in relative time. So much in her life had changed. Perhaps things would change more.

After they passed through the town and approached the coast to take the ferry, Eithne studied the houses. Such a desolate place. The port seemed busy enough, but the land looked full of barren rocks and sand, worse than in Donegal.

The ferry ride itself made her grip hard on the rails. She disliked the deep water but mustn't let the ferryman or her servants see her fear. When they arrived on the island, she wrinkled her nose at the stink of fish. South, the Tinkers had said. But which road headed south? Three started in that direction.

Eithne must ask someone local for help. *Bother.* She didn't want to deal with the locals.

With a spark of inspiration, she turned to the coachman. "Ford. Inquire about a Tinker named Seán Fitzgerald. Tall, dark hair, lanky. Late twenties. I'm looking for his wife, Esme, my twin sister. They live on the south of Achill. I shall wait here."

"Yes, mum." He nodded and scurried off to find an inn.

Eithne sat back, closing the carriage curtains. When she found Esme, how would she approach her sister? Should she demand the brooch and be done with it? No, that wouldn't have worked ten years ago and it wouldn't work now. She'd need to be cunning. Not that Esme had any sophistication about manipulation, but she got stubborn and righteous. If Eithne offered peace, though, Esme might be optimistic enough to believe her. Her sister might even invite her to stay. And if that didn't work, she'd filch it once Esme left her house.

Eithne shuddered. Given what she'd seen of Achill so far, Esme must live in a hovel, scraping her existence from the land like their parents. Would getting the brooch even be worth a night in such a place? The blasted thing haunted her dreams every night now. If she didn't get it soon, the stupid thing would drive her mad.

She thought of her three boys, home safe with their nurse, in a palatial home. Their windows covered with lace curtains and plenty of food in the pantry. The memory of their cherubic faces made her smile, except the youngest, with Hugh's eyes. They deserved their great-grandfather's legacy. God knows he'd given them nothing else.

Besides, that brooch should have been Eithne's, as the eldest. She meant to have it.

When Ford returned with his gathered information, they embarked south to a town called Derreen.

Esme

The bog dream returned. She picked her way down an unfamiliar path, jumping from stepping stone to stepping stone across an acrid, steaming bog. If she strayed from the path, she'd be lost forever.

One stone wriggled beneath her weight. Her heart raced as she held out her arms to regain her balance. She jumped to another stone as the first sunk beneath the stinking mud with a loud, disgusting smack. A bubble of sulfur belched where it sank.

Shivering, Esme jumped to the next stone as her current boulder shifted. She must hurry, though she didn't know why. Stone by stone, she leapt from one to another. Some rocks sank more quickly than others, with no rhyme or reason.

A cruel laugh echoed across the bog. Her own face mocked her, orchestrating her torture. Eithne.

Esme woke, cold sweat dripping down her neck. Her heart raced and her throat scratched raw. The pre-dawn light crept into the small cottage as she washed her face and cradled her growing belly, now six months pregnant. After coaxing the banked fire into a cheerful glow, she stared at the mesmerizing flames. They called to her in a new way, almost as if beckoning her closer. Blinking, she backed away, but they drew her gaze once more.

A noise outside interrupted her fascination. Had her grandfather returned already? He'd just left a week before. Checking to see that Katy still slept in her bed, she rushed to the cottage door. Just as she reached the front, the back opened, and Aisling entered with Aoife in tow. Esme nodded to her friend and flung open the door.

A large black and gold carriage led by two white horses stopped in front of the *clachan*, but no one emerged. Curious, Esme stepped outside. The curtain pulled aside, and she saw her own twin, Eithne.

Am I dreaming still? What would Eithne be doing here?

Eithne stepped out of the carriage with all the grace and splendor of a duchess. "Well, don't just stand there like the country bumpkin you obviously are, Esme. Come and greet your sister."

Under her dark cape, Eithne's pink dress had lacy frills, and she wore an outrageous feathered bonnet. Pink and rose ribbons fluttered in the ocean breeze, glittering in the early dawn.

Esme stared at her sister like she saw a shade, something out of her nightmares. She wished her house was cleaner and bigger, and her clothing more beautiful. With clenched fists, she resisted the temptation to cross her arms and cover her berry-stained apron. "What in God's sweet name are *you* doing here?"

Eithne straightened her spine and looked down her nose. "That's a fine way to greet family, Esme. You've lost whatever manners you might have once had. Oh, I see you're breeding again. Lovely. Grandfather mentioned you had a daughter. Perhaps you'll have a son now, so that husband of yours can find some pride. Don't just stand there like a damsel who just discovered her fiancé is a pirate. Stand aside and fetch me some tea."

Esme stood, stunned.

Aisling poked her head out of the cottage, her eyes darting between the two sisters. She ducked back in, and Esme heard her rummaging through the dishes.

Eithne studied the cottage and around the landscape, lip curling up. "I don't know how you can stand it, Esme. Even for you, this is base squalor." Clicking her tongue, she stepped through the door with ginger steps, picking her skirts up high.

Her sister would find fault in a pile of gold. She'd be spoiled for choice on her criticisms of Esme's house. Esme clenched her jaw, trying to make her legs go into the house. Perhaps, if she stayed out here long enough, Eithne would give up and leave. But Eithne had never been one to abandon her purpose.

Finally able to move, Esme stalked inside after her sister. She had no patience for niceties. "Eithne, you didn't answer me. What are you doing here?"

Eithne's smile oozed sugar and no substance. "Esme, since when does a sister need a reason to visit?"

After shutting the door, Esme crossed her arms. "You always have a reason for what you do, Eithne. Stop evading."

"Yes, you're so smart, Esme." Eithne took the cup Aisling handed her. With a roll of her eyes, the blond woman left the cottage.

As the other girl left, Eithne raised an eyebrow. "At least you've got a servant, though how you can afford her, I can't comprehend. She's a lovely thing, with that white-blonde hair."

"She's not my servant, she's my friend. I'd introduce you if you didn't act so spiteful."

Eithne dismissed that with a wave of her hand. "Oh, do calm down. You're always so excitable. I would have thought so many years living in *this* would have made you a bit more mature."

"Mature!"

"Hmm, yes. So where's your dark pirate? Did you manage to run him off already?"

Esme's heat rose, but she refused to let her sister bait her. She took a deep breath and clenched her fists. "No, he's well, as opposed to your husband. A farming accident, I hear?" Her voice took on the sickly sweet quality her sister used. Esme hated hearing her own voice say such wicked words, but Eithne always brought out the worst in her.

Eithne took a sip from her tea and spoke in a bland voice. "Yes, well, he got rather careless with his equipment."

Esme recognized truth in any statement with no effort now, even without being near the brooch. If she pushed hard, she'd draw the truth out, even if they resisted. The pushing made her physically ill, and she hated using it. Eithne either evaded or lied, so she pushed. "Why are you here, Eithne? After all this time?"

"I needed to get out of that horribly suffocating house. A trip around the country suited me, and I heard you moved here. Is that so hard to believe?"

Yes, it is. "No. Tell me the truth, Eithne."

"I..." Her sister struggled to say nothing, or to evade again, shaking her head.

Esme's stomach churned, but she clenched her muscles and pushed with the brooch's power again. "The truth."

Eithne looked as if she'd swallowed a pine cone. "I... I've been having some dreams."

Her face shone with truth, but not the whole truth. Esme pushed some more. Eithne paced the small room, but Esme didn't ease up. "What else?"

Eithne stopped pacing, swirling to face her sister. "Fine! I came to find something."

Esme'd never met anyone who resisted her as much as Eithne. Esme's head pounded, but she pressed on. "Find what?"

Her sister took a deep breath and let it out before answering. "The brooch."

Esme stared at her twin with horror. So she *had* remembered it. Still, Esme must not give away anything. "What brooch? Stop being mysterious, Eithne."

Eithne scowled at her. "The brooch that Grandfather gave you. I know you have it. I saw it. You hid it somewhere, but you can't have gotten rid of it. I'm eldest, and it should be mine by birthright."

Esme shrugged and turned to the hearth to pour herself more tea. She wouldn't lie, but she refused to let Eithne get the upper hand. "I had it, yes. But Seán made some poor trades a couple of years back."

"You're saying you don't have it? You're lying. I can... I can sense it's here."

After spinning around, Esme narrowed her gaze. "What do you mean, you can sense it?"

A blue glow shone through the wall to the bedroom, and she prayed Eithne couldn't see that. Esme had wrapped it in its velvet bag, at the back of the bottom drawer of the press. But *she* had attuned to it years ago in Donegal, and a few times at the local standing stones. How on God's green earth did Eithne sense it?

Her twin shrugged, her tone full of nonchalance. "I just do. It's somewhere here. It's calling to me."

Esme glared at her, willing her to go away and never come back. She must bluff her way out of this, or her sister wouldn't give up. "You're mad, Eithne, gone utterly insane. I need you to leave now."

Her sister's voice dripped with bitter resolve. "I'm not leaving until I get that brooch."

"And I'm telling you to get out." Esme shoved power and will into her demand.

Eithne's face clouded with anger and frustration. If her sister didn't leave, she may have to push her out. She didn't want to risk her pregnancy with a physical fight, but she might have to threaten Eithne with something heavy. Esme eyed the hearth tools. What if Eithne started rifling through her things?

Her sister evidently valued her dignity more than the brooch. She placed the tea cup down and, with a haughty sniff, swept out of the cottage. Esme held her breath until the carriage rattled down the path. Trembling, she ran to her press, pulling out the precious brooch, wrapped safe and sound. She searched for a better hiding spot and found a hidden niche in the wall under her bed. Her stomach protested all this movement, and she finally gave in to the nausea. She knew Seán couldn't see the glow, so others shouldn't either. It would be safe here.

Esme had just wiped her mouth when Aisling came in. "So, that's your sister? What a harpy. I'm so glad you moved here rather than her!"

Eithne

The blasted brooch was *there* in that ridiculous hovel. She knew it. She'd come so close! Eithne wouldn't be defeated so easily, not after days of stinking, spine-jarring travel to this godforsaken place.

After the coach rounded the mountain, out of sight from the cluster of huts, she told Ford to stop. When darkness fell, Eithne waited. She stayed until the moon rose, bright and shining in the dark, velvet sky. Stars winked at her as she waited.

Eithne didn't understand how someone would choose to live in such a barren, thankless place. With no good farmland, how did they eat? The ceaseless wind tore at her clothing, and the raucous seagulls grated on every nerve.

She had some other tasks to take care of when the morning dawned and she visited her dear, sweet sister once more. Even if she found the brooch, and it offered the power her dreams promised, it would do her no good if Esme just stole it back. Eithne must ensure her sister didn't follow her. If she arranged to have Esme locked away for some heinous act, Eithne could rest easy with her prize.

Ford asked if he should let the horses loose from the harness, but she refused. She must visit the priest first. Then, as soon as she finished her task tomorrow morning, they must be ready.

After that task was completed, Eithne drifted in and out of sleep, but being so close to her goal kept her from true rest. Every rustle in the wind, every seagull's cry, and every shuffle from the horse startled her awake.

When the sun rose in the dim, windy morning, she walked from the coach and back around the mountain until the huts came into view. A small trail of people descended the hill toward the shore.

A smile crept across Eithne's face. *Time for Sunday Mass.*

Her sister's bright-red hair bobbed down the path with her blonde friend. As they walked out of sight, Eithne stole toward the house.

The village sounded deserted, but she wouldn't have much time to search. It must in the bedroom, of course. She'd have sensed it more strongly in the larger room. The bedroom had several drawers and shelves, but none held the brooch.

Shutting her eyes in frustration, Eithne forced herself to calm. She breathed in and out, tasting the air for the power from her dreams. She pulled in her concentration and reached out to sense the brooch.

A cold, blue light shone through her closed eyelids. There, behind the bed, inside the wall. A small chink in the plaster revealed a velvet bag. As soon as Eithne touched it, a slow smile spread across her face.

Success.

After pulling it out, she traced her fingers along the exquisite knotwork. Her fingers tingled with anticipation and power. The gold and silver filigree pulsed with warmth while the aqua-blue gems glowed in the dim morning light.

Hearing a sound, she hastily stuffed the brooch back into its velvet pouch and secured it inside her bodice. She must flee before someone found her.

As she placed her hand on the door, she spied a piece of fine needlework on a frame by the door. It must have taken hours for her sister to create the beautiful piece. With a wicked grin, Eithne scooped up a handful of soot from the hearth and smeared it across the design. Then she hurried back to her coach.

She'd done it. She found the brooch. Only her sense of dignity kept her from whooping with triumph as the carriage clattered along the rough path.

Esme

The day after Eithne's visit, Esme still hadn't been able to get her head around Eithne's appearance. As she dressed, she glanced at where she'd hidden the brooch in the wall. She stepped toward it, to keep it with her, but Aisling arrived at that moment. They walked out to brave the February winds to the chapel.

Halfway down the hill, Aisling halted with a sour expression. "I'm not feeling so well, Esme. Go on without me." Aisling had been so withdrawn since Cormac disappeared. Aisling helped if someone sought her for healing, but she used to make rounds to the different villages. Now she stayed at home and rebuffed offers of company. Esme watched her friend disappear into the *clachan*, and grew determined to speak to the priest.

The wind whipped hard and she tied her scarf around her head. Gossip drifted on the wind from the women walking in front of her. Mistress Lynch clicked her tongue. "They say someone poisoned the Father, so they do."

Mistress McEnella scoffed. "And who'd poison a priest?"

"Her with the red hair, of course. She can't even keep her husband home."

"Drove him off with a witch's hex, she did."

The two ladies shared a cruel laugh. "Oh and he's a Tinker, is he no? Better off, he be well gone. Thieves, the lot of 'em. Keep an eye on your sheep, pet. The girl might steal one in the night."

And what would I do with a stolen sheep? Didn't they all graze on the same mountain? She'd have no way to hide such a theft. Her chicken coop showed signs of sabotage on a regular basis now, and she'd found one of her lambs dead in the field. And they were supposed to be wary of Tinkers, were they? Their hypocrisy maddened her.

Then the import of the women's gossip sunk in. Someone poisoned the priest? Had he died?

After slipping on the narrow, steep, pebbled path, Esme concentrated on her footing until it grew flatter. It wouldn't do to twist her ankle now. Her pregnancy weight made her awkward. She must relearn how to balance when she walked. If she hurt herself, how would Seán find out?

A dusting of frost sparkled on the old church roof, but no snow lay on the ground. At least the warm Atlantic winds kept it from snowing too much in the winter. Getting snowbound in such a place would drive her mad.

More people milled outside than usual. No one seemed to have gone inside yet. If the priest had fallen ill, there might be no Mass today.

She arrived just as two of the older fishermen did. Mr. Clooney gave her a long look, up and down, lingering on her growing belly. His lip curled up in a sneer. Her face burned with embarrassment, though she'd nothing to be ashamed of. She had a husband, even if he barely came home.

The second fisherman ignored her. Mr. Pike resembled the nasty fish. The two looked as crabbed and weathered as the stunted trees along the coastline, wrinkled and bent from the wind and the sea. She almost missed Mr. Quinn. At least he'd give her a nod.

A fisherman's wife emerged from the chapel, her head bowed. A sigh swept across those gathered, and everyone lowered their gaze to clasped hands. Most crossed themselves first. Esme hastened to do the same. The priest must have died, after all.

Esme crossed herself and said a brief prayer for his soul. While she didn't speak with any of the other villagers, she felt sorry for the old priest, and didn't wish to be disrespectful to his work or memory. Esme hoped he found peace in heaven.

When she dragged herself back to her cottage, something felt twisted. She glanced around, but nothing seemed out of place. Then her gaze fell upon her embroidery, and she covered her mouth, letting out a horrified gasp. Black soot smudged across the piece, a cruel piece of sabotage.

Esme's eyes grew wide, and her heartbeat raced as she ran to the chink in the bedroom wall. *Gone! She stole the brooch! May the devil make a ladder of Eithne's backbone, to pluck apples from a tree in hell!*

Her grandfather had trusted her with this legacy. She should have kept it safer. Why hadn't she kept it with her? Esme pounded her fist against the wall until the pain turned to numbness.

More than a month later, word came that Father McNulty's replacement had arrived. Esme looked forward to Mass this time. Despite her disgust with the other villagers, and the rampant gossip about her involvement in the priest's death, nothing had come of it. Sure, the women whispered about witches as she passed, but she held her head high. She'd done nothing and therefore held no shame.

Still, the long walk down to the shore got more lonely every day.

The church smelled dank and musty. Thin, narrow windows didn't let in much light even on sunny days. The overcast winter sky made the interior dim and small. Twenty people sat in murmuring clusters.

Esme had offered to watch Aoife while Aisling went to church, but Aisling refused. Mother and daughter shared a fierce bond, stronger than Esme ever had with her own mother or her child. Even Katy preferred staying with them.

Perhaps they grew so close because Aisling had little to do but take care of the girl. Cormac had planned well for the winter, so they had plenty of food. Barrels of dried fish, seaweed, potatoes, turnips, and grain, as well as the herbs and edibles from the garden, chickens, and pigs.

With Cormac gone, though, what did Aisling's future hold? What would they do once the bounty ran out? Aisling earned trade from her healing, but not enough for them to survive.

Her attention turned back to the church. From what Esme could gather, a mysterious illness snatched Father McNulty's life last month. No one knew what happened, but death came fast. Rumors of poison bounced around the community. Aisling did her best to stamp out the ugly rumors, but Esme still heard the whispers.

The priest's door opened in the back of the church.

Everyone craned their heads to glimpse the new priest. Esme had to stand to see him at all. He stood tall and thin, almost skeletal. His long face reminded her of a horse, topped by thick, black hair. Esme couldn't see more from her vantage point in the back of the church. He shuffled in and opened the large, ancient Bible on the podium.

After clearing his throat several times, he spoke in a high and breathy voice, like a young girl's. It seemed incongruous with his tall frame.

"*Dia daoibh*. My name's Father Duggan. I welcome you to my church. Let us begin."

Father McNulty, for all his surliness, had a particular talent in public speaking. He spoke with humor, an engaging banter of a homily and a strong, booming voice. Father Duggan did not have this talent. Perhaps he felt nervous in his new post, but his speech grew reedy and halting, with pauses to collect his thoughts. His sermon became disjointed and difficult to follow.

People in the church shuffled and fidgeted, drowning his soft, thin voice further. It faded behind a barrier of random noises, as if the wind snatched the words from his mouth and scattered them. Only the occasional word fought its way through.

The sermon seemed to last forever, with no structure or purpose. It rambled and bounced along. He peppered his sentences with "ah" and "um" and few complete thoughts. Esme found it almost painful to listen to after the polished storytelling from her father and Seán.

When the priest finished Mass, the congregation breathed a communal sigh of relief. The singing came as an enthusiastic break from the tedium. Esme sang with more vigor and intensity than she'd ever done in church. It earned her a few glances, but she didn't care.

Afterward, she hung back to speak with the priest about Aisling. Her friend would appreciate a visit, and the new man should know one of his parishioners was recently widowed. Esme waited until the older women chattered and clucked over the new priest. His long face and lines turned into a pleasant smile. He did this for each of the elder hens and finally glanced up to see Esme hanging back.

His handshake felt warm and firm. "How do you do? I'm Father Duggan."

"I'm Esme Fitzgerald, Father. My husband's Seán Fitzgerald, but he's off on a trade at the moment."

"Ah, then, I'll meet him another time, so." He turned to see the next person, but she'd been the last.

He stood, awkward, until Esme spoke again. "There's a young widow up on the mountain who didn't come down for services. I thought she might benefit from a visit from you?"

With a gulp, he glanced toward the cottages. "Ah, yes, well, I should be going around to greet folks anyhow, yes. I'll include her on the, ah, rounds. What's her name, then?"

"Aisling O'Malley, and her daughter is Aoife. Her husband, Cormac, disappeared at sea during the Christmas storm."

"That's fine, then. Thank you. I look forward to meeting them soon." The lie shone in his eyes as he turned, escaping toward the manse house, leaving Esme standing alone in the wind.

Why should he lie to her about that? But then again, what had she hoped for? An instant confidante and ally? Someone she might talk with, perhaps. Father Duggan didn't seem like someone interested in talking. At least she'd be able make her confessions again. Her last fight with Seán weighed on her soul these last few weeks.

Seán went out trading for a month or longer. He'd come home, and life would be lovely for a few days. Then he got restless, and she resented him being underfoot. They'd argue over some small, silly thing, get into a fight, and he'd leave in a rage. She shivered and hugged herself in memory of the last one, as she trudged home up the pebble path.

This fight had been bad. He didn't leave right away, as a storm raged outside. She'd used that knowledge to heap all her fears and anger upon him, like piling dirt on a grave. He lashed back with his own furious rants, until they stood nose to nose, every muscle tense. Well, nose to chest, since she stood so much shorter.

This last argument had been nothing new. Esme glared at him with old anger. "Are you off to abandon me in the morning, then?"

"I've half a mind to, the way you harp on about it!" But after a moment, his face softened. "I'm sorry, my love. Truly, I am. I want to give you everything you desire. But I can't do it staying here. I *must* be on the road. I'll bring you back something pretty, I promise."

Esme sneered. "You can't buy my affections with cheap gifts and think it'll all be fine when you're gone for months!"

He pushed her, and she almost fell. She stumbled back to the wall, rage sparking from her eyes. Seán pinned her and forced a kiss as if this would fix things. Esme paled at the memory. The kiss fixed nothing. It just made her angrier, but she had little strength to fight back.

He pinned her wrists against the wall and bruised her lips with kisses. Not gentle kisses, but intrusive, punishing her with his love. Everything seemed twisted and wrong to her. She shook just thinking about that night. She worried he would take her there, but he gave up when she refused to respond. He threw her wrists down with disgust and stalked into the storm.

He disappeared at first light, when the wind calmed.

Esme couldn't talk about the fight to Aisling. To a woman who lost her husband, even a cruel one would be a treasure. Father Duggan heard her confessions and gave her advice, but he said her husband had a right to any affection, forced or not. He also agreed Seán needed to do what he must to support his family.

It sounded so reasonable when put that way, but it didn't *seem* reasonable on the cold, lonely nights.

Esme thought back to her youth, when her grandfather wandered by every few months, laden with gifts and stories. They loved seeing him, but never resented him leaving again. She'd begged him to stay, as all the girls did, even Eithne. But a husband should be different. Grandfather's wife died long before her parents got married, so he had no ties to keep him bound.

Seán had a family. He could trade on the island and be home twice as much, even three times. But he chose to go further and further afield, to hunt down the perfect trade, the magical train of commerce for instant wealth. Esme knew this to be a silly dream, or her grandfather would have found it. Her grandfather always had luck with trades and gambling. He never seemed to be in dire straits or short of funds.

The baby kicked, and she placed her hand on her belly. "Am I upsetting you, wee tadpole? I'm sorry."

This pregnancy had lasted longer than the last four, but her bones ached from fatigue. When Katy ran by, full of energy, she watched in wistful envy. Aisling now took care of Katy more than Esme did, especially as her belly grew. She just didn't have the strength.

Perhaps she needed another trip to the stones. A visit calmed her mind and her heart. Would it work without the brooch? The emptiness left a hole in her soul.

Eithne stole it, and Esme's heart grew sick about the theft. Could she not even trust her own twin? Of course not. She never could trust Eithne except to behave in an underhanded, selfish manner. Esme still steamed over the damage Eithne had done to her embroidery that day. She clenched her fists again at Eithne's duplicity and her own stupidity.

Did she even need the brooch anymore? Esme still spied the truth in people's eyes without it, though not as clearly. Perhaps the stones would still heal her fatigue. She must do something, because some mornings, she could barely rise from her bed.

The next day, making sure Katy stayed with Aisling, Esme trudged out to the other side of the island. Low mist and soft rain made her question her decision on the five hour trek, but once she started, she was determined to finish her quest.

The stones rose through the turf as stark gray sentinels against the late afternoon light. The rainy fog still clung, and the low sunlight painted them a sullen gold. They seemed lonely, somehow, or full of sorrow. Esme touched the altar stone and jumped back.

It stung as if she'd touched a peat log still hot from a burning fire, smoldering with heat and pain. She touched it again with a tentative finger.

The stone burned, and she stepped back. While closing her eyes, she tried to quest deeper, into the earth beneath the stones, as her grandfather had taught her. An oily, disgusting slime coated her mind and everything around her. The land cried out, cold, tired, and ill. Pushing against this filth, she dredged up images of fresh spring lambs gamboling across the green grass, daisies beneath their feet, and butterflies flitting through the air. The bright colors and powerful images pushed against the slimy cast and eased the pain. While using different scenes of life and growth, she repeated this process several times to banish the evil. After five times, she dropped to the grass, exhausted but happier. Now, she let the stones heal her in return.

Esme curled up around her pregnant belly, pulling her cloak over her like a blanket. She slept under the fresh-cleaned altar stone. After slumbering for hours, she pulled much-needed strength from the very stones she helped.

Chapter Thirteen

November 1796

Eithne

Eithne kept the brooch with her at all times. She cradled it in her palms, as if it might scuttle away if she let go. She wore it within her bodice, wanting the warm precious metal and gems against her skin every day.

When she made her assignation with the foreman, Mainey, several weeks after her sojourn at Esme's house, she chose the old stone circle.

With Hugh gone, she no longer needed to be so secretive about her lovers. But since Mainey lived on the property, she preferred not to take a chance. Even if she ruled her domain, she must maintain appearances.

Eithne arrived before her lover, and walked around the stones, casually caressing each one as she passed. Moss and lichen covered their surface, and she made out odd shapes rustling in the darkness. Still, Eithne had nothing to fear from things in the night. Let the superstitious servants believe in tales of the Good Folk. She had too much sense for such twaddle.

Mainey arrived, blond hair shining in the moonlight. She loved his long, silky smooth hair against her skin. After melting into his arms, she raised her face for a kiss. His warm lips made her shudder in delight.

They made passionate love on the soft grass, delighting in the secret freedom of the evening.

Afterward, he rushed back to his duties while she lingered, enjoying the warm glow of satiation. The stars above twinkled as she lay in the cool night.

With a start, Eithne sat up. How long had she been there? The stars shifted positions, and yet she still sweated. The wind blew chilly enough that she ought to be freezing.

Eithne touched the brooch within her bodice. The piece of jewelry radiated warmth. She extracted it from the fabric and almost dropped it with a cry.

It glowed orange.

Eithne studied the piece of ancient jewelry with curious eyes. She turned it around and held it up in the moonlight, but the thing still pulsed an angry orange-red. Then she placed it down on the ground in the center of the stone circle.

She stumbled back as the orange glow radiated out and touched each of the standing stones until they, too, glowed in the night sky. Fire-glow burned each of the ancient carvings, radiating with heat. The power surged through her and she let out a cry. Rather than a cry of pain, though, she shouted out of sheer delight.

Eithne twirled in place with her arms outstretched, reveling in the intensity. Her skirts billowed out as she laughed. She had been right to covet the brooch. Something alien and new tingled through her arms and toes.

The possibilities swam in her mind. What could this artifact do for her? Her grandfather always droned on with his stories of faeries and wishes. Perhaps the daft old man's tales held some truth.

Eithne pointed at the brooch, using her will to manifest her command. "Wealth! Bring me wealth and power. I want to be in control!"

The orange pulsed brighter once, twice, and a third time, flashing red before it faded. The tingling became a burning, buzzing pressure in her mind. It crackled and burst into a thousand orange fragments, fizzling down to the earth and dying like a kicked fire. Then the power and the glow faded away.

Eithne burned with more vitality than she'd ever possessed in her life. Her laugh echoed in the night.

Esme

Esme waddled to the communal garden, stopping to stare at her plot. She should bend down and harvest the herbs, then hang them up to dry in her cottage. But she must bend over or kneel, neither of which she felt up to at the moment. Tomorrow would be no better, so she shuffled to the stool. She got hold of the sage and the rosemary, but the chervil remained out of reach.

She leaned farther, the stool tipping. *Just a little more... there.* She creaked and groaned until she stood again and pressed her hand against the small of her back. The ache seemed worse today, but chores needed doing and Seán left again the week before.

Their fights became almost a game now. She'd yell at him, and he'd get angry and leave anyhow. He never got violent since that time in February. Since she developed this balloon in her belly, he didn't touch her. Not even affectionate cuddling. He fetched her food and drink, and did all the chores, but gave her no tender caress.

Esme ached for a loving touch. She sniffed back the impending tears, willing them to disappear. Tears fell often and for no real reason.

Aisling sat on a chair next to her back door, rocking with Aoife. Despite being older, Aoife remained fragile and in need of care. In Esme's opinion, if Aisling let the child play on her own, she'd grow stronger, but she daren't say a thing. The healer would know better than Esme. Besides, Aoife wasn't Esme's child, and she had no place to speak. She'd also risk Aisling refusing to help with Katy.

As Esme turned toward her own door, a spasm gripped her back. She pressed the heel of her hand against the base of her spine, hoping to ease the pain.

She let out a low moan, which got Aisling's attention. The other woman yelled across the garden. "Esme? Are you all right?"

When Esme didn't answer right away, she rushed over, Aoife in tow. "Esme? Does your back hurt?"

Frustration and pain made her snap her words. "My back has hurt for the last month, but yes, it hurts worse now. I need to go lie down."

The cottage looked a mess, but Esme didn't care. Katy played with some bits of straw and small stones near the hearth. She'd strewn things all over the floor, things Esme didn't have the strength or gumption to pick up. Later, she would deal with it all later.

The pain deepened but she made it to her bed. Esme didn't lie down right away. She waited until the spasms stopped seizing up and down her spine and the back of her legs. She closed her eyes and breathed, but it didn't help.

Aisling patted her arm. "Stay here, Esme, I'll be right back."

Stay here? Where in God's sweet name would I go? Her eyes drooped like lead weights. She certainly didn't plan on hopping on a horse to go galloping across the countryside.

In the brief respite between pains, Esme caressed her belly, humming to herself. Did the baby hear? It didn't move. Too quiet. She tried to remember the last time it had kicked. Yesterday. Panic rose as she waited for Aisling.

When the healer returned, she dragged her healing satchel and blankets. "What's all that for?"

Aisling's eyes widened. "For your birth, silly girl. You're going to have your baby."

Now? But Seán wasn't here. Panic rose in her heart. "But he hasn't moved since yesterday. Is something wrong?"

"No worries about that, Esme. Babies go quiet before they are born. Now, lie back here. I'll put down blankets to save your bed from a soaking."

Before Esme could move, a strange, earthy scent filled the air. Warm rivulets dripped down her legs and off the edge of the bed in a disgusting trail of slime.

Aisling mopped up the excess with a blanket and swung Esme's legs around, making her lie back.

"What do I do?"

"Nothing, yet. Don't push. Let me look at you."

Aisling poked around her female parts. It didn't arouse her, but it felt… curious. Almost detached, as if it happened to someone else.

Aisling made a strange noise. "What? What's wrong?"

"Nothing's wrong. You aren't as ready as I thought you'd be. This child will take time, I'm afraid. We might be in for a long night."

Night? Noon just passed. A stabbing pain shot through Esme's back. A ripple contracted through her belly, an earthquake of flesh and muscle. She let out another moan.

"I'll be back soon, Esme. I'll get willow bark tea and hot water. The hearth at my place is cold, but I'll get yours going. We'll need it."

Worry clouded the truth in Aisling's eyes, but the other woman vanished before Esme asked more information. Any birth took a lot of work. Esme didn't remember Bridey's birth, but she'd seen cows and sheep give birth. A neighbor had a difficult birth once. The hoarse screams in the night frightened her, and she burrowed into her da's arms. Her ache intensified with her fear.

The urge to push came so strong. Aisling said not to push, so she tried not to. She clenched until her muscles twitched with each spasm. When she let go, the pain flooded back. It started at the base of her spine and radiated around her belly, her shoulders, even down to the tips of her toes. She wanted to howl, and then the pain eased again.

Sweat poured down her face, despite the cool April air. It pooled into her ear, and she shook her head to get rid of it. Another pain began, and she forgot such things as sweat droplets.

Esme remembered the pain, the sweat, and the screaming, but little else. Aisling stayed by her side. She cried out for Seán so many times, thinking him close. Her delirium waxed and waned from rational speech into fevered garbling. Aisling moved between Esme and the girls, taking care of both. She'd keep Aoife and Katy occupied until Esme moaned again and she had to switch focus.

As dawn approached, Aisling wore a grim look.

During a clear moment, though she hated doing it, Esme pushed her friend for the truth. "What, Aisling? What is it? You must tell me." Esme had no energy left, but she gripped her friend's arm. She wanted to rip the child from her belly and be done with it.

Aisling shook her head. "Naught to worry yourself over, Esme. Relax. Here, let me get you more tea."

Aisling lied. That showed bright in her eyes, even with the brooch's diminished power. "No more tea, Aisling. I'm sick of tea. I'm sick of this child. Tell me what's wrong, now!"

Aisling didn't answer, but mopped Esme's forehead with a cool, wet cloth. "Shh. Rest now."

She had so little strength, but she pushed one more time. "Aisling…"

The healer bit her lip. "I may be wrong, but I think the baby…"

"What, what's wrong?"

"I think the baby might not… he might be gone already."

Esme's mind didn't absorb the sentence. The words didn't seem real. She wanted to undo the pushing. She didn't want the truth anymore. The meaningless words floated around her mind like a carousel, out of her grasp. If she reached for them, she might catch them. She stretched her arm out, touching Aisling's face. Tears glinted on her friend's cheek.

Aisling's expression broke Esme's last grip on reality. She drifted in and out of a cloud of nonsense. Sounds and visions swam in her head.

Aisling brought another pot of the tea, with seaweed to help with labor.

One more big push and the baby's head popped out with a liquid sound. The healer scrambled to grab a blanket and pulled the rest of the baby from Esme's body. Aisling fussed with the pathetic form, slapping it on the bottom, fishing around in its mouth, scooping out mucus.

For a brief, shining moment, life stirred in the child, but it flashed out, like a will-o'-the-wisp. Aisling took a deep breath, tied off the cord, and cleaned the baby up. Esme's heart surged into her throat and then she drifted off again.

Esme roused as the afterbirth came out. She struggled to sit up. "Where's my baby? Is it a girl or a boy?"

Aisling cradled the tiny bundle in her arms, cooing. She glanced up with an exhausted smile. "He's small, and very weak, but he's alive."

Esme's heart soared. A son? She'd borne a son. Sean would be so thrilled. "Give him to me! I need to hold him."

With tender care, Aisling laid the swaddled babe into Esme's eager arms. She peered at his tiny face, all red wrinkles. The dim light made him look almost dark-skinned, but she only saw her wee son. She cried as she held him close, rocking to her sobs. She wept with tears of joy, bearing another live baby after losing so many.

After she got him to take his first drink, Aisling took him back. "You need rest more than he does, my dear. Sleep, now. I'll take good care of the wee one."

Esme imagined walking along the beach with Sean and her son. What would she name him? Maybe Éamonn, after her grandfather. Or Brian, her da. Seán may want to name him after his own father, Oisinn. A name from the legends.

Her dreams crowded with bright colors and laughter.

A shout woke her. She shook the sleep from her head and rubbed her eyes. Her belly ached, and she placed a hand there out of reflex. Then she remembered she'd birthed her baby. Her little Oisinn. The cot wasn't next to the bed. Pushing herself to her feet, she stumbled to the next room. Aisling sat in the chair, facing the fire, her back to Esme.

"Aisling? The babe must be ready to eat again. How long have I slept?"

Her friend didn't answer, just continued to stare at the hearth.

"Aisling? Aisling, what's wrong?"

The healer rose, holding the swaddled bundle. She shook her head, unable to meet Esme's eyes. "Esme, I tried everything, I swear I did. He didn't make it… I'm so sorry."

"No! I don't believe you! He's alive! I fed him!"

Esme reached to take the babe, then winced as pain sliced through her abused body.

With a deep sigh, Aisling squeezed the bundle. The other woman brought the pitiful corpse, swaddled in a flannel blanket, to his mother. "Here, Esme, here's your boy. It's better if you see him yourself."

Esme unwrapped him to count ten fingers, ten toes, translucent eyelids and a tiny, blue mouth. Why blue? He looked perfect. Would he suckle with a blue mouth?

The truth of the situation slammed into her chest. Her baby, her sweet baby had died, all for nothing. She tried to cry, wanted to cry, but she had no tears left from the long night's labor. She howled with a dry and cracked throat.

Aisling settled on the soaking wet bed and hugged her, cradling the dead child between them.

Eithne

While she instructed her cook on that week's menus, pain shot through her belly. Eithne gasped and clutched her middle.

Something struggled against her power over the brooch. She didn't know what she fought or how to counter it. Almost as if someone slugged her in the stomach.

The cook bowed and exited without a word. Eithne had trained her well. A servant had no place witnessing their mistress's distress.

The sensation faded, but something serious had happened. Her mind flooded with distress, but not her own. She rushed to the locked safe in her study. The brooch sat there, well and good. But it felt… lighter. It seemed more insubstantial, as if it weakened. Eithne gripped it so tightly, the edges of the brooch bit into her hands. The jewelry was solid, right here in her palm. How could it fade away?

Still, something happened. Something she had no control over. Did Esme have a way to wrest the power back from her? Did Esme even know it had power? Of course she did. Her twin might be naïve, but not stupid.

The traps she'd left for her twin must not have worked. She'd need to try something else.

Eithne had no wish to kill her sister. Even she balked at such an extreme measure. But how would she break her twin's hold on the brooch? Maybe the brooch held onto Esme's sickly sweet good nature.

What if Esme became somehow corrupted? Maybe if she stole something valuable or cheated on her husband? If that became known, it would remove Esme's holier-than-thou righteousness. She had such a tender conscience. An act of such perceived depravity might sink her into a sullen despair. Esme wouldn't have the will to work a retrieval spell with such a millstone hanging around her neck.

Eithne had some ideas, but she must find the right conspirator.

Esme

Esme regretted not borrowing a horse, though riding would have increased her pain too much. She slogged along the sodden path, her boots squishing in the marshy areas. She'd left Katy with Aisling and regretted leaving her daughter with every step. The rain washed away or buried the stepping stones. As she concentrated on her footing, she did her best not to slip and fall.

In the weeks since she'd lost her baby, Esme lived in an exhausted fog. The difficult birth, the death of her baby, and her pushing Aisling for the truth drained her of all strength. Even the needs of her daughter hadn't been enough to pull her from the abyss. One thing she knew, though, she shouldn't push again. Pulling the truth had become dangerous, both to her body and to her mind. The brooch's power may have even killed her baby.

Aisling fed and washed Esme and took care of both daughters. Her friend moved in with her. Some nights, she only got rest because Aisling slept with her arms around her, comforting her like a sick child, kissing her head and cheeks when she cried.

A child. That's what she'd become.

Seán hadn't returned and nothing seemed real. Esme flickered from bad dream to nightmare and back again. She hadn't left the cottage in what seemed like an eternity.

Today, Aisling insisted she go out. And what did she do, her first sojourn? She tramped halfway across the bloody island to the stone circle. Deep in her bones, Esme knew she needed strength from the stones.

She brought a cloak, a shawl, and a scarf, as the air grew icy in the wind. The blanket of fog mirrored the dream-like quality of her life.

The silence seemed unnerving. A loud plop sounded behind her, and she whirled, ready for an attack. She let out a nervous laugh when a marsh bird dropped mud he didn't want to eat. The bird unfolded his wide, white wings and flapped off into the mists.

Did she travel the right path? She followed the map in her mind, from a half-dozen journeys over the years. Her memory clouded with pain.

She harbored a strange, wild hope Seán, or better yet, her grandfather, waited for her at the stones. This futile hope kept her going through the marshes.

Amorphous forms emerged in the dim white. Dark, wet, and massive, with splotches of white lichen splashed in random places, as if someone threw paint at them. They both comforted and menaced her.

Esme caressed the largest stone. She shut her eyes, concentrating on the land beneath the stones and her own soul.

After opening her eyes, she marched around the circle as her grandfather showed her. Step by step, clockwise, she sensed the stones to her right. Tendrils of her own essence burrowed into the soil like roots, not pulling her, but supporting her. By the time she reached her point of origin, she became part of the circle, buoyed by a mystical net. The white mists glowed a greenish-blue and pulsed with her heartbeat.

A hint of dank evil clung to the earth, but she imbued it with healing joy, and it faded to almost nothing. She had no strength to clean it further. Today, she must take her own healing.

Esme sat on the flattest stone. The surface radiated warmth. She concentrated on the glow and on the power.

The glow passed through her, up into her head, out to her fingertips and toes. It pulsed in and out, healing and fixing, like a salve to her broken soul. A form appeared to her in the mist. The shining human form she'd glimpsed before. It approached with slow, gliding steps. She reached out to touch it.

At the point of contact, the dam burst. Light and love flooded her, as well as terror and pain. Tears ran down her cheeks, and she cried for her lost child in a way she couldn't before. She wept herself out, then breathed in deep. The sweet tang of the fog, the slight rot of the marsh, and the salt sea in the distance tickled her nose. The stones smelled chalky and wet. She lost herself in the swirling odors, almost visible in the mist. Confused glimpses of people, places, and objects she once owned spun in her memory. Her sister Eithne glared at her with angry eyes.

Esme's bum had turned to ice, though the stone remained warm. She wiggled her toes to bring back feeling. They tingled and pricked with reaction. She smiled for the first time since Seán last left.

Despite the long trip, Esme knew she'd done the right thing coming here. She'd come alive again, ready to face the world, or at least the trip home. The walk to the circle had taken her half the day, and despite the new energy, her body still craved rest. She considered stopping in Dugort on the way home. She didn't fancy walking all the way back tonight, and Dugort had an inn.

Esme descended the boggy hill to the beach. After removing her muddy boots, she splashed in the water, squishing her toes into the sand. Why did sand feel so much nicer than mud? The walk along the shore restored her almost as much as the stones had.

A few hardy souls took advantage of a windless day at the beach. The weather remained cool, but the sun burned through the scattered fog. A couple sat near the end of the beach and a lone man rode a fine horse toward her. Seán had given her lessons on judging horseflesh. The roan thoroughbred cantered down the sand. His rider looked to be enjoying the trip as much as his mount.

They slowed as they reached Esme. The older, stout man sat the horse well, no stranger to riding. "Good day to you miss." The gentleman, for so he must be, tipped his riding hat to her.

Esme did her best to curtsy, which she had never done without boots on. Careful to modulate her voice into her practiced posh accent, she answered, "Good day to you, sir." She hid her bare feet under her skirts, but since she held her boots, it made little difference.

"Have you moved to the area, or are you visiting? I'm sure I would have noticed such a lovely thing as you before this." He gave her a disarming grin and her cheeks grew warm.

The healing energy of the stones made her as giddy as a child. "I live on the south side of the island. I came up for a visit, and I wanted a walk on the beach."

"Ah! I see. And what's your name, young lady?"

She bobbed again. "I'm Mistress Esme Fitzgerald."

"And I am Lord John Sweeney, at your service, Mistress Fitzgerald. Do enjoy your day." With a tip of his hat, he rode away, his lovely horse flinging up bits of sand.

Esme stood, flabbergasted. She just met a lord? In a mud-bedraggled skirt, barefoot and threadbare. A mixture of shame and delight flashed through her. He seemed a decent sort for a lord.

Before he died, Aisling's husband, Cormac, had mentioned a Sweeney, but hadn't the first name been Carrick? They must be father and son. She felt the fool staring after the retreating form.

As Lord Sweeney disappeared, she hid a secret smile. She'd finally met a lord, and hadn't embarrassed herself with her low-class words. Her practice had paid off.

Cormac had suggested she take her finer work up to the grand house to trade. The idea had merit, but she had no skill in barter. Seán always handled the trades. Perhaps when her husband returned, she'd ask him. *Whenever that might be.* Her thoughts turned bitter.

The day seemed to dim. Thoughts of her errant husband brought her back to reality after the euphoria of the stones. The sand on the beach now seemed gritty and irritating rather than wonderful. She wiped off her feet and ankles and put her boots on. Her idea of staying overnight at the inn no longer held any appeal, and the walk home would be long.

Should she tell Seán about the brooch and the stones? Esme debated the thought many times. But her grandfather told her to tell no one. Witch hunts still happened, and communing with faeries wouldn't be Christian. Not that Seán would ever betray her for being a witch, but she shouldn't take the chance. Not with her parents gone over the ocean. She swallowed in memory of her parents, her sister, gone forever from her.

Esme missed her family horribly, especially on dark, lonely nights. Her wish of filling the empty cottage with children seemed a faraway dream. She filled it with song, or told herself stories aloud. It helped break the silence.

Her sister, though. Esme would have to go after Eithne and get the brooch back. Its absence left a hole in her soul that seemed to get bigger every day. Besides, their grandfather had given it to Esme, not Eithne. She must not let her sister win. To do that, she'd need her husband's help.

On the long walk back, Esme sang waulking songs, repetitious verses to help with working wool. She sang a sad song of Deirdre of the Sorrows, and sweet songs of love. Her father loved battle songs, so she sang one and remembered him. She ignored her stinging tears, singing through a throat tight with nostalgia.

Dusk chased her as she took the final turn toward the *clachan*. Her eyes lit when she noticed their cart, with Nuala grazing alongside. She quickened her step, eager to see her husband after so many weeks' absence.

By the time she climbed the stony path, full dark embraced the island. The gentle wind caressed her. The stars sparkled and winked in the clear black night sky.

Esme stood outside, nervous to see Seán again. She breathed deep, smelling the homey scents of the horse, the garden, and peat fire. Damp thatch added to the smells, so it must have rained today. Fresh-turned earth in the garden. Another aroma swirled around her, salty and savory. Had Seán made supper?

Esme put her hand on the door just as Nuala whickered. As she turned toward the horse, the door flew open to reveal Seán.

Dirty and unshaven, her husband had aged ten years in the few weeks since he left. He stared at her as if he saw a ghost, a fetch come to take him away to the Land of Ever Young, *Tír na nÓg*.

He clutched her tight, hugging her so hard, she yelped. His breath reeked of whiskey. He gripped her close and wouldn't let go. She struggled to get a breath and wriggled until she got her arm free.

He jumped back, eyes blazing. He looked slightly crazed and definitely drunk. "What in the name of Sweet Mother Mary are you about, Esme? I got worried sick about you. Where did you go?"

"Then don't yell at me when I get back!" She rubbed her upper arms. They ached, and she knew it would bruise.

He looked down at her belly, almost as flat as before she'd gotten pregnant. "And where's the baby?" He glanced back into the cottage, as if he'd previously overlooked an infant.

Emotions slammed into Esme. Her throat closed with anguish. She gritted her teeth, trying not to sob, and choked the words out. "The babe came, but he didn't live more than a few hours. I went walking." Esme refused to let the pain show on her face. If she let any emotion through, it would take over like a tidal wave. She didn't want to let that out.

Seán's face turned blank, his eyes glistening with tears. "Ah, God, Esme, I thought ye were dead! No one knew where you'd gone or what happened. I've been up and down the mountain looking for you all day!"

Did he not care their child had died? "Aisling knew where I went."

Seán gave a bitter laugh. "That one. She'd say nothing to me. She just said you'd gone walking." He waved his hand in a vague gesture toward the road. His eyes narrowed. "Or did you meet with someone?"

"Meet with someone? That's silly, Seán. Well, I did meet someone, but not on purpose, just pure chance. Did you hear what I said? Our son died!"

A sharp, unfamiliar anger burned behind his eyes. "Oh, so you did meet someone then? And what's the fellow's name?"

What on God's green earth did he have to be jealous about? She raised her head and mustered all her dignity. "If you must know, I met Lord John Sweeney."

Esme didn't know what reaction she expected, but at this point, she didn't care. She'd had enough of his moods and tempers and would be damned if she'd cater to them.

Seán grabbed her by the arms again, lifted her into the cottage and slammed the door. She struggled to get free, but he had an iron grip on her. He flung her onto the bed. She yelped when she cracked her head on the bedpost. In a flash, he'd pulled up her skirts and jerked at her petticoats, trying to shove them out of the way. She struggled with him, trying to get out of the bed, but he had pinned her down with his weight. "No! No, Seán, you can't! Stop!"

"Quiet! I'll show you who you should be meeting! You're my wife!"

She crossed her legs and kept them tight, sobbing in fear and rage. He struggled with her skirts, but couldn't get through. Instead, he hit her. He slapped her in the face, and the pain shot through her as if he'd stabbed her. He hit her again, her head cracking against the bed frame once more. She blocked his next blow with her arms, so he punched her in the stomach.

Esme screamed for him to stop, but more blows rained down. Not all of them connected, but enough found their mark. She fell into a fog of fear and betrayal.

Sometime later, the hail of pain stopped. When she woke, the cottage echoed with emptiness.

He'd gone.

Seán

Hours later, Seán woke from a drunken stupor in the back of his cart. His mind filled with flashes of memory, fear, and shame. He didn't remember what happened. He held his head in his hands, trying to remember. Pacing around the cottage, sick with worry, looking for his wife. Had she given birth yet? Where did the baby go?

The drink helped to stave off the fears. Had she wandered off into the marshes? Gone down to the church? He almost rode Nuala into the ground searching for Esme across the mountainside.

Then she returned, and his heart had leapt into his throat. She stood in his foggy memory, declaring she met Lord something-or-other. Met him? Swived him, she meant. Anger clouded his memory, a rage of jealousy. His lovely, dear, sweet wife, sleeping with another man. Her declaration pounded against his aching head, and his heat rose again, then turned into shame.

Did he have a horrible dream, or had he hit his dear Esme? "Oh God, what have I done? Esme, our baby… Oh God, Oh God!"

Seán wailed, head in his hands. He rocked back and forth until his head spun. Rushing out of the wagon, he made it to the grass just as the sickness erupted. He vomited until his insides felt dragged out and run over by a team of horses. After looking up, he blinked in the dawn light. His horse, Nuala, stared at him. A long piece of grass stuck out of the side of her mouth.

He grunted and patted her on the flank. "Ah, Nuala, what a mess I've made of things. What can I do?"

The stolid horse still stared at him, as if she considered eating his shirt.

Seán glanced down at himself, curling his lip with disgust. His clothing stank, and he needed a wash. As if clean clothes and a shave would make this any easier.

When he steeled himself to enter their cottage, he flung the door open, ready for Esme to fly at him in a rage. But she'd left. *By all that's holy, she must be at Aisling's.*

With straightened shoulders, Seán marched himself to Aisling's cottage. He must settle this now. More waiting would only make things worse.

He hesitated before knocking. What would he say? That he was sorry? Of course. That he acted like a brute and an idiot? The truth pained him. That he'd never do it again? Why would she even believe him?

Seán tried so hard to be a success for his dear Esme. He just didn't seem to have his father's knack. While he might seek his Da out to ask for help, his shame kept him from that. He'd failed his beautiful bride. His future slipped through his fingers, and he just made it worse by the day.

He rapped the wooden door with his knuckles three times. It sounded weak to him. Did they even hear that inside? Seán raised his hand to knock again when the door flew open.

Aisling stood, hands on her hips, staring at him with fire in her eyes. "And what exactly will you be wanting, then?"

Anger made her formidable. A far cry from the blathering young lady he first met, intent on nothing but her child. She cared for Esme and Katy, and it brought out a fierce mothering instinct in her.

"I'd like to… Esme… I need to talk…."

She stepped into the doorway, filling it with her tiny presence, puffed up like a mother hen with ruffled feathers. "You'll not be talking to Esme. Tell me what you want to say and I'll pass it on."

Seán gulped at her angry words, but that would only be fair. "Please, then, tell her I'm an eejit. I'm sorry. I'd understand if she never wanted to see me again, but to please, please, come back and see me." He didn't know what else to say.

Esme's voice came from a gloomy corner of the room. "It's all right, Aisling."

Seán focused on the spot and saw Esme cradling Katy, though the girl looked uncomfortable. His wife's face looked a colorful mass of bruises, with her left eye swollen shut. His heart ached at the sight of her.

She rocked, cooing at the child. She might be holding their new baby, but she lost it. And he, like a brutal coward, beat her when she needed comfort. His cheeks grew warm with shame.

Aisling didn't move an inch. "Esme?"

She didn't look at him but remained entranced with Katy. "Let him in. For now."

Aisling looked rebellious but gave way. She glared as Seán ducked his head to walk into the tiny cottage.

Barrels and bags of food stacked in one big corner, including dried fish, apparent from the stink. Herbs and flowers hung drying from the rafters. Seán got one posset in the eye as he turned, then he crouched down to avoid more. A sleeping pallet sat along the far wall and a hearth on one end of the room. Other than a table and a few chairs, that was the extent of the furniture.

Seán stared at Esme, taking in every detail of her. She still wore the dress from yesterday, muddy at the hems and torn. Had he done that?

Had she been unfaithful? Did she have a lover? His flush faded, but now jealousy replaced it. He tamped down, knowing it to be a mistake. Seán couldn't be angry now. He must be kind. Esme deserved kind. She deserved the life she wanted, with a husband who stayed home, too.

Could he leave the life of trade and be a farmer? Sean shook his head. He knew nothing about farming. It took real skill. Look at how Esme's father had failed, and that farm had been bigger than their tiny garden.

His wife glared at him, and he knew she'd seen his flash of jealousy. "Well?"

Seán dropped his gaze. "I… I don't know what to say, Esme. I behaved like a monster. Can you ever forgive me?" He pleaded with his eyes, his body, his very soul. He loved her dearly and couldn't bear the idea of losing her. Yes, they fought like cats and dogs, but that had become part of the thrill. Their rows were part of the wild ride, a part of them.

Esme continued to stare at him, saying nothing. Her silence grew unnerving. A pressure pushed on his soul. He let it push through to whatever he had within him. Seán wanted her to yell back like a spitfire cat, claws out and ready to ravage his face with long scratches. This calm Esme confused him, and he didn't know how to react.

Her hair tangled like a bird's nest, russet in the dawn light filtering through the window. Glimmers of copper and rust shimmered, giving her an unearthly aura. The bright blue of her good eye shone from under her tangle of red.

She glanced at Aisling, who took Katy from her. The older woman hovered near Esme for several moments before letting out a growl and leaving them alone.

Esme's jaw clenched before she spoke in an ice-cold tone, almost as hostile as her sister's. "Never again. Is that understood? Never, not so much as a slap."

His knees grew weak that she might forgive him, that he might have his Esme back. They got so weak, he fell down in a pitiful gesture of begging. "Never, never again, I swear, Esme."

She stared at him hard, as if peering into his soul, but he meant it. His horror and disgust with his own actions made him stare at the ground. He'd become the worst sort of monster, a man who beat his wife.

Sean had known men like that. In the past, he'd always considered it a horrible weakness. Men who never controlled their own tempers behaved no better than animals. And here, he'd done the same thing on the whiff of mislaid jealousy and a burst of temper.

Esme nodded in judgment. "I believe you. But I need time. I'll come home later."

Hope flowered in his chest and withered again. He had no choice. Shoulders slumped, he left the cottage, as if she had beaten him with a strap. In a way, she had, and he deserved it. Seán had tortured himself all day yesterday, terrified his wife had left him or died. He took out those frustrations and fears on the very wife he worried about. Unforgiveable.

Now she'd pull them back up out of the muck. She didn't need to, but she would. Seán hoped he had the fortitude to remain with her for the journey.

December 1796

Aisling

It was touch and go for a while, Aisling thought, *but she's a survivor, despite everything.* She hung the fresh-washed clothes from the day before. Most of the blood came out, but one dark-brown spot refused to go, scrub as she might. Perhaps she should tear it into rags? Best let Esme decide.

Esme remained so weak from her last pregnancy and the emotional drain of losing her son. She couldn't sit up for more than an hour at a time and only sat to read. She didn't get good rest unless Aisling slept beside her. While Aisling enjoyed their loving nights together, Esme needed something more. Aisling had done everything she could for her. The rest would be up to Esme.

Esme always lit up when Seán arrived. They snarled at each other's throats within an hour of his arrival, but at least it gave her something to fight for. Esme'd lost five babies now. Aisling knew herbs, such as thistle or wild carrot seed, to prevent her friend from getting pregnant again, but should she tell Esme? Such a horrible thing to lose a child, but each pregnancy gave her hope.

She reached high to pin the last washed blanket. As she did so, a pain shot up her calf. She dropped the blanket and massaged her muscle and tendons. Perhaps she just pulled the wrong way. Shrugging, she bent to pick up the blanket, and the pain returned. Her tendon jumped beneath her skin. After rubbing it a few times, she rose again, stretching her back.

"Would you like help with that, Aisling?"

Aisling recognized the male voice. She whirled, spying Seán leaning against the cottage wall, one side of his mouth curled up in a smile. He had a bundle in his arms.

She cocked her head. "When did you arrive? I heard no horses!"

"Sold the last one and carried the cart myself. My shoulders are aching!" He had a disarming charm. The bundle squirmed.

She narrowed her eyes. "Have you seen Esme yet?"

"No, should I have? I just got here and saw you dancing with the laundry, or so it appeared. What were you doing, anyhow?"

"Nothing. Let me warn you about Esme before you go inside."

A look of alarm and concern flashed across his face. "Warn me? What?" He straightened, abandoning his casual stance. The bundle unwrapped and revealed a nose.

A nose? The nose of a puppy. A grin escaped her control.

When he strode to the door, Aisling ran to him and put a hand on his arm. "Go gently, Seán, go soft. She's still quite weak. We almost lost her this time, too. Here, let me take the wee dog while you talk to her. Save him for later, aye?"

Seán's face shifted, expressions of fear, frustration, and anger flitting across his face, damped down as he gave her a curt nod. After handing her the puppy, he tiptoed into the cottage.

Despite her rage at Seán after his last visit, Aisling felt sorry for them both. At least Esme had a husband still. It must be heartbreaking to keep trying and never succeed. She unwrapped the squirming dog and two soulful brown eyes gazed at her. A border collie, black with a white belly and legs. He yipped and licked at her face, eliciting a giggle.

Aisling looked for Katy and found her playing in the dirt next to the garden. She had a streak of mud across one cheek and built several piles of dirt. She held a stone, moving it like a horse cart, winding through the dirt piles. As she crouched next to the younger girl, Aoife whinnied, and Aisling waited for Nuala's answer, forgetting for a moment Seán said he'd sold the horse.

Sold off Nuala? That man loved that horse more than his own daughter. He'd never do such a thing unless desperate. Seán always seemed so cock-sure of himself and his trading abilities. Why would he sell off Nuala?

Aisling placed the puppy in her basket and finished her hanging, then walked out around the cottages to the front, where Seán left the cart. It held a few bags of food but nothing more. A sack of flour, a bushel of apples, and a barrel of smoked meat, not close to what he ought to have brought home. Perhaps he had coin instead of goods.

Aisling felt like a burden on the couple. She made some fees with healing and kept Esme company while Seán traveled. She looked after Katy, almost more than Esme did herself. Perhaps she should live in her own cottage more and put less of a demand on Esme and her meager resources.

She should pull away, leaving Seán and Esme time to heal. It broke Aisling's heart whenever they fought. Esme ended up a right wreck every time. Aisling ached to hold her and make it all better, as when Aoife fell from the rock wall and skinned her knee.

Gathering Aoife and Katy from their piles of dirt and the puppy in his basket, she brought them inside her own cottage and started a hearth fire. She'd make stew for supper and leave Seán and Esme alone.

Chapter Fourteen

May 1797

Seán

S eán opened the cottage door to nothing but darkness. He let his eyes
acclimate before entering. Once he made out the loom by the hearth,
a project half-finished and the faint odor of peat smoke and copper
blood, he walked in. The dirt floor splashed with mud, but he kept going
to the bedroom, finding Esme lying on the bed.

She lay so still, as if dead. Terrified for a moment he had lost her after
all, Seán put a tentative hand on her shoulder. She felt cool but not cold,
and he let out the breath he hadn't realized he held.

Seán experienced incredible guilt every time he left. He wished he'd
been here when she lost the baby, but he'd returned now. At least he'd been
home for Katy's birth. Especially now that he'd lost Nuala.

He pushed the thought away and gave Esme a shake on the shoulder.
His wife moaned, shifting in her sleep, but didn't wake. Not wanting to
disturb her rest, he sat on the stool and studied her.

She'd aged in the five years since he took her to wife, but he'd aged
even more. Though he counted but twenty-seven years, his hair showed
a few silver strands. She had no silver. Her red curls danced as unruly as
ever, carefree and beautiful. But deep lines etched on her face, tense even
in slumber.

Seán ached to smooth the lines of worry, to give her the peace of mind
she deserved. He wanted to give her the baby they both craved, a child to
salve her broken heart and bring joy to their lives.

Sure, they had Katy, but why couldn't they conceive another child?
He'd lain with a girl or two before he met Esme, and none came forward
to say he fathered children. But Esme got with child. She just didn't hold
on to them. Except this last one, and he'd died almost as soon as he lived.

A sharp pang of loss shot through his heart at his son, lost and buried.
Sean wanted to name him Brian, for Esme's father, but the child hadn't

even lived long enough for baptism. His poor, wee lad. A teardrop landed on his hand and soon, more tears dripped down his face.

Esme stirred but still didn't wake. He wanted to stroke her cheek. She'd grown so thin and sallow, almost like a stranger. How had she lost so much weight in so little time? He only left a few weeks ago.

These last two weeks had been hard. He traded most of his goods for a string of donkeys, but the donkeys got a chill and died, one by one, along the road. Nuala looked ill as well. Seán spent most of his remaining coin for a healer, but she died a couple days past. He mourned for his horse almost as much as he mourned for his son. She'd been a good horse. His first, solid and dependable.

Now he had almost nothing, with a sick wife and a daughter. He must pick up again and try to rebuild his trade string.

Unable to resist any longer, Seán stroked Esme's cheek, a gentle caress which spoke of his love and tenderness for his wife.

Her eyes fluttered at the touch, a slow smile spreading on her lips. Her gaze widened when she realized who sat next to her. "You're home?"

Who did she think touched her if not him? "No, darling, I'm merely a fetch here to frighten you." He grinned to take the sting out of his sarcasm.

She smiled back, a weak, wan smile which melted into a sad frown. "Seán…"

He picked her thin hand up from the bed covers and cradled it in his own. "I know, *mo chroi*. Aisling told me. My dear, sweet wife." She seemed so delicate, as if her bones would break under the slightest pressure.

"I'm so sorry, Seán. I tried to be careful, I did."

"Let me get you supper, my darling. Would you like stew, or perhaps stew? I can also make stew, if you'd like." They'd long since discovered he had no talent for cooking, but he could manage basics.

Esme let out a weak chuckle. "Stew would be grand, Seán. Did you bring back any bread? I'd love to soak up the juices."

Seán gave a mock frown, shaking his head. "Alas, I have flour, but not yet baked into edible form. How about oats to thicken the stew? I brought you another surprise, though."

"That will do fine, my love. What surprise?"

"You'll have to wait and see. Aisling is holding it for you until you're stronger."

She closed her eyes again, exhaustion clear in the lines of her face. Seán walked to the hearth to start their supper.

Yes, he brought flour and oats, but only enough food to get them through a month or two. He had little coin left and no other trade goods. He didn't even have any more fabric for Esme to make into clothing. Seán made a nice side trade with her clothing and embroidery. The sturdier items sold at the monthly market in Achill Sound and other fairs. She sold the finer embroidery to the factor up at Carrick House.

While he stirred the iron pot, Seán remembered the first day they brought goods to the big house. Esme didn't want to go on her own, so he traveled with her. After all, she had no training in trade, and Seán didn't want the factor to cheat her.

They filled the cart with her creations, adding other things to make the cart seem full. And if Lord Carrick appeared, he'd feel better being there. Esme explained their innocent meeting, a couple of minutes on the beach, but he couldn't get rid of the irrational jealousy at the notion of Esme with someone else.

As they approached the white house with black trim around the windows, Esme's face lit up with delight. She'd seen few grand houses, and this one glittered in the bright May sunshine. The building stood three stories tall, with a crenelated tower in front, and real glass windows with lace curtains. They aimed for the stables and the servants' quarters around back.

Seán approached the rear door to knock when it flew open and a young girl dressed in a white apron, around twelve, barreled out with an enormous tub of laundry. Her flight almost knocked Seán over. After a hasty apology, she hurried to a stone-fenced area next to the stables. Seán glanced at Esme and shrugged, lifting his hand to knock on the door.

His efforts brought out a large woman, a bright patterned kerchief tied around her head.

Her gray hair framed an impatient look on her sweaty face. "What will you be wanting? No deliveries today. Wednesdays only."

She moved to shut the door, but Seán shoved his foot in the way. "We'd like a word with the factor, if you please. We have luxury goods to sell, made by my good wife there." He gestured to Esme, who nodded in a genteel manner.

The woman gave him a glare, nodded, and then disappeared. She hadn't closed the door, though, so Seán waited. Esme's eyes darted from the big house, to the stables, to the girl hanging the laundry.

After a long ten minutes, a young, clean-cut man in a black suit arrived, looking from Seán to Esme and back again. "I'm told you have goods to offer. What have you got?"

Seán handed him a pillow as an example, one of Esme's best creations. "Fine embroidery and needlework." Bright, bold colors, a cardinal on a winter branch, embroidered with fine detail. White floss showed the snow on the buff cloth, and bright red berries of mistletoe dotted the scene. She'd backed the pillow with deep burgundy velvet.

The factor took the pillow and examined it. He brought it within two inches of his face, looking at the quality of the stitches and materials.

He fluffed the pillow, punched it a few times, and nodded to Seán. "Your wife's work?" He inclined his head at Esme, but didn't look at her or acknowledge her in any other way.

"It is. We live on the south end of the island. I'm away on trade, so she'd be coming up with more items, if you've an interest."

The man pursed his lips and nodded. "I am. Lady Carrick has a passion for such things. May I?" The factor, for so he must be, strode to the cart and rummaged through the baskets of completed items.

Within twenty minutes, he made a pile of his selections. "How much for this?"

Seán and the factor fell into a haggling session, and Esme followed the proceedings with avid interest. She'd suggested to Seán that she learn how to bargain, so she might do this on her own in the future.

Afterward, Esme traveled across the island every few months with a selection for Mr. Walsh. He wasn't friendly, but he paid a fair price. He never cheated Esme, though the last time, he bought fewer items. The factor explained that Lady Carrick spent less time at Carrick House now, and more time with her sister in England. The lord's son still had no wife, so business slacked off.

The stew boiled over, causing the peat log to hiss, which made Seán return to his task. He added turnips and grains to the stew, and the bit of bacon left from the last slaughter. Now to let it simmer for a while. He added a generous pinch of salt for a finishing touch. They had plenty of salt this close to the ocean. He wished he had a dab hand at herbs like Esme did, but his stew should at least put meat back on her bones.

When he checked on Esme, she slept again. He almost fell asleep himself, watching her breathe in and out, her chest rise and fall in rhythmic time. What if he'd lost her? He thought of his son, another young soul lost to heaven. As he held back a sob, Seán pulled the thought out and worried at it like a sore tooth.

What did he offer her, anyhow? He didn't have the knack of trade which came naturally to his father. He did well enough at first, but a series of poor decisions left them on the brink of poverty. This last trade mission left him in despair.

Last week, after several years of searching, he'd finally found his cousin, Tomás. They'd shared a long evening of ale and stories. Tomás said the village pushed him out of the *clachan* after an embarrassing incident with a fisherman. He wouldn't go into detail, but Seán guessed the cause. Tomás always had an eye for the ladies and precious little discretion. Still, he wished he'd known about it before he moved Esme there. Maybe they should move somewhere else? But she found a staunch friend in Aisling.

After the night of drunken camaraderie, Seán traded his last horse to Tomás for a wagonful of food, and they parted as friends. Tomás promised to come see them the next time he came near. Seán knew that wouldn't happen. Half of the goods had been rotten, and the rest only a few days off from it. Seán began to suspect the villagers had a point in their mistrust of Tinkers.

His wife brought in a steadier income than he did, despite him being the man of the family. And bringing a puppy seemed a puny gesture. He'd found it wandering alone on the side of the road, half-starved and bedraggled. Even poor, Seán wouldn't let the wee thing die alone.

Seán couldn't look at her any more. He loved her so much he thought his heart would burst, and he failed her. He shuffled outside instead and unloaded the meager contents of his wagon. Food and supplies, but not much of either. His stake had disappeared, except a few coins. The urge to disappear, to start all over and build his trade up before she knew how badly he'd failed, flashed through his mind. No, he couldn't do that to his Esme. That would be even more of a failure.

Seán finished his unloading. He'd nurse Esme back to strength. Perhaps, someday, they'd enjoy time together, without the constant need for work to keep mind, body, and soul together.

June 1797

Esme

On a glorious day in June, both families trundled down to the beach for a day of sun and fun. Aisling had Aoife in tow and Esme strapped her toddler, Katy, to her back. Cú Chulainn, the collie puppy, trotted along beside them, his tail wagging. They hadn't seen Seán in a month, but at least he'd left on good terms this time.

Seán had stayed for several weeks, and for the first time, her husband showed genuine tenderness and joy. They shared more than arguments, even spending some time together, walking along the shore.

Despite this idyll, the other villagers still snubbed them, and anonymous damage happened to their pens and garden. After so many years, they'd accepted Aisling. Her healing skills earned her a grudging respect. They even said hello as Aisling passed. Esme and her family remained unwanted strangers.

After a huge chunk of thatch ripped from the edge of their roof, Seán lost his temper. He stomped from cottage to cottage, demanding to know who did it. No one answered, only giving angry glares. Frustrated, he worked through a hailstorm to repair the damage, muttering curses under his breath and throwing his tools around.

With spring came new growth and a new spirit. Seán traveled with his meager stake, bolstered by Esme's efforts and creations. He built up a decent stock to trade again. He left as soon as the roads became passable, pulling his cart behind him. First, he needed to find a donkey or horse. Esme wished he could find Nuala, but she'd be too old now for such work. Besides, he wouldn't be able afford such a fine mare.

They all needed a rest on this brilliant day, so they traveled down to the shore. As the women and their daughters approached the beach, white sand reflecting bright sunlight almost blinded them. The wind blew strong, and they stayed out of the water, as the tide had a powerful pull. But the children played in the sand while the women relaxed in the warmth.

A few of the older boys played on the rocks off to one side, Donal Patten and Tony Molloy, with Tadhg Duggan, the priest's nephew. Esme waved to them, but they ignored her. When Aisling waved, they nodded.

Sandblasted by the wind, Esme stretched on a blanket just above the high water mark. She wanted to dig her toes into the cool sand. Aisling set up their meal of bread, fruit, and cheese.

Esme roused herself from a pleasant drowse when Aoife shrieked. The girl hopped around, shaking her leg, something dark wrapped around her ankle. Worried it might be dangerous, both mothers jumped got up to see what frightened the child.

"Get it off! Get it off!"

"Aoife, stop jumping about! Hold still, let me get it." Aisling brought a stick and poked at the eel-like creature. Cú Chulainn barked at it, leaping as if trying to dance with Aoife.

"Whassat, Ma?" Katy pointed at the thing while Aisling pried its mouth off from Aoife's twitching foot. Aoife sobbed, her face puffy and red.

"I don't know, dear. I think it's an eel."

"It's a lamprey, Katy. Come here, I'll show you the teeth."

"Teeth?" This got Katy's attention, and she scrambled over to watch the operation.

Esme shuddered. It sounded nasty, and she wanted no part of the creature. Aoife stopped crying and hiccupped. The eel left a round, red mark where it attached.

"See, it's got a ring of teeth all the way around."

"Ewww! Thas icky!"

"I quite agree, Katy. Come, let's build a sand castle. Aoife? Will you join us? Or do you want to stomp on more piles of seaweed?"

Aoife scampered away from the pile, giving it a resentful look and shaking her head.

Esme pointed to the discarded eel. "Aisling, can we eat that?"

"Sure and you can, but you must be careful and clean it well. It does well boiled in a seaweed stew, nice and salty."

Dried fish might be the only meat left after a long winter. She'd try it, at any rate. Esme scooped up the offending eel and dangled it in front of Aoife. Cú Chulainn jumped for it, wanting to be part of the game. A satisfying squeal and a deep chuckle rewarded Esme's efforts. The child still fell sick much more than most children and never seemed to gain weight. She might blow away with the next strong wind.

Just as she thought it, a gust of wind threw a blast of sand and grit into Esme's eyes. She spluttered and spat, trying to get the gritty stuff out of her mouth. She groped for a cloth to wipe them, and Aisling handed her one, laughing.

That night, when she tasted her eel stew, she decided she liked the flavor. It didn't taste fishy, but oily. She should comb the beaches for more. The fishermen didn't bring them in. They considered eels to be bad luck and tossed them back.

Esme placed her hand on her stomach, which fluttered. Three months ago, she missed her courses. She hadn't mentioned it, afraid it would hex her baby. A tiny tickle, like eels wriggling in her stomach. Would this one be a boy? A young son to help Seán trading, someone to pass on the knowledge to. A brother to protect his older sister.

When Seán returns, I'll tell him the good news. We can celebrate with a night alone. Aisling would take Katy. It had been months since they'd shared an intimate evening. While she carried a child, Seán worked hard to be considerate.

Would it stop him now? The thought distressed her. She wanted to enjoy her husband, but would it endanger the child inside? But plenty of women had relations while pregnant. She wanted happiness, for herself and her husband.

Esme ran out of blue embroidery thread with no way to get more until Seán returned. She cursed her lack of foresight and switched projects. The collar she worked on would be uneven with a different color. She might pick it out and do the entire project in another color, but she didn't want to waste all that work. She'd have to finish it another time. What to work on next?

With a critical eye on the loom, she decided she didn't want to weave now. The day still held plenty of light and she wanted to put it to good use. She should work on the large piece.

Esme uncovered the wooden frame in one corner of the room. The tapestry had a unicorn in the center. She'd seen the drawing in her hedge teacher's book, many years ago. Mostly black, stylized trees and flowers stood around a low wooden fence. Inside sat the unicorn. As a child, the piece had enchanted her and she strove to recreate it from memory. She'd blocked out the design in charcoal and sewn the unicorn portion first. Esme ran out of black embroidery thread and given up on the job until she bore Katy.

After removing the fabric wrapped around it, Esme stared at the sweet unicorn's face, gazing at her with magical eyes.

"Ma? Whassat?"

"It's a unicorn, sweetling. See? Like a horse, but with a long horn on his forehead."

Katy tried to touch the tapestry, but Esme lifted it out of reach. Biscuit crumbs still covered her daughter's hands, along with bits of drool. She didn't want that all over this precious creation. After Eithne smeared the ashes all over it, cleaning took months of painstaking work. Esme didn't want to go through all that again.

Such a spiteful act, and typical Eithne, to ruin something beautiful. Esme stowed it away again. Best not try until Katy grew old enough to know better. Besides, she had no inspiration to work on anything, as if sewing lost all luster and excitement after remembering her sister.

Instead, Esme picked up her loom. She had plenty of red thread to finish the work. She'd just set the shuttle when a jangle of metal and the whinny of a horse came from outside, setting Cú Chulainn off. She froze. Had Seán come home already?

She stashed the shuttle into the loom and picked up her daughter. After opening the door, she saw the cart, but no Seán. His new horse, Donas, a great black brute who kept trying to bite her, stood on the grass. Where did her husband go?

A loud crash from behind caused her to whirl. Seán flung open the back door and dropped a bucket on the ground. Apples rolled from the bucket, scattering all over the winter cottage. His eyes flashed dark and darting, his long hair unbound and matted. He looked unshaven and his clothing grimy. His sour scent filled the cottage as if he hadn't washed for weeks.

As she held tight to her squirming daughter, she asked, "What are you about, Seán?"

His eyes darted around the cabin, searching. "Where is he?"

Esme blinked several times. "Where is who? What are you talking about?"

"Don't fool with me, Esme. I heard about it all the way down in Achill Sound." He advanced on her, none too steady on his feet. He must be drunk.

She placed Katy on the ground behind her, shielding her daughter into a corner. Cú Chulainn crouched and growled, sensing the tension. "Heard about what? I've done nothing!"

"Heard about you off with some fisherman in Mweewillin, that's what. They say you're over there every week and sometimes overnight!"

She laughed at him, loud and startling in the tense room. "That's not me, you great fool! That's Aisling. She found a young man, Padraig, and she's been with him. I predict they'll marry before another month's gone."

He stared as if unwilling to believe her.

Esme let out a deep sigh. "It's true, Seán. Haven't you gotten this through your thick skull? I'd never take another man over you. You must believe me."

She wished he saw the truth as clearly as she could. Much good it had ever done her, but at least he'd know she didn't lie.

Suspicions flickered across his face in a parade of mistrust. "Aye, well, maybe that's true…"

"It *is* true, Seán, believe me. Besides, I wouldn't risk losing another baby with too much activity of that sort." She wanted to hold the news back longer, but she needed something to defuse the situation with hope.

"Activity? Another baby? You're with child?" His eyes widened, and he looked both scared and proud now. His face no longer reminded her of a sinister pirate on a rampage.

"I am, and I'll thank you for not scaring me to death with pointless theatrics, if you please." With the danger past, she could afford flippancy.

"Ah, Esme, my dear darling." He walked toward her but stepped on an apple. He windmilled his arms, trying to keep balance, but fell straight toward her. Esme tried to scoot out of the way and catch him at the same time. She failed in both efforts. He collapsed on top of her. She screamed in pain, and Cú Chulainn barked his head off as they both tumbled to the dirt floor. Her hips and backside ached. Her eyes darted around for Katy, but the child had scooted to safety.

Despite his drunkenness, Seán scrambled to his feet. "Esme! Are you okay? Here, I'll help you to the bed."

Esme struggled to rise, slapping his hands away. She pushed Cú Chulainn's nose away as well, as the dog tried to help. "I can walk on my own, you great blundering eejit. Haven't I handled myself whenever you leave? I'm no baby to be coddled."

She hobbled to the bed. Esme had to lay on her side, but the pain lingered. The ache stabbed deep into her lower back.

When it moved to her middle, she whimpered and clutched at her stomach. "Go get Aisling, Seán."

Seán

After banishing Seán, Aisling spent a long time in the cottage with Esme. He paced outside, wearing a path in the thin grass. Every sound made him glance up, hopeful for good news.

When she emerged, she spoke to him in a firm tone. "She'll be fine, and the babe's fine, as far as I can tell. However, she must rest. That means no fighting, no worries, no working, and no cooking. You must take care of her as if she broke both her legs. If she tries to get up and work, you need to stop her. Can you do that?"

Seán nodded, his fears for Esme keeping his voice silent.

The other woman eyed him, skepticism plain on her face. "Well, you do your best. And no more drink. You must stop until the bairn arrives, for Esme's sake. I'll check in on her every day. If she bleeds at all, come get me at once, understood?"

Another nod.

"Then get inside there yourself and give her a welcome hug. And stop with the mistrust! She told me what you accused her of. As if she would ever have eyes for any but you." She clicked her tongue as he scuttled into the cottage.

He did well enough at the home tasks, at first. Seán's restless nature made him want to move, and frustration at staying in one place made him prickly. But while they got into arguments, Katy and Cú Chulainn offered comic relief. Their antics broke the tension and allowed them to back down with grace.

Sometimes he'd compare things they did with his own tales. These became stories Katy asked to hear over and over again. She loved "The Day Nuala Raced Across the Bridge Without Da in the Wagon," almost as much as "The First Time Da Saw a Bull," or "When Da Met Ma," her favorite.

Aisling and Seán formed a cautious friendship from the shared need to care for Esme as she rested. He told her tales of his travels and trades, while she reminisced about her late husband, comparing Cormac to her new suitor.

"Cormac, now, he was a smart man. He could read, you know. He loved his books. Almost as much as he loved being on the ocean."

Seán sipped his tea and nodded. "A traveler of the sea, rather than the land. I can appreciate the draw."

"Sometimes he seemed too smart to marry the likes of me. He and Esme would talk for hours about things, and I didn't understand a word of it. But he loved me well, and I miss him."

Seán shoved down the erupting surge of jealousy, ugly and green in his mind. If Aisling didn't worry about it, he shouldn't.

"Ah, now, Padraig, he's not what I'd call smart. And he pouts like a hurt puppy when I need to go healing. But he dotes on me."

"Is that enough, then? To take care of you?"

"Aye, it's enough. To be treasured, that's a rare thing indeed. And one any woman craves."

Seán glanced toward Esme, sleeping in their bed. He vowed to make his wife feel treasured. For he did treasure her above all else.

They spent most of the summer in this routine. Seán ached to get back onto the road. He kept eyeing the cart and the horse. Esme caught him loading up the cart a few times, as if getting ready for a run, but when he noticed her standing there, he removed the items with a sheepish look, and brought her a book or her needlework to change the subject.

They told stories in the long summer evenings. Seán met a Scotsman on his last trip and regaled Esme with tales of the *Cailleach*, the hag of the winter and of kelpies, a water horse. Esme's father used to tell stories of selkies, a seal who shed her skin and walked like a human.

A selkie made an excellent wife, so the stories said. If her husband hid her sealskin, she wouldn't change into her seal form. She'd go out on his boat with him and he'd bring back full nets. She'd give him fine babes. But if she found her skin, she returned to the sea, abandoning any children she had.

Kelpies lured men to their deaths by appearing as a comely mare. If a man tried to ride her, she'd take him into the water and drown him, feeding upon his flesh.

Esme raised her eyebrows. "Perhaps the Scottish lakes are more dangerous than our seas?"

Seán shrugged and gave her a sly smile. "That would be the difference, aye. Or their horses are more fractious than our women are."

"Donas must be a Scottish horse, then." Their shared laughter felt good. Almost like when they'd first met, young and in love.

Since the evening sky stayed clear and the weather warm, they ate stew in front of the cottage, watching the dusk rise from the sea. Esme taught him seasoning tricks, so his stew tasted better than barely edible.

Aisling made them rye bread to sop up the juices. Katy curled up in Seán's lap, fast asleep. Cú Chulainn slept on Esme's feet.

What life could be better than this? Seán felt content for the first time in years.

Esme

Seán cleared his throat once, then again.

"What's wrong with you, Seán? Are you choking on your stew, or do you have a frog in your throat?"

He swallowed, his jaw clenching. "I have a gift for you, Esme."

With raised eyebrows, she put her hands on her hips, skeptical of his gift. "A gift for me? For what, pray tell?"

"Your birthday, of course."

Startled, she counted the days. She hadn't even remembered. Twenty-three years old. How had she gotten so old?

Seán fumbled in his pocket and presented to her a small package.

She stared at it. "What is it, Seán?"

He placed it in her hands. "Open it and find out."

Esme untied the twine and unwrapped the dark linen. She kept unwrapping it until she came to a velvet bag. With a glance at Seán, she poured its contents into her hand. A silver triskele knot pendant on a fine silver chain lay in a puddle in her palm.

Tears burned behind her eyes, but she blinked them back. "Seán, It's lovely!"

"As are you, *mo ghrá*, as are you."

She glanced down to the pendant, unable to move. "But how can we afford this?"

Seán plucked it out of her palm, affixing it around her neck. He held her shoulders and smiled. "Ah, that sparkles and shines like your eyes. It suits you."

"But Seán, this is such an extravagance. Didn't you have more practical things to buy?"

"And what's more practical than making my wife weep with joy?"

They spent the rest of the balmy night in bed, trying not to wake Katy or the dog.

July 1797

Esme didn't have the strength to deal with another quarrel. She sat next to the fire with her eyes closed while Seán huffed and puffed, speaking of every slight issue and blowing it up out of all proportion.

This time, he objected to her closeness to Aisling.

Esme snapped, tired of his harping. "And who do you think takes care of me while you're traveling across God's green earth? She's there for me, when you aren't, Seán. There's nothing wrong with that."

"Aye and I'm grateful enough, but when I'm here, you should be with *me*. I'm your husband!"

She shut her eyes and prayed for patience. "Seán, please, I don't want to argue about this. I know you're restless. We don't need more supplies, but if you want to go out, go! Having you about is like… like having a resentful puppy at my feet."

"A resentful puppy, am I? I work hard to feed you, clean the house, take care of our poor Katy, and feed the animals, while you lounge around and call me a puppy?"

She clutched at the arms of her chair, digging her fingers into the wood. "And what do you think I do while you're away? I do all that and more, and you don't hear *me* complaining. You're a fine, strong man. You should be able to shoulder such responsibilities with grace and ease."

Seán let out a humorless laugh. "Grace and ease? Like you falling down this morning?"

"I tripped over Katy's doll, which you should have picked up."

"Me? Why can't Katy pick it up? It's hers!"

Esme rolled her eyes. "Katy's four years old. She's still learning. You are a full-grown adult and should be able to keep up with a toddler when she… Oh!"

The familiar deep ache had returned. Esme willed it to go away. *Not now. Not now!*

"When she what?"

Cú Chulainn growled as she spoke in a soft voice. "Seán, get Aisling, will you?"

Her husband's eyes grew wide. "Are you… wait here."

As if I would go walking like this. They didn't permit her out her door, though she had no wish to wander. The ache stabbed sharp and then turned into a dull pain.

By the time Aisling arrived, blood stained her skirt. Katy sobbed, which upset the dog, and Seán's gaze shifted back and forth, helpless.

Aisling shooed them all out the door. "Go take Katy and repair the pigpen. Leave us be."

Seán took his daughter's hand and left, with Aoife following.

Katy asked him a question and his deep voice responded, but she couldn't make out the words. "Is it happening again, Aisling? So soon?"

"I'm afraid so, Esme. You might get lucky and keep it, but given your history, you shouldn't hold on to much hope."

Esme tried hard not to blame Seán for this. If he hadn't fallen on her weeks before or left the toy for her to trip on… foolish thoughts. Both things had been accidents and nothing done on purpose. Still, she might have been fine if he hadn't returned. She got so lonely when he left, but when he came back, he seemed out of place, a stranger.

Esme couldn't see the other side of the long night. The pain gripped her with intensity, more than the last time. Not more than childbirth, not the physical pain. The emotional pain, that grew past endurance.

As a girl, Esme dreamed of a large family. Children running around at her feet, screaming and playing around a big farm. She pined at the idea, knowing now she'd never achieve it. At least she had Katy.

Thoughts of Katy didn't rescue her from the incredible loss. She stared at a black hole through the red haze of pain, blurred by tears.

Seán

For days, Esme barely moved. She didn't speak or look at Seán at all. She'd accept food from Aisling or Aoife. All day, she stared at the rough stone wall of her cottage. Sometimes, she allowed Cú Chulainn to curl up next to her on the bed.

Seán mourned his old wife. She'd been so vibrant and alive when he met her, such a bright force in his world. But he had to watch helplessly as she faded into a shell of her former self.

Aisling told him Esme didn't sleep all day. *At least she got rest.* He stayed out of the way and spent the evenings in Aisling's cottage, with the girls. Aisling joined them after she fed Esme and they enjoyed an odd sort of camaraderie, these people who all cared for Esme.

He clenched and unclenched his fists several times before he built the courage to ask. "Will she recover, do you think?" He'd put it off night after night, but he must know. Anything he might grasp onto for hope.

"I truly don't know, Seán. She might. She's young and healthy. But she may not want to."

He furrowed his brow. "Not want to? She has a daughter to care for. She can't just, what, let herself die?"

"If she's determined, she might. She's eating, though, so I don't think that's the case."

He took the encouragement and grabbed it, keeping it deep within his soul as a salve. "What can I do to help?"

"What you're doing. Staying out of the way. She's angry at you, perhaps blaming you for her losing the baby."

"Me? But it wasn't my fault!"

Aisling said nothing but rose to sweep the ashes from the hearth.

He had fallen on her, and he wasn't a small man. *A big, lumbering brute, you are. No business with a delicate blossom like Esme.* He *had* left the doll on the ground. He saw it and ignored it. How would he know it would rob him of his child? Perhaps even rob him of his wife.

If he needed to stay out of the way, he'd do so.

The next morning, he harnessed Donas to the cart, packed the items Esme made since the last trip, and headed toward Achill Sound. Cú Chulainn climbed into the wagon with him, but he placed the dog back into the cottage. Esme needed the hound more than he did. He'd make a trip out to Leenane or even Louisburg and bring back a lovely gift for his lovely wife. By the time he returned, she'd welcome him into her arms once again.

The mists swallowed him as he rode down the hillside.

Chapter Fifteen

August 1797

Esme

Esme hadn't seen him in two days and finally unfroze enough to ask Aisling about Seán.

At first, Aisling just shook her head, but Esme kept asking. Finally, she threw her hands up in frustration. "I don't know where he went, Esme, he just left one morning. From the things he took, I'd say he left on a trade trip. Besides, it's not like you'd been speaking to him."

I can't even keep my husband by me when I'm ill. Her life had turned into a disaster. Her dreams became tiny, broken shards, a shattered mosaic which she'd never piece back together.

Esme felt a sudden, desperate need to hold her daughter. "Where's Katy?"

"She's down with Aoife, weeding. Aoife is good at that, now, and she's teaching Katy."

And everyone else can take care of my daughter. What good am I, then?

Esme turned her face back to the wall, willing Aisling to leave. The dog whimpered and whined until Esme let him up on the bed. His warm body comforted her. She slept, holding the dog as a substitute for her lost child. A boy with raven-black hair like his father, waving to her from the water. She ran along the beach, trying to reach him, but sand bogged her down. She tossed and turned, moaning in her sleep until she finally woke, less rested than before.

Aisling did her best to make the household cheerful, despite Esme's black moods. She built a fire and set a pie to bake. With a glance to Esme in bed, she turned to the two girls. "Aoife, which story do you want? What's your favorite?"

"The swans, Ma, tell about the swans."

"The Children of Lír, is it, then? I can do that. Have I told you this one before, Katy?"

Esme turned to look as the toddler shook her head, mute. After her dream, the last thing she wanted to hear was a story about children being cursed into the sea. Her voice sounded hoarse, even to her ears. "I've told it, sweetling, but you may have been too young to remember."

At her mother's voice, Katy ran and curled up on the bed, head on her mother's shoulder. Esme closed her eyes, comforted by her daughter's warmth and love.

Aisling pursed her lips and leaned back in the rocking chair. "Once there lived King of the *Tuatha Dé Danann* named *Bodb Derg.* He was a great king with two daughters. He had a rival, though, named *Lír.* Lír grew angry after he lost a battle, so Bodb gave him one of his daughters, the beautiful *Aoibh,* to be his wife. Aoibh bore Lír four beautiful children named *Fionnuala, Aodh,* and the twins, *Fiachra* and *Conn.*

"After several years, his lovely wife died. Both Lír and his children mourned their mother day and night, for they loved her dearly. Lír needed a new wife, to keep his home and raise his children. To keep them happy, Bodb sent his other daughter, Aoife, to marry Lír."

Aoife piped up, her eyes shining. "That's me!"

Esme beamed at the child's excitement despite herself. Aisling grinned at her daughter. "That's right, dear, it's your name, as well. This Aoife wasn't as nice as you, though. She grew jealous. Jealous of the love Lír had for his children, and jealous of the love they had for each other. She paid a servant to kill them, but the servant refused her command. She tried to kill them herself, but couldn't go through with it. But then she used magic."

Aisling paused to let the drama of the last statement build. Cú Chulainn wriggled down to lick Katy's face when she stopped talking, eliciting a giggle from everyone.

"Aoife used her magic to enchant the children into swans. When their grandfather, King Bodb, learned of this treachery, he cursed Aoife, turning her into an air demon, to ride the winds and never touch the earth again for all eternity.

"However, once Aoife became an air demon, she couldn't cancel her spell, forcing the children to remain swans. They lived for three hundred years on the waters of Lough Derravaragh. Next, they lived for three hundred years on the Sea of Moyle, fighting the tides and storms every day. They spent another three hundred years on the waters of *Irrus Domnann.*

"In order to return to their proper forms, the spell said they'd need to be blessed by a monk when a church bell tolled. Once they completed their transformation, Saint Patrick himself converted them to Christianity."

Aoife knew the story but asked anyhow, her eyes shining with excitement. "What happened then?"

"By now, they'd lived for nine hundred years. Once they'd broken the enchantment, they withered and died, poof! They turned to dust on the spot."

Katy's eyes grew wide. Her mouth turned into a tiny circle, and she let out a squeal. Esme hugged her and she snuggled back into her mother's embrace. "It's not a happy ending, is it, Ma?"

"No, darling, it isn't. The Irish aren't one for the happy endings. We do love our misery, so we do. It keeps us strong."

"Am I strong, Ma?"

"You are indeed, my dear. We all are strong women and nothing can bring us down." Cú Chulainn made sure they knew he was strong as well and nosed his way into Esme's lap.

Aisling glanced into the bedroom, her eyes glittering in the firelight. She locked gazes with Esme, and then the latter stared at the floor.

Seán

As much as Seán loved being on the road, the thrill of the trade, the need to be free, Seán thought long and hard about Esme's needs. He concluded he might survive living most of his time at home if he set up a permanent trading post in the village. At first, he'd need to spread the word along his routes, but folks might travel out to Achill. *It'll make Esme so much happier.* He'd also stop with the drink. Esme deserved a sweet husband, not an angry one.

If it didn't work, they'd find another place to live. With Tomás gone, nothing held them there except Esme's friendship with Aisling. They might convince Aisling to come with them. She stayed a staunch friend to his wife and took care of her when Seán didn't.

The fair in Louisburgh held over fifty vendors. As Seán pulled up in his cart, he kept a tight rein on Donas to keep him from spooking. The strong odors swept over him. The stench of people, animals, waste, and rot hit Seán without mercy, but tantalizing odors of fresh-baked meat pies and roasting pork made it better.

He stabled his horse and unhooked his cart, paying the stable lad a coin. After striding into the marketplace, he took a survey of everything on offer.

The first stall sold woolen goods, rough pieces with no sophistication. Nothing like Esme made. He touched one plaid and stroked the rough texture. A rough weave worked if done well, but this weave felt crude and bumpy. He moved on.

Glassblowers filled the next stall, sturdy shelves with colorful wares sparkling in the late afternoon sun. Dust motes floated and added to the sparkle, like faery dust sprinkled everything. Seán grunted and looked to the next space.

Ah, delicious meat pies. His mouth watered as he fumbled in his pouch to pull out a coin. When he bit into the warm pastry, meat juices dribbled down his chin, but he mopped them up and licked his fingers, not wanting to waste the savory treat. Crumbs of pastry fell on his shirt, so he wetted a finger to catch them as he walked.

When he looked up, he bumped into a towering, burly man, twice Seán's weight, who glared at him. A horrible stench rose from his clothes, the acrid odor of pig shit. The man looked familiar, but he couldn't put his finger on it.

Seán mumbled an apology and tried to move around the man, but the crowd didn't give him any chance to do so.

The man clamped a hamfist hand on his shoulder. "'Ere, now, you ought be more careful, you should."

The smaller man nodded and tried to duck past.

The other man didn't release him. "This is no place to be knockin' folk about, now, is it?"

Seán's shoulder already ached. "I agree, sir, I'm that sorry. If you'd excuse me?" He tried to extricate himself and duck under the man's arm, but the grip remained tight. Seán only had a few coins in his pouch. He'd sewn the rest into the lining of an inside pocket. Did the man want a fight, rather than money?

"I don't take kindly to folk bumping into me in my own market."

Now Seán remembered the smell. The man who tried to convince him to come to the Louisburgh market instead of Westport, so long ago. "Your market, is it? A fine market, too. I'm headed to that stall down there." Seán pointed to a stall behind the man, hoping he'd turn.

The other man didn't comply. "I think you need a lesson."

Seán cocked his head, trying to seem affable. "Ah, the wise man can always learn more, I say. What sort of lesson would you have in mind?" He might still talk himself out of this fight.

"A heavy one." Something pounded him on the back of his head. The world spun and went dark.

When he roused, someone carried Seán into an alleyway behind the meat pie stall. Deserted and quiet. He tried to move, but his body wouldn't obey him. They relieved him of his pouch and his shoes.

They searched other parts of his pockets when he groaned. "What... what happened?"

"None of your business!" The big man hit Seán on the head again, and it cracked into the brick corner of the building. A sickening pain flashed through his head and down his spine.

Chapter Sixteen

March 1798

Eithne

Eithne's children grew, the farm prospered, and her power increased. She didn't hold as many soirées as she used to. When she invited guests over, she preferred young, attractive noblemen, with the occasional artist or wealthy businessman thrown in for flavor.

Eithne kept the brooch close. She visited the stone circle often, delighting in the surge of power and joy that coursed through her. Even when she didn't come to the stones, it pulsed in her very blood, an almost sexual ecstasy. However, it faded when the link with her twin sparked. Esme used the power herself, even without the blasted brooch. Eithne must sever the link, but she had yet to find someone to corrupt her sister into uselessness.

The power grew more intense if her own passion peaked at the stones. Sometimes Eithne brought her foreman lover, but he grew afraid of the place, muttering about the Good Folk and their curses. No matter. She'd continue to use the place. It had brought her everything she wanted. She had other lovers, less given to fear.

She didn't wish to confront Esme again. The last visit had been terrible, like Esme had delved into her soul and rifled around, discovering her innermost secrets. Eithne shivered at the memory. A horrible sensation, and one she'd never repeat. Somehow, she'd repay her sister for that violation.

The guests for the afternoon's event began to arrive. As she glanced around the bright ballroom, she made sure the chandelier gleamed and the butler had decanted the brandy. New painted wallpaper in robin's egg blue and white filigree covered the walls. Much better than that dark, dank Scottish plaid Hugh had used.

Today's guest list included an actor from Dublin, a businessman from Liverpool, and a young lord from County Mayo. The latter lived in

London for many years but just returned home via relatives in Derry. She hadn't met him yet, but looked forward to his arrival. Rumor had him quite handsome.

Eithne sipped her brandy as she waited for the first guests. Her businessman arrived first. Once her butler brought him into the drawing room, she gave him a curtsey, putting out her hand for a kiss. "Mr. Wyatt, so pleased to see you. Did you have a pleasant journey today?"

He bowed over her hand as he held it, brushing her knuckles with his lips. "Quite sunny, I'm glad to say. Much better than the voyage across the Irish Sea. It's as if every tempest in the world had gathered for a party!"

She simpered at the older man, knowing him to be a landlubber. For all that he made his wealth from slave traders, he couldn't handle a sea voyage.

Her butler arrived with a message that her actor wouldn't make it. Such a pity. If her lord proved to be ill-favored, Mr. Wyatt would be a poor third choice. Eithne only included him on the invitation for the modicum of respectability the older man offered her party. She took another sip of her brandy and turned as the door opened.

Lord Carrick Sweeney stood tall, with blond hair and hazel eyes. Eithne quite forgot about Mr. Wyatt.

She adored men with blond hair, and he'd tied his back in a pale blue ribbon, matching her new wallpaper. His dazzling smile promised she'd be having a lovely evening, after all. "Lord Carrick, do please join us. Would you care for some brandy?"

Her footman poured a glass and Sweeney smiled, lifting her hand for a kiss. "You are utterly charming, Mistress O'Hagerty. I'm off to my estate tomorrow, and it would have devastated me to miss your company."

Wyatt lifted his own glass. "And where do you call home, Sweeney?"

"I've lived in London for ten years, but my parents own a country estate on Achill Island, in County Mayo. It's in the middle of nowhere, and I despair of any local society, but my father needs me. He's quite failing in health." He rolled his eyes and shrugged, taking a canape from the passing footman. After he took a bite, he raised his eyebrows and nodded at Eithne. "Delicious."

Hope and a plan burst in Eithne's heart. Her voice took on an over-sweet tone. "Achill Island? Why, my twin sister lives there!"

Sweeney raised his eyebrows. "Does she indeed? And is she as stunning as you?"

The afternoon dragged on for much too long. When Eithne finally convinced Wyatt to leave, she turned to Sweeney. "And must you run off as well? Or could you tarry for some conversation?"

He gave her an admiring look and a knowing half-smile. "I'm sure you can persuade me to linger, my dear."

Esme

As they took advantage of the balmy April afternoon, Esme slapped the wet dress against the rock with vigor, getting her frustration out on the laundry. "It's been five years. You'd think the other villagers would at least say hello to me once in a while."

"They nod. They acknowledge your existence, don't they?" Aisling washed both girl's clothing. She grabbed a dress from the pile, clucking her tongue at the long rip in the skirt. "I'll have to repair this again. Aoife's more boy than girl. She falls into every patch of bracken on the island, I swear."

"You don't keep her busy enough. She has too much time on her hands. One of these days, she'll take a tumble off one of those rocks she climbs, with none around to help her." Esme slapped the dress again, taking satisfaction in the wet smack as it hit the rock.

"Katy follows her around like a puppy, closer than a shadow."

Esme wrinkled her nose. "I caught her climbing the stone wall up the hill the other day. I can't keep her from climbing, following Aoife all the time."

"They'll both be fine, I'm sure. Their clothes, I'm not so certain about."

Esme looked at the next dress in Aisling's pile. She pointed to a huge, dark-brown stain on the bib of Aoife's apron. "What on earth caused that?"

Aisling laughed. "Oh, this? It's just blood."

Esme stopped her wringing. "Blood? What in God's sweet name happened to Aoife?"

"No, not Aoife's blood. Mistress Swain's. The old biddy who moved in with Mistress Lynch."

Sure, they accepted that newcomer right away. The new woman acted as barmy as Mistress Lynch did. They deserved each other. They still treated Esme like a stranger and snubbed Katy. "Did she die? I hope so."

Aisling made the sign of the cross and her eyes darted around, searching for anyone who might have overhead the remark. "Esme Fitzgerald, you take that back!"

"Oh, fine, I take it back. I hope she's grand." Esme smacked the rock extra hard, speaking with poor grace.

"She just cut her forehead when she walked into the cottage. She forgot to duck." Aisling tried hard not to giggle, but it came out in a snort. Esme's lips twisted to keep her own in, but soon they burst out laughing.

As short as Esme stood, she never had to duck. But for most others in the *booley*, one learned about the low doorways. The roof peak gave headroom in the middle, but the edges, with walls and doors, stood five feet tall. Mistress Swain stood at least five foot four.

After they recovered from their mental images of the tall woman smacking her head on the doorframe, they sighed and picked up their next piece of washing. "Where are the girls, anyhow? We could use the help today."

Even without Seán home, the girls burned through an enormous amount of washing each week. He'd gone away longer than normal, a full seven months. Esme pursed her lips, half-expecting him to arrive as if nothing had happened. As the days passed, the possibility seemed more remote.

Aisling moved back to her own cottage with Padraig. They'd gotten married several months past, and she expected a baby. Padraig strutted around, proud as a mother hen with her first egg. He may not have the cunning wit Cormac had, but he loved his new wife. He didn't have many stories or conversation, but Aisling could depend on his sweet mood and reliable work.

Esme missed the warm companionship Seán offered when home, despite their fights.

"Now, why are you sighing? The laundry won't get dry with your breath. You must hang it up like this."

Esme threw a wet cloth at Aisling, but her friend ducked and laughed, now splattered with soapy water. "I'm sighing because, well, I miss the stories. You remember the ones Seán used to tell? And Cormac? My father and grandfa used to tell stories and sing songs. I just miss them." She missed all of them.

Aisling wrung out the last of Aoife's dresses and hung it up on the clothes line. "Well, I've a surprise for you, then."

"What surprise?"

"If I told you, it wouldn't be a surprise, now, would it?"

Esme narrowed her eyes, but finished her own task. They dumped the dirty water into the creek below the line of cottages and watched it trickle down along the burn. Swirls of white soap bubbles danced along the surface until they sunk and disappeared.

Aisling grabbed Esme's arm. "C'mon, we must get ready."

Esme refused to budge. "For what?"

"For the surprise, of course, silly. Get a move on, girl!"

Aisling led Esme stumbling back to her cottage and rifled through her clothing. She held up a deep-brown dress, studied Esme, and shook her head. "No, no, this one won't do. Have you nothing bright and pretty?"

Esme crossed her arms. "Not until you tell me why we're getting dressed up." She might push Aisling for the answer, but didn't want to wind up passing out for the evening from exhaustion. Besides, she didn't use the brooch's power much anymore. It hurt too much to fight Eithne's grip on it.

A slow smile came across Aisling's face, and she returned to Esme's dresses. "Ah, now this one's lovely! It's an intense blue. Have you ever even worn it? I've never seen it on you. And such lovely green flowers on the collar!"

Esme yanked it from Aisling's hand, remembering how Seán always loved her in blue. "That one isn't mine. It's a piece I made to sell."

"Well, you can keep it and wear it tonight, can't you? It suits you well." She held the dress up to Esme's neck for inspection. "Yes, it will do. Put it on." She tossed the dress to Esme and moved to the drawer where Esme kept her jewelry.

Esme changed into the dress. It hung a little long, but not so much she tripped.

Aisling pulled out the silver chain, with the silver triskele. "How about this? The silver would contrast well on the green and the neckline's right for it."

Esme's good mood disappeared. "Seán gave that to me."

Giving her friend a sad look, Aisling sighed. "How long has he been gone, Esme? Do you really expect him back after all this time?"

She didn't want to answer that, so she stayed silent.

Aisling ignored her and put the necklace on Esme. "Yes, that will work. Now, to your hair."

Esme placed a hand on her locks, wild with the heat of the laundry water. Usually, she pulled it back into a harsh bun, or washed it fresh and hope for the best. Aisling grabbed a brush and pushed her down onto the stool.

"Aisling, what are you doing? Ow! Stop pulling!"

"It will pull. Sit still. I'm doing up your hair. You want to look nice for the surprise."

After much yanking and cursing, Aisling tamed Esme's hair into a decorative bonnet. She stood back, cocking her head to survey her efforts. She pulled a few strands loose from the bonnet, so they framed Esme's face with red curls. With a nod of approval, she grabbed her shawl. The afternoon chilled with an ocean breeze.

"I'll be back in about twenty minutes, then we'll go, aye? Eat something first. You might not get a chance later."

While munching on a handful of early strawberries, Esme couldn't imagine why she'd need to get dressed up. Few people held fêtes or parties in this remote outpost of civilization. There hadn't been a gathering at the *síbín* since the owner died last year. What could be going on?

Esme studied her hands, still reddened by the lye soap. She rubbed them, but they showed only a few wrinkles. At age twenty-four, she'd aged well. Age reminded her of Katy. Where'd she gotten to? She stood at the window, spying Aisling with Aoife and Katy, entering her own cottage, Cú Chulainn trotting behind. The dog followed them both like, well, like a lovesick puppy.

When Aisling returned, she'd braided her own reddish-blond hair into a long braid with a green ribbon. Her dress, a light spring green, lacked the fine embroidery on Esme's. Her face glowed with fresh scrubbing and a secret smile.

Esme glanced behind Aisling. "Isn't Padraig going?"

"No, he's not back yet. Aoife will watch Katy, never fear. Come, let's step lively. The surprise is down in the village."

The two women picked their way down the worn mountain path from the summer *booley* to the few buildings along the dock. The church stood next to the dock building, which always reeked of fish guts. The building next to it, the *sibín*, had been dark and crumbling the last time Esme visited.

It had transformed in the last few weeks, painted bright yellow and filled with people. She stopped dead in her tracks.

"Come on, no need to be afraid. You said you wanted stories and singing, did you not? Well, this is where we get them!"

Dusk rose on the seaside buildings, while the warm glow of a peat fire beckoned. Many folks from the surrounding villages sat inside. Mistress Lynch sat with Mistress Swain on the barrels along one wall, giggling. Mr. Pike and Mr. Cooney, both older fishermen, chatted out front. All four stopped and stared at Aisling and Esme.

Esme balked, but Aisling grabbed her hand and dragged her through the doorway while the four older residents stared. Esme wanted to glare at them, stick out her tongue to make them acknowledge her as a resident, but she walked by with her eyes straight ahead.

Aisling prodded her in the side with her elbow. "It might help if you said hello to *them*, once in a while."

"I used to, when I first moved here. I grew tired of the icy glares and silent faces. They still think I pushed the old bat down the mountain." Her voice sounded full of bitterness. When had she grown so cynical?

"Ah, look, there's Donal Patten, tuning his fiddle. We'll have music, then." The tall, lanky Donal sat with two men from another village. She'd seen them before, but didn't remember their names. Donal pulled his bow across the strings and fussed with his tuning knobs. The little McCann girl sat next to him, looking up at Donal with lovesick eyes. They'd be a match soon if he could stand her simpering.

Aisling found a place to sit on a low bench. "So, this is why we got dressed up? Who are we trying to impress, so?"

"You'll see, I'm sure."

After rolling her eyes, Esme concentrated on the folks gathered. The Ginleys ignored each other as usual. They'd sit together, but never speak.

Tony Molloy arrived, with his *bodhran* in hand, and sat beside Donal. He met Esme's eyes, but she dropped hers, embarrassed at staring. A blur of dark, straight hair caught her eye and she steadied her gaze. Seán? Could it be? No, another man from a nearby village.

Tony had a lovely voice. Weak in the chin, but he stood tall and sturdy. Younger than Esme, but not attached either. She risked a glance up again, but he peered off to his left at a shuffle in the doorway.

She glanced in that direction, too. Tadhg Duggan arrived, drunk already and belligerent. He had a reputation for being nasty when he drank, and everyone gave him plenty of elbow room. However, the tiny building offered little space for such antics. He crashed into Eileen McCann, then almost landed on Donal's fiddle. Donal snatched up his precious instrument just in time before Tadhg landed on the hearthstones with a grunt. After a moment of stunned silence, Tadhg's snores filled the room. Nervous laughter scattered across them.

Still laughing, the men at the hearth carried the drunk outside and washed him up. When they returned, they began the first tune.

The strains of Drowsy Maggie jangled at first, but the boys soon learned to stay in tune together. No one danced, as the night was young and no one had drunk as much as Tadhg. Feet tapped, and a few people talked and laughed.

Several tunes later, Eileen McCann stood and sang in a sweet, clear voice. At first, people continued talking, but their friends shushed them. She sang a sad love song about Gráinne and Diarmuid. Esme remembered the story, but not this song.

Gráinne had been engaged to another man, Fionn mac Cumhaill, hero of the Fianna. However, she didn't wish to marry her much older fiancé. She fell in love with the young, dashing Diarmuid. At first, loyal to his hero, Diarmuid refused to run away with her, but she placed a *geis* upon him, and they escaped together. The Fianna pursued them in many places, but Diarmuid's brother interceded, begging a pardon for them.

A rare Irish love story, this one almost had a happy ending. They settled in Kerry and bore several children. Many years later, a boar wounded Diarmuid and Fionn delayed healing him until he died. Gráinne pined away in sorrow for mourning him.

Esme caught herself recounting the tale in her head, in her grandfather's voice, with all his turns of phrase and dramatic pauses. She lost track of Eileen's song. As it ended, slow clapping came from the doorway, loud and staccato in the hushed, crowded room.

A tall man with blond hair and a dazzling smile clapped. He looked like he belonged on the stage. Esme had never seen him, and his dress looked much too fine for him to be a villager.

He walked toward Eileen, still clapping. She stared at him, dumbstruck, as he took her hand in his. As soon as Eileen realized she was staring, the girl dropped her gaze, her cheeks flaming red.

"What a delightful voice, my dear gel. Do honor us with another."

Eileen giggled and tossed her head in what might be a flirt. In reality, it only swung her mop of dark curls around and mussed them. Esme thought she looked silly.

Donal scowled and pursed his lips, but he struck up a tune with words, *Mo Ghile Mear*. A lament in the Irish by the goddess Éire for Bonnie Prince Charlie of Scotland. It reminded Esme of her pet name for Seán, *mo ghrá dubh*—my black-haired darling.

Eileen's voice sang soft and tentative at first, but she gained momentum and confidence.

Sé mo laoch mo Ghile Mear
'Sé mo Chaesar, Ghile Mear,
Suan ná séan ní bhfuaireas féin
Ó chuaigh i gcéin mo Ghile Mear.

When the song ended, the blond man clapped again. "I didn't understand a word, my dear, but you sang them beautifully." He bowed over her hand and kissed it. After striding to the hearth, he searched for a place to sit. One young man scrambled to offer his stool. The posh man nodded thanks, accepting it.

He dressed in a fine, deep-blue jacket, and breeks, with silk stockings and a jabot at his collar, snow white and fluffy. Esme wondered where he came from when he turned. Their eyes met, and one side of his mouth curled up into a smile. She looked down at her feet, flushing red. Why did she stare so at this blond lordling when she had her own handsome husband?

Aisling whispered in her ear. "And that's why we got you all dressed up."

Amazed, Esme stared at her friend in astonishment. "You mean him? And what would I be to him?"

A sly smile crept across her friend's face. "Why shouldn't you be anything to him?"

"I'm married!"

Aisling shrugged. "Seán left seven months ago, Esme. He's never stayed away this long before. What if he's gone forever?"

Esme gritted her teeth. "He'll be back."

Her friend gripped her arm. "He might be dead, Esme. Wouldn't he let you know if he lived? When Cormac died, you were there for me. I must return the favor."

With a roll of her eyes, Aisling nodded at the newcomer. "Well, in the meantime, you've someone nice to look upon."

Careful not to turn around and look at the man, Esme asked, "Who is he when he's at home, then?"

"Who is he? Why, that's the Lord, it is. Up at the big house, near Dugort."

"It is not! I've met Lord John Sweeney. He's much older. Fat, too." This man looked thin and muscular, perhaps even lanky, but not fat.

Aisling waved her hand. "Oh, that must have been his father. His son has taken over. He's doing his rounds about the island, so everyone says. He's stopping in each village to see what his new home is like."

Esme's gaze flickered to the man. "How very 'Lord of the Manor' of him. Does he think he owns us?"

"Well, he *does* own our land."

They all rented from some disembodied landlord. They paid their rents to the priest, who acted as a local factor. Esme never considered what happened after that. The priest must pay the factor at Sweeney House, Mr. Walsh. She'd been dealing with him for years and never made the connection. With Seán gone, Esme fed them with her embroidery work. She wondered if it would halt now the old Lord passed on. The thought stirred feelings of helplessness and resentment in her heart.

The close quarters of the *síbín* became too much for her. She needed air.

Esme threaded her way to the door, breathing in the cool air when she emerged. The fresh night soothed her spirit. She'd felt smothered and trapped.

Aisling hadn't followed her out, but someone breathed behind her.

She spun to find the new Lord silhouetted in the golden rectangle of the door. "Was the music not to your liking, fair lady?"

Esme blushed again, but hoped it wouldn't be apparent in the gathering gloom. "I only needed fresh air. It's crowded in there for my tastes."

"A lover of open spaces, are you? As am I. I'm Carrick, and I'm very pleased to meet you." He bowed low, showing a bald spot on his head. It disappeared when he stood, but she smiled at the imperfection in the man.

"I'm Esme. Esme Fitzgerald."

"At your service, Mistress. Is your husband not joining you this evening?"

"No… no, my husband is not here." Aisling's earlier comment haunted her, and for a moment, Seán's certain death loomed over her. She shook off the worry. Alive or not, he wasn't here now.

"Ah, that's all to the good, then. It leaves you free to enjoy my company." His smile oozed with charm. His intense gaze captivated her.

"I… I'm so sorry, but I must go." She turned to leave, but he placed a hand on her forearm. She turned, her heart beating faster.

Carrick gave her a sweet, almost apologetic smile. "May I accompany you somewhere? Were you bound home? I have a carriage, and it's grown quite dark."

She'd heard tales of landlords who took advantage of their tenants, especially their attractive female tenants. Esme wasn't a young girl, but she didn't wish to trifle with her virtue or her reputation. "No, no, I just needed fresh air. I'll be grand."

"A pity indeed." He spoke in a soft voice as he looked her over, appraising her, which both flattered and repulsed. "With your permission, I shall rejoin the festivities. I'm pleased to have made your acquaintance, Mistress Fitzgerald. Your servant." With a faint emphasis on the word "Mistress" and a curt bow, he strode inside.

Esme let out a breath she hadn't realized she held. He *was* a pretty man. He had pale eyes, but she couldn't make out the color in this light. His polished manners kept her on edge, but he also made her act like a giddy girl. At least she'd learned how to speak well.

If he hadn't left, she might have done something foolish.

Flustered from the encounter, she blew out a breath, as if trying to dispel cobwebs. Esme had no desire to enter the *síbín* again. She climbed up to the cottage, alone in the deepening velvet night.

On a bright Sunday morning, the villagers descended the mountain to the church. Groups of people walked like a string of mottled pearls along the path. Katy and Aoife skipped down, holding hands, jumping over rocks and clumps of grass.

Aisling couldn't keep the laughter out of her voice. "Slow down, girls! You'll trip if you go too fast and tumble all the way down into the sea. Padraig will catch you up in one of his nets, and we'll have ye for supper on a Friday!"

Esme giggled despite her recent funk. Her leaving the *síbín* last week resulted in renewed rejection by the village. Esme tried everything she could think of, including bringing baked goods to each cottage and offering to watch oldsters. Nothing made any impact.

She might speak to the priest about it again. She'd tried in the past, and he told her it would take time. Despite being even newer to the area, they accepted him. Priests enjoyed an integral place in any Irish society. Apart from the fact he collected the tenants' rent, he acted as the community confessor, organizer, and moral compass. He'd never warmed to her, always acting nervous and distracted when they spoke.

Moral compass, indeed. She heard from Aisling that his nephew, Tadhg, wasn't truly a nephew, but a bastard son. So much for moral fortitude. She didn't even need the brooch to learn that.

As if she summoned him with the thought, the young man in question leaned against the church door as they arrived. Despite looking disheveled, Tadhg still dressed in nice clothes for church. He could stand a shave, though.

Tadhg pushed away from the door as Aisling and Esme approached and nodded to them. Esme could swear someone touched her hip as she passed by. Someone stood too close behind her as they found their place.

When she sat, Tadhg spoke into her ear. "You're looking mighty fine on the morning, Esme."

She dropped her gaze at the compliment. Tadhg seemed a nice enough man, but she'd already learned what drunken men become in their cups, and had no wish to deal with another.

"Are you doing aught after church? I'd love to take you out on a walk along the beach."

"Tadhg, I can't. I'm working at the house."

Esme didn't quite lie, but had no interest in spending time with him. She disliked her own hypocrisy, but couldn't stand the man. She didn't want to offend anyone with rudeness to the priest's "nephew," but he felt slimy and had a sly smile. He had attractive curly brown hair, always messy in a roguish sort of way and light-hazel eyes. Still, he made Esme's skin crawl.

Tadhg sat next to her, their thighs touching. He didn't have a "normal" seat, as he drifted about like a piece of flotsam. He didn't always attend, but he always put her on edge. Aisling didn't seem to mind, but she had a visible husband. Tadhg arrived after Seán disappeared, so to him, Esme seemed available and game for his attentions.

His arm brushed against hers, and she resisted the urge to rub her skin. She glanced sideways at Aisling, who rolled her eyes. At least Tadhg didn't smell like a brewery this morning. He smelled of soap and peat smoke.

Father Duggan arrived and marched to his pulpit. He spoke today of moderation and the evils of strong drink. A jagged barb at his "nephew." Esme daren't risk a glance to see if he took the lesson to heart.

After the service, Esme told Aisling she needed to speak to Father Duggan. The long line of thanks seemed interminable, but she waited. Tadhg disappeared into the crowd.

Seán had plenty of faults. After he lost control that night, he kept himself in moderation. And he never lied to her, never once. Honesty made up for the rocky marriage. She missed Seán with an aching heart, wishing against hope his cart would be in front of their cottage when she returned home.

Esme took a deep breath and walked to Father Duggan, having received thanks from the last villager. He put out his damp hand. "Esme, how are you today?"

"Hello, Father. I wanted to thank you for your words today. Quite on point, I think."

"Indeed, I thought so as well. A man must understand his own limits." He put a finger to his temple.

"I agree. As well should a woman."

He lifted his eyebrows. "As well, yes. Had you a question for me?"

Esme took a deep breath. "Well, I did, yes. I'm still having a tough time gaining acceptance into the village. You said to give it time. Is six years not enough, then?"

The priest gave her a sad smile. "Esme, I wish I could help. Now and then, I've talked to the folk, urging them to include you. I've worked to ease the rift as best I can."

She blinked at him. His blue glow proved he lied. He did none of that. Esme kept her expression frozen, lest he witness her skepticism.

"Perhaps a change of routine would help?"

While she seethed at his perfidy, his words refocused her attention. "What sort of change would you suggest?"

He shrugged, frowning. "Perhaps you should travel? Go and visit other villages?"

So, he wanted her to move away. She understood now. Did he encourage the alienation? She kept her temper tight and her lips tighter, and pushed with the brooch's power. Maybe he'd tell her the real reason. "Other villages?"

Sweat bloomed on his brow, despite the cool day. "Sometimes a person belongs better in a different community. Each village is different. They have differing values and beliefs."

Different values. Different beliefs. What did he mean? Despite her misgivings about the brooch's magic, she pushed more. "I'm not sure I understand."

"I just think... well, perhaps you need a less Christian community." He tugged on his collar, as if it cut into his throat.

Less Christian? Her blood grew cold. Had he learned about the brooch and the stones? But Esme no longer had it. Eithne stole it. Ever since, Esme had an empty spot in her soul, something eating away, draining her energy. How would Father Duggan have known? Unless Eithne had said something. She remembered the whispers about her being a witch, about her poisoning the prior priest. She'd dismissed those as nonsense, but something didn't need to be true to be believed. With sudden decision, Esme nodded. "Perhaps I shall. Thank you, Father. Your insight has been helpful."

She whirled and stalked away, trying to keep her temper from exploding. No wonder she'd always been so isolated. Why hadn't she seen it before? She'd grown to rely on her talent of seeing the truth, but she never outright asked him.

By the time Esme reached the sanctuary of her home, her rage had transformed into another black mood. Aisling played with the girls in the garden, so she gave a half-hearted wave.

Once behind the safety of her own door, she flung herself onto her bed. It wasn't fair. She'd worked hard to be a valuable member of this community. She helped with the livestock, the garden, helped others repair the common areas, and supported herself and her daughter. Even after Seán's disappearance. If the trade from Sweeney House ever dried up, she'd be in serious straits.

The thought of Sweeney House brought up the image of Lord Carrick Sweeney, with his blond hair and smooth manners. It wouldn't be a good idea to run into him on the long walk to the factor's office, on a lonely, windswept moor. What if she brought Katy on her next visit? Children sometimes worked for putting off men bent on pushing their affections.

Esme stared into the hearth. The peat needed a new log as the embers died. It smoldered in shapes, beckoning her closer, but she had no desire to join them. She had no desire to do anything.

The day before, Mistress Lynch made a nasty remark about Seán abandoning her. Then the woman she spoke to retorted that Esme must have killed her husband herself, to rid her of the Traveling lout.

The horrid remark danced in her mind, bouncing inside her skull, until it consumed her every thought. She could think of nothing else but Seán. He left half a year ago, and he'd never been gone more than a few months. He must have decided the arguments hurt too much, and left her forever. The idea paralyzed her. She wouldn't sew, she wouldn't wash, and she barely slept.

When the fire died, the cold roused her enough that she stumbled toward her bed. The familiar wall beckoned her.

Aisling

Aisling entered and spied the dying fire. She scraped up the ashes around the hearth. Soon the thick, earthy smell of peat burning filled the cottage.

The other woman then pulled out a pot, potatoes, and the dried fish. Tonight, Esme should have made dinner, but she'd ignored the task because of her black mood.

Aisling had dealt with Esme's moods many times. Her friend would emerge from them, given time. She chopped up onions and potatoes.

Aoife and Katy peered into the doorway, the rising moon silhouetting them against the darkening sky. "No, Katy, leave your Mam alone. She needs to rest now."

"But I want to give her a Sunday kiss!"

"You can give it later, sweetling. Here, want to help me peel an onion?" Aisling placed an onion on the low table in front of the child.

"No, I want to go to Mam."

"I said, not now. Here, start with the end, like this, see?" She cut off one end and peeled the skin off in strips.

The child pouted, but touched the papery texture of the onion skin. Soon she played with the discarded bits while Aoife and Aisling finished preparations. Aoife prepared tea and brought a steaming cup to Esme, setting it next to her on the bedside table.

The aroma of rosehips and chamomile curled in the air. She willed Esme to come to her senses and drink some, but her friend didn't move. She refused to respond to a touch on her shoulder but continued to stare at the wall.

By the next morning, Esme remained in the same position. Aisling decided it had been long enough. No tragedy sent her into a downward spiral this time. The woman needed to come to her senses, and past time.

Aisling shook her friend's shoulder. "It's morning, Esme. Come to breakfast. You need to eat."

Esme jerked her shoulder from Aisling's hands and grunted.

"Come on, Esme, time to rise. It's a bright, new day, after all. We've things to get done. You've the commission to finish, remember?"

Esme didn't budge.

In frustration, Aisling used more physical force to turn her over. Esme turned, sent her an icy glare, and twisted back into her ball position against the wall.

With a deep sigh, Aisling finished breakfast preparations. The cottage seemed too quiet. "Katy, where's Aoife?"

The child built a strange, ethereal structure from last night's dry and brittle onion skins. Cú Chulainn kept sniffing at the delicate structure, destroying it with his breath. "Out."

"Out where?"

Katy shrugged and built her tower again, placing one more on top. The entire structure fell again. Her face crunched and turned red before letting out an enormous howl of frustration.

Aisling exhaled again. The child acted half her age. Katy learned things slower than Aoife had, which maddened both mothers. She scooped the bawling child up and patted her back. At five years old, she should be past this stage by now.

With Katy in her arms, Aisling went outside to scan the area for her own daughter. After Padraig's babe died stillbirth, Aoife became her world again.

The mists curled thick around the mountain, and the sounds muffled with the damp. "Aoife! Where are you, Aoife?"

The sun had been up for an hour, but hadn't burned through the fog. Near midsummer, the nights grew short and the sun rose early. Even the cows slept.

"Aoife!"

The dog barked and sniffed the doorway.

Aisling's breath grew quick. She tried to gain control on her mind, spinning with panic. "Cú Chulainn, find Aoife. Can you find Aoife?"

A sound came from the front of the cottage, so she rushed to the other door. Darkness surrounded the hillside.

The dog rushed off and Aisling spied a flash of bright in the fog. Was it Aoife? She put down Katy and moved toward it. When she noticed it didn't move, she ran. While crouching near the still form, she shook her daughter with growing panic. "Aoife? Aoife, wake up! Aoife!"

Her daughter didn't move, but her skin was warm. Still alive, then. The dog nosed at her as if trying to pry her up from the grass. The child breathed. Aisling couldn't find any injuries or wounds. After pushing the dog away, she lifted her daughter and trudged to the cottage. Cú Chulainn whined at her heels, almost tripping her in his frenzy.

At eleven years, Aoife weighed almost as much as an adult, built tall and solid like Cormac had been. Katy trundled after Aisling back to the cottage.

Once inside, she examined her daughter, moving her from side to side, lifting her arms, and examining her skin. No wounds, no bites, no stings. No broken bones, no blood, no bruises. Aisling touched a soft area of Aoife's scalp. Had she fallen and hit her head?

She laid her daughter on a pallet and propped up her head with two pillows. After piling blankets over her, she brewed tea. Comfrey for knitting broken bones and willow bark for the headache she'd have. What if she didn't wake enough to drink? Aisling shoved the idea far into the back of her mind as the tea steeped.

Katy poked her unconscious friend. "Whas wrong wif Aoife?"

"I'm not sure, sweetling. I think she fell and hit her head. Here, eat while I work on her." She handed the child a heel of bread from last night's supper to keep Katy occupied while she worked.

Aoife's heart beat strong, but she wouldn't rouse at all. She should have woken when Aisling carried her, if she only slept. Aisling's own heart beat faster, sweat dripping from her forehead.

The water took forever to boil.

She crouched beside Esme's bed. "Esme? Esme, I need you. Aoife's hurt. I need you to help me, please?"

For a long moment, Esme didn't move, but she turned over. Her face looked drawn and immobile, as if she wore a strange mask. "What?" Her voice echoed, like from the depths of a dank cave, her words muffled and sticky with phlegm.

"Aoife fell, and she won't wake up. I don't dare leave her side. I need fresh herbs. Can you pick chamomile and comfrey for me? I don't know what else to do, Esme. I really need your help. Please?"

Esme grunted and struggled to a sitting position. She shuffled to the door, wrapping a shawl over her wrinkled, dirty shift.

The act of rousing Esme helped to calm Aisling. The water finally came to a boil.

When Esme returned with bedraggled herbs clutched in her fist, she looked no more awake than she had when she had gotten out of bed. With a shake of her head and a word of thanks, Aisling added the fresh herbs to the steeping tea.

Aoife hadn't yet moved. Aisling lifted her torso and grabbed a pillow to prop her up. She put the steaming mug under Aoife's nose, hoping the aroma would wake her. It didn't.

Aisling tried to get a sip into her mouth, but it dribbled down her chin. She tipped Aoife's head back and trickled it down her throat. The girl choked but still didn't wake, her head remaining limp. Aisling added honey to the tea.

After several dribbled sips and failed attempts, she gave up. Perhaps a quarter of the mug had made its way down Aoife's throat. That would need to be enough.

At a loss for what to do next, Aisling focused her attentions on Esme. She hadn't returned to bed, but sat in her hearth chair.

"Let's get you cleaned up, Esme. You look a fright. Here." She handed the rest of the tea to her friend. "I'll get you something to eat. You're skin and bones already."

Aisling didn't want to stop working, as that might allow her fears to take over. She fed Esme and Katy, cleaned the cottage, then weeded the communal garden. She tended the animals then organized Esme's thread and fabric collections by color.

She gave up and collapsed into Seán's chair. Esme still sat in hers, staring at the hearth, cold mug of tea in her hand.

Aoife still hadn't roused.

Some internal voice, some alien thought, niggled at her brain. *Esme can help.* She argued with the voice. What would Esme be able to do? She had no healing skills. Still, the thought wouldn't leave her. Aisling gave in to it and tried to rouse her friend. "Esme, I'm worried. What can I do?"

Esme didn't answer.

"Esme? Are you here? Or has your shade gone wandering in the faery lands?"

Aisling joked, but concern for her friend grew. She left a shell of her body behind as if no one was home. Or she shuttered her windows and wouldn't let any light inside. If Esme walked with the faeries, pulling her back again too quickly might prove dangerous. But Aisling needed her.

Esme's voice came from the other side of a long tunnel, echoing with far away voices and impossible dreams. "Hmm?"

"Esme, I need your help, please come back?"

As she blinked in the light, Esme shook her head, like a dog ridding itself of water. She glanced around, then peered at Aisling, as if trying to remember her friend's face.

"Esme?"

"I… what… what's wrong?"

"It's Aoife. She's still not awake."

Esme furrowed her brow, her expression still muzzy. "Aoife?"

"Yes, Aoife! She hit her head and has been out all morning." While pointing an impatient finger at her daughter, Aisling physically turned Esme's head to look at the child.

Finally, Esme woke fully, staring at her friend. "And what do you think I can do? You're the healer!"

Aisling sat cross-legged on the floor, her head in her hands. "A voice in my head told me you could help. Can't you think of anything?"

Esme stared into space, and Aisling thought she'd gone away again. With a deep sigh, Esme looked into Aisling's eyes. "I might I have an idea. But we need to bring her to the other side of the island."

After quelling the hope bursting in her heart, Aisling nodded with desperate vigor. "Yes, we have a cart. We can borrow Tadhg's horse, to be sure. Now?"

While squinting at the long beams of light coming in the window, Esme asked, "What time is it?"

Her panic rose again, worried that Esme would postpone the trip. "Late afternoon, at least."

The redhead shook her head. "No, we can't go until the morning. Traveling across the bogs at night would be suicide."

Aisling stared at her daughter, Aoife's pale face shining in the dim cottage. "But... Aoife..."

Esme gripped the arms of her chair, her knuckles turning white. "I can't risk the bogs at night, Aisling. I'm not even sure if it will help, but it's the only thing I can think of."

"What are you hoping to do?"

Esme swallowed and stared back into the fire. "I can't explain, I just have to try it. And I need to be there, at that particular place."

Suddenly, Aisling had enough of Esme's vague statements. She jumped to her feet and paced around the room. "Are you mad? Esme, this doesn't make any sense. I can't drag my daughter across the island on a whim."

Esme glared at her friend. "It's not a whim, Aisling. It's, well, it's something my grandfather gave me, but warned me never to speak of it. It might help."

The questions pushed and jostled in her mind, but Aisling shoved them down and bit her tongue. She hated waiting, but she could do it. If Aoife survived the night.

Chapter Seventeen

April 1798

Esme

A quagmire of despair and loathing trapped Esme. Her fear and pain stuck her in the swamp. She tried to extract one arm, but it snapped back to the ground. She lifted a leg, but it sucked back in the same manner. Her head felt immovable, sluggish, and trapped. Struggle as she might, it drew her in, the pull of the ache, the emptiness.

A thin wail penetrated her bubble of emotion. Katy. Her daughter needed her. She latched onto the tentative, high-pitched lifeline. It dragged her, inch by inch, out of the bog and into the light of the day.

After shaking her head of sleep, Esme sat up. She never remembered the details of her dreams, except for the terror. Before she got out of bed, she recovered her breath and sanity. Katy cried again.

Aisling shushed the child, and Katy whined. Esme listened for Aoife's clear, high voice, but heard nothing.

Once she rose, she staggered to the washbasin. She brushed out her hair, splashed cool water on her face, and rubbed her teeth with a frayed branch.

Now that she felt human again, she turned to face Aisling. "How is Aoife?"

"Unchanged. I got more honey tea into her, but I'm terrified, Esme. She can't live long like this. We've got to do something."

"Did you get Tadhg's horse?"

"Outside and hooked up. I packed food for the journey. Is there anything else you need?"

Esme's hand contracted as if she held the brooch. Why hadn't she confronted Eithne after she stole it? Because she had Katy and then Seán left, and she just never did. Well, she'd have to remedy that later. If this worked without it.

Esme hoped the stone circle would help Aoife, even without the brooch. The circle still brought her peace and energy. It might do so for Aoife. She'd ask whatever lived in the circle for help. Her grandfather said the power was for the family, but she must try. Perhaps Aoife had faery blood. She *had* foreseen old Mr. Quinn's death, hadn't she?

The soggy morning made the trip seem interminable. They left Cú Chulainn at home, not trusting him to stay in the cart through the marshes. They trudged their way over the mountain pass, through the bog and to the circle, mist clinging to the stones. Esme's own energy flagged to nothing. Her life had lost purpose after Seán disappeared.

Well, she had a purpose now. Esme helped Aisling lift Aoife from the cart. The girl remained unchanged and inert. They carried her into the center of the circle, laying her on the flat stone. Katy watched, wide-eyed, from the cart.

Aisling looked at the stones, looming sinister in the mist and the rain, with narrowed eyes and a pinched expression. "Now what?"

"I'm not certain, but I need to try this on my own. Can you wait with Katy?"

Aisling swallowed, her eyes growing wide, and gave a nervous nod. She picked her way back to the cart.

Esme walked around the circle, as her grandfather did when he first attuned her to the stones. Her skin tingled, which gave her confidence as she walked past each dark stone in the misty rain.

By the time Esme reached full circle, the standing stones glowed blue, pulsing in the dim light. The magic reached down through her to the earth, a conduit of energy up and out, down and in. She crouched beside Aoife in the center, bundled in wool blankets against the damp.

Esme placed her glowing hand on Aoife's head. The light suffused the child and sank into the earth below. It flickered between blue and green, with hints of purple and red, like half a rainbow, pulsing and quickening.

At the entrance to the circle, the figure appeared, as she'd half-hoped, half-feared. It glowed brighter than the sun, hurting her mind. Fear washed over her, urging her to run, run away fast and fleet across the moors. *Flee and never look back.* But she wouldn't leave, not with Aoife so ill.

She must ask for help. *Le do thoil, an féidir leat teacht chun cúnaimh orm?*

Agus in íoc mo shaothair?

Cold fear tightened around her heart. What sort of payment would a faery want?

The answer came into her mind in a flash. *Píosa de do shaol.*

A piece of her own life? The fear turned to ice and threatened to shatter. However, she had little choice in the matter. She nodded.

Ní mór duit é a rá. You must say it.

Aontaím. I agree.

The fear flew away, leaving her heart warm and joyful. With a light heart, Esme danced with the fire. She became part of the earth power, a circle between the ground, her body, and Aoife. The energy scrambling in her mind and Aoife's. As if icy fingers fiddled with the pieces of Aoife's soul, putting the puzzles back together, fitting them into their patterns.

A brief flash rippled across her mind, a vision of her husband. She reached for him. He smiled at her, his beautiful dark smile, and then he faded into a million pieces. A rip, a snap, a crack, and Esme fell back. Her own soul seemed colder, somehow, as if turned to stone, or as if a piece had been taken.

When Esme looked up, Aoife's eyes blinked open, confused and frightened. Aisling cried out in relief from beyond the circle, but her friend didn't enter. Esme struggled up from the rain-soaked peat and knelt by the girl. "Aoife? Are you all right?"

"I'm not sure, Aunt Esme. I'm so cold and my arms don't want to listen to me. I was dancing, dancing forever and I saw you, but it wasn't you, and she danced, too, but now I'm just so cold."

"Come, let me help. Your legs are just stiff."

Esme clasped her hands around Aoife's chest, helping the girl sit up. Her skin looked blue, but not from any faery glow. Aoife's teeth chattered, and so did Esme's. It might have been May, but her body didn't believe it.

Aisling ran to her daughter, picking her up into a fierce embrace, spinning as she cried in relief. "Thank you, thank you, thank you! How can I repay you?"

Esme glanced at the largest stone. "It's not you who will pay."

Aisling didn't reply, still intent on hugging Aoife. She asked no further questions until they packed their supplies and started home. "Esme, what happened back there? Are you... are you a faerie?"

Esme laughed, shaking her head. "No, I'm human. It's a family thing. Grandfa Éamonn gave me a brooch and taught me how to use it. Eithne stole it, but I can still touch the stones. They never did that, though. I had to try something." She smiled at her friend and put her hand on Aisling's arm. "I'm very glad it worked."

Aisling's face cleared, and she smiled back. "Me, too."

She hugged Aoife closer, kissing her forehead, though the girl squirmed to get away. "Ma, I'm fine, you can stop smothering me now!"

Esme laughed, her own mood greatly improved, despite her missing piece. She no longer balanced on the brink of the abyss. "Aisling, what do you say to a stop by the beach on the way back?"

Dugort was just a few miles away, and she ached to dig her toes into the sand.

"Let's rest for the night at the inn first and then go in the morning. I want to put Aoife to bed." The girls got excited at once, always up for a day at the beach.

Aoife whined. "But I'm not tired!"

After some argument, Aisling gave in. They pulled the cart into the inlet and unharnessed the horse. He seemed glad for the holiday, snorting and stamping at the sand while they removed his tack.

Esme patted his neck. "Leave the bridle on, in case we need to catch him. He may not want to come back!"

"I don't think I want to, either. What a delightful place! I'm glad we stopped."

They pulled out a bag of apples, giving one to the horse, and sat back to watch the waves lap the sand. The gloomy sky held an odd glow, similar to the greens and purples of the faery light. They relaxed and dug their toes into the sand while the girls ran along the shore, looking for shells. Tadhg's horse explored the succulent grasses growing on the hillock behind the beach, content in his treat.

That morning, Esme felt as if she walked on clouds. Her dreams no longer oppressed her soul, and her fears lightened. Not gone, not completely, but pushed into the back of her mind.

Hooves echoed on the stone track behind them with the jangle of tack. The sound made her think of Seán, but she chided herself with foolish hopes. Esme looked back and gasped, transfixed. Aisling heard her and glanced in that direction.

"Look, Esme!"

Esme turned back and fixed her eyes on the surf, determined not to lock gazes with Lord Carrick Sweeney, resplendent in a bottle-green velvet jacket and buff riding breeks, on his graceful roan mare. His blond hair fluttered in the strong ocean breeze, but it didn't diminish his looks one bit, instead giving him a rakish air. Esme pushed down the thought. Attractive, yes, but also dangerous. She had no interest in becoming his lover, only to be discarded when she became pregnant, or when he found a wife of suitable class. She wasn't her sister.

Esme poked her friend in the ribs to get her attention. "Will you stop staring? He'll see you."

Aisling's voice teased. "He already has."

Esme risked another glance. He'd dismounted and strode toward them, confident and strutting. She growled deep in her throat, a visceral sound. She searched for Katy and Aoife, but they built a sand castle off to the left, well out of earshot. *Thank sweet God for small miracles, at least.*

He gave them a low bow. "Mistress Campbell, I believe? We met at the party last month, down in the *sibín*. You are looking lovely in this unearthly light."

Esme still wouldn't let herself turn around while Aisling and the Lord chatted. She concentrated on her daughter, playing in the wet sand. Her dress would be filthy, but Esme didn't care.

The Lord's voice cut through her reverie. "And Mistress Fitzgerald? Is that correct?"

She turned and blinked, as if just noticing him. "Why, yes, Lord Sweeney. I felt certain you wouldn't remember me."

"How could I forget such enchanting blue eyes? You would chase the clouds away with one glance. And please, Lord Carrick is the proper way to address me." He reached for her hand, but she kept both hidden.

Prickling at the correction, she drew back. "You wouldn't have seen the color of my eyes. You met me outside, in the dark." She sounded churlish, but didn't want to give him an inch.

Instead of taking offense, he laughed, a full and booming sound, surprising for someone so slim. One of his front teeth looked crooked, forming a gap. "I noticed your eyes when I first arrived, Mistress Fitzgerald, while inside." He emphasized her title. His own eyes sparkled a pale hazel, green flecks mixing with light brown, with long, thick lashes.

Unsure of how to respond, Esme didn't want to encourage him further.

Aisling came to her rescue. "My daughter fell ill, so we brought her up here for a break and sunshine."

"A fantastic idea, my ladies. Might I join you?" He tipped his hat.

Esme ached to say no, but daren't put her only source of income at risk. She forced herself to nod and gestured to a spot next to Aisling.

Her friend must have noticed her discomfort as she opened the conversation. "Have you lived at Sweeney House long?"

"As a child, until my tenth year. Then Mother trundled me off to boarding school in the Lake District in England. I've only just returned three months ago. The place has changed so much, but in some ways, it's just as I remembered it." He gazed at the ocean as if conjuring up his childhood recollections.

Esme cleared her throat. "And are you planning on staying, or are you just passing through?"

He looked surprised at the question. "I must stay, of course. My father, well, his health isn't as good as it used to be, you see." His eyes looked drawn, and Esme recalled the bluff older man she had met so many years ago, on this very beach.

Her voice turned gentle. "I'm grieved to hear that."

"And your wife?" Aisling inquired with an air of innocent curiosity. She didn't fool Esme in the slightest.

If Esme thought he looked bleak at the mention of his father's health, he looked morose at the mention of his wife. "She's not with me here. She lives in London, now."

He spoke in short, clipped syllables, making it apparent he didn't wish to discuss the issue further.

The three of them sat in awkward silence while gulls screeched on the sea breeze. Katy came running up to them, slowing when she spied Lord Carrick, remembering her manners. She curtsied to the man despite her sand-soaked dress.

"How do you do, Mistress…?"

Esme spoke up. "Katy, my daughter. Katy, this is Lord Carrick, from Sweeney House, where I sell my needlework and clothing."

The child's eyes grew wide at the title. She nodded in another curtsy and backed away to the elaborate construction she and Aoife created in the sand. After a flurry of furious whispers, the girls sent furtive glances at the visitor.

This elicited a chuckle from Lord Carrick and helped to ease the tension.

He turned to Esme. "So you sell your creations to the House? I'd learned my mother had a local seamstress but I didn't realize you were the artisan."

"I'm probably not her only supplier, but she purchases items every few months. Pillows, dresses, aprons, bonnets. I bring up a selection to the factor. He returns those items she doesn't like, paying me for those she selected. I've never met her in person."

"We shall have to remedy the lack forthwith, I think. Would you like to come to the house after your beach holiday?"

Panic seized Esme. Meet the Lady of the house, like this? Grubby in worn clothes, filled with gritty sand?

Her panic must have burned on her face, for Lord Carrick recanted. "No, no, I suppose it won't do after all. You'll want time to bring your girls back home, I'm sure. Let's arrange a meeting, then. Perhaps in three days? Come up with your wares, as you normally would. I'll give you the grand tour. Perhaps I can show off my own musical skills. You didn't give me the chance to when last we met."

Esme's head swirled. How would she get out of this?

Once again, Aisling saved her. "What sort of musical skills, Lord Carrick?"

"Oh, nothing too impressive. I can play the pianoforte well, if I do say so myself. I understand you can sing, Mistress Fitzgerald?"

Esme still hadn't regained control over her thoughts, so she kept her voice neutral. "I enjoy singing, yes."

"Excellent. I'd be honored if you would sing for me during your visit. I'll invite a few of my friends, so do wear something lovely."

He said this with all the gallantry of a medieval knight, asking for his Queen's favor in a tournament. Esme stammered as her cheeks grew warm.

Esme wanted to withdraw into a shell, blot out the terrifying prospect of a visit to Sweeney House. A grand house, with her all grubby and dirty. She had no business in such a place as anything but a servant.

What would he want in return? What sort of payment would this slick and casual Lord require of her? Her stomach churned at the possibilities.

She'd never been with any man but Seán. Since he disappeared, she'd barely spoken to any other men, much less spent time with them. Those few she'd been friends with, such as Alan and Cormac, had no romantic interest in her. The affection she shared with Aisling differed from what a man wanted.

A sharp sting of attraction spiked her memory. It reminded her of the time Seán courted her. A spark crackled between them, and she couldn't deny his attentiveness. She sensed an underlying danger, subtly threatening. She couldn't put her finger on it, but she must remain cautious. Esme considered pushing at him, to find if he lied. But without having the actual brooch, she didn't trust the power.

She shivered, which earned a curious look from Lord Carrick. Esme wrapped a blanket around her shoulders in explanation. May winds in Achill normally blew cold, especially on the beach, but the sun made the wind warm today.

Hugh O'Hagerty's face flashed into her mind. Had her sister loved him? He'd been a man of property, someone with a high status and wealth, like Lord Carrick, though from merchant stock rather than noble blood. But Esme doubted her sister loved anyone. Her twin would never be satisfied with what she had. Her sister always needed to grasp farther, deeper, for things she didn't possess. At least Eithne always commanded her own destiny.

Did wealth and power ever bring joy? With wealth, one had the leisure to pursue pleasure. What if one got so caught up with the wealth, one had no time to enjoy it? Where was the line between quality of life and quantity of wealth?

If born to it, with enough wealth to buy anything, leisure came easy. It's what the Lord Carricks of the world did. Folks like her, like her sister and all the "common" folk around the world needed to scratch wealth out of the dirt, bit by bit, to enjoy the few moments of joy they garnered in the cracks. A day at the beach, perhaps, or an evening of song.

Esme squared her shoulders. If Lord Carrick wished to offer her joy, why should she reject him out of hand? She'd keep a firm grip on her heart and virtue, but she missed singing. Perhaps he'd lift her spirits with a song.

On the trip home, Aisling poked her in the shoulder several times with a sly smile.

Esme poked back. "Aisling, it's just an invitation to sing. He'll have me performing at a party, hired entertainment of some sort."

"Oh, you think so, do you? I saw how he looked at you."

She rolled her eyes. "It doesn't matter one whit how he looked at me. I'm married, and so is he. There's nothing to be done about either situation, so the point is moot."

Aisling raised her eyebrows. "I don't think the point is as 'moot' as you claim, Esme. He's a lovely man and rich. Why are you so against enjoying his company?"

Exasperated at the suggestion, especially as it mirrored her own thoughts too closely, she answered with a flippant tone. "Because I'm married and shouldn't be alone with a married man?"

"And what does it matter, when it's all said and done? Besides, Seán's gone, Esme. You can't deny that anymore."

"He hasn't. He wouldn't. If he... I don't know, Aisling." Tears burned behind her eyes, and she brushed at them, willing herself not to cry. She straightened her spine and glared at Aisling. "Nothing is said, and nothing will be done. I'm not interested in an affair. My reputation is in tatters as it is, thanks to the gossips in the *clachan*. I don't want to be one of those women. I'd never live that lie. Truly. It would... I just couldn't, that's all."

"Well, I think you're being foolish. He'd give you all sorts of delightful gifts. And he's got lovely eyes, did you notice?"

Esme stared forward without answering, but thinking, *Yes, he has lovely eyes.*

The next night, the sky growled, dark and forbidding. The sun set late and rose early this close to summer. However, the clouds dimmed the sky to the point of dusk. Wind and rain whipped across the mountain *booley*, forcing villagers into their cottages. They secured the shutters and lay in supplies while they waited for the storm to pass. Esme shivered in her shawl as she closed the cottage door. At least Katy already slept with the dog curled up next to her.

She brought in more peat bricks than they normally used in a night, anticipating a long evening. She stirred the stew, smelling the aromatic summer herbs and lamb meat. After she added chopped turnips and potatoes, she added fresh chervil. Dried seaweed gave a salty tang to the flavor and her mouth watered in anticipation.

It still needed to steep for at least a few hours. Esme swung the cauldron back over the flames and pulled out her sewing bag.

Esme wanted to finish the embroidery on this bonnet in time for her visit to Sweeney House. She'd resigned herself that she must attend, but refused to arrive looking like a poor slattern. She laid out her best outfit, the chemise of fine, ivory muslin, with detailed rose vines along the sleeve hems. With a deep, emerald green overdress, it should look lovely. Green dye came cheap, but it faded fast. Esme had fresh-dyed the dress and embroidered rose vine details along the neck and hems. She braided a leather belt to go over her stays and finished the pale green bonnet with ivory details now.

At least her outfit should make a decent impression on the Dowager Lady Sweeney.

Esme swung between fear and anticipation. While she craved a glimpse into life for the landed gentry, she remained terrified of making a fool of herself. Even worse, of arriving as if a guest, and ending up a servant. Or shown as a comical spectacle, a clown brought out for entertainment. "See how the peasants pretend to be grand!" Even worse, to be made into some sort of lord's plaything.

Esme wished she'd asked questions when he'd invited her. She might have gauged his intentions with a few leading queries. At least she'd have a better idea of what he expected.

After the visit to Westport with Séan, she'd worked to enunciate her own speech. It took lots of practice, but she spoke well enough, and avoided her country idioms. Her parents taught her respect for priests, lords, soldiers, and other classes of authority. Thanks to her hedge teacher, Mr. Connell, she read and wrote in both English and Irish. She'd learned her figures and her history, but no French or German, philosophy or art.

No, she'd seen some art. Alan showed them all paintings in the hotel in Ardara by an English painter. Landscape scenes, pastoral with soft light for the sky and sheep dotting the countryside. What had his name been? Turner. J-something Turner. One by a man named Constable. She'd asked Alan if he'd been a constable and if that was his title. Eithne had told her not to be silly.

The door burst open to admit Aisling, Aoife, and Katy, rousing her from her musings. "Where have you all been? The devil's loose tonight, to be sure. You're all soaking wet! Come in, come in. Here, take this." Esme handed Aoife a blanket to wrap around herself. All three shivered, their teeth chattering with the chill.

"We had to find the last lamb. He wandered off. We'd have lost him!" Katy's eyes grew wide. They loved the wee lamb.

"Is he safe in the other cottage, then?" Since Padraig had gone fishing, they crowded in the larger cottage for the night.

Aisling nodded, glancing toward the sea. Her face looked pinched with worry.

"Padraig will be fine, Aisling. He'll find a cove and stay safe until it blows over. The storm signs are obvious. He's a good fisherman. He'll be prepared."

Esme bundled Katy up with a thick wool blanket and got one for herself. They settled down in front of the hearth.

Aisling spoke, though her voice sounded flat with no emotion. "I remember a night like this. The dark demons of the sky flew loose and wreaked havoc on the land and sea."

Aisling never discussed that night. Esme set her needlework down to listen while cuddling Katy closer. The girl squirmed, not wanting to feel smothered. She settled with her back to her mother's leg. This tenuous contact acted as a comfort to her mother.

Her friend spoke into the hearth fire. The peat didn't burn with strong flames but shimmered and glowed with the heat of the brick. Aisling didn't move her eyes from the embers, mesmerized by the patterns. "Aoife was about four. That day dawned fine and clear. The sky lowered in the late afternoon, and wind whipped along the shore. Gulls, startled by the strong wind, screeched and complained. It brought me out of my garden to look."

The crackle of the peat filled the awkward pause.

"Cormac had left three days before. Since he knew how I worried and fretted, he promised to always come back after three days."

A single tear slid down her friend's cheek, unchecked. It glittered in the firelight, sparkling like a diamond. Such a thing of beauty to herald such sorrow.

"I dreamt of him on the boat. The waves crashed over and swamped it, as if the sea smacked me in the face, over and over. My breath caught and I choked on the sea. I woke up in a panic, knowing he'd drowned."

Esme remembered the same dream from that night. The same experience of choking on water, slapped by the sea. Did Cormac send the images in his final moments, a last message? That might be where Aoife's talent came from.

"I lie in bed, frozen with terror. I had no way to bring him back. If I didn't have Aoife, I would have walked out into the sea to join him."

The simple statement of fact held no emotion. Aoife stared at her mother, tears running down her face. She jumped up from under her blanket and wrapped her thin arms around her mother's neck. She sobbed while Aisling sat, eyes now dry, still staring into the fire. Cú Chulainn whined at their feet, trying to push his nose into her lap.

Esme placed a hand on Katy's head, stroking the silky soft curls. Her hair might stay blonde, with thin, flyaway ringlets all around her face. Katy leaned into her mother.

What would have happened to her and Katy, if Aisling had walked into the sea that night? She wouldn't have survived without her friend.

Even before Seán disappeared, Aisling had always been there. When Seán attacked her that night, Aisling comforted her and helped her to heal. When it became apparent he wouldn't return, she'd lost so much hope.

Had Seán died? She'd gotten so used to knowing the truth, Esme didn't know how to deal with not knowing. An old internal argument for which she never found a good answer.

A crash outside startled them. A cow mooed, followed by the sound of rushing water. More racket from both animals and humans shouting. The thin drain passage through the center of the cottage rose to a torrent. They rushed to shore the edges.

Floods came often in the summer *booley*. The rain fell on the mountain and sometimes the creeks and rivers couldn't handle the flood. Everyone had a routine to counter the damage.

Everything the water might damage sat on the bed, tables, or shelves built into the cottage walls. A few things hung from the rafters under the thatch, but a leak made that risky. They fetched a pile of hay and packed it around the drain passage and the uphill door in the back of the cottage.

The drain didn't get worse, but the crash might have been another cottage's thatch falling in. It might be any of the *booley* houses.

The waiting grew oppressive. Action kept their imaginations from what might be. Katy hugged her leg, clamping down like a donkey on a bit. "Ma? I'm scared."

Esme hugged her daughter, realizing lies sometimes helped. "It's all right, *m'iníon*, we'll all be fine."

Aisling looked up, back in the present. "Maybe a story would help?"

Esme's mind turned blank. All the stories she'd heard, and not one came to mind. She glanced at Aoife, curled up at her mother's feet. "How about Aoife and Strongbow?"

Aoife grinned at her favorite story, the tale of her namesake.

With a smile, Esme settled in to tell the tale. "Many years ago, the land of Ireland was at war. The men of Ireland love conflict. However, one man, Dermot Mac Murchada, searched for outside help. His rivals cheated him of his throne to be the High King of Ireland, though his grandfather was the great Brian Boruma. By his reckoning, he had the right to sit on the throne of his famous forefather."

Aoife had heard the tale many times, but she sat, enraptured as she carded wool, while Esme told the story. Katy worked on spinning, sitting at her mother's feet. She didn't enjoy spinning, but neither Aisling nor Esme tolerated idle hands. It reminded Esme so much of her own childhood, her throat caught.

"His rival, the High King, worried that Dermot would oust him, sent an ally to conquer Dermot's lands. They slaughtered his cattle to force his people into starvation, and this began twenty years of war and revenge between the two factions.

"Later, the man who had slaughtered Dermot's cattle came to power. This new High King exiled Dermot, who then sought help from the King of England and France, Henry II.

"Henry II, a mighty king, was used to power. He told Dermot to recruit his nobles to help, but he demanded a price. The man who agreed to organize the invasion, Richard de Clare, had the nickname Strongbow. Dermot's daughter, Aoife, would marry this man, and their child would inherit the kingship of Leinster when Dermot died. She couldn't be forced under Irish law, but she agreed to the match, and Dermot returned with his allies.

"This pact would be a disaster for Ireland."

Aoife's eyes remained glued to Esme, though the girl might recite the story herself. Esme tried her hardest to look dramatic for this part.

"Strongbow's campaigns regained the throne of Leinster for his father-in-law, Dermot. His wife, Aoife, would conduct charges on his behalf, earning her the name Aoife Rua, or Red Eva. She became a warrior woman in the tradition of the great war teacher, Scathach." Aoife grinned fit to crack her face, but Katy rolled her eyes and kept spinning.

"Dermot's son died in the wars, leaving him a broken man. He died months later, leaving Strongbow as the King of Leinster.

"And thus, the first Englishman ruled land in Ireland. Henry II used this foothold to launch his own invasion and the English have ground their foot on the throat of the Irish ever since."

Esme wondered what Aoife's life had been like, told to marry a man she didn't love, and one who brought about her own land's doom. Did she find affection for him? Esme missed cuddling in Seán's strong arms.

After the two girls fell fast asleep in their pallets, Aisling and Esme found relief in each other's arms, like so many nights before.

Chapter Eighteen

April 1798

Esme

Aisling put her hands on her hips. "It would be best for me to take Katy to Achill Sound, at my great-aunt's tavern. Can't you see that?"

Esme rubbed her temple with her fingers. She tried to think couldn't string her thoughts together in anything resembling logic.

Her friend placed a hand on her shoulder. "I'll go there with the girls and the dog, then you can go off to the Big House with yon Carrick. That way you don't have to worry about hurrying back that night. It'll just be a few days."

Aisling's plan sounded logical. A full round trip after such a long day would be tiring. But she couldn't shake the feeling something would go wrong.

"Where would I stay overnight, Aisling? I can't afford to stay at an inn, not unless I sell everything I bring. Even then, that money's far more useful for things we need, like a new cooking pot."

The large pot they used every day had seen better days. It must be at least two hundred years old, as Aisling's family owned it for several generations. Last week, Katy poured in too much cold water and it cracked. Not a large crack, but it would widen with use.

Aisling patted her shoulder. "I'm sure you'll be able to stay at the Big House, Esme. They'll have a place for you."

"You make it sound like I'm going into service or something." Esme shivered at the idea. Service held no shame, but a servant in a big house needed training. Even worse, she might be something other than a servant. Esme blocked out the notion, as she had so many times over the last three days.

"Or something." Aisling teased.

Exasperated, she gave in. "Fine, take Katy to your great-aunt's house. I'm sure I'll finish with whatever I'm doing in a day. Should I meet you in Achill Sound?" She tried to keep the bitter defeat from her voice, with limited success.

Aisling waved her hand. "No, no, we'll be back in a few days, never fear. I'll show the girls the festival on the mainland. Enjoy your time, learn new things, sell your wares, and live a little. Just be careful."

"Careful?"

Aisling's gazed dropped. "You don't want to risk getting with child. You know how dangerous that would be." Then she lifted her face, her smile brighter. "But that shouldn't keep you from having a posh day in a big house with lots of food and attention. You'll be grand, Esme."

Esme flashed her friend a narrow look. What would be grand about the whole thing? Lord Carrick had trapped her into this venture. Sure, she'd bring all her best creations to sell. If Lord Carrick held a party, she'd entertain them. Then she'd take her leave and travel home. That would be the end of it, she hoped.

Butterflies tickled in her belly. They'd gotten so active, and she wished they'd fly off and leave her alone.

The journey to the other side of the island took forever and not long enough. Esme thought of Seán as she trudged on. His silky, black hair, his roguish smile. The times they laughed together. The way he brushed her hair out in front of the hearth.

Once, when he finished brushing through her hair, his hands strayed down to her waist then to the front of her shift. She'd enjoyed the novelty of not seeing him as he touched her. Esme closed her eyes, remembering his hands, the warmth of the fire on her face, with him pressed up against her back. She missed his touch. It had been so long.

When she arrived at Sweeney House, she walked around back, as always. The factor's office sat tucked in behind the potting shed and the laundry room. He worked in a decent-sized room, kept in precise order. Piles of papers covered the table, all squared in even stacks along a table near the window.

Mr. Walsh bent over a letter but glanced up at her entrance. He nodded to the chair near the door. The *scratch-scratch* of the quill came in soft counterpoint to the bird calls outside and the occasional bang or crash from the nearby kitchen.

Esme studied the factor as he wrote. Tall, thin, and punctilious in his dress, he looked as if he belonged in a Dublin law office rather than a grand house in the back of beyond. He had thinning fair hair and dark eyes, shaded against the late morning glare from the windows. He'd always been fair to her, and she hoped he'd be her ally in the current situation.

Her current situation. What a loaded phrase. She didn't even know how to define her current situation, other than "complicated."

Mr. Walsh finished with his letter, put the ink away, and sanded his sheet, blowing on it to dry. He folded the paper into three sections and inserted it into an envelope. A drop of sealing wax and his master's seal completed the process. He folded his hands, ready for his visitor.

He blinked several times, looking her up and down. "Mistress FitzGerald, how nice to see you. I didn't expect you for at least another fortnight. Have you special items to offer?"

"I...." She hadn't even planned how to explain her early presence. "Yes, well, I'm here by invitation, I suppose."

One blond eyebrow rose at this statement, and he waved his hand for her to continue her explanation.

"I encountered Lord Carrick the other day, and he invited me today for a gathering. I brought my wares for you, in case you should want anything while I... visited."

It sounded so contrived to her own ears, but Mr. Walsh nodded. She opened her bag and lay out the creations on his desk, careful to avoid the ink. She pulled out the pillows first, one made in deep midnight-blue velvet with white and green embroidery, a night scene in the winter, pine branches with silver snow. A single blue jay stood on the branch, lighter blue bright against the dark velvet sky. Walsh chose that one and placed it to one side.

"The Dowager has requested items in deep blues. It's as if you've read her mind." With anyone else, this might be banter. For Mr. Walsh, he made an observation of fact.

Tea towels came out next, followed by a set of fine petticoats and a sturdy overdress of pink and white chintz. He passed over the towels, accepted the petticoats and held the dress up to the light.

"I'll have to get approval for this one. She wants a workaday dress, and this might do. However, for such items, she'd best decide. Can you wait here? Or must you get on to your... invitation?"

Her cheeks grew warm, certain he considered her visit salacious. She swallowed and gathered her dignity to act professionally. "I... that is... Lord Carrick did not set a time. He said to come after my business with you concluded."

Mr. Walsh left without another word, carrying the chintz dress over one arm. Esme let out an exasperated breath. How would she ever get through this day if she couldn't even handle Mr. Walsh? She'd worked with him for years.

The sun dimmed as a cloud floated by, and she stood by the large casement window to watch the sky. A single bird soared above, riding the winds off the Atlantic. She envied his freedom, the ability to flap his wings and fly away from impossible choices and improbable situations. The way Seán always escaped.

While looking back to the room, Esme blinked several times. She wouldn't admit to tears, even to herself. Just dust floating in the air.

Footsteps approached, so she returned to her chair. She expected Mr. Walsh to return with a verdict on the dress, but Lord Carrick Sweeney entered, dressed in a faun riding jacket and jodhpurs, smelling of horse. As he removed his hat, his blond hair looked dark with sweat, sticking up in mussed spikes where it escaped its ribbon.

"Ah, Mistress Fitzgerald. I am so glad you made it. Why would you come to the back door, though? You're a guest, and you should come through the front as any other guest."

His smile grew infectious, and she returned it. "Ah... well, I had business with Mr. Walsh, of course, so it made sense to me to come to him with my wares."

"A woman with beauty, talent, *and* a business sense, how rare! And he's abandoned you here? My dear, please, come in through to the drawing room. I shall have refreshments brought. I must go change and wash, but you should relax." He took her hand and pulled her into the next room. She snatched up her bag of wares before she found herself in a library. A brief impression of books from floor to ceiling, red-leather overstuffed chairs, and a mahogany desk flickered by before he brought her to a brighter room.

Blasted with a riot of decoration, Esme couldn't take in the entire space at once. She had too much to look at. Instead, she stared at the table in front of her, which held three arranged leather-bound books, an empty tea tray, and a fine china vase containing a single pink rose.

"Are you comfortable, my dear? I shall return soon. Help yourself to tea when it arrives." Lord Carrick hurried out the door, his bootheels clicking down the hallway before she could utter a word.

Now that Esme had a chance to catch her breath, she studied the room. Varying shades of gray and pale blue decorated the space. She daren't touch a thing, for fear she'd break it. Several long sofas and single chairs clustered around tables with precious ornaments of glass and china. A lace-maker must have exploded in the room, as lace doilies nestled under each ornament and object d'art, doilies along the marble mantelpiece, lace curtains on the windows, even lacy designs on the thick carpet under her feet. Wouldn't Eithne be envious of this room?

Esme stood to examine the brass figurines on the mantelpiece when footsteps sounded. They were too light to be Lord Carrick's or Mr. Walsh's. She sat again, folding her hands in her lap and straightening her back. Perhaps the Dowager?

A maid, no older than sixteen, arrived with tea. She'd pulled her dark hair under a white mob cap. She wore pale blue livery with a lace-edged apron. After placing the tea tray on the table, she curtsied once and disappeared. Esme let out a long breath.

Lord Carrick *had* said she should help herself. Esme reached out a tentative hand for a sugared biscuit on the three-tiered tray. Yet more lace sat under each tray of sweets and savories. Esme twisted her mouth in a wry smile. Someone loved their lace. If she learned to tat, she'd have a lifetime customer.

Esme glimpsed red out of the corner of her eye. The pillow on the chair next to her had been the first one she sold Mr. Walsh, with the cardinal. Such an odd, surreal sensation to find her own handiwork decorating this grand room, with its myriad collection of exquisite ornaments. Someone treasured her creations. Her back straightened again, but this time, from pride.

She poured a cup of tea with shaking hands, adding several lumps of sugar. She'd first tasted tea when Alan's father made them some. While Esme loved tea, it remained an expensive luxury. She liked it sweet with plenty of milk.

A novel savory followed the sugary biscuit. It had bread, meat, and unusual spices. Perhaps lamb? She chose a third morsel when someone else entered.

Guilty, she dropped her hand from the tea tray. Mr. Walsh returned with the chintz dress.

"Ah, Mistress Fitzgerald. The Dowager Sweeney would love this dress, as well as the other selections I've made. Shall I bring you the payment in here?" His expression remained neutral, but Esme caught a hint of censure. His tone implied that business shouldn't be conducted in the drawing room.

"No, I'll return to your office." She stood and almost knocked over the tea tray in her haste. As she reached out to steady the tower, she brushed her sleeve into her teacup, dragging the warm liquid across the white doily. She gasped in horror, but Mr. Walsh intervened with a white handkerchief, dabbing the errant liquid away.

Esme had already ruined expensive lace. She'd likely knock over a priceless china vase next. She used tiny steps, keeping her body rigid as she followed Mr. Walsh back into his office.

They worked out the details of the bill as usual, but Esme detected a change in Mr. Walsh's manner. He'd always been fair, but detached. An expression flickered across his face, a lingering look, as if he saw her in a different light. It made her uncomfortable.

Once they completed the transaction, Esme packed the rejected items into her bag. She stood to return to the drawing room.

"Would you care to leave your bag here? You may collect it later, if you like."

She hadn't mistaken the tone. He implied she wouldn't leave soon, which, in turn, implied other things.

Esme breathed in deep, placed her bag under her chair for safekeeping, and gave Mr. Walsh a haughty nod. She gathered what grace she had and returned to the drawing room.

To her relief, Lord Carrick hadn't yet returned. Perhaps more over-sweet tea would drown the butterflies in permanent residence in her stomach.

Ornate decorations adorned the cornices and the candle chandelier above her. She wondered who lit those dozens of candles. They must need a long candlestick, or perhaps a ladder, to reach each one.

As she grinned at the image of the young maid perched on her tiptoes, trying to light a tiny high-perched candle, a sound behind her made her spin, the smile still on her face. Turning, she spied Lord Carrick, fresh-washed and combed. He wore a stunning deep-burgundy velvet jacket over ivory jabot and riding trews. In addition, he'd pulled back his blond hair in a velvet ribbon matched to his jacket.

The lord flashed a grin in response to hers, his teeth dazzling. "Such a lovely sight to return to. Tell me, my dear, what has you so delighted?"

To tell him would expose her as a bumpkin. Instead, she gave him a shy smile back. After obvious consideration, she chose another morsel from the tea tray and popped it into her mouth.

He let out a chuckle. "You'll be fine tonight, my dear. Perfectly fine. That frock is lovely, but it needs something else. Do you have a brooch, perhaps? Something delicate would set it off."

Esme shook her head, mute. Esme wouldn't have dared bring her brooch to this… whatever it would be… even if she still had the jewelry.

The lord frowned, shaking his head. "Ah well, it can't be helped. Now, would you like to sing with me before others arrive?"

She'd been right. He wanted a showgirl, a spectacle for entertainment.

Esme always loved singing with her family, or at gatherings. But she felt more comfortable with friends and neighbors. This performance would be for strangers. Rich, noble strangers, at that. The butterflies hadn't drowned. In fact, they'd multiplied.

Lord Carrick strode to the pianoforte in the corner, with deep, polished wood and a padded stool. He uncovered the keys and fluttered his fingers over the ones in the higher register, like faeries dancing on dewdrops.

The priest in Ardara had a pianoforte. She'd loved the rich sounds the keys made.

His hands perched over the keys, ready to play. "What song shall we play, my dear?"

He hadn't called her by her name once since she'd arrived. Had he forgotten it? She abruptly forgot every song she'd ever learned. Her mind went blank with panic. It must have shown on her face.

"Do you know 'Fare Thee Well?'" He played the first few bars on the keys and Esme nodded, swallowing against her dry throat. She lost her voice with her memory.

Esme coughed and cleared her throat. She reached for her teacup to down the last cold sip of creamy liquid. As she did so, the lace from her sleeve caught on the filigreed edge of the tea tray, pulling it over and knocking the remaining sweets and morsels to the floor. Powdered sugar exploded on the thick carpet, blending into the grays and blues of the Turkish design. She gasped in horror at her own clumsiness.

Lord Carrick chuckled under his breath and yelled out, "Rose!" The girl who'd placed the tea tray rushed in. She surveyed the situation and whirled out without a word. Seconds later, she reappeared with a dustpan and brush. Esme stood beside the disaster, struck dumb with horror, in the spot where she dumped the sweets. She moved aside for the maid.

Her blush rose hot and fast. "I am so sorry, Lord Carrick, you must think me hopelessly clumsy. Is there anything I can do to help?" She thought that's what a lady might say in apology, and it sounded right to her.

"Please, think nothing of it. If you must assist, you can help by calling me Carrick. The Lord is my father." His grin widened and he reached for her hand. Hers had turned icy, but his felt warm and soft like a girl's, unused to hard work.

Esme swallowed. She wanted to pull her hands away, but he held them fast. "Certainly, Lord… Certainly, Carrick." She choked the words out, her voice a whisper. The whole situation had become ridiculous. Did she think this a tale from ancient history, where the comely maid swoons in the master's arms, then they end up riding off together into the sunset, and society be damned? That sort of thing didn't happen in actual life. Not to a married woman.

The reminder of his marriage stiffened her spine, and she extracted her hands. She covered her gaffe by walking to the pianoforte and picking up the music. She held it up as if she could read it.

Esme knew words and numbers, but had never even seen written music. The dots and lines seemed like a foreign cipher, an ancient language of a forgotten race, like the faeries. Perhaps that came close to the truth. Turlough O'Carolan, the last great Bard of Ireland, had supped with the faeries. He brought hundreds of tunes into the human world.

She hoped she knew the same version of this tune, Lord Carrick… the same version Carrick did. It seemed so strange calling him by his first name, like a lad down the street, as opposed to the lord of a fine manor house. Esme pushed the thought aside and looked at the title. Yes, she knew this song, another one her father loved and sang to her mother on her birthday. Nostalgia for that part of her life, and missing her parents, gripped her heart so hard, she almost cried out.

While handing the sheets back to Carrick, she spoke with firm determination. "I'm ready when you are. Would you mind playing a refrain first, so I know your timing?"

His eyes twinkled with mischief as he sat on the padded stool with a paisley pattern in cut velvet. Such a fine fabric for an occasional piece.

Carrick played through the melody once and then started again. This second time, Esme sang along. Shy and light at first, she gained confidence in her voice and her place.

The room had tall ceilings, so her voice bounced back until sound surrounded her. Such a wonderful feeling, almost as thrilling as the buzzing of the stones. She floated on the wings of song. When it ended, she felt bereft, as if she'd lost a precious jewel.

Carrick gazed at her with a new appreciation. Before, he gave her admiring looks, as any man might an attractive woman. Now it seemed different. Perhaps respect?

"Such an exquisite voice, Esme. We don't need further practice at all. Do you play the pianoforte?" He scooted over and patted the empty spot on the bench.

Esme shook her head. She'd never played anything with keys. She might coax a tune from a tin whistle, but nothing like her father. He played anything he picked up. Her grandfather told her his own father had been a talented musician.

A brief frown flashed across his face, but disappeared so fast, Esme might have mistaken it. "Ah, well, your singing is accomplishment enough to satisfy even the harshest critic. Have you had enough tea? We'll have other guests arriving soon, I shouldn't doubt."

"How many are coming?" She hoped only a few came. The butterflies must have had babies.

"Just a few, perhaps five. Society isn't robust in this backwater, after all." His brow furrowed. "Not like London, or even Dublin. This is more like I imagine America must be. Isolated and desolate, but with fewer savages."

Savages in America, with her parents, her sister Bridey and Níamh. Would they get attacked by savages? She'd heard of Indians, primitive folk who scalped men and kidnapped women. Esme shivered at the thought of Bridey kidnapped and living with the savages.

"Are you cold, Esme? Here, let me get you a shawl." He rummaged through an armoire and brought out a tweed shawl in muted greens. She hadn't been cold, but she accepted and used it as a luxuriant shield.

Carrick glanced toward the door as he sat at the pianoforte again. "I will warn you, stay out of arms' reach of old Judge Fraley. You might say he's unconcerned with personal morals."

Just as he played the opening notes for another practice song, the butler arrived at the entrance archway. In a sonorous voice, he announced the first visitor, the aforementioned judge. In walked a large, sallow man well into his sixties and from the red-veined, bulbous nose he sported, fond of the drink. The butler announced another tall, thin man, but Esme couldn't see him past the Judge's bulk.

As others arrived, Esme sat in the corner, watching them mingle. She didn't know what to do with her hands. She tried not to fidget, but the butterflies turned into dragons.

Carrick laughed with an elegant older woman, a loud, boundless laugh. When his mirth faded, he glanced over and caught her gaze. He gestured to the woman he spoke with, and they both approached her corner.

Carrick's eyes sparkled as he spoke. "Esme, may I introduce The Honorable Lady Violeta Trudeau? She's on holiday from Le Havre, in France and looks forward to your singing this afternoon. Lady Trudeau, this is Mistress Esme Fitzgerald, one of our local artisans."

Esme curtsied as she'd seen others do, hoping she did it right. "I'm quite pleased to meet you, Lady Trudeau." She swam in the turbulent sea with no boat around to rescue her. *Artisan? What a grand word for a seamstress.*

The short, plump woman peered at her through a pair of tiny eyeglasses, which she held on a stick. "Oh, dear, what lovely embroidery on your dress! Did you do that yourself, then? It's exquisite." The lady traced her finger, not touching, along the rosebuds and vines on Esme's overdress. Esme blushed, but she gave a quick nod.

Lady Violeta wore her hair swept up into an amazing coiffure, filled with dried flowers and a stuffed bird. Esme had never seen such a display. The woman's own dress, though of fine, pale-pink watered silk, seemed plain next to her outrageous hairstyle.

Carrick spoke to Lady Violeta again, leaving Esme a chance to observe her. She must be older than she'd seemed from far away. Fine wrinkles fanned out from her eyes and around her lips. The skin on her hands looked so thin. She had a heavy, hooked nose, upon which she perched her tiny glasses when needed. It made her look like a near-sighted raptor.

A knot of three men talked to the Judge near the pianoforte, one of them thumping on it with a massive hand, accentuating whatever point he made in his argument. Esme winced at the violence to the delicate instrument.

Carrick said something to her, but she hadn't been listening.

"What? I mean, I'm sorry, I didn't hear that?"

He raised an elegant eyebrow. "I asked if you were ready to sing, my dear Esme?"

"Oh! Yes, of course." She walked over to the pianoforte, where several men watched her. They didn't move out of the way, so she stopped short of the instrument. Unsure, she glanced back at Carrick.

He stood right beside her. "If you would excuse us, gentlemen? We should like the use of the pianoforte."

The youngest of the group gave Carrick a disdainful, almost resentful look, but sat on the nearest divan. The Judge lingered. Mindful of Carrick's warning, Esme didn't come within arms-length. Carrick drank his glass in one gulp and gave a few experimental taps on the keys, then played the refrain from the song they practiced.

Esme opened her mouth, but nothing came out. She half-expected enormous butterflies to burst from her throat, but only a strangled croak escaped. She swallowed, cleared her throat, and nodded to Carrick, who once again played the tune.

Her voice wavered at first but she soon shut out the audience and their grand clothing, fancy hair, and languorous manners. She soared through the song on the wings of a nightingale, dipping and darting back and forth. While singing like this was a joy to her, a joy she should indulge in more, she'd rarely sung since Seán left.

Thoughts of Seán almost robbed her of her singing breath. She concentrated hard to finish the song. Her throat shrank with tears she mustn't shed now. Esme tamped down on the memory of her missing husband and finished her performance with a sweet trill.

The applause from the audience made her glow hot with pleasure. She'd done it! She showed talent and aplomb. Now she might escape. Esme made a curtsy, then glanced to Carrick. Would he require another tune from her?

A hand touched her waist, and she whirled to find the huge red nose of the Judge about three inches from her eyes. She flinched, but the pianoforte at her back stopped her from retreating. She knocked her heel on the leg, forcing a stifled cry.

His breath stank thick with sour whiskey, despite the early hour. "Lovely, lass, just lovely. You are quite the enchantress with your voice. Will you sing another?" Esme almost gagged at the stench. To extract herself, she sidled along the edge of the pianoforte until she reached Carrick, perched on the bench with a fresh glass in his hand.

Lady Violeta came to her rescue and inserted herself between Esme and the Judge. "Judge Fraley, you unhand that young woman. You've frightened the poor thing half to death."

Esme gasped in fresh air, searching for a window.

"Now, then, child, you stand there, and I shall maintain a guard. Please, *do* sing another song. Your voice is indeed delightful."

With a shy smile to her rescuer, she turned to Carrick.

He showed her the music page. "How about this one?" Esme didn't recognize the title and shook her head. He handed the book to her, so she flipped the pages until she saw one she recognized, squinting at the fancy script.

Carrick nodded and played the refrain again. She knew this one well, a sad love song. Though an English song, the Irish loved their misery and adopted anything sad for their own.

Esme sang several more that afternoon, and then Lady Violeta sang a song. She had a husky, almost furry voice, warm and sweet. Relieved not to be the only performer, Esme felt less like a pet monkey on display.

One of Lady Violeta's remarks made her laugh, and she covered her mouth in horrified embarrassment, but no one seemed to care. She had little interaction with the men as they clustered around the Judge, but Carrick and Lady Violeta kept her company. After Carrick plucked another fresh glass of wine from the servant's tray, he told a rather off-color joke. A young man in blue livery lit the candles. It had grown dark without her noticing.

Esme entertained the notion she'd been unfair to her host, that he had honorable intentions. He might have invited her to bring her into society. She'd never heard of such a thing, but she may have been too cynical. Esme wished she could ask him outright, to judge his truth. But without the brooch, she wouldn't rely on its power. She needed to get that back from Eithne.

As several guests left, Esme glanced around. If she returned to Mr. Walsh's office, she might collect her bag, and escape. She wandered toward the entrance to the library as the last male guest left.

Carrick came from behind her and took her hands tight in his grip. "Esme, you aren't leaving so soon, are you? I've a supper set." She didn't dare pull loose. He stood too close to her and her heart beat faster.

Lady Violeta tutted several times. "Carrick, you naughty man! Don't corner the poor child. You're as bad as the Judge. Esme, dear, I shall join you both. It should offer you some safety, at least. Bonner!" She called for the butler as if she lived there herself. "Set *three* for supper, if you please."

Carrick's smile didn't fade, but his jaw muscles tightened. That flash of resentment quieted any qualms Esme had. He must not be used to being thwarted, despite his polished methods. The steel in his face boded ill for any plans of escape. Perhaps she could leave with Lady Violeta. She would have to abandon her bag. Mr. Walsh might hold it for her next visit. If she came back.

As they entered the dining room, Esme had never imagined such a meal in her life. The table glittered with china, silver, and a massive candelabrum. Tall pillar candles flickered on stands near the walls, making the room glow and sparkle. Esme counted at least twenty covered dishes on the sideboard. All this for just three people? Esme's eyes grew wide at such extravagance, as she ate two simple meals a day. She must eat sparingly, since she'd filled up during tea, and didn't wish to get ill.

Esme recognized some dishes as the footmen served. Roast pheasant and potatoes au gratin, stewed eels, and a creamy oyster stew. Others looked strange, such as the odd breaded balls and sticky, stewed fruit.

Lady Violeta gestured to the footman. "Those are dates in honey, dear. Do try them, they're delicious."

Esme ate one, uncertain how to keep the sticky mess from her clothing. Between the soups and candied sweets, everything tried to fall or drip on her dress. She contented herself with tiny bites and half spoonfuls. Was this why high-class people ate so daintily?

The Lady passed her another delicacy to try. "Where do you live, Mistress Fitzgerald? Are you nearby?"

Conversation would be safer than trying to eat more oyster stew. "No, I live on the south end of the island, past Achill Sound, perhaps ten miles away."

Lady Violeta's eyebrows reached for her hairline as she swiveled to her host. "I didn't think anything lived on the south end, Carrick. I thought you called it a barren area?"

He dabbed a napkin on the corner of his mouth. "It is, Violeta. Some crofters scrape out a living with sheep and fishing, but it's not a hospitable place for any industry."

Esme's jaw clenched. The village did well enough. They may have never accepted her as one of their own, to be sure, but none of them starved. They had food enough to enjoy their lives. To hear Carrick disdain their efforts infused her with anger and pride, but she kept her peace.

"I *have* considered setting up a warehouse for shipped goods, but it doesn't seem worth the cost. The amount of production in the area is so low, they have little surplus to sell on. I might set up a storefront to offer goods for sale. I would have to find a suitable factor, though."

The idea of being able to purchase items from other places, like needles or fine thread, sounded fantastic. However, the notion of this outside baron swooping in and taking their hard-earned money stuck in her craw. Seán might work as a factor, with his skill in trade... if he lived.

When the footmen, matched in size and livery, emerged with the sweets, Esme stifled a burp. They carried a cake in the shape of a castle, complete with drawbridge and moat, as if someone sculpted a medieval fortress from frosting.

Lady Violeta clapped her hands. "Oh, how delightful! It seems a shame to cut into such a piece of artistry."

The cake tasted even sweeter than the honeyed dates. It must be pure sugar, with more sugar spread on top. She picked at it rather than stuff more into her already full stomach.

Carrick raised a silver fork. "Do you not like it, Esme?"

"It's delicious, but I'm so full from supper. I have no room for more." She hoped she didn't offend him. She'd never left a plate so full in her life, but if she ate any more of the sugary treat, she'd be sick.

Esme sat in silence as Carrick and Lady Violeta discussed artwork she'd commissioned last week in Dublin. None of the artists' names sounded familiar, nor did the words."Cheearoskurro" must be a foreign word, maybe Greek. Esme picked at her frosting.

Lady Violeta let out a deep sigh and clasped her hands. "Well, I believe it must be time for me to leave. Mistress Fitzgerald, would you be so kind as to accompany me?"

Carrick shook his head. "Now, Violeta, the girl still has business here, and her home is on the other side of the island. She has goods in Mr. Walsh's office to sell to my mother. I'll get her home safe, never fear." He used a wheedling tone Esme had never heard from him. That last statement shone bright as a bald lie, and her stomach churned with fear and doubt.

Lady Violeta scowled. "Nonsense. Mr. Walsh is efficient. He would have concluded any business before the party started. Bonner!"

The butler arrived as if by magic. "Mum?"

"Fetch Mistress Fitzgerald's things from Mr. Walsh's office. He'll be there, I'm certain."

The butler disappeared without even glancing toward Carrick for confirmation. He returned in short order with Esme's grubby-looking bag of creations.

Carrick rose as Lady Violeta took the bag from Bonner's hands. "I must protest. I've a room made up for the girl here."

She sent him a withering look. "I'm quite certain you have arranged everything to *look* seemly. But she acts like a frightened deer, and no wonder. I'm sure you gave her little choice in this arrangement." The woman turned to Esme. "May I see your work, dear? Are these goods you've made yourself?"

Esme nodded, unable to speak, as Lady Violeta pulled out several items. She held up a bonnet with blue marigolds embroidered around the edges. "Oh, look at that! Delightful. I'll have to commission you for a gown. My seamstress is decent enough, but not at all imaginative. You enchant with your skill and your voice. Come, Mistress Fitzgerald. I shall take you home."

Carrick half-rose from his seat, his arm out. "But…"

Lady Violeta raised a hand. "No, Carrick. I shall not allow you to get your claws into this sweet, *married* young lady. Go about your business now. Shoo!"

With a bustle and a flutter, a dazed Esme found herself outside and handed into Lady Violeta's coach by the footman. She barely had time to nod thanks before they sped off, clattering down the gravel driveway into the dark of the night.

Lady Violeta patted her hand. "Now, if he troubles you again, you come to me. I'm staying at the hotel in Dugort, and you can stay with me this evening. I shall take you anywhere you like in the morning. Unless you prefer to stay and take your chances with Carrick?"

Esme found her voice. "Oh, no, Lady Violeta! I'm so grateful for your intervention. I didn't know what I'd do on my own."

"You're safe now. He likes to pretend he's genteel, but his conquests are legend. He *does* have a wife, but she's been locked up in an asylum for years in London. She's quite lost to him, so he searches elsewhere. Usually, he finds a young widow or the like. But your husband's still alive, yes?"

"I believe so, but he's been, well, gone for some time now."

"Hmm. How long?"

Esme gulped. "Eight months."

The older woman exhaled and rolled her eyes. "Long enough for Carrick to decide he's got an open season on you. But we shan't let that happen. Now, tomorrow morning we shall get some shopping done, discuss that commission, and then I'll take you back to your home."

"But it's several hours' ride each way, Lady Violeta! I can travel home on my own, I'm used to the trip, but you--"

Lady Violeta laughed. "I've ridden the width and breadth of this country and England and France as well, Mistress Fitzgerald. May I call you Esme? Please, call me Violeta. A couple hours' drive in the country will do me a world of good. It's musty in the hotel."

How had she gotten so lucky? Without Lady Violeta, she'd have had no choice but to become Carrick's mistress. Now she might have found a new patroness and a way to escape his advances all rolled into one. Once again she drifted on fate. For once, she drifted in the right direction.

The hotel room looked almost as sumptuous as Sweeney House. Esme took the maid's room off the main one with gratitude. She curled up into the soft bed and fell into instant sleep.

Esme woke in the night, her stomach roiling with pain. She rushed to the chamber pot in time to throw up the rich meal. Once her stomach emptied, the stuffiness of the room smothered her. She must get outside in the cool air. Lady Violeta snored faintly behind her bed curtains. Esme pulled on her shawl and crept out of the room.

Faded, red velvet covered the stairs and floors in the hotel, with well-polished mahogany balustrades. As she exited the building, dawn approached, bringing thick fog. Esme breathed deep, relishing in the fresh air, quelling her nausea.

Only a few people walked on the street, servants or apprentices, scuttling about in the morning mist to their masters' bidding.

Esme breathed deep again and almost busted out of her stays. Her stomach settled more with the sweet morning fog. She felt reborn, with a new outlook on her future. She held her hope tight, for with hope came joy. Such a simple concept. Esme might no longer be reliant on Sweeney House for her patronage. Perhaps Lady Violeta would even help her find Seán, wherever he might be.

The sun struggled to burn through the heavy mist, and a warm beam shot through. Esme strolled down the town's main street, peering at closed shop windows and dreaming about what the future might hold.

A dim figure emerged from the mist. The set of his shoulders and his gait made her catch her breath. She could have sworn Seán walked toward her. As he got closer, details became clearer. Long, black hair, a disarming smile, but no, the figure disappeared, dissolved into fog. Esme shuddered, convinced she'd just seen the shade of her dead husband.

A clatter behind her made her spin. Carrick stepped down from his carriage. He wore an unpleasant frown and slapped his gloves against his thigh.

Esme's gaze darted around for a way to hide. The storefronts attached to each other, revealing no convenient alleys. She froze in place while he marched toward her, anger in every line of his body.

He grabbed her by the upper arm, fingers digging into her flesh. "How fortunate I decided to arrive early. The hotel clerk swore you'd already left, but I thought he lied. I'm happy to be wrong. Now, girl, you needn't have run away so fast. I'll be gentle, I promise."

Even if Esme had no magic, his eyes belied his words. She pushed to get a more truthful reaction. "What do you mean to do?"

"As if you didn't know! You seemed pleased enough yesterday to be in my parlor. And this is how you repay my kindness, by running off without so much as a 'by your leave?' You ungrateful little wench! Come, your protector isn't around now, and we've business to conclude."

Carrick jerked on her arm, and she fell toward him, stumbling into his embrace. He wasn't an imposing man, but he had more strength than she did. Without difficulty, he shoved her into his carriage. She tried to exit out the other side, but he'd locked it, and the latch must be on the outside. She curled up in the seat corner.

"Did you think you'd just run away like that? You have much to offer, my girl, and I mean to take that offer."

"I'm not offering! I just want to go home. To my husband!"

He rolled his eyes and smiled, but not sweet like yesterday. "Your husband is long dead, Esme. I looked into it after our first meeting. He disappeared months ago, and he'll never be back. Be thankful you'll have a man in your life again." As he spoke of Seán's death, that hint of kindness flickered again, but it disappeared with the last cruel sentence.

Her breath caught as she tried not to cry.

"Oh, do leave off, girl. It's not as if it hurts. Afterward, I'll take you to your home. Then my payment will be complete."

"Payment?"

The cruel smile returned. "Indeed. I understand you have a quite charming twin sister in Ardara."

Esme's eyes grew wide as a sickening suspicion grew in her heart. "How do you know Eithne?"

The grin he gave showed too many bright white teeth. "How do you think I found you? She told me where you lived. And that your husband wouldn't interfere."

How did she ever consider this man attractive?

They arrived at Sweeney House in a few moments. He yanked her out of the carriage and toward the front door. The footman who'd helped her into Lady Violeta's carriage the night before gave her a sympathetic look. Esme wanted to cry for help, but he worked for Carrick. She'd have to help herself, for once.

Esme stomped hard into Carrick's instep. He bellowed as he dropped her arm. She scrambled away, ripping her dress from where it caught on Carrick's belt. She pelted down the back of the house and into the peat bog behind it. Esme didn't know how to find Lady Violeta's hotel from here, so she ran. She'd rather drown in the bogs than be forced into Carrick's bed.

Though she stumbled twice and fell once, she heard no pursuit. In no time, her fine dress got muddy and bedraggled, torn in several places, and one shoe lost in the muck. She slowed her pace as she picked her way through the bog. A bog would suck someone down in an instant. She moved from tussock to tussock, now testing each step.

Her old nightmares returned to haunt her. Stuck in her endless swamp, mud sucked at her feet, lost forever to wander among the muck. If she wanted to banish her nightmares once and for all, she must find her way out.

Could she find her way out to the other side? Slievemore Mountain lay past the bog. From there, she'd find her way to the stones, and then home.

The long, lonely, cold, and wet slog through the endless marshes stole all sense of time. Esme slipped and slid, soon getting covered in muck. She should have circled around to get back to the hotel, to Lady Violeta's room, but got well lost by the time she thought of this. So onward she trudged, step by step, squishing and chilled.

Esme plopped onto a clammy rock, utterly lost, miserable, and about ready to give up and let the bog consume her. The buzz of an insect flitting into her ear made her think of the stones buzzing with the brooch's magic.

What if she tried to *sense* the stones? Her grandfather never mentioned such a thing, but she must try.

Esme perched on a clammy rock jutting out of the mossy bog and closed her eyes. She quested along the bog for those tendrils of heat and light which connected her to the stones. As the stench of rotting mud tickled her nose, she cast about in desperate jumps, searching for that bit of magic.

The jingle of tack echoed in the swirling mists. Her heart skipped a beat. Had Carrick found her? Or had Seán returned to rescue her, like an outlandish heroic tale, after so many months? She snorted at the fancy. Her own imagination ran wild.

While shoving these fantasies aside, she quested out once more. Was that a glimmer of heat? No, just a marsh bird. Esme needed something heavier, full of the ponderous magic of the earth itself. She caught a whiff of chalky damp and there! She found them! After opening her eyes, she scrambled through the wet reeds to the pulsing magic. When the shapes in the mist resolved, she cried out in relief. She found her standing stones.

How had she known they were there? Had *they* known *she* was there? Had they called to her? For her to find them with no sense of direction or location seemed amazing.

They hummed.

Esme crept to the altar stone, her shaking hand stretched out to touch it. For a moment, terror seized her and she hesitated. The warmth radiated so strongly the heat traveled up her arm and into her heart. "Sweet God in heaven…"

After leaning forward the last inch, she gasped with the impact. Nostalgic images of home raced through her memory. Safety, love, comfort, all warred within her mind. Esme draped her entire body over the stone, spread eagle, to draw all the delicious warmth into her body. For the first time in what seemed like forever, she felt safe and calm.

Esme lay for an endless time, melding with the earth magic of the stones. When she rose, her muscles screamed with pain, bruised and battered. Something sickened within her, maybe within the stones themselves. A rotten, corrupt edge to what used to be whole. Though the stones healed her, she felt more hollow than before.

The faeries must have taken another piece of her. She shivered. How many pieces did she have left?

The mists hid the daylight. She must get back to her home, back to Aisling, Katy, and Aoife. Had they even returned yet? Still at Aisling's great-aunt's house, most likely. It didn't matter, she must return. She hoped the fog would remain, to hide her.

Esme dusted off her hands, tugged her dress in place, and scrubbed off the worst of the mud. She began the long, barefoot journey to the other end of the island.

Eithne

Eithne woke with a start. *What was that?* A noise, someone crying out for God. Eithne grunted. As if that would help anyone.

The dawn light just edged through the window. Had Carrick corrupted her dear, sweet sister yet? She smiled at the image of her oh-so-righteous sister tangled in a compromising position with a married man. With that stain on her reputation, no one would care if she disappeared. Eithne wouldn't have to worry that her sister would pop up some day to reclaim the brooch.

With this lovely image, Eithne rose to complete her morning ablutions. After choosing her outfit with care, she chaffed at the daily chores she must go through until she heard word.

Yes, she had patience. She'd learned patience from being married to Hugh. But even her patience had limits.

Chapter Nineteen

April 1798

Esme

T he cottage stood cold and empty, and yet it offered Esme a safe haven from the tumult of her nightmares. She shook with chill by the time she stumbled inside and coaxed a reluctant fire from the hearth. Her feet got bloody from the walk across rocky roads, her second shoe long since sucked away by the bog.

Esme sat with a plaid woolen blanket wrapped around her shoulders, shivering hours after her body warmed to a toasty glow. She cleaned her throbbing feet and bound them with cloth. While she might repair the dress, she wanted nothing else to do with it after what almost happened. However, she couldn't bring herself to burn it. She shoved it into the back of her drawer.

She wouldn't find safety here. Carrick would come to her house. Esme must hide. She must leave. Would Lady Violeta still be in town? No, she'd head back to London soon. The patroness wouldn't be a permanent solution.

Should she go into service as her private seamstress? Service seemed such a different life than she'd ever known. Such a position had a pride of place. Her family had never been in service, and Esme held an unspoken qualm about entering a life of servitude. The work wouldn't be any worse than what she did now. But she'd be giving up on her ability to care for herself. She'd relied on others far too much. And what would become of Katy? Great houses didn't permit girls in service to be married or have children. Besides, Lady Violeta said she already had a seamstress. She couldn't put someone else out of work like that.

No, she'd take what she could carry and leave. Her mind swam with confusion when she considered where, so she shoved that decision away. First, she'd find Aisling and the girls in Achill Sound. Aisling might have some ideas.

A crash came from outside. Had Carrick come already? Her eyes darted around in a panic, searching for a hiding place. The small cottage had nothing. Fear paralyzed her. She stood like a statue.

When muffled curses followed the jangling tack, Esme gasped. She recognized that voice, and a faint glimmer of hope crept out from under her blanket of mourning.

The door burst open with a spray of wind and rain. Seán, her own dark pirate, stood in the doorway, soaking wet from the storm and looking like he hadn't shaved in months.

She leapt at him, her arms wrapped around his neck, almost knocking him over. "Seán! Oh, Seán, you're alive!"

He laughed and wrapped his strong arms around her, swinging her around and around. She lost all her fears in his embrace. "Oh, Esme, *mo chroí!*"

Esme pulled him in, still hugging, and slammed the door behind them. "Oh, come in, you great lumbering fool! You're letting in the storm."

After she served him some stew, Seán told his story. "I didn't remember anything after they hit me. I knew my name, but not the name of our town, or where I lived. I remembered you, and I described you to anyone who would listen, but Esme is too common of a name. They put me in that hospital in Galway, Esme. But no one would help me find you or let me out."

Esme shook her head. "We'd just about given you up for dead, Seán."

"So had I, *mo chuisle,* so had I."

Esme sat curled in Seán's arms, spooned against him in front of the hearth. She never wanted to leave his safety.

Their reunion began with exploring each other's bodies again, with almost as much tenderness and consideration as their first time. His hand caressed her back, down to her waist, and over her hips. She delighted in brushing her hands through his thick, dark hair, and digging her fingers into his chest. When she moved her hands to his buttocks, she pulled him close. His kisses made everything else disappear.

Esme shoved all memories of Carrick aside as they melted into their love-making.

When she cried out, Seán filled her mind, her heart, and her body. They fell asleep entangled together, thankful to be one again.

Esme wanted nothing more than to descend into Seán's arms forever, but after her trip to the other side of the island, her garden needed tending and the house needed cleaning. Aisling hadn't returned from Achill Sound with the girls, so she had time.

As she pruned the weeds from her plot, as well as Aisling's, she heard a hiss behind her.

Startled, she turned to see a neighbor. Esme straightened to face the old woman. "Did you say something, Mistress Lynch?"

In wicked, spitting words, the old woman said, "Go back, ya wee witch. Go back to whatever hell spawned you. Can't ye figure yet we don't want you here?"

Esme swallowed, but stood to face her accuser. "I pay rent, just as you. I belong here. I've lived here for years. My daughter was born here."

"Aye, and she's a witch-spawn. Ye're evil, the lot of ye! And if you don't go on your own, we'll make you wish you did."

She hobbled off before Esme formed an answer to the horrible words. After letting out a deep breath, she finished her weeding. The words kept running around in her mind, though.

With such poison in the village, leaving might be the best idea, after all. She'd need to get the brooch back, but why move back here afterward? They'd only moved here because of Seán's cousin, and he had left before they arrived.

But first, she needed to tell Seán about the brooch and her need to get it back.

Seán shook his head as he stirred their dinner at the hearth. "A magic brooch. Esme, have you hit your head or something? Are you listening to yourself?"

"I *know* I sound mad, Seán, but I'm telling you the truth. The brooch is a family heirloom. Grandfa gave it to me years ago, and the thing has power. Eithne stole it when she visited. I need to get it back."

He set his lips in a thin line at the mention of Eithne. "Why? Why not just let her keep the blasted thing?"

"She's doing something, something wrong. I'm not sure what, but I can sense the wrongness. We have this connection between us. I'm connected with the brooch, too. The land in the stone circle has turned slimy, dirty, corrupt. If I don't fix this, something will go horribly wrong. Seán, please believe me!"

Seán crossed his arms. "And what about Katy? You can't bring our daughter on this madcap quest."

Esme waved away that issue. "Aisling said she'd care for her while we're gone. She planned to spend some time in Achill Sound with her great-aunt, and Katy can spend some time in a real town."

Seán gathered her into an embrace, kissing her forehead. "You may be as mad as a hare, but you're still my wife. If you need to go haring off to Ardara to get back a chunk of jewelry, then who am I to stand in the way?"

He held her at arms-length to gaze into her eyes. "But how will you get this brooch back from Eithne? That one isn't going to hand anything over. She wouldn't give a cup of water on a rainy day."

Esme took a deep breath, looking north toward Ardara. "I haven't figured that part out yet. But we've got days to come up with a plan as we travel."

He stroked her hair with gentle hands and gave a wry smile. "Aye, that we do."

The rain fell in a constant torrent, making roads treacherous and the travel slow. Esme didn't own one dry thing and her skin chaffed with the damp. They'd lost the wagon awning during Seán's string of bad luck, but she didn't want to bring that bad time up, so she suffered in silence.

When they pulled into town, she glanced at the old bakery, hoping to glimpse her dear friend, Alan. He'd be a grown man now, of course. Her last memory of him flashed as a lanky lad, wispy blond hair, almost white in the sun.

Esme spied the McHugh's pub and dragged Seán to the door. They walked in, dripping and shivering, as the landlady brought them mugs of ale and meat stew.

The only brilliant idea they'd thought of was to enlist some local help. Esme felt a pang of loss that she wasn't a local any longer. She swallowed her bite of stew and sniffed back the sadness.

"Esme? Are you all right, *mo chroí*?" Seán lifted her chin with his fingers. She put on a brave smile. A cry would do her no good. She had her family and she'd find a new place to call home. No sense in sobbing over the past.

With a shake of her head, Esme took a sip of ale. "I'll be fine, love. I'm just cold and long for a warm bed."

"Aye, I'm for that myself. Let's get settled in a room for the night, and tomorrow we'll look up Alan."

Seán hadn't liked the idea of calling on his old rival, but Alan might have some way inside Eithne's house. They had no other notions.

When they reached the privacy of the room, Esme fell back on the large, warm, and most importantly, dry bed. After they laid out their damp clothing to dry, they cuddled together in thankful body warmth. Esme held him close, not wanting to let him leave ever again. Even if she had to go on the road with him on his trades, she wouldn't let him out of her sight.

The next morning, Esme and Seán dressed in their best. They walked three doors down to Alan's bakery.

Esme experienced a stab of doubt. What if Alan had moved? Or died? She would have left Katy all alone for nothing.

As soon as they opened the door, the sumptuous aroma of fresh-baked bread caressed them. Esme took in a deep breath, nostalgia and hunger vying for her attention. Alan's father had just pulled a fresh batch of loaves from the oven when he did a double take.

He looked her up and down and shook his head. "By Mother Mary herself, I thought you were a ghost! Sure and I'd never see Mistress Eithne dressed like that. That must be Esme herself! Come here, sweet girl, and give me a hug. I haven't seen your lovely face in years."

Esme's smile almost cracked her face as she gave Mr. Gallagher an enormous hug, wallowing in nostalgia at the scent of flour and yeast on his well-used apron. "Mr. Gallagher, it's wonderful to see you! Is Alan around?"

"Alan? Ah, but you wouldn't have heard, would you?"

"Heard?" Her earlier thoughts came back to stab her heart. "Heard what?"

Mr. Gallagher's face twisted up in disgust. He took a ball of dough off the counter and pounded the mass on the table with vigor. "That one's gone and converted, he has. He's a… a minister!"

Esme almost laughed with relief. A minister! Well, far better than dead. She held her tongue, though, and kept her expression horrified for the older man. At least now she knew where to find her friend.

After a promise to give her love to the rest of his family, they left the bakery and headed toward the inn. They'd have to travel back to Donegal Town. Ardara held no Protestant churches, and ministers wandered amongst the parishes. Alan's father said he lived and worked near Laghey.

Six weary hours later, they pulled their cart into the town of Laghey, an hour past Donegal Town. The Church of England spire rose from the center of town. When Esme peered into the building, the space seemed achingly empty. She leaned back against the wagon in defeat.

Seán put his arm around her shoulders. "It'll be grand, *mo chuisle*. If we can't find Alan, we'll think of another way. Let's head back to Ardara, aye? Let's see where your sister lives and what we'll have to contend with."

With a deep sigh of frustration, Esme pushed herself from the cart and jumped into the seat. As she did so, she spied a man walking toward them with an odd yet familiar gait. Alan? It must be! He'd filled out, but his shaggy blond hair remained the same. She hopped back down and ran toward him, wrapping her arms around him as his eyes grew wide. "Alan! Alan, it's really you!"

"Whoa, whoa, hold on! Wait… Esme? By all that's holy, I never dreamt to see you again!" He held her in a tight hug for several minutes.

Seán cleared his throat with pointed purpose.

With no embarrassment, Alan released Esme and held his hand out to Seán. "Oh, yes, of course. Seán? How nice to see you again."

Her husband glared at Alan's hand before shaking. The two men tried to out-squeeze each other but soon relented. Seán gave in to a grin, as did Alan. All seemed right in Esme's world again.

Alan turned back to Esme, his hand clapping her shoulder. "Whatever brings you to this lonely place, Esme? Have you been up to Ardara yet?"

Her expression turned serious. "I have, Alan, and I heard the tragic news."

"Tragic news? What news?" The look of horror on Alan's face made keeping her joke difficult.

She giggled. "About you becoming a minister, of course!"

"Oh! You must have talked to Da. Yes, well, he didn't care for my choice, that's true enough. But in the end, being a minister is a great deal more satisfying than kneading bread all day." He gave her a wry smile. "God above, it's good to see you. If you saw my da, does that mean you needed me?"

Esme rewarded him with a half-smile. "I do, my old friend. Eithne's been a sneak once again, and we need to fix things."

He rolled his eyes. "That one. I'm your man, Esme, as always. How can I help?"

Alan raised an eyebrow. "A brooch? Esme, there are easier ways of getting jewelry. Like walking through a nest of snakes. Why do you need the one Eithne stole?"

Esme gritted her teeth. What would Alan, a Protestant minister, say to a magical brooch? She didn't want to risk losing her childhood friend, not after finding him again after so many years. "This brooch is special, handed down through our family for generations."

His expression turned to a scowl. "And is Eithne not part of your family? She has several sons to pass her wealth on to when she goes."

She shook her head. "You don't understand. You won't understand, not even if I tell you."

With crossed arms, he said, "Try me."

Esme glanced at Seán, who gave her a shrug. She took a deep breath to quell her churning stomach. She'd just found her best friend after years. Would he hate her after this? No, no, she couldn't, but she wouldn't lie, either. "Grandfa told me tales about the brooch, a gift from the Good Folk. I don't want to risk angering them."

"Well, as a minister, I can't admit belief in them. However, as an Irishman, I understand you can't discount the Good Folk, and you don't abuse their gifts, no matter what. So, I suppose I need to help you. This won't be easy, though."

As they discussed the plan over supper, Alan suggested a classic distraction technique. He'd call on Eithne as a minister to discuss a charity project. She contributed to a food kitchen, and he'd question her on the poor quality of her donations.

While that happened, Seán would cause mischief in the fields. Seán bit his lip. "What sort of distraction? I don't want anyone hurt."

Esme put a finger on her lips. "A fire would be the most useful. If she heard a fire alarm, she'd run straight to her most precious items. Knowing Eithne, that brooch would come before even her own children."

Alan nodded, his mouth pursed in thought. "Aye, that's typical. But even if she gives away the location, what then?"

Seán took a bite of soda bread. "If she's in charge of the estate, she'd need to attend any major disaster. She'd run off and handle things, even if she has a competent foreman. That should give you time to secure the brooch."

Alan frowned, his face growing pale. "I'm willing to provide a distraction, but I can't, in good conscience, steal from her."

Esme jumped up from the table and paced. "But you wouldn't be stealing! She stole the brooch from *me*. Grandfa gave it to me years ago. Katy should inherit it. Eithne has no right to it!" Speaking her daughter's name made her voice catch in her throat. She missed her so much.

Seán grabbed her hand, halting her pacing. "Shh, *mo chuisle*, we'll get the brooch back for you. Alan, if you tell us the hiding place, Esme will slip in once Eithne leaves. I'll watch the outside of the house after I set the fire. If she heads back to the house before Esme gets in and out, I'll think of something else to keep her away."

Alan still didn't look pleased. "Not the best idea in the world, but I suppose it'll do. If aught goes wrong, we regroup at the standing stones. Seán, do you remember the place?"

He glanced at Esme. "I remember."

Eithne

Tonight might be a good time to visit the stones again. Eithne hadn't been up that hill for some time, and she had several issues at the estate an adjustment of the power might fix. She needed to deal with the lazy workers and negligent farmers. A nudge in the right direction often pushed their labor to a more profitable pace.

She started planning her afternoon when the butler came in with a visitor card. Alan Gallagher? The minister, here? He'd never visited her at the house. Sometimes she noticed him in Ardara or Donegal. She waved at the butler to let him in. Eithne hoped he didn't prattle on too long.

Amid the ceremony involved in afternoon tea, she stifled a yawn. He seemed unimpressed with her donations of culled produce. Did he expect her to give salable food to the poor? What was the point of that? Such a silly, sentimental fool. Still, her duty as a Christian and a Protestant demanded she keep up appearances of charity. With some reluctance, Eithne agreed to increase her donations to a standard he deemed more suitable. Not that she had any actual intention of doing so.

Just as they finished tea, a yell came from outside. Chaos drifted into her drawing-room window, with shouts of "fire." A column of smoke formed in the distance, near the older hay barn.

The minister cocked his head. "Will you need to attend to that, Mistress O'Hagerty? I'd be pleased to remain here and wait, in case I can be of help."

She waved away the suggestion. "No, no, my foreman will deal with all of that. He'll come if he needs my help."

"Hadn't you better see for yourself?"

Eithne narrowed her eyes. "I see no need." He *wanted* her to leave. Very well, she would, but not until she rid herself of him. "As delightful as your visit has been, Reverend Gallagher, I do need to attend some other tasks. Do stop in again when you need something." She rang for the butler to show her guest out.

"Yes, well, certainly, Mistress. And thank you for the tea." His eyes darted around the room before he allowed the butler to escort him out.

Now, what had *that* been about? Eithne must have missed something. She turned around and pushed aside the portrait of her husband. A small hole in the plaster housed the silver and gold brooch. She took out the piece and pinned it inside her chemise. If the fire spread, she'd rather have this on hand. Besides, if she planned to go out to the stones tonight, she'd be prepared.

Eithne checked with the foreman, but he'd already doused the fire. Several hay bales smoldered in an empty barn. The horses hadn't even been in danger, out on the exercise field.

As the sun dipped toward the horizon, Eithne prepared for her trek to the stone circle. Despite being May, the hill grew frosty when the wind blew. The brooch reacted more strongly around the old fire feasts and sun feast days. Their grandfather had told stories about such times. Samhain on the first of November, midwinter, Beltaine on the first of May, and midsummer. Beltaine had been just two days earlier.

As Eithne climbed the hill, something rustled behind her. She hadn't arranged to meet with her lover tonight. Had he followed her anyhow, hoping for an assignation? She'd disabuse him of that notion. They only met on her terms, not his. She peered through the bushes to find the source of the noise, but a bird squawked and fluttered away. Eithne let out the breath she'd been holding and continued her trek.

Eithne reached the circle and prepared to prime the brooch. She hummed and touched each stone in turn, clockwise. No one had taught her any ceremony, but she'd experimented and learned some actions increased her power. The tingling shot up her toes and fingers. The humming grew and the glow burst forth, orange and red in the deepening twilight.

She watched herself walk into the center of the circle and did a double take. Herself? Esme! How dare *she* intrude? *How dare Esme try to steal my power! Esme will never take it from me!*

With a growl, Eithne pulled the surrounding power into her hands. She threw the sparkling energy straight at her sister.

Esme blocked the surge with glowing blue power, quenching Eithne's sizzling orange fire. The edges crackled and sparked as they pushed against each other's wills. The pressure pushed against Eithne's ears with sharp pain in her temples. She shoved the discomfort aside.

Her sister cried out with a pathetic plea. "Eithne! Stop this! Don't you realize what you're doing here?"

Eithne forced her will harder. The orange glow inched closer to her sister. It pulsed forward in waves, each time gaining purchase. Eithne smiled at this proof of her superior strength. "Esme, go away! This isn't yours. The power is *mine!*"

Her sister's blue power pushed back, and Eithne staggered. Why would Esme be so strong without the brooch? That made no sense.

"You're killing this place, Eithne. Can't you sense the sickness in the land?"

Eithne laughed. "Don't be ridiculous, Esme. You're a sentimental fool. No wonder you couldn't handle this. You're too weak!"

"You're hurting the stones! And they're killing the land!"

Didn't Esme know her by now? Even if spoke the truth, what did that matter? This pile of ancient stones meant nothing to her. Dozens of circles covered Ireland like spots on a young man's face.

While gathering her will, Eithne thrust once more, gaining ground. Esme staggered this time. With renewed glee, Eithne rammed harder, bracing her feet and outstretching her hands to focus.

Behind Esme, two other figures arrive. The tall figure of the minister stood to Esme's right, his eyes wide at the sparkling energy. That explained his odd behavior this afternoon. On her left, a tall, dark man. Esme's husband, the dirty, stinking Tinker. Old pain returned, making Eithne seethe in anger and jealousy.

That inane cretin had turned her down and chose Esme the weak. Esme the pitiful.

Eithne gathered all her frustration and anger, rolling the rage into a tangible ball of power. She might not break Esme's barrier, but she could go around. With a cry, Eithne clenched her fists, gathered the energy, and threw the crackling orange sphere straight at Seán's chest.

The ball exploded into a million shards of fire. His handsome face contorted in fear as Eithne smiled. He let out a soundless scream, his back arching, silhouetted against Esme's blue fire.

A horrible screech cut through the air. The voice invaded her mind, scraping her soul and filling her bones. Pain shot through her body, up from the very ground she stood on.

Eithne pushed back with her will, shoving her sister's invasion away, down into the dirt where she belonged, but her sister's power resisted. How did Esme resist her? Esme had no grit or strength.

She clenched her fists until her nails bit into her palms and drove her power straight into Esme's shield.

A small glimmer of doubt crept in.

Sparks of orange and blue lightning crackled between them. The stone circle hummed with power and flashed with the baleful glow of their magic. The Tinker sprawled on the ground, a large smoking spot on his chest.

Now, the minister grabbed Esme's shoulder, pointing at the Tinker's body. Even from this distance, she saw the change on her sister's face. Instead of fear, though, Eithne recognized the rage bubbling up inside her twin. For a moment, Eithne's eyes grew wide. Had she underestimated Esme?

The old connection between them sparked back to life as her sister shrieked. Esme raised her hands, now crackling with blue energy. She pointed them straight at Eithne.

Every inch of Eithne's skin burned. She refused to cry out. She'd never give Esme the satisfaction. The blue glow surrounded her, pressing against her eyes until she saw nothing.

Something wrenched within her, something essential and deep. She fell, tumbling into a dark, dank place with no light or warmth.

Eithne woke the next morning, soaking in the dewy grass. She immediately touched her pocket. Esme had disappeared with the brooch. Eithne cried out and pounded her fist on the ground in frustration.

Esme

Esme just wanted to stop the pain. She curled up on the floor, unable to move a muscle. Alan brought her to his manse, but she made him leave. Whatever she'd done to Eithne, the pain gnawed at her.

Esme had pulled on the brooch's power to cut her sister away, from her life and from her soul. She didn't want to touch her twin's mind ever again. All her life, she held tight to a small glimmer in her mind, a piece of her twin. She shoved that away last night, destroyed the hope, ripped the bond from them both.

She paid for that now. Esme didn't move for hours. When she did rise and look around, blinking in confusion, the details from the night before flooded back. Alan's parlor dissolved into painful memories.

Even covering her face with her hands didn't stem the torrent of tears.

When Esme emerged from her grief, an endless time later, she packed her things with Seán's. She had no tears left for that task. The only thought which kept her moving was Katy.

Over the next few days, Alan helped her deal with Seán's burial. Throughout the process, she remained numb, unable to face the hope and terror of the last few days. Not now, not yet.

Esme returned to Achill on her own. Dull day followed dull day as she let the horse head home. When Achill came into view, she perked up enough to get the horse and cart on the ferry. Her heart rose at the prospect of seeing her daughter, clouded with the danger Lord Carrick still posed. With the brooch now in her possession, she might keep from falling into his power again, but she would rather be nowhere near him.

She hadn't been to this part of the island in a while. A new blacksmith banged his hammer at the forge on the edge of town. The old one had died in a smelting accident the year before. The inn painted its façade white rather than pale yellow. She searched for the side street where Aisling's great-aunt Honora ran her inn.

Sandwiched in between two other town houses, she found the thin building. The great room on the ground floor had a hearth and sitting area with sleeping rooms up a pair of rickety wooden steps.

Aisling jumped up from the bar as she came in. "Esme! You're here? What happened? Where's Seán?"

She must look a fright. Esme had taken little care for her appearance since that night at the stones.

Esme's voice came in a bare whisper. "Can we talk, Aisling? In private?" She nodded down to Katy, who hugged her with fierce intensity.

"To be sure. Come upstairs. Girls, tend the fire, and sweep up around the hearth."

Aoife whined. "But we already swept this morning!"

"Then sweep again, and do it right this time."

The girl grumbled but grabbed the short wire-bristle broom near the hearth. Esme heard Seán's name and spun back around, grabbing Aoife by the shoulders. "What was that, Aoife? What did you say?"

Aisling clutched her arm. "Esme! What in God's name are you doing? Leave her alone!"

Aoife only gave a defiant glare.

"Aisling, she said something about Seán, I swear!"

Aisling yanked Aoife out of Esme's grip, and held her in a tight embrace. "And so? That doesn't mean you can hurt my daughter!"

Aoife stuck her chin out. "I said, Uncle Seán's dead, and Aunt Esme killed him!"

Aisling calmed her voice, smoothing her daughter's blonde hair. "Aoife, dear, you're babbling."

The younger girl shook her head, burying her face in her mother's shoulder. "He died far away, in a wicked, pagan place, and all because of her." Aoife pointed at Esme, her face pinched with judgment.

Esme fell to her knees, her face distorted in grief.

The other woman pushed her daughter out the door, steel in her voice. "Aoife, take Katy outside, now. And we'll discuss this later."

Esme's mind swirled a maelstrom of guilt, her loss breaking through the wall she'd built around her sorrow. Her need for the blasted brooch had killed Seán. He'd never come back for her. She had no one left in this world, no one to love her, no one to embrace her. First, her parents abandoned her. Now, Seán left, too. And she had only herself to blame.

Aisling's soothing voice penetrated her fog of grief. She perched Esme on one wooden stool while Aisling took the other. "Esme, what was that all about?"

Through the last vestige of hiccups, Esme stared at the door. "Aoife... she knows when people die, or are about to."

Aisling rolled her eyes. "Don't be daft, Esme. That's..."

"She knew when Mr. Quinn would die."

The other woman waved her hand. "Everyone knew that. Aoife's just resentful of you ordering her around. She's gotten so bold. But what happened with Seán, Esme? Tell me what happened."

Esme wanted to tell Aisling about Cormac's last vision, but she took a deep breath instead. "We went to get back something Eithne stole from me years ago. Seán helped me. We ran afoul of something dangerous, and

Seán died. He never would have been there but for me. Oh, sweet God in Heaven, Aisling, Aoife is right. Seán is dead because of me!"

Aisling let out a deep breath. "He came of his own choice, no? You don't have control over his decisions, wife or not. Have you seen your grandfather yet?"

"Grandfa's here?" Hope bloomed in Esme's heart. She couldn't bear to face the stones again. But if her grandfather had come, he could use the brooch to heal the land. She wouldn't have to.

"Aye, and looking for you these past few days. I told him you'd gone up north, but not where. I didn't want to send him on a wild goose chase."

Esme jumped off her stool, pulling on her shawl. "I must see him, Aisling. Where is he? He'll know what I should do."

When she tracked him down, playing dice down at the docks, he listened while Esme described what happened in Donegal.

He tapped his lip, staring toward the sea. The wind blew strong, making choppy, white waves across the gray water. "We need to get up to the stones, right away. Eithne will have lost her power, so this is the best time. The magic may seep back to her if we don't."

"I can't, Grandfa, not now. I can't face another one after what happened with… what happened…" Esme sobbed again, but her grandfather pulled her into a tight hug until she stopped.

"You must, don't you see? By using the brooch's power to her own selfish purposes, she's twisted the very land beneath us. She's corrupted the brooch. I can feel it, but as her twin, you're the only one who can fix what Eithne's broken. As much as I'd love to take this burden from your shoulders, my dear granddaughter, this is something only you can do."

Esme shivered in the cool night, pulling her shawl tighter. "But must it be now? I have to mourn, Grandfa. I must take care of my child and mourn my husband."

He gripped her shoulders, shaking his head. "It must be now, child, and I'm sorry for that. The longer we wait, the harder it will be. You may not even be able to do it later. The sickness will grow even without Eithne feeding it."

"What sort of sickness? You said you can feel it?"

"A sickness of the land. It's why the harvests have been poor these last few years. Why people are fighting, rebelling, feeling the strife in the very earth. It's affecting us all, and you're the only one who can heal it."

"I don't want to be the only one! That's not fair! I'm just a… a poor widow." She couldn't stop sobbing.

Her grandfather held her tight again. "You're far more than a poor widow, my dear Esme. You're the child of my heart. In addition, you're descended from a magical legacy, a friend of the Fae. You are Esme. You are strong."

She didn't believe him, but the truth shone on his face, and she had no choice.

Esme took in a deep breath and squared her shoulders. "Very well, Grandfa. Show me what I must do. Then I will be done with it."

His eyes turned sad as he locked gazes with her. "My dear child, you'll never truly be done with it. It's a part of you. That's what the brooch is, both a blessing and a curse."

Esme pulled it from her pocket, holding it out to her grandfather. "I don't want it anymore! Here, you take it back. It never did me much good, anyhow."

While folding her fingers back over the piece of jewelry, he shook his head. "No, child, you must keep it now. It's part of you. Even giving it away won't do any good, until it is time. And that time is not now."

June 1798

Her grandfather stood at the largest stone, his hands placed on it like he greeted an old friend. "This is the best time of year for such work. Midsummer holds a great deal of power."

"Midsummer and midwinter, right? And the fire feasts, such as Beltaine and Samhain?" A large chunk of Catholic guilt almost made her choke on reciting the pagan feast names.

"Aye, when the veil between this world and that of Faery is thinnest. This is the easiest time to ask for their help."

Esme pulled her shawl more tightly around her shoulders. "Do we ask them to heal the land?"

"We can ask for help, but we must do it ourselves, child. It's your sister who violated the natural balance, so we must make it right again."

Her hands clenched around the edges of the shawl. "That's not fair! I did nothing wrong!"

Her grandfather furrowed his brow. "You allowed her to get the brooch and pervert it to her uses."

Tears of frustration and injustice welled up. "I didn't know!"

Éamonn gathered her into a warm hug. "How could you? I never told you. I didn't know myself it could be done. My sweet dear, sometimes we must pay for things we don't do. Life is not so fair as all that. This can't be a surprise."

He let go and looked deep into her eyes, his glittering pale blue in the dim light. "Sometimes you must give up everything for what is right. Sometimes life gives you no other choice."

She nodded, hugging him again, safe within his arms. "I've always known life wasn't fair, Grandfa. I grew up with Eithne, remember?"

He laughed as he stroked the back of her head. "So you did, child, so you did. Come, let us right her wrongs."

Her grandfather marched around the circle, clockwise, chanting in that ancient not-quite-Irish language. The stones glowed purple and blue, cooling, healing colors. He chanted louder as he reached the center. Together, they held the brooch up as an offering. It glowed and pulsed in greens and blues, sparks of purple flying into the air. Scents of burnt metal and rotten vegetables assaulted her. Her feet grew hot, the ground itself burning with unnatural fire.

Nebulous figures appeared behind each stone. They shone bright and hard to focus on, and each one chanted, echoing her grandfather's words. Their voices sounded powerful and terrible, ripping through her ears and mind like a tempest. The sound thrummed in her head, and she couldn't escape.

The chanting morphed into a song. This wasn't a sweet song, full of lovely melodies, but a strong, martial song, with fire and purpose. Esme shook, wishing above all else she could flee this space, to run away from the brooch and all it meant.

The songs pounded into her head, the words buffeting her, punishing her for all the wrongs of the world. They twisted through her mind and tore bits of her memories asunder. It scraped and slashed at her sanity until she cried out in frustrated pain.

Her grandfather shouted over the voices. "Now! Pull in that heat. Let it out through the brooch. Send it to the land."

"How?"

"Let it roll across the countryside, like fog on a chilly morning."

Esme drew the heat through her feet and legs. It grew so hot, she shifted from foot to foot, trying to cool the fire. Through her torso, out her hands, into her fingers. The brooch dazzled with light, a sun peeking over the horizon at dawn.

The ground grew scorching as the brooch pulsed and the faeries sang. It undulated, pitching her back and forth, bubbling as it drifted across the land.

Over each mountain, each valley, into every river, the healing fog flowed. As it touched the land, it gurgled and popped, killing the rot and soothing with healthy power.

Across Achill Island, Esme sent her healing power. To the mainland, farms and towns, cities and the wild woodlands.

After what seemed like days, the power reached the epicenter of the corruption, far north in Ardara. Here, Esme felt Eithne's resistance. It fought the fog, slicing through the thin power. Esme grabbed her grandfather's hand for strength as her twin struggled against the magic.

A new glow brushed through her, a strange, uncomfortable power. This came from the stones, and the beings chanting around them. The Fae lent their support.

If she took it, she'd lose another portion of her soul. Esme knew that as firmly as she could see truth shining on someone's face. Would it be worth it? She might stop now, short of a full healing, and let Eithne alone to her corner of rot.

But her grandfather taught her to never leave a job unfinished. She wasn't her father. She couldn't stop now.

With a last squeeze on his hand, Esme accepted the Fae help. A flood of power coursed through her, coating the land in a deluge of healing. The torrent rushed across Eithne, knocking her away from the battle.

The song faded. Exhausted, Esme let go of her grandfather's hand, falling to the ground in a faint.

When she could open her eyes again, he glowed as brightly as the Fae. He shone so bright that she couldn't see him, as if she stared straight at the sun.

With a cry she scrambled back, letting go of the brooch. The amorphous, shining forms of Fae danced around the circle, one by one, winking out of existence at the altar stone.

Her grandfather strode toward the stone behind the last Fae. As he got closer, her heart grew cold. He didn't glance back at her, but at the stone. An echo of his voice called for Katie, his dear wife, Katie.

The stone flashed so bright, her eyes shut in pain. When she opened them, the glare had disappeared and everything was silent.

Her grandfather had disappeared. *"No!* No, no, no, no! You can't take Grandfa from me! Please! Bring him back, bring him back!"

Esme screamed and pounded her fists on the altar stone. She sobbed and pleaded, asking them to return her grandfather, but she received no answer. A faint howl on the wind whispered her name, but her beloved grandfather never reappeared. She pummeled the stones until her hands ached with blood and bruises.

If Esme thought she'd mourned for her husband, that had been nothing to the wave of despair engulfing her soul at her grandfather's death. She howled in pain, sounding more animal than human. The pain ripped through her like a claw, stealing her mind. Her eyes remained full of pain, but no relief of tears would come.

Chapter Twenty

July 1798

Esme stared at Aisling, unable to believe her ears. "Katy? Leave her here forever? How could I do that? *Why* should I do that?"

"The road's no place for a young child, especially one as trusting as Katy. She'd be prey to every man who came along, with her pretty face and those wide eyes. Then what happens when you arrive and find a position? And having a child would make that impossible, especially without a husband in sight. What about the dog? They should stay together. No, leave them with me, Esme, for now. Auntie Honora is happy to let us help with the tavern. Padraig is off fishing most days, anyhow. Then, send for them once you settle down. It'll be better this way, to be sure."

Leave her only child? How? Katy was one thing she had left of Seán. Her throat closed, but the tears refused to come.

Aisling turned thoughtful again. "I have an idea. It's not much of one, but it's a start."

Esme furrowed her brow. "What is it?"

"Well, there're a group of Tinkers in town. Even if they didn't know Seán, you might travel with them to find his parents?"

The sudden bloom of hope died as Esme shook her head. "No, they both passed last year from a fever."

Aisling tapped her lip. "Hmm. Perhaps, then, they can take you to some of my own relatives."

Esme shook her head. Aisling's family would all be on Achill Island. It wouldn't take long for Carrick and Eithne to find her. Anywhere here would be too close.

Aisling lifted a finger. "I've got a cousin down in Kenmare. She runs a clothing store. You can work for her as a seamstress!"

"Kenmare?" Esme had never been further south than Galway. Her grandfather told her stories of Kenmare, with lovely gardens and sunny weather, but it seemed so far. Kenmare might be far enough away to keep her from both Carrick and Eithne, though.

Tears threatened again at the thought of her grandfather, but that pain remained too raw. She couldn't cry for him yet. "What's your cousin's name?"

"Úna. She's my mother's cousin. Úna Downing. She's about sixty, I'd say, and a strong woman. Strict, but fair. She'll take care of you and be glad for your talent, to be sure."

What a mad idea. She'd been frightened just moving to Achill with her husband. Now Aisling wanted her to move halfway down the coast, alone? However, Esme had few other options. Lady Violeta had returned to England. Aisling mentioned seeing her go through Achill Sound on the ferry to the mainland.

One thing Esme knew for certain. She needed to take control of her own life. She'd drifted along on the tide ever since her marriage to Seán. She'd let her husband uproot her to a new place, where they'd never been welcome. Then, she'd let Sweeney House dictate how she spent her days. She'd let Eithne define her goals. Now, she must take what remained of the threads of her life and weave her own tapestry.

As she held tight to her daughter, whispering "goodbye" into her shining blonde hair, Esme let the tears fall.

Katy buried her face in her mother's chest. "I don't want you to go again, Mam."

She pulled back and stared into her daughter's eyes. "I don't want to, either, sweetling. But you're safer here. And when I get to the new place, and earn some money, I'll send for you. I will. It won't be too long."

"You promise?"

"I promise."

Esme returned to the *booley* to pack what she might carry. Then, she'd travel with the Tinkers to Kenmare. Once she found a position with Aisling's cousin, she'd send word to Aisling and have Katy join her.

At least she'd learned how to travel. She remembered the first long journey to Achill, that wild, sodden trip south with her husband. Her heart ached for Seán's strong arms to wrap around her.

After shoving painful memories aside, Esme pulled everything she owned onto the table. She had no horse or cart, though she had enough to fill one. How to pare her life into one bag? Bread, cheese, and a packet of dried mutton and fish. Her embroidery tools and finished goods. She'd need to earn her way, in Kenmare or wherever she ended up. She agonized over the large loom but settled on breaking down the smaller one, and strapping it to her growing pack.

The rest would have to go to Aisling. She wrapped the druid's brooch into its velvet bag, placing it in the hidden pocket beneath her skirts.

A huge pack lay on the floor, with leather straps to secure it to her arms. She wanted to take more, but she only had so much room. Aisling would keep the rest for Katy. With a last sigh for this place where she'd spent all her married life, Esme walked out the door.

Seven of the villagers faced her, angry scowls on their faces. Esme stumbled back, her eyes darting from one to the other. Mistress Lynch stepped forward, leaning on her cane. "We told you to go. Ye didn't go. Now we're going to make you."

Esme held up her hands. "I'm going! See, I'm all packed. You'll never see me after today."

A few exchanged glances, but another growled. "Not good enough. We need to cleanse yer evil away. You've tainted this place with yer spells."

Her blood grew cold. "Spells? I've done no spells."

Mistress Lynch spat to the side. "Me daughter saw you! You glowed blue when you stood at the Fairy Stones."

The Fairy Stones? How would Mistress Lynch's daughter, a quiet woman with a pale face, have seen her at the stones? But truth or tale, it didn't seem to matter to the angry folks now surrounding her. They stepped closer. She couldn't get any further away, as her back hit against her front door.

With Seán gone, and her grandfather disappeared into Fairy, who did she have left to help her? Not even Aisling, as she was in Achill Sound with her aunt and the girls. Esme only had herself.

She had no physical power, but she did have something else. With sudden inspiration, she turned to Mistress Lynch. "And what sins do you have in your past? Tell me the truth!" She pulled hard on the brooch's power, harder than she had in a long time. She must impel the old crone to spill her secrets, to distract the mob from harming Esme. "Tell me!"

With wide eyes, the older woman stepped back. "I... I have no sins."

Esme almost let out a smile at the bright blue glow that shone on Mistress Lynch's face. "That's a lie, and you know it. What did you do?"

The other woman glanced back and forth to the others, looking for some avenue of escape, but declared in a halting voice, "I had lovers. Dozens of them, when my husband went fishing."

"Ha! And you, what are your sins?" Esme turned to point at the closest man, a burly fisherman with black, curly hair.

He backed up several steps, shaking his head and drawing a cross on his chest. "No, no, you won't put yer spells on me!"

"Tell me the truth!" Nausea churned in her stomach at using the power, but if it gave her an escape, she didn't care.

"I left a girl. She carried my baby, and she died after I left." He covered his face with his hands as he stumbled away.

The remaining villagers stepped back, only a few at first, but when Esme searched the faces for her next truth, they dissipated almost as quickly as they'd gathered. Soon, only Mistress Lynch remained, who had stood her ground after her confession.

The woman glared at her as she strode past her. Esme ignored her. *Crazy old bat. I hope everyone shuns you for being unfaithful now.*

Esme's stomach churned into knots and as soon as she rounded the hill, she threw up into the gorse on the side of the road. She felt disgusted with herself for her actions. But at least she'd escaped their anger, once and for all.

The rain had stopped, but the weather stayed soft and dismal. Muzzy light hid the sun. The last days melded together in a fog, much like her haze of grief.

While standing on the shore one last time, Esme pulled out the wish-stone she'd found her first days in the cottage. It reminded her of Bridey's stone, the one Eithne tried to steal. What did Bridey and Níamh do now? Her grandfather had never heard from them in America. Had they died on the journey? Did they have families of their own in the wilds of Ohio?

After pushing the idea aside, Esme clutched the faery stone as she concentrated on her wish. She might have used the magic so many times. To keep a baby, to bring Seán back. But she'd always saved it, not daring to use it. Nothing seemed right before. This time, since she left the place she found it, the time felt right.

Esme considered wishing for a better life in Kenmare, but she would make that happen with her own efforts. She had some control over that. Instead, she wished that Katy would thrive. Then she spun three times sunwise, tossing the stone into the ocean. The tiny *plop* seemed anti-climactic after all her years on Achill Island.

With a deep sigh, Esme turned to walk along the coast road toward Achill Sound, toward her daughter, toward Aisling, and toward what the future held for her.

Esme hadn't walked more than a mile before she spied someone riding toward her. She tensed, her heart beating faster. As the figure grew closer, she recognized him with a cold heart.

Carrick.

She had nowhere to hide. No trees or houses stood along this lonely road. Only the mountain above her and the sea below her. However, he also had no one with him. No carriage, no driver.

As he pulled closer, she clenched her jaw and kept her face down. Maybe he wouldn't recognize her under her massive pack. He might mistake her for a stranger.

"Esme."

So much for that hope. She kept walking.

"Esme, I must speak with you."

As if she had anything to say to him. She kept walking.

He pulled on his reins as she passed his horse. The beast turned, the jangle of the tack reminding her of Seán returning after a long trip. Esme swallowed against the hope that sound invoked and kept walking.

Memories of Seán and what Eithne did to him infused her with frustration and fury. Eithne plotted with this man to bring her down. She'd had enough of both of them. When he dismounted and grabbed her arm, she jerked away, turning to glare at him. "Go away, Carrick. I'm leaving and I never want to see you again. May the devil make a ladder of your backbone, to pluck apples from a tree in hell!"

The rage in her face and her curse made him back away, his eyes wide. Her gaze slipped away from him, as if he deserved nothing more. She stalked away to Achill Sound, to Aisling, and to her new life.

For a wonder, he didn't pursue her.

Two days later, Aisling introduced her to the Travelers. The leader of the tribe, a short, stocky man with bad breath and a keen eye, looked her over. When he noticed the enormous pack on her back, he nodded to one of the women.

The woman, about her own age and sporting a gap-toothed smile, led her to a wagon painted with red and yellow flowers. "You'll stay with me for the trip. I'm Banba. What's your name?"

"Esme. Banba? As in the goddess? Truly?"

The girl grinned, showing a missing eyetooth as well. "Sure and it's true. Me mam was a great one for the tales, she was. Here, let me take that." She lifted the heavy pack off Esme's shoulders. The relief from the removal of the pack, and from Banba's friendship, made her feel young and free again.

They left the next morning, a train of a dozen bright-painted, round-topped wagons. The leader, Ferdinand MacDillard, seemed a gruff, taciturn man. He kept everyone in line and moving at a steady pace. Esme felt content to ride in relative comfort.

If only her journeys with Seán had been so comfortable. The gorgeous hills of Connemara rose and fell around them, stark and beautiful in late summer brilliance. Wild ponies stood atop one hill and the other Tinkers talked of staging a raid to capture the graceful beasts. Esme hid a smile when they decided against the venture. Such a shame it would be to harness that wild splendor. The herd gamboled along the ridgeline. She both admired their beauty and envied their freedom.

The rocking motion made her queasy, so she leapt down to walk alongside the train. Banba joined her, and they enjoyed the fine, warm morning.

Turning to her new friend, Esme cocked her head. "Have you been a Traveler all your life?"

The woman nodded, shaking her dark hair out of her bonnet, then twirling it up again inside. "Da up there wouldn't have it any other way, to be sure. It's a good life. We meet many people and see much of the land. We're not tied down to grubbin' in the dirt for our food, either."

Esme never considered farming as "grubbing in the dirt," but she understood the other woman's point.

"Do you know of my husband, then? His name is Seán Fitzgerald. He had a string of horses he traded, though he sold other things. He's..." She dredged the image of him from memory, aghast to discover how hard it was to picture him. Would she lose his face?

"He's tall, six feet at least. Long, straight, dark hair, like your da's. He wears it in a ponytail. His skin is darkish, from the sun and brown eyes. He tells everyone he's descended from a Spanish pirate. I would love to find some of his family."

Banba's mouth pulled up on one side. "He does sound familiar, but your description might match half the Travelers on the west coast. I'll ask the others tonight when we make camp."

That night, as they sat around a crackling campfire, Esme related tales Seán's father, Oisín, had told her, stories of horse trades gone sour. Esme wished she had more recent stories, relevant to her search. None of the Travelers had heard of them, or any relatives.

Waves of depression and hope alternated in her heart, lifting her high and low in turns. She missed her husband with an aching heart, and her grandfather even more. At least she had faith that Aisling would take good care of Katy, but she missed her dear daughter. The memory of her abandoned child—and she did abandon her, no matter what Aisling said— dimmed her smile. Katy would be far better off with Aisling. She must convince herself of that or lose what tenuous grip on sanity she still possessed.

A man told a story about a fair he'd attended, one with a rat race. Several Travelers entered their "contestants" into a wooden run, urging their individual rats to run down the path. Instead of racing, the rats attacked each other. In the end, the storyteller said, it became a bloody mess, in every sense of the word. Everyone laughed at the punchline and toasted his story. Esme's gorge rose.

The fire glowed amber and gold, dancing in the center, reflecting into the surrounding faces. Young and old, the Travelers loved to laugh. They held tight to a zest for life the farmers in the booley lacked. Perhaps she'd been wrong all those years ago to forgo the traveling life for a settled home.

How would her life have been different? Would they have fought less? Or driven each other mad with proximity? Would she have died in childbirth? She came close with Katy, with no guarantee they'd have been near a healer.

Would she have been traveling while with child? Then she noticed a heavily pregnant woman walking with a man, glowing with health and happiness.

I can't play the what-if game. What if I never met Seán and instead went to America with Mam and Da? Or if I married Alan and stayed in Ardara? What if Eithne and I had been friends instead of... whatever we are?

Esme might spend her life dreaming of scenarios that would never happen, could never happen, with nothing to show but discontent. Better to live her life in the here and now, plan for the future and accept the past.

Her grandfather would have agreed.

Four days later, they arrived in Ballyvaughan. Other than that first night, the rain never let up. Esme hid inside the covered wagon, grateful for the dry sanctuary. She emerged to help with the horses when they made camp and did her share of cooking and cleaning. This wouldn't be a free ride as a lady of leisure. She received protection and companionship from these people and owed them a great deal.

The wagons bounced too much for needlework, but she did weaving on her lap loom. She worked on belt strips, easy enough despite the jouncing. It didn't feel right to sit idle.

With dark and sodden nights, most of the Travelers remained in their wagons when they stopped. This limited the songs each night, but didn't stop them all. Sometimes they backed the wagons into a circle around the central fire, burning hot enough to survive the rain. It only worked on soft evenings but provided welcome warmth, light, and camaraderie.

Ballyvaughan had little more than a dock, a pub, and a general store. However, it commanded a fantastic view of the cold, choppy Galway Bay. Farther and farther south she traveled. Would she walk off the southern tip of Ireland and drown in the sea? Would she find Hy-Brasil or Tir na nOg?

Despite being small, Ballyvaughan had a market fair. Fifteen wooden stalls and tables, selling produce, livestock, baked goods, and tools. Several hawked their wares with loud, annoying voices, while others just sat at their table, watching those who passed with passive gazes. They'd only rouse when someone looked interested in buying.

Esme hadn't been to a market off Achill Island in years. She watched as one of her Traveler companions haggled with a drover for kine. He told outrageous lies to get a better price. The drover lied as well. They deserved each other.

Banba caressed linen on sale at another table, dyed a rich, emerald green. That color dye always faded fast. The vivid shades never lasted. Esme opened her mouth to mention it, but the other woman switched her attention to a blue piece. She haggled the price to half the original ask. The Tinker girl lied as well. Banba didn't need it for her poor, sick grandmother. Even without the brooch's power to show her, Esme knew. Her grandmother died years ago, Banba said as much last night.

Frustrated at the duplicitous nature of people, Esme turned to find something hot to eat. Perhaps a meat pie? She whirled around and crashed right into a tall, blond man.

He held her at arms-length, a huge grin on his face. "Whoa, now, girl. Where are you off to in such a hurry? I know we just saw each other two months ago. No time for a hug for your poor, lonely friend?"

Amazed, Esme clung to him tight and wouldn't let go. "Alan! Oh, I'm so happy to see you!" If she let go, he might disappear. "But what are you doing here?"

"Part of a learning trip. We're to visit several parishes and work with them for a month before moving on. This month, three of us are here in Ballyvaughan. Careful, Esme, you'll crack me in two if you keep on like that!"

She didn't let go, but she loosened her grip. Even that made her worry she might lose him, too. She ached to have a man's arms around her again, even if only a friend.

After a long time, Alan held her back to look at her. "Talk to me, *mo chara*. Tell me all that's happened. Where's your wee daughter?"

"Katy's safe, Alan. Sit, and I'll tell the tale."

She let it all out, like a confession at church. He already knew the story of what happened in Ardara, so she spoke of Carrick Sweeney and his attentions, of her grandfather's death, of Aisling's offer to raise Katy, and of her trip south with the Travelers.

As she finished, Esme sobbed on his shoulder. Her oldest friend put his arm around her, gathering her close.

"Shh, *mo chara*, shh. I wish I could bring Éamonn back to you, my dear, I truly do."

Esme never mourned for her grandfather. She hadn't allowed the terrible grief to take over, as she'd been on the run since it happened. But hearing her friend, Alan, optimistic and cheery at the worst of times, put her grandfather's death into words, gave them power. She sobbed in his arms for a long time.

She didn't stop crying, and Alan, unsure what to do, led her to the inn he and his fellow clergy stayed at. Esme descended into a terrible state. She keened and whimpered until her voice croaked and her eyes burned with anguish. She rocked and rocked, refusing to speak to Alan or anyone else.

Esme cried for more than her lost grandfather, who meant the world to her. She cried for her husband, who had loved her. Esme cried for Katy and for Aisling. She cried for her parents and Bridey and Níamh and even for Alan. She cried for the babes she had lost, souls who never got a name. And above all else, she cried for the life she'd wasted, living on that desolate mountainside, waiting for a husband who, in the end, died because of her.

Esme recovered her senses several hours later. This wasn't the Traveler wagon. A room at an inn somewhere. She peered out the window at the choppy water of Galway Bay in the early morning dawn, hints of pink and purple in the distance heralding a new day. Her mouth tasted like ashes. A pitcher of water on the table helped to wet her throat, and memories of yesterday flickered back.

Alan had brought her here. She remembered now. They even spoke that evening, talked about her plans, her hopes, her pain. She nibbled on the loaf of bread, though she didn't feel hungry. She must keep moving.

Esme didn't want to continue with the Traveler band. She liked Banba, but the girl had lied so much when buying that fabric. What else had she lied about? Esme didn't dare examine her face with the brooch's power. Lies might be necessary for people to live together, but she still detested the un-needed casual deceptions. However, at Alan's suggestion, she traded some of her goods for a horse and cart, so at least she wouldn't have to walk the entire trip. And her ability to see the truth helped her secure an excellent bargain.

Alan needed to go to Limerick, and he had a map to Kenmare. He also had a surprise for her, but refused to tell her what. The anticipation helped pull her out of her gloom. At least she hadn't lost her oldest friend.

Once Esme packed her things again and shouldered her heavy pack, she went to the church to find Alan. She pulled on the bell and waited for him to open the door. Traveling south with him would be such a wonderful adventure. They had so much to talk about, to reminisce with. She still wanted to ask him about his relationship with Bridey before they left. Esme hid a secret smile.

The door opened, revealing… not Alan. "May I help you?" The mousy young man blinked in the morning light.

"I'm looking for Reverend Gallagher. He said to come meet him."

"I'm so sorry, Mistress. He's gone up in the hills, you see. A parishioner needed him, she's quite ill."

She blinked in confusion. "Gone? But he wanted to travel with me to Limerick today!"

"Oh! Yes, he mentioned you. He left something." He shut the door and opened it again almost immediately, handing her a packet. "Here. He said to give you this, and Godspeed on your journey."

He closed the door and Esme's hope died again. Why did all the men in her life have to leave her? When she opened the packet, she found two maps and a note.

My dearest Esme,

Many apologies, but I am called to my duties. I might be days, even weeks, so I urge you to go on without me. I promise I'll seek you out when I can, after I'm free here. Be safe on your journeys, and God bless.

Your friend,

Alan

One map had a clear path down to Kenmare, through Limerick. However, the other map seemed older, more curious. It only showed a path through the Burren, the rocky area south of Ballyvaughan. This paper showed a path winding south, with arcane symbols about halfway through. This must be Alan's surprise. She studied it, tracing her finger along the path through the county, south toward the Shannon River.

Esme girded her determination with renewed purpose. She was, for the first time in her life, alone in the world. She no longer had a father, husband, or grandfather watching over her. Esme would live, or die, by her own efforts. The notion both invigorated and frightened her. She stomped the frightened part of her soul into a quiet corner of her mind and told it to be quiet and let her alone. Surprisingly, it even listened.

With the horse and cart she purchased from the Travelers, she traveled south from Ballyvaughan. This area, called the Burren, was a study in natural stone sculpture, a wondrous, stark landscape, filled with shapes and faces. As if God played with liquid stone one day, then turned up the heat and baked it into odd shapes. It reminded Esme of the baked goods in Alan's Da's bakery, all humped and crusty, with cracks and crikes running down the center. Her grandfather once told her the rocks formed after a fight between giants during the time of the Fomorians. Memory of her grandfather made her chest tight. At least no one would see her cry here in the wilderness.

Esme fancied faeries peered at her from hidden cracks. While she spied movement at the edge of her vision, she didn't look too closely. If she whirled around, all motion vanished. She laughed at her own folly like a foolish young girl, and not an old married woman of twenty-four, with a child of her own. Katy would have loved playing among the rocks, searching for faeries.

Thinking of Katy, Esme fell into a quiet mood again, her thoughts tangled. She no longer searched for faery faces in the rocks.

To be fair, calling this a road would be too generous. More like a dirt path winding through rocky outcroppings and through scant passes in the mountains. All day she traveled, with little to break the monotony of the stony ground. Esme caught glimpses of precious dots of color, flowers pushing their way through the dirt in the bottom of the crevices to find precious sunshine. She kept tight hold of the reins to keep the horse from eating every clump they passed.

By the end of the first day, the map brought her close to the arcane symbol. When she rounded a bend, she gasped. A huge dolmen stood in a central plain, looming ominous even in the bright sunset. The massive structure sat on a slight rise in the unreal landscape. A huge table-shaped stone tripod, its top askew for eternity. As she drew near, evening mists rose, and her flesh tingled with chill and anticipation. This must be Alan's surprise. She might draw energy here, as her grandfather taught her. Her breath choked again in heartache, but she pushed the pain away. This place would help heal her sorrow.

After shedding her pack, she hobbled the horse. Esme pulled her brooch out of its hidden pocket. The jewelry had become a part of the fabric of her soul. The stone beneath her feet thrummed as she stepped up to the monument.

This place seemed different than the stones on Achill. She remembered the circle in Ardara, but each one had a different personality. This time, the stones glowed purple and pulsed with a slower beat, almost drowsy. Was this one older? Perhaps it housed different faeries. Her eyelids drooped here, rather than being energized.

Last year, Aisling went to the mainland to visit a friend in Leenane. She mentioned a hot spring where they bathed, soothed by the steaming waters. This felt like floating on mineral-laden waters into a deep, restful sleep.

Her legs grew weak, and she needed to sit. Esme chose a place along the upright inside the structure. Almost instantly, she fell into a deep, healing sleep, undisturbed by nightmares.

Chapter Twenty-One

July 1798

Three dusty, trudging days later, Esme arrived in Kenmare. After a horrible storm, the rest of the trip felt blessedly dull. She traveled through towns and villages, argued with sheep for the right of passage down roads, and did tentative trading at fairs and markets along the way.

When she arrived in Kenmare, Esme felt at home. It reminded her so much of Ardara, the place she'd left so many years before, that tears of homesickness pushed behind her eyes. After swallowing them down, she took a drink of water from her canteen to clear her throat.

As the sun touched the sea, she stopped at an inn called O'Donnabhain's and paid for a room for the night, with a bowl of hearty stew, and a huge mug of sour ale. She mopped up every drop with the wheaten bread. She wanted more, but she already regretted the extravagance. Now that she'd arrived, she should trade the horse. If she didn't get a position with Úna, she'd have to find other work. Her savings and remaining goods would only last her so long.

The inn looked clean and comfortable, but Esme's mind raced, refusing to rest. Her grandfather said her mother's father lived in this area for a while. Might she have distant relatives here? What would Úna be like? Would she be kind? Would she allow Esme to bring Katy here?

The possibilities crowded into her brain, refusing to let her rest. Jumbles of scenes played out, ranging from warm welcome to outright rejection. What if her work disappointed Úna? If she had a posh reputation, she might not want a Traveler in the establishment.

When exhaustion finally took over, Esme slept. She didn't get much rest, but it at least kept her from imagining worse disasters.

The morning dawned foggy. Kenmare clustered around a triangular town center with streets radiating out in a spoke pattern. Esme wandered up and down each street, looking for Úna's shop. The thick mist of the morning caressed everything as she peered into a large meeting house, a tin shop, a cobbler, two bakers, and an apothecary. The scent of leather mixed with baking bread. When she walked down the third spoke, she spied a tailor's shop.

Esme had expected a man's tailor shop with a corner for women's clothing. In all her limited experience, women didn't own shops for clothing, at least not in the country. Perhaps London or Dublin had enough business to cater to women.

However, with expensive plate-glass windows, this appeared to be a shop dedicated to women's dresses. Wooden forms in the window showed a tableau of two women sitting to tea, both with full-ruffed dresses of watered silk. One wore a bonnet on the featureless wooden head with deep red ribbons tied under the "chin." The other wore a more casual mob-cap, fringed in delicate lace.

When Esme opened the door, a sense of industry confronted her. One woman worked at the front desk, writing in a ledger. Three bent over tasks behind a low wall. Two stitched fine embroidery while another worked on a vast array of petticoats.

The woman behind the desk stood as Esme entered. She smiled with large teeth, her white skin setting off ink-black hair. Her dark gray serge dress made her seem monochrome. A touch of deep blue ribbon peeked through her lacy mob-cap.

Esme noticed she had a moon-shaped scar over her left eye. "Good morning to you, Mistress, and how may I help you today?" She spoke in a strong, determined voice.

"Hello and good morning. I'm looking for a Mistress Úna Downing?"

The woman arched a quizzical eyebrow. "I am Úna Downing. May I ask why you are seeking me?"

Now for the hard part. "My friend, Aisling, sent me. Aisling O'Malley, on Achill Island. She said you might need—" Esme broke off. She shouldn't ask outright, should she? No, she'd vowed to take control over her life. She steeled her spine, looking up at Úna. "I'm requesting a position if you've one going. I'm an excellent seamstress, with especially fine embroidery skills. Aisling thought you might have work for me."

The woman gave Esme a long, lingering look. Úna stood tall and solid, at least seventeen stone. She took careful note of Esme's dress, bonnet, and the shawl she wore against the morning chill. She'd worn the best she had for this meeting.

"Did you make your own clothing?"

Esme nodded, mute. All the horrible scenarios of the night before crowded into her imagination.

Úna extended her hand to the embroidered work on Esme's sleeve. She asked, "May I?" Esme nodded again, lifting her arm to aid the examination.

The woman looked at the front and back of the stitching, clicking her tongue now and then. "Hmm." She pushed the design with her fingers, tugged at it for strength, and checked the hems of her sleeve. The memory of Lady Violeta doing the same at Carrick's house made her shudder.

"As it happens, I do have a position available. One of my girls is getting married and wants to farm with her new husband. I shall offer you thirty shillings a week to start. If you impress me, I will give you a rise. If you disappoint me, you shall have to find another position. I expect you to work on time and sober every day but Sunday. I allow no gentleman callers or lewd behavior. Is that acceptable?"

Esme swallowed against the knot in her throat and nodded. Úna moved like a storm, unstoppable and formidable.

"Excellent. Tomorrow morning, one hour past sunrise. You will bring what tools you have and we shall supplement what you're missing. If you've creations already made, bring those. I can purchase them from you for sale in the shop, if they are acceptable."

Esme kept her voice even, though her heart surged with victory. She had a place. She could stop running. "Thank you."

With a brusque nod, Úna returned to her ledgers.

One girl twittered, and Esme tried to figure out which. Úna sent a silent glare toward the workshop. The twittering stopped. The girls bent to their tasks with mindful industry. Esme left in a daze.

Within the course of the week, Úna installed Esme in a flat above the shop, which she shared with another girl, Annie. Annie seemed rather simple, but made excellent stays. Maire had skill as a milliner. The girl who repaired the cloud of petticoats, Múireann Ferriter, did best with the larger projects. The girl who'd gotten married also made stays, but did decent embroidery. Esme's handiwork soon outshone her predecessor's efforts, and Úna gave her a rise in pay.

Úna was a strict taskmistress, and her imperious attitude sometimes reminded Esme of her sister, Eithne. The confidence and bossy manner brought her twin to mind often. *Odd how the things which annoyed me as a child bring comfort as I get older.* Though Úna demanded precision, she proved to be generous in her praise. She took care of "her girls," and protected them. She was a force in the town, despite being a widow. No one crossed her.

Esme related her story to the entire group over several nights. She told of her childhood in Ardara, her parents' trip to America, and her marriage to Seán. She ended with her parting from Achill and the reason for it. Úna got so indignant at Lord Carrick's behavior, she seemed ready to hitch up a wagon and go slap the man herself. Regardless, Esme had found a home in this new place.

As they exchanged stories, Esme discovered that Úna's grandfather was Esme's mother's father. A tradesman named Theodosius lived in town for several years, married a local girl named Tamara, then when she died, left without a trace. That must have been when he traveled north to marry Esme's grandmother. No one here heard of him again, but there wouldn't be two people with such a name.

This meant she and Aisling were distantly related. This discovery made her glow with pleasure. She wrote to Aisling with the news and to Katy. Tears stained the paper as she wrote that Aisling must keep Katy, at least for now. While Úna treated everyone fair, she also maintained strict standards and permitted no children in her shop. Esme couldn't ask for Katy to come join her.

On Saturday evening, she walked down the street to a stone-walled park. Annie told her about a stone circle in the park, right in the middle of town. Esme hadn't visited yet, wanting to approach it alone.

No moon shone tonight, but the stars twinkled bright, offering a faint glow over the tops of the trees. She walked through the gate and past the tall hedges. There, just discernible in the dark, stood a large ring of stones, spots of black against the gloom. Her memory flashed visions of her swamp nightmare as she crept forward. But each step got more confident as she reached the largest stone. Esme placed a hand on the monolith, ready for angry sparks or icy cold. The stone almost jumped out at her, pulling her into their community.

The warm, sizzling buzz she'd grown to love and crave rushed through her, like when she made love to Seán. The sensation sparked into her body and flowed through her arms and legs, up around her head and into her heart. The ghostly figure of her grandfather stood next to her and lent her strength. Together, they banished the dismal swamp of her nightmares.

These stones had been waiting for her.

Esme stitched in the back room when the bell above the door tingled. She glanced up, but she knew Úna and Maire worked in the front room, so she needn't stop her work. However, when the customer spoke, she froze, her heart beating faster.

Carrick's voice drifted through the curtain. "I understand you have some very skilled seamstresses here, Mistress Úna."

"I have a reputation for fine work in my shop, sir. Did you require something specific? Something for your wife, perhaps?"

He hesitated before answering. "No, not my wife. But I do wish to purchase a gift. Something with embroidery. Do you, perhaps, have someone skilled enough to create designs like birds or trees? Nature scenes."

Esme shrunk back, certain he searched for her. She glanced around, anxious for an escape, but the shop had no back door to the workroom. Her only exit lay through the front. She rushed to the rack of clothing waiting for repairs, and hid behind the voluminous skirts, her hands trembling.

Everything she'd worked for here seemed so fragile. Had Eithne tracked her down somehow and sent Carrick to fetch her? What would he do if he found her? She clutched hard to the brooch, sewn into her dress pocket for safekeeping. The edges of the metal bit into her hands. If only she had some defensive power, something physical to repel his advances.

Úna's voice came closer. "We have several fine embroiderers, sir. Here's a sample of the work you describe. If this piece doesn't suit, I can always commission something to your specifications. How soon would you want the finished product?"

Esme wiped the sweat from her brow. She couldn't breathe behind the fabric, but she daren't push away from her hiding spot. Steps got louder.

"Have you, by chance, a young woman in your employ, about so tall, with red, curly hair? I'm searching for my cousin's wife. I learned she settled in the area, and she always did lovely work."

He sounded so close. Esme held her breath.

"I don't believe so, but I will enquire of my girls if they know of someone of that description."

Esme let out a slow, shuddering breath at Úna's words.

Carrick sounded confused. "Hmm. That's odd. I'm certain they said this shop."

Úna's voice turned to steel. "They, whom, sir? I would be grateful to know who recommended you."

He didn't answer at first. Instead, rapid steps approached. Esme shrunk back further into the corner, her back up against the closet wall.

Someone flung open the workshop curtains. Úna's tone became even more implacable. "Sir! That area is not open to customers. I must ask you to leave my shop."

Through a gap in the dresses, Esme glimpsed him, searching the workroom for her. Múireann and Annie stood as one, blocking his view of her, hiding in the clothing. Maire stood next to Úna, whose crossed arms and severe expression might have curdled milk. "You will leave this place, sir. I have no wish of your custom."

He spun on her, his eyes blazing. "I know she's here! I saw her walk in myself, this morning!"

Úna's expression turned to stone as she pulled the curtains aside. "If you do not leave, I shall call the constable."

He glanced at each of the girls, finding no help from any of them. Then he stalked out of the shop. The bell jingled cheerfully as he left.

Esme breathed again.

Úna's voice turned more gentle than she'd ever heard it. "Esme? It's safe, dear. He's gone."

They gathered her into an enormous hug. Tears flowed, but they were happy tears. Tears of relief. Tears of home.

Esme had always dreamed of a big family, especially after her own moved to America. But family might be more than those related by blood. Family can be those who care for you, no matter their relation.

That Sunday, Esme attended church with Úna and the other girls. The church looked simple but elegant, with the back room crumbling. The age of the stones and smooth-worn pews embraced her.

Older priests tended to be posted to larger towns while younger priests learned their vocation in smaller villages and isolated outposts. This one looked younger than Esme and had a thick mop of curly brown hair. His long face animated with conversation as he spoke with two elderly aunties on their way into church. Maire claimed to be smitten by Father Trant, for as much good as it would do her.

When Father Trant asked for volunteers to help at a church social next week, Esme asked Úna if they might help. Úna frowned at the idea, as they worked on Saturday, but Esme convinced her they could take shop wares to display.

Esme seldom attended such gatherings, but she'd seen a rare, precious quality in Father Trant. A quality she valued in Úna. A particular feature she'd sought for all her adult life and rarely found. Seán had it. Her grandfather had it. Aisling had it.

They told the truth.

Epilogue

sme found happiness in her work at Úna's shop. She found a family with the other women, and a place she called home. She still dreamed of Seán, and sometimes of Alan. Aisling sent word that Carrick still lived in Sweeney house, but remarried.

She hadn't gotten word of her twin sister, Eithne, for many years. Other than that she still lived in Ardara, not much news reached this far south. Aisling sent word that Katy married a fisherman named McGinty, and no longer wished to join her mother. Esme cried a great deal when she got that message, but she must let her daughter live her own life.

In all the years after their departure, she'd never received word from their parents, or Bridey, or even little Níamh. She'd long since concluded they must have died on the trip, in one of the horrible so-called "coffin ships."

Esme also learned a hard lesson, that lies didn't have to be terrible. She avoided those who lied as much as possible, but now understood lies might be a kindness, to smooth relationships. The unbridled truth sometimes created more harm than a white lie. Such as telling a woman her face looks horrible after a recent illness, or a man the fish he caught was too small to feed his family. They already understood these truths. Reminding them only caused pain. Small untruths made the gears of social interaction work better.

Esme still didn't like it.

When he falls for a woman promised to another, can an enchanted family heirloom aid his quest to Scotland and his ardent desire?

Will the lovelorn young man's hopes be dashed upon a storm of heartbreak, or will he find his one love across the sea?

Buy *Legacy of Luck* to take a risky leap of faith today!
books2read.com/LegacyofLuck

Thank You!

Thank you so much for enjoying Legacy of Truth. If you've enjoyed the story, please consider leaving a review to help others discover the magic of Ireland and Esme's adventures.

If you would like to get updates, sneak previews, sales, and get a FREE short story and a FAMILY TREE, please sign up for my newsletter.

Monthly Newsletter Signup and homepage:
www.greendragonartist.com

Other Books by This Author

See all the books available through
Green Dragon Publishing at
www.GreenDragonArtist.com/Books

Read Now

SONG TRANSLATIONS

BANRÍON SÍ
Written by Turlough O'Carolan (1670-1738)

Irish

Ciste nó stór go deó ní mholfad,
Ach imirt is ól is ceól do ghnáth;
Taoim ar baois fá mhnaoi 's mó ró-mhaith dhodlaim,
'S nach truagh sin duine ar bith beó mar táim?

'Sé fáth mo thuirse nach bhfágham do chuideacht,
A mhaighdean tséimh má's gnaoi leat mé,
Suidh go dlúth le mo thaobh is tabhair póg dhom bhéal,
Is coingigh dhuit féin ón mbás mé!

English

Treasure or store I would ne'er advise,
But play and drink and music to frequent;
Fits of folly for a woman mostly is my cause for excess drinking,
Is it not sad that one such as I exists?

The cause of my weariness is I do not leave your company,
O gentle maiden if you love me,
Sit close by my side and kiss my mouth,
And save me from death for yourself!

BROCHAN LOM
(traditional puirt a beul, or mouth music
from the early 18th century, when the Irish language was banned)

Irish

Brochan lom, tana lom, brochan lom na sùghain
Brochan lom, tana lom, brochan lom na sùghain

Brochan lom, tana lom, brochan lom na sùghain
Brochan lom 's e tana lom 's e brochan lom na sùghain

Brochan tana, tana, tana, brochan lom na sùghain
Brochan tana, tana, tana, brochan lom na sùghain
Brochan tana, tana, tana, brochan lom na sùghain
Brochan lom 's e tana lom 's e brochan lom na sùghain

Thugaibh aran dha na gillean leis a' bhrochan sùghain
Thugaibh aran dha na gillean leis a' bhrochan sùghain
Thugaibh aran dha na gillean leis a' bhrochan sùghain
Brochan lom 's e tana lom 's e brochan lom na sùghain

Seo an rud a gheibheamaid o nighean gobh' an dùine,
Seo an rud a gheibheamaid o nighean gobh' an dùine,
Seo an rud a gheibheamaid o nighean gobh' an dùine,
Brochan lom 's e tana lom, 's e brochan lom sùghain.

English

Porridge thin and meagre, porridge thin from sowans.
Porridge thin and meagre, porridge thin from sowans.
Porridge thin and meagre, porridge thin from sowans.
Porridge thin, it is meagre and thin, it is porridge thin from sowans.

Meagre and thin porridge, thin, thin, meagre porridge
Meagre and thin porridge, thin, thin, meagre porridge
Meagre and thin porridge, thin, thin, meagre porridge
Porridge thin, it is meagre and thin, it is porridge thin from sowans.

Give ye bread to the young men with sowans-gruel,
Give ye bread to the young men with sowans-gruel,
Give ye bread to the young men with sowans-gruel,
Porridge thin, it is meagre and thin, it is porridge thin from sowans.

This is what we used to get from the smith's daughter at the Dun
This is what we used to get from the smith's daughter at the Dun
This is what we used to get from the smith's daughter at the Dun
Porridge thin, it is meagre and thin, it is porridge thin from sowans.

SEÁN O'DUIBHIR A' GHLEANNA
John O'Dwyer of the Glen
The tune appears in A General Collection of the Ancient Irish
Music
by Edward Bunting, c.1796.

Irish

Ar m'éirighe dhom ar maidin,
Grian a' tsamhraidh 'g taitneamh
Chuala 'n uaill dá casadh,
'Gus ceol binn na n-éan;

Bruic is míolta gearra,
Creabhair na ngob fada
Fuaim ag a' macalla
'Gus lamhach gunnaí tréan

An sionnach rua ar a' gcarraig
Míle liú ag marcaigh
Is bean go dúch sa' mbealach
Ag áireamh a cuid gé.

Anois tá 'n choill dá gearra
Triallfaimíd thar caladh
'S a Sheáin Ó Dhuibhir a' Ghleanna
Chaill tú do chéim!

Is é sin m'uaigneas fada
Scáth mo chluais dá ghearradh
An gaoth aduaidh ag leathadh
'Gus bás ins an aer.

Mo ghadhairín suairc dá cheangal
Gan chead liú ná aisdíocht
Do bhainfeadh gruaim den leanbh
I méan ghil an lae.

'Sé rí na h-uaisle 'r an gcarraig

An céafrach buachach, beannach,
Do thiocfadh suas ar aiteann
Go lá deire 'n tsaoil;

'S dá bhfaghainn-se suaimhneas tamall
ó dhaoinimh uaisle 'n bhaile
Do thriallfainn féin ar Ghaillimh
Agus d'fhágfainn an scléip.

Táid fearann ghleanna 'n tsrotha
Gan ceann ná teann ar lochtaibh
I sráid na gcuach ní molfar
A sláinte ná a saol;

Mo loma 'luain gan fosga
Ó Chluain go Stuaic na gcolum,
'S an gearrfhia ar bhruac an Rosa
Ar fán le n-a ré.

Créad í an ruaig so ar thoraibh,
Buala buan a mbona?
An smóilín binn 's an londubh
Gan sár-ghuth ar ghéig;

'S gur mór an tuar chun cogaidh
Cléire go buartha 's pobail,
Dáseóla 'gcuantaibh loma
I lár ghleanna 'n tslé

Is é mo chreach ar maidin
Nach bhfuair mé bás gan pheacadh
Sar a bhfuair mé scannail
Fá mo chuid féin -

'S a liacht lá breá fada
Thig úla cumhra 'r crannaibh
Duilliúr ar an dair
Agus drúcht ar an bhféar.

'Nois táim-se ruaighthe óm fhearann

I n-uaigneaas 'bhfad óm charaid
Im luí go duairc faoi sgairtibh
'S i gcuasaibh am tslé;

'S muna bhfagha mé suaineas feasta
Ó dhaoinibh uaisle 'n bhaile
Tréigfidh mé mo shealbh
Agus fágfad an saol.

English

When once I rose at morning
The summer sun was shining,
I heard the horn awinding
And the bird's merry songs;
There were badger and weasel,
Woodcock and plover,
And echo repeating
The music of the guns.
The hunted fox was flagging,
The horsemen followed shouting;
Counting her geese on the highway
Some woman's heart was sore;
But now the woods are falling
We must go over the water-
Seán O'Dwyer of the Valley
Your pleasure is no more.

There's cause enough for grieving,
All the woodlands falling,
The north wind comes freezing
With death in the sky;
My merry hound's tied tightly
From sporting and chasing
That would life a young lad's sorrows
In noondays gone by.
The stag is up in Carrick,
His antlers high as ever;
He can enjoy the heather,
But our day is o'er;

Let the townsmen cease they prying,
And I'll take ship from Galway-
Seán O'Dwyer of the Valley,
Your pleasure is no more.

The homes of Coomasrohy
Have neither roof nor gable,
In Strade where birds are silent
No man recites its praise;
From Clonmel along the river
There is no shade or shelter,
And hares amid the clearings
Run safe all their days.
What is this thud of axes,
Trees creaking and falling,
The sweet thrust and the blackbird
In silence everywhere?
And - certain sign of trouble -
Priest and their people
Flying to mountain valleys
To raise the word of prayer?

My only wish on waking
Is that I had ceased from caring
Before my own demesne lands
Were cause for my grief;
For through long days of summer
I rambled through their orchards
And oakwoods all green
With the dew on the leaf;
And now that I have lost them
And lonesome among strangers
I sleep among the bushes
Or mountain caves alone,
Either I'll find some quiet
To live as best contents me
Or leave them all behind me
For other men to own.

MO GHILE MEAR
Written by Seán Clárach Mac Domhnaill, c. 18th century

Irish

Sé mo laoch mo gile mear
'Sé mo Shaesar, gile mear,
Suan ná séan ní bhfuaireas féin
Ó chuaigh i gcéin mo giile mear

Bímse buan ar buairt gach ló,
Ag caoi go cruaidh 's ag tuar na ndeor
Mar scaoileadh uaim an buachaill beo
'S ná ríomhtar tuairisc uaidh, mo bhrón

Sé mo laoch mo giile mear
'Sé mo Shaesar, gile mear,
Suan ná séan ní bhfuaireas féin
Ó chuaigh i gcéin mo gile mear

Sé mo laoch mo gile mear
'Sé mo Shaesar, gile mear,
Suan ná séan ní bhfuaireas féin
Ó chuaigh i gcéin mo gile mear

English

My dashing darling is my hero
He's my Caesar, a dashing darling,
I've got no rest and no pleasure
Since my dashing darling went to a distant land.

I'm incessantly sorrowing each day,
Lamenting sorely and showing signs of tears
As the lively lad has been separated from me
And no news from him is told, my sadness.

My dashing darling is my hero
He's my Caesar, a dashing darling,
I've got no rest and no pleasure

Since my dashing darling went to a distant land.

My dashing darling is my hero
He's my Caesar, a dashing darling,
I've got no rest and no pleasure
Since my dashing darling went to a distant land.

SONGS IN ENGLISH

THE COLLEEN RUE/ AN CAILÍN RUA/THE RED-HAIRED GIRL)
c.1790s hedge schoolmaster song

THREE RAVENS
Published in the song book Melismata by Thomas Ravenscroft, England
Recorded by James Child (1825-1896) in 1611
Recorded by Francis in The English and Scottish Popular Ballads in 1882–1898

OLD ARBOE
Literacy and Orality, c. 18th century

ARE YE SLEEPIN', MAGGIE?
Written by Robert Tannahill (1774-1810)

NELL FLAHERTY'S DRAKE
Written by Eoghan Rua Ó Súilleabháin (1748–1782)

FARE THEE WELL

18th century English ballad, c. 18th century

Historical Note

Dear Readers,

As you embark on the enchanting journey within the pages of "Legacy of Truth," I wanted to share a glimpse into the historical tapestry that serves as the backdrop for this captivating tale.

Set against the mystical landscape of Donegal in Ireland, the story unfolds in the year 1795—a time when shadows dance, secrets whisper, and the mystical meets the mundane.

The house Eithne lives in, Woodhill Estate, is a real place that existed in Ardara at that time and still stands today. I've not only visited, I've stayed in the Bed & Breakfast.

Travelers are called many names: Tinkers, an lucht siúil, Minkiers, gypsies, pavees, paddies, pikeys. They are itinerant ethnic groups in Ireland and Scotland, with a long tradition of customs. They speak English but have their own languages such as Shelta, Gammon or the Cant. Ethnically, they are not related to the Romani gypsy tribes from Eastern Europe, though the two groups have some things in common. Their origins are shrouded in the mists of time, but they have been a separate group for probably at least a thousand years, according to DNA testing evidence. Their numbers greatly increased during the Great Hunger of the 1840s.

The book describes Hedge schools, which were often the only way Catholic Irish children could learn, as there were Penal Laws that forbade those of "non-conforming faiths" to go to school. Those Penal Laws, though revoked shortly before, were still followed, and kept Catholics from inheriting land, holding political office, acting as police, and many other ways of keeping them out of any modicum of power.

The village of Derreen on Achill Island and the summer booley homes were also drawn from historical fact. Carrick House, however, I invented from one of the names for Kildavent castle, Carrickkildavnet, a stone tower associated with Gráinne Mhaoil, the Irish pirate.

The stone circle in Kenmare, like almost all of the Neolithic monuments in my books, is a real place, as well, though not nearly as close to the water as in the book.

I hope you find joy in the emotional intrigue, fairy enchantments, and the poignant struggle of Esme Doherty as she navigates a world where truth carries profound consequences.

About the Author

Christy Nicholas writes under several pen names, including Emeline Rhys, CN Jackson, and Rowan Dillon. She is an author, artist, and accountant. After she failed to become an airline pilot, she quit her ceaseless pursuit of careers that begin with the letter 'A' and decided to concentrate on her writing. Since she has Project Completion Compulsion, she is one of the few authors with no unfinished novels.

Christy has her hands in many crafts, including digital art, beaded jewelry, writing, and photography. In real life, she's a CPA, but having grown up with art all around her (her mother, grandmother, and great-grandmother are/were all artists), it sort of infected her, as it were.

She wants to expose the incredible beauty in this world, hidden beneath the everyday grime of familiarity and habit, and share it with others. She uses characters out of time and places infused with magic and myth, writing magical realism stories in both historical fantasy and time travel flavors.

Social Media Links:

Blog: www.GreenDragonArtist.net
Website: www.GreenDragonArtist.com
Facebook: www.facebook.com/greendragonauthor
Instagram: www.instagram.com/greendragonartist9
TikTok: www.tiktok.com/@greendragonauthor

www.ingramcontent.com/pod-product-compliance
Lightning Source LLC
Chambersburg PA
CBHW050015120726
47903CB00006B/1781